By Laura Moore

Making Waves
Once Touched
Once Tasted
Once Tempted
Trouble Me
Believe in Me
Remember Me
In Your Eyes
Night Swimming
Chance Meeting
Ride a Dark Horse

Making Waves

Making Waves

A Beach Lane Novel

LAURA MOORE

BALLANTINE BOOKS
NEW YORK

Making Waves is a work of fiction. Names, characters, places, and incidents are the products of the author's imagination or are used fictitiously. Any resemblance to actual events, locales, or persons, living or dead, is entirely coincidental.

A Ballantine Books Trade Paperback Original

Published in the United States by Ballantine Books, an imprint of Random House, a division of Penguin Random House LLC, New York.

BALLANTINE and the HOUSE colophon are registered trademarks of Penguin Random House LLC.

ISBN 978-0-425-28482-7
ebook ISBN 978-0-425-28483-4

Printed in the United States of America on acid-free paper

randomhousebooks.com

987654321

Book design by Diane Hobbing

\

In memory of Maxim Daamen (1948–2013), a friend who taught me about NVUs and so much more

CHAPTER ONE

"Maniac" blared from the front pocket of Dakota Hale's zipped hoodie. She ignored it. Whoever had invented designated ringtones was a veritable genius.

"That's call number four," Rae observed, exchanging a sponge for a micro-duster. Rae was doing the Friday shift with Dakota, a marathon of house preps, errands, and inspections before the owners arrived for the long weekend.

It was the fifth time Piper had called, and that wasn't including the quick conversation they'd had earlier this morning, but who was counting?

Dakota replied with a noncommittal *hmm* and continued stocking the Ellsworths' kitchen from the grocery bags that were next to her sock-clad feet. Ron and Myrna and their three kids had a weakness for Doritos and huge bottles of Diet Coke. She hoped their diet was healthier in New York City than when they came out to their East Hampton country home.

"You suppose it's an emergency?"

Rae Diaz, the oldest of six children, had a heart of gold.

"Of course it is." Dakota opened the cupboard next to the refrigerator and placed two boxes of spaghetti—never linguini, because Ron had a thing about only eating spaghetti—next to a bag of white rice. "Everything's an emergency with Piper. She can't find her new sunglasses. It's an emergency. She's forgotten her password to her favorite shopping site. A major crisis. Her favorite dress isn't hanging where it should be. Time to call the cops." She kept her tone light and amused as she rattled off a carefully edited list of items that Piper routinely treated as an SOS.

"You'd think she'd figure out that Fridays are our busiest days."

Dakota shrugged. "The concept of work doesn't register with her." She placed a bag of Italian-roast coffee beans front and center on the shelf, where it would be easily spotted. "If it's really urgent, she'll leave a message." She shut the cabinet door firmly. "I'm teaching her the concept of boundaries."

"Good luck with that, girlfriend. We have three more houses to go. She may set a personal record just to show you what she thinks of boundaries."

As if on cue, "Maniac" began again.

With an I-told-you-so lift of her brows, Rae shimmied her hips, twirled her dust cloth in the air, and pranced across the ceramic-tile floor in a fairly decent imitation of Jennifer Beals to give the gleaming glass doors of the double wall oven a final swipe. Rae had been dancing a lot today.

And Dakota had been gritting her teeth and refusing to press the answer button on her phone. The obvious solution would have been to turn it off, except then she'd have been unavailable to the people who did need to reach her—her employees and clients. Premier Service, the concierge business Dakota had started four years ago, was founded on the premise of being available to clients and providing exceptional service. If they wanted something, Premier Service was there to provide it. For Dakota, solving any problems her staff might encounter on the job was equally important. Impossible to do if she couldn't answer their calls.

Repeating the word "boundaries" to herself, she opened the refrigerator door and scanned its contents, double-checking that in addition to the Diet Coke there were two bottles of champagne chilling to accompany the appetizers she'd picked up at Loaves & Fishes, a gourmet food shop in Sagaponack, which sold everything from flaky croissants to boeuf bourguignon to assorted salads and sides for the beach crowd.

Next she inspected the freezer and made sure the pints of cookie-dough-and-chocolate ice cream for the kids were fresh—no freezer-burned contents to gross out the young Ellsworths—and aligned neatly on the top shelf.

She'd brought up two bottles of a Bordeaux from the temperature-controlled wine cellar in the basement—Ron's pride and joy—to go with the entrée and the dessert of chocolate mousse—Myrna's favorite.

All good with the food and booze.

Turning around, she adjusted one of the daisies in the vase she'd placed in the middle of the counter, then surveyed the rest of the kitchen. Everything was in its place and spotless, as with the other rooms in the sprawling home.

"Our work is done here. On to the Morrisseys," she told Rae.

"Okay, boss."

While Rae stored the dust cloth and cleaning products in the utility closet, Dakota scooped up the empty canvas shopping totes and from her leather hobo bag fished out the bundle of keys for the day's visits. Together they walked to the front door, where Dakota stepped into her Uggs and Rae her clogs. Then Dakota punched in the security code she knew by heart; the Ellsworths were long-standing clients. The alarm system on, Rae opened the front door, and she and Dakota stepped out of the house, whose design always made Dakota think of children's building blocks stacked haphazardly and then held together with clear packing tape. It was not an uncommon architectural style for the Hamptons. After all, fabulous wealth didn't mean good taste. But at least the Ellsworths' home was hidden by trees and not sitting exposed, smack dab in what used to be a potato field, like so many other Hamptons properties.

"Maniac" sounded again.

"Will she never quit? You know, I used to love that song." Rae's tone was mournful.

"I'll find another one for her," Dakota promised.

"Don't bother. Piper and 'Maniac' are forever linked. Besides, switching ringtones will only ruin another great tune."

It was one thing to ignore people who couldn't control their speed-dial impulse. Annoying her smart, dependable employees was not good business practice, and Rae was her very best.

With an inward sigh, Dakota resigned herself to her fate. She'd simply have to stay calm and refuse to get swept up in whatever drama Piper was currently starring in.

Wise words, but often difficult to put into practice.

"Right. You drive to the Morrisseys, I'll call Piper."

"Excellent plan."

She tossed Rae the keys to her old Toyota Land Cruiser. Rae caught them and climbed in behind the steering wheel while Dakota settled herself in the passenger seat.

"I can only imagine what it's like, dealing with her," Rae said. "But she does have her good points. She can be funny as hell."

"I know she can." Maybe she'd luck out and catch Piper in a humorous mood. One that wasn't cringe-worthy.

"But," Rae continued, "if she's calling because she wants to wheedle another free cleaning out of Premier, you hand that cell over to me, stat. I'll set her straight. Because that is just wrong."

Dakota pretended to laugh along with her.

Since Piper often spent the day with a phone attached to her ear, she answered immediately. "Hello?"

"It's me. I saw you called."

"Dakota, I've been trying you for *ages*!"

"I know, I'm sorry. I'm at work."

"Your clients, they take up so much of your time."

"Yeah, they can be funny like that." Dakota stared out the window as the car sped past oak scrub with the occasional spindly pine breaking through the brown canopy. Every few thousand feet a driveway cut into the woods, a pebbled or sandy drive marked by a small white wooden sign with black lettering—hands down the Hamptons' favorite style—and the house number. Rae was driving east. Soon she cut across Route 27 to the coveted area known as "south of the highway," where tall elms stood and, closer to the ocean, the narrow roads were bordered by potato and corn fields, and privet hedges screened the multimillion-dollar houses within. Whether north or south of the highway, every house she and Rae passed represented potential customers. Dakota was determined to add as many of them as she possibly could and expand the business she'd built.

But it was October. Already the Hamptons had an abandoned feel to them. While she loved the uncongested roads and quieter tempo of the off-season, the businesswoman in her worried about making payroll.

Her mind on the upcoming slow months, she went on, "There's nothing wrong with being busy when you run a business, Piper. It's much better than the alternative."

Piper made a sound that conveyed her complete disinterest in the topic of Dakota's work—successful or not. "Have you tried that eye cream I told you about?"

Piper's new favorite serum made Iranian beluga caviar look cheap. "No, not yet."

"I'm sure it would help. You look so—"

Since she really didn't want to hear how tired she looked, Dakota quickly asked, "Was there a reason you called?"

"Oh God, yes! It's the worst, Dakota. I can't believe it. What will everyone say?"

Dakota pressed the acupressure points below her brows. "And we're talking about . . . ?"

"Elliott, of course. He sold the house without even telling us. Mimi's fit to be tied. How could he do this? What was he thinking?"

Elliott was Piper and Mimi's older brother. Upon their mother's death, he'd inherited the family manse, Windhaven, a six-bedroom shingled "cottage" near the end of West End Road in East Hampton that came with a guest house, pool, manicured lawns, and mature plantings. The property was further graced with sweeping views of the ocean on one side and the tranquility of Georgica Pond on the other. In the hotbed of the Hamptons real estate world, Windhaven would command top dollar.

"Well, he did say maintaining Windhaven was becoming too time-consuming." Which was Elliott-speak for the house being too great a financial burden. Admitting that something was no longer affordable wasn't in the family's vocabulary.

"Yes, but I didn't believe he'd actually go and sell our family home! Surely he could have come up with an alternative."

Not if he needed a large infusion of cash. The stock market had taken some serious hits recently, and that might have shaken the investors in the Templar Group, the hedge fund Elliott managed. If they'd grown nervous and decamped, he might have been left scrambling. But mentioning the topic of Elliott's finances, his unlucky investment strategies, or anything that hinted at the waning of her family's fortunes would only ramp up Piper's agitation. Better to stick to the immediate mini-crisis at hand.

"I'm sorry. Really I am," she said, opting for a palliative response. "I know you liked the house."

"I loved it. There's no place like Windhaven on the East End.

Or anywhere. An enduring symbol of my family's history is gone, gone forever." Piper was obviously in a Scarlett O'Hara kind of mood. "Mimi's beside herself, absolutely furious."

"Yes. You mentioned that. Do you know who bought it?"

"Elliott may have told me. Some nouveau riche type."

Dakota's sympathy dipped toward the empty mark. "Well, again, that's too bad about the house. I'll call tomorrow—"

"You have to come over today. Mimi's driving out. You know what she's like. After five minutes I'll be exhausted, and I have a dinner with Duncan tonight. I want to be at my best for him." Duncan Harding was Piper's latest lover. They'd met at the Southampton Social Club, a trendy restaurant and dance club.

Dakota's surfboard was strapped to the Land Cruiser's roof. A gear bag holding her wetsuit and neoprene booties sat in the trunk. She'd been hoping to head out to Montauk after work and catch some waves.

"Pretty please, Dakota? I need you," Piper said with a sweetness that never failed to exasperate, since it was only employed for one purpose.

And yet she gave in. Again. Irritated with herself as much as with Piper, she asked in a clipped tone, "What time?"

"Five o'clock."

"I'll try to make it."

"Oh, good. I knew I could count on you. I love you, sweets."

Even though it was expected and tacitly demanded, Dakota's reply was nonetheless sincere. "Love you, too, Piper."

"Oh, one more thing. Can you pick up a bottle of vodka? Mimi will be wanting her martinis."

"Sure." As Piper's requests went, this one was easy.

Disconnecting, Dakota stared at the blank screen and wondered how long she would have to hear about the latest family tragedy.

Rae's voice jolted her out of her abstraction. "So, how was Mommie Dearest?"

CHAPTER TWO

The last three visits on the day's schedule didn't take long. At one, an indoor pool heater needed to be switched on so that the water would be at the stipulated seventy-five degrees upon the owners' arrival. The couple also liked to have their bed turned down, fresh flowers set on each of their bedside tables, and the fire laid in the fireplace, ready for the match. Another property had several newly planted specimen trees that required watering. Then Dakota had to check that the handyman she'd hired had installed the shelving in the garage per the owner's instructions. At the last house—a converted barn in Wainscott—all that was required was a vacuuming and dusting and for the extra glassware to be wiped with cloths and set out on the sideboard. The owners were throwing a party on Saturday night. Serious foodies, David and Nina Greenfield did their own shopping and cooking. But they'd hired Rae, along with Lupe and Jarrett, two other employees of Dakota's, to work the party. With the Hamptons' social whirlwind dying down, it would provide a nice chunk of change for the three of them.

At each house Dakota left a complimentary vase of flowers for her clients, each arrangement coordinated to match the interior.

The ease of the last three jobs made it difficult for Dakota's mind not to wander back to her mother and their conversation. Piper Hale was many things. A beautiful social butterfly, she flitted from one Hamptons scene to the next, with the odd dash into the city for a party that was sure to end up in the style section of the *Times* or better yet, "Page Six" of the *Post.*

She was also a drama queen par excellence. But for all Piper's over-the-top declarations, Dakota knew her mother must truly be upset over the sale of Windhaven. First and foremost, it would be embarrassing to face the inevitable questions about why her older brother had sold the house that had belonged to the Hales for generations. And it was where Piper had grown up. Its rooms, which carried the tangy scent of the sea, were also filled with memories. According to Piper, they were good ones.

Except, of course, for the prolonged period reminiscent of winter in Siberia, beginning with Piper's announcement that she was expecting but couldn't name the man who'd impregnated her and continuing when she went against her parents' wishes by keeping the baby. Even after the birth of her child, the freeze endured. Such was the wrath of the Hales.

Since Dakota was the flesh-and-blood reminder of Piper's filial defiance, she had no fond memories of Windhaven to mourn. No birthday parties were thrown for her by doting grandparents. Thanksgiving meant being shunted to the end of the table, yet even from that distance, her grandfather's disapproving glare and her grandmother's audible sniffs reached her.

For all the lights and tinsel and cups of heavily spiked eggnog imbibed by the adults, Christmas was an equally stiff affair, with everyone in attendance—Piper and Dakota included—pretending not to notice the disparity between the single gift Dakota received and the colorful boxes with her cousins' names scrawled on the tags. Except for its size, Dakota's present from her grandparents never varied: a Fair Isle sweater in an improbable pink. Since they'd failed to deny her existence, they were determined to disguise her. As if having her don a preppy sweater might make her pale skinned, blue-eyed, and blond, like them.

Luckily, the Thanksgiving and Christmas memories at Windhaven had stopped when Dakota turned thirteen. That was the year her grandparents began spending winters in Palm Beach, the warm climate easier on her grandfather's failing health, his liver finally succumbing to decades of heavy drinking. Even the spring and summer visits to Windhaven dwindled to a few unpleasant occasions. Dakota learned to seize either schoolwork or her part-time jobs as a babysitter, plant-waterer, and dog-walker as excuses to stay away. Her regrets were relayed by Piper and accepted without question, and everyone was happier.

While the sale of Windhaven evoked no sense of nostalgia in Dakota, she did wonder who its new owner was. She knew her curiosity would be satisfied soon enough. Where the ever-flighty party girl Piper Hale couldn't be bothered to recall or even be troubled to ask for the most crucial of names, her older sister, Mimi Hale Walsh, could recall entire family trees—and then hack them to pieces with a few choice anecdotes. Bitter and resentful that life hadn't given her everything on her wish list, Mimi liked nothing better than to see others fall. Not even family members were exempt.

After she and Rae wrapped up at the Greenfields, Dakota drove Rae over to the East Hampton Citarella, a high-end grocery store, where her boyfriend, Marcos, would pick her up in the parking lot. Rae and Marcos had a place in Hampton Bays, just past the Shinnecock Canal. A distance of about twenty miles, in the off-season the drive took a little over a half hour. When the summer folk flocked to the east end of Long Island, the trip could clock in at over an hour. Not even sticking to the back roads to avoid Route 27, the artery that connected the Hamptons and ended at Montauk, the easternmost point, shaved off many minutes. Rae and Marcos were hoping to move closer, but housing prices eastward became exorbitant fast.

Pulling into a parking space, Dakota said, "See you Tuesday, Rae. Hope the party goes well tomorrow night. Call if anything comes up."

"Most def." Rae climbed out of the SUV and patted the bag protecting Dakota's surfboard. "May the waves be cranking, D. And say hi to that crazy lady Piper."

"Will do." She, too, got out. A trip to the market's deli was in order. Essential to refuel before tackling the double headache of her mother and aunt. From there she'd pick up the bottle of vodka at the liquor store and, if she timed it right, arrive at her mother's house on Dunemere Lane after Mimi's opening rant. There'd be plenty more to follow.

To avoid the line of customers ordering lox, sliced deli meats, and salads for the long weekend, Dakota went straight to the refrigerated shelves that held prepared sandwiches. She was bent over, her fingers around a turkey and avocado wrap and deciding between peach and lemon iced tea when a finger poked her in the side.

A freckled strawberry-blond girl in pigtails, an orange fleece jacket, and jodhpurs gave her a gap-toothed grin and waved. "Hi, Dakota."

Her own face split in a smile. "Well, hi there, Gracie! Good to see you. Are you going riding?"

"Just finished," Gracie's mom, Gen Monaghan, said. She was holding on to three-year-old Brooke's hand. "We're picking up dinner—Alex is flying in later."

Gen Monaghan was one of Dakota's favorite people. A talented painter, she was married to Alex Miller, who had his own roots in the Hamptons, though his weren't as deep as the Hale family's. They lived in Georgica in a house Alex had inherited from his great-aunt Grace Miller.

Dakota had met Gen and Alex through that aunt, soon after she started Premier Service. Gen and Alex had needed help organizing their beach wedding, which, in spite of Alex's wealth and connections, they were determined to keep a low-key affair. Aunt Grace had recommended that they turn to Dakota.

Gen claimed that Dakota's success in corralling her many relatives and providing perfectly chilled champagne, raw clams and oysters, steamed lobsters, *and* a wedding cake free of a single grain of sand was nothing short of a miracle.

"We were in the produce aisle when eagle-eyed Gracie spotted you, which is terrific, because she's saved me a telephone call." Gen ruffled her daughter's hair. "But if you're rushing off to a job, I'll catch you later."

"No, I'm heading over to Piper's. Elliott's sold Windhaven, and Mimi is not happy. I've been summoned to listen to the Hale sisters' lament."

"That's sure to make for an interesting concert."

A mild and restrained response, considering that she must know that Mimi and, to a less acute degree, Piper hated that Gen, a Massachusetts "nobody," had invaded their turf.

"Funnily enough, that's exactly what I wanted to talk to you about, too," Gen said. "Windhaven's new owner? His name's Max Carr, and he's an associate of Alex's. Max is looking for a company to help with the house, and so of course Alex thought of

Premier Service. Would you be willing to talk to Max? He could be a good client for you."

But at what cost?

The eruption would be full-blown, with the toxins lingering in the atmosphere long afterward, once the family heard that she was helping Windhaven's new owner. She'd be working for the enemy. That no one had forced Elliott to sell the ancestral home to this Max Carr would be immaterial.

At Dakota's hesitation, Gen asked, "Would it be ridiculously awkward?"

Dakota gave a little laugh. She'd be labeled a traitor. But Mimi had already stuck so many labels on her, what was one more?

"It might get sticky. But you and Alex have been really wonderful to me." After the wedding, they'd sung her praises to anyone within earshot. With Alex's connections, she'd tripled her list of clients. "I'd be happy to talk to him."

"Oh, good. Do you have time to meet tomorrow?"

Damn. As Rae liked to say, the shit was getting real. She'd assumed he'd simply call and she'd spend a few minutes on the phone, perhaps pass on some names if she decided that negotiating the family minefield wasn't worth it. "Uh, sure. I could meet him at Windhaven at ten o'clock."

"Thanks, Dakota." Gen stepped forward and hugged her. The front of her down vest opened like the wings of a blue jay. "I know how complicated your family is."

"Complicated" being the polite term for dysfunctional.

Dakota didn't do sympathy well. Whatever her childhood had been like, she was an adult now, financially independent, and fairly well adjusted. In the grand scheme of things, what were a few lingering hang-ups, especially when they were perfect for her chosen profession? Being a hyperorganized control freak accustomed practically since birth to demanding egotistical types held distinct advantages in the concierge business. "Happy to, Gen. Give Max Carr my number in case he can't see me at ten." It was possible he'd prefer one of the ludicrously expensive concierge services operating in Southampton, the kind that provided chauffeurs to drive Manhattan hairdressers out to the Hamptons so they could give eight- and nine-year-old boys a haircut because the mother claimed that was "simpler."

Too much money could seriously damage a brain.

"I'll have Alex give Max your info and tell him it's a go. Oh, and are you free for Sunday brunch? We'd love to see you."

"Thanks, I'd like that."

"Hope things work out between you and Max."

Dakota pictured the outraged expressions on her relatives' faces and tried for an answering smile.

CHAPTER THREE

With her coloring, most people assumed Dakota was named for the Native American tribe. There had been a period as a kid when she would correct anyone who remarked on her name that no, as far as she knew, her father wasn't a Native American. Nor was her mother fond of the states, either North or South. Piper was one of those "everything is fuzzy west of the Hudson River" types. The Dakota that she'd been named after was the prestigious apartment building in New York City, the one where John Lennon had lived and where, on the sidewalk, only steps away from its imposing arched entry, he'd lost his life.

Any attempts to explain the origin of her name had ended when she was twelve. The reason wasn't that she'd grown sick of people concluding that her mother must have been a John Lennon groupie. Her decision had stemmed from a talk Piper gave her. Not just any talk. The Talk.

From her friends, Dakota already knew about the one most

parents gave. A cautious speech, it was sprinkled with soothing words like "respect" and "love" and phrases like "it's perfectly normal."

Piper, in her inimitable fashion, chose to personalize it.

Dakota was sitting in the smaller living room in the house on Dunemere Lane, the house Piper had bought when her parents delivered their final ultimatum—no bastard grandchild would live under their roof—watching a rerun of *The Brady Bunch.* She'd loved that series: the kids and their squabbles, the way they made up, the way they talked to each other, Cindy's dorky pigtails, the way Mike and Carol hugged. Weirdly, her favorite character was Alice, the housekeeper. Practical Alice kept it together, calmly sliding casseroles and baking sheets dotted with carefully arranged mounds of cookie dough into the waiting oven while the eight family members succumbed to whatever crisis was unfolding.

It was the same with *Batman.* She adored Alfred. Batman and Robin might be out scaling skyscrapers to catch the Penguin; ever-unruffled Alfred carried tea in on a silver platter.

Longing for a father was taboo, drilled into her time and again by Piper saying, "It's just you and me, doll. We're a team." And while it would have been wonderful to have a brother or sister to help her try to make sense of the reckless adults around her, what she yearned for even more was a stalwart Alice or phlegmatic Alfred, someone on whom she could depend.

She had been fully immersed in the Bradys and their happy, love-filled life when Piper wandered into the room, a glass of wine in hand. She was back from a cocktail party and still in her leopard-print leggings, high-heeled black suede booties, and a tuxedo shirt fastened with a single button. With her blond hair teased into a wild mane, she could have passed for a blue-eyed Kate Moss.

She sank down on the ivory twill sofa next to Dakota. There was no "Have you done your homework?," no "Have you picked up your room?," no "Have you eaten?" That wasn't Piper's style.

Besides, the questions asked by other parents—Carole and Mike Brady included—weren't necessary. Dakota always did her homework, picked her clothes up off the floor, and brushed her teeth. She also made her own breakfast and brewed Piper's coffee, carrying it carefully so the hot liquid wouldn't slosh onto her hand as she climbed the stairs and entered the darkened bedroom.

Caffeine was essential to counteract the alcohol and whatever else Piper had ingested the night before. Without it there was no way Piper would get out of bed in time to drop her off at school. Piper had even taught her how to turn on the car so that the interior would be warm when, bleary-eyed and in a puffy down parka zipped over her Hanro camisole and cotton lounging pants, she would drive her to the middle school in put-upon silence. The second the car rolled to a stop near the brick building, Dakota would jump out with a quick "Bye," and her mother would drive home and go back to bed, rolling out of it for the second time closer to eleven o'clock.

"Well, that was dullsville. Why do I ever think Ann Clark can throw a party? And what is this?" she said with a nod at the TV.

"*The Brady Bunch*."

"Oh God, again? How trite." Her free hand reached for the remote lying on the glass coffee table that was shaped like a blob. "Really, doll, there must be something better."

"No, don't! I like this show."

Piper sat back with a huff of displeasure. For a few minutes they watched in silence.

Maybe her absorption in the sitcom posed a challenge. Maybe the reason the party had been "dullsville" was that no one had paid Piper proper court. Or maybe it was seeing Mike and Carol Brady in their striped pajamas in bed, a chaste foot of space separating them, that provoked her.

"I ran into Jenny Hollins at the post office today." That was Chip Hollins's mother. He had zits that he covered with gobs of Clearasil and he liked to tease Dakota about being John Lennon's love child, which showed how stupid he was since Lennon was shot in *1980.* "She said you're learning about sex in school."

Dakota went hot with embarrassment and stared harder at the TV screen. "It's called health class," she muttered.

"It's probably as sanitized and boring as this show. The *Joy of Sex* is over there, you know." She pointed to the built-in bookshelf to the right of the fireplace. "Though the book *I* learned about sex from was *Fear of Flying.*"

Dakota prayed for sudden deafness.

"Thank God for Erica Jong." Piper took a long sip of her wine. "The sex I had with your father? Straight out of *Fear of Flying,* believe me. It was glorious and wild. No questions asked, just two strangers coming together. Of course, ours wasn't a zipless fuck."

Dakota wasn't supposed to swear. *Oh, Dakota, must you be so vulgar?*

"Erica Jong coined the term 'zipless fuck,' you know. That book, it freed so many women from stupid social conventions about sex. And did I ever 'fly' with your father. Over and over again." She smiled and stretched, arching her back against the sofa cushions.

Only the word "father" kept Dakota from plugging her ears or, better yet, racing upstairs and escaping. Not that retreating would by any means have ensured the end of the conversation. If she'd been in the mood, intent on finishing her tale, Piper would simply have followed, not bothering to knock when she entered. Ms. Penelope Worth Hale decided what rules and etiquette applied to her.

"So you met my father at the Dakota, right?" she asked as casually as she could.

"I was living in New York, subletting an apartment in Greenwich Village while I studied at Parsons. My teachers thought I was quite brilliant. If I'd stayed in the program, I'd be selling in Barneys and Neiman Marcus." She gave a heavy sigh and raised her glass to her lips.

"But the Dakota is uptown, right?" she prompted.

"Seventy-second Street and Central Park West. Not exactly the hippest neighborhood, but the Dakota, well, it's an amazing place. The group I ran with, we were always being invited to gallery openings, clubs, and parties all over town. And if we weren't invited, we simply crashed. The party at the Dakota was thrown by some friend of a friend of Sara Pryce's. Sara's never really liked me. Jealous, I suppose. I would have skipped it and gone directly to the other happening on the night's calendar—an outdoor bash at Battery Park, which I knew was going to be a mad scene—but Nina Chappelle, who was my *real* friend, had heard that Michael Douglas was going to be at the Dakota party. Or maybe it was some other actor. Whoever it was, Nina was obsessed with him. She loved to make it with celebrities. Still does, though since she's gained so much weight she has a hard time attracting anyone at all. I don't know what I'd do if I ever lost my looks. . . ."

Following one of Piper's monologues was like following the trajectory of a ping-pong ball slammed too violently. It bounced all over the place.

Piper paused to sip her wine and perhaps contemplate the terrible fate of being as fat as her friend. Then she shrugged.

"Anyway, Nina begged me to come with her, promising me she'd heard the apartment was simply out of this world. So I went."

Dakota sat very still so as not to distract Piper.

"It was unreal, Dakota. I'd been in some incredible digs in London, Paris, and Rome when I traveled after graduating from boarding school, but this apartment was fabulous. Totally over the top. Priceless antiques mixed with the most amazing collection of photographs and contemporary paintings. Glam beyond belief. And let me tell you, the people there were as wild as the apartment. They knew how to party.

"Enormous as it was—the owners, whoever they were, must have combined two apartments into one—the place was packed, with people streaming in and out like it was Grand Central Station. The music was blasting so loud I felt it in my bones. So of course we followed it to the source. And get this—adjoining the vast living room was a ballroom! Nina and I started dancing. I was wearing my hair longer then and I'd found this super-sexy black leather mini in a shop on Bleecker and paired it with a fitted sequin bustier.

"Nina and I always drew looks when we danced together. The same thing happened at the party. Everyone in the room was watching us. But I only felt one pair of eyes on me. His. Before the song had even ended, I left Nina twirling and swaying and went over to him."

Dakota held her breath.

"It was perfect. We didn't exchange a word. We just stared into each other's eyes and I felt as if I was going to explode. Silently he took my hand and led me through the throng and then down a hallway that was crammed with people smoking, drinking, necking. But this man, he had *presence.* They all made way for us.

"There was a door at the end of the hall. He opened it and there was a couple inside, doing lines of coke—" Piper broke off her tale to glance at her. "Oh, come on, don't look so shocked, Dakota. Coke was everywhere back then. And believe me, we didn't 'just say no.' "

"So what happened?"

"Well, he only had to lift his chin like this." Piper demonstrated. "And they split like that," she said, snapping her fingers. "We stepped inside. Lord, even the bathroom was outrageous in that apartment. Huge, and decorated with this sublime wallpaper that was covered with peacocks and birdcages and climbing roses. Classic Schumacher. I'll never forget it." She sighed happily at the memory.

"Anyway, he was the perfect screw. Strong as a bull and relentless. Masterful. I remember giggling with Nina afterward because I could barely walk. We had to go to the Odeon and have steak frites so I could recover my strength. Then we went to that bash at Battery Park, though honestly, after the Dakota it was kind of anticlimactic." She laughed at her pun. "After that, we hit the Limelight. What a night. Definitely one for the books. I've often felt I should have written to Erica Jong about it."

Ugh. "But what about . . . my dad?"

Piper looked at her blankly. "What about him? And really he's not your dad or even your father so much as a sperm donor—not that I was in the market for a baby, believe you me."

The microwaved macaroni and cheese Dakota had eaten for dinner bubbled unpleasantly in her stomach. "So you never found out who he was?" Her voice cracked as she asked.

Piper frowned in annoyance. "Why should I have? That was the whole point. For all I know he was a Mexican millionaire, an Arab sheikh, or a Brazilian diamond mine owner. Who cares? I wasn't interested in his identity. I wanted the *experience.* And that's what you want when you have sex with a guy, Dakota. Pure animal lust. It's the ultimate. You'll see. Don't listen to anything the teacher in that stupid sex ed class tells you."

Dakota wasn't going to lie. That ten-minute discourse of her mother's on "how I met your biological father" messed her up for quite a while. It was kind of tough knowing that the only parent she had enjoyed sexploits with anonymous men, and that her carelessness extended far beyond not bothering to cook dinner. It hadn't even occurred to Piper to ask this flesh-and-blood sex fantasy for his name in case nine months later a little bundle of awkwardness came along.

It was one thing to live with the knowledge that she'd been conceived in a lavish bathroom, and quite another to come to terms with the fact that the bathroom wallpaper had left a more lasting impression on her mother than the man who'd rocked her world. Dakota supposed she should be eternally grateful Piper hadn't named her Schumacher.

But being grateful for that—as well as for the fact that apparently Piper's bathroom tryst was the only sexual adventure she'd had that night—was pretty paltry. It was no match for the anger that ate at her.

Luckily, she'd sorted herself out. Her friends helped. And she learned to take full advantage of Piper's indifferent parenting, staying away from the house on Dunemere Lane until the fury inside her subsided. Thanks to her buddies who one day drove her out to Ditch Plains, lent her a surfboard, and then taught her how to stand on it, Dakota discovered the best place to let go of the hurt and pain.

Balanced on her board, she learned how to catch a wave, find a path, and cut through the cresting, rolling ocean. She learned how to carve, slice, and roll back as she shifted and balanced on the fiberglass surface. She practiced until she'd mastered how to create something beautiful out of a force that might otherwise have crushed her.

Now she reminded herself of all she'd learned and become as she pulled up in front of Piper's house. Mimi's Audi was parked next to her mother's Mercedes, so she knew she'd be walking into a Hale-brewed storm. She would have to use all her acquired skills to ride this wave, too.

CHAPTER FOUR

Max Carr picked up the phone on the first ring. "Yes?"

"It's Roger Cohen on the line, Mr. Carr. I told him you were just about to leave the office for the Hamptons. He says it's important."

"Put him through, Fred. And tell the driver I'll be down in five minutes." Whatever the lawyer had to say, he could make it brief. Max didn't want to keep Alex Miller waiting. Miller was one of the few people he actually liked. For some reason, Miller seemed to reciprocate the sentiment. He was giving Max a lift to East Hampton in the helicopter he'd chartered so that Max could visit his new beach house—a property Max had bought thanks to a tip from Alex.

"Very good, sir. I'll connect you."

"Thanks, Fred." He waited a second, and then Roger Cohen's voice came over the line.

"I have good news and bad, Max. Which do you want first?"

"I'll take the good news first, but make it fast, Rog."

"Yeah, Fred told me you're on your way out. Your administrative assistant looks after you like a mother hen. Going to see the new house? Congratulations, by the way."

"Thanks."

Roger got the message. Clearing his throat, he continued. "You were on the money about Chiron. It's ripe for a takeover. You've talked to your partners?"

"We had our investment meeting. I told them we'd put Steffen in charge of the company."

"That must have made them happy." Roger's tone was dry. Chris Steffen was a wunderkind in the pharmaceutical world. "So you've got the green light."

"Yeah, I just heard. They're sold. I'll get my team to hammer out a proposal that you can look over. We'll want to move fast."

"Got it. Oh, and I looked into that company, ZTron. Hemorrhaging dough."

Not all of the businesses that Max targeted were big-ticket, splashy ones like Chiron. That deal promised to make Max's private equity firm, the Summit Group, an even bigger player in the pharmaceutical world, and land Max at the top of Forbes's "Forty Under Forty" list. But ZTron, a robotics company that specialized in factory automation, while ineptly managed, had a good R&D department. They were working on some innovative designs that had the potential to be used in a variety of fields. With the right kind of restructuring and planning, with the right kind of vision, ZTron could take off. Max wanted in.

"Thanks. I'll do some more research over the weekend. Let's plan to meet Tuesday at nine o'clock. And the bad news?"

"Right." Roger hemmed. "That email you forwarded to me? No two ways about it. Your ex-girlfriend isn't feeling warm and fuzzy toward you."

"She wasn't my girlfriend." He didn't do girlfriends.

"And I can only say thank God for that. She fully intends to sell the sex tape she made of you two unless you make it worth her while. She mentioned a million dollars as possible incentive to changing her mind."

"That's extortion." He swiveled in his office chair to stare out the bank of ceiling-to-floor windows that formed the corner of his office. Most people would consider his sleek Park Avenue office as imposing as any stateroom. He supposed it was. At times it also felt like a tempered-glass and reinforced-steel cage.

"Yes, it is. Unfortunately for you, the lady—and I'm using the term loosely—doesn't seem to be worried overmuch that she's breaking the law. Fortunately for you, while she wasn't shy about filming you and her together, it didn't occur to her that turnabout might be fair play."

"You've got her blackmailing me on tape?"

"I do." Roger chuckled. "Ms. Ashley Nicholls's Valley Girl–speak clangs as clear as a bell. Do you want me to turn what we've got on her over to the authorities?"

He tried to remember Ashley's face. Not easy, since he hadn't seen her in over a month, and after a while the women he hooked up with—even for repeat encounters—tended to blur, one leggy blonde into the next.

The women he dated knew the score. Max wasn't looking for any kind of commitment or long-term relationship. When he was seeing a woman, he was generous with his body and his wallet, but that would never lead to a set of keys to his Tribeca loft.

He should probably be angry that Ashley had decided that the sex and dinners at Bouley and tables at the 40/40 Club or Marquee weren't enough, and that she had figured hiding a small video camera—or even her cellphone—in her bedroom to record them fucking would be a better going-away present than the Harry Winston bauble he'd offered when he ended things between them.

But for some reason he couldn't summon the appropriate outrage at the shakedown. Perhaps it was because he understood that with each business deal he successfully negotiated, he became a bigger target. He was accustomed to that. It wasn't unlike when the defense had attempted a blitz or tried to bring him down with a humiliating sack.

But the tactics were different now and the stakes higher than when he'd played football. When he met a woman at a bar or club and within minutes of their flirty exchange she excused herself to fix her makeup, he pretty much figured she had her cell out to Google him and calculate to the last penny his net worth before she'd even reached the ladies' room.

Now Ashley Nicholls had upped the firepower.

Not that it would do her any good.

"No police," he answered. "Who knows what might leak out of a police station. Just explain to Ashley how many laws she's broken and what kind of jail time she's facing and how hard we'll come down on her if she goes through with this. And make sure she understands that this is a threat and a promise that won't go away."

As the firm's leading rainmaker, Max was the favorite of Bob Elders, Summit's CEO. Max didn't want that to change. Bob was a pretty rigid guy, still married to his high school sweetheart, and would flip if a tape of Max and Ashley doing the dirty became public. It might put an end to the increasingly frequent hints Bob had been making that Max was his first choice to replace him when he grew tired of the game.

"Will do. And may I make a suggestion?"

Max checked his watch. "Shoot."

"First, consider installing a metal detector in your bedroom."

"What, so no phones or video cams can pass the threshold?"

"Precisely."

"Pointless. Ashley never got an invite to my apartment. She

must have set up the camera in her place. Besides, certain metal objects have their use in a bedroom. Handcuffs, for instance."

Rog made a choking sound. "Ms. Nicholls didn't seem restrained in any way in that video," he said once he'd recovered.

"No." He didn't think her enthusiasm had been an act for the camera, but hell, maybe thoughts of the million dollars she'd planned to swindle out of him had fueled her sexual hunger. *Christ.*

"Which brings me to my second suggestion. Try going out with women who are . . . well, let's just say nicer than Ms. Nicholls."

"Not interested." Nice meant he might end up caring. Nice meant he might feel something, and Max couldn't do that. "We'll talk Tuesday."

The helipad was between FDR Drive and the East River. Max carried his leather weekend duffel and his briefcase into the terminal. From the exterior it looked nondescript, but inside it was urban chic, with low-slung leather sofas and chairs, and a stainless steel bar. Industrial lights illuminated the dark-painted walls.

Max had just set his duffel and briefcase down next to one of the barstools when Alex Miller entered. Alex was in his early forties, blond-haired and with piercing blue eyes. He was about six feet, a couple of inches shorter than Max, and his build was lean and wiry. His reputation as a killer squash player matched his reputation as an investor.

"Good to see you, Max."

"Likewise." He shook Alex's hand. "What are you drinking?"

"I'll take a whiskey, neat."

"Any particular brand, sir?" the bartender asked.

"Macallan."

"And I'll have a Grey Goose," Max said.

"Macallan and Grey Goose coming right up."

"Good week?" Alex asked him.

"Yeah, for the most part. I've got a couple of interesting deals in the works. Some other stuff . . . well, shit happens." He left it at that. Alex Miller was happily married. He had a couple of young kids. Telling him about Ashley Nicholls's blackmail attempt would be awkward. Embarrassing.

The bartender placed their drinks before them. "You gentlemen will be boarding the helicopter in ten minutes."

"Thank you." Max pulled out his wallet from inside his gray flannel jacket and handed him his credit card.

"Thanks for the drink, Max."

"Thanks for the ride."

"Anytime. Here's to your new house." Alex clinked the rim of his whiskey glass against Max's.

Max took a healthy swallow. Ice cold in his mouth, the vodka burned a fiery path to his stomach. He hoped that by the time he finished his drink, the odd, sick feeling left in his gut by Roger Cohen's phone call would be burned away.

"Where are you staying?" Alex asked.

"At the house."

"You could stay at our place if you want."

He knew Alex well enough. This man loved his family and hoarded his time with them, a precious commodity in their world. He'd be butting in.

"Thanks, but after I signed the papers, I had the realtor turn on the water and electricity and deliver a mattress and bedding and a couple of towels. My assistant called a local dealership. I'll have a car waiting for me at the airport."

"Still, kind of bare-bones. We at least have chairs."

"I'd kind of like to get a feel for the place. And I don't mind roughing it." He gave a quick smile. "As long as it's temporary."

"Well, come to Sunday brunch and get a solid meal. We're

having a few friends over. It'll be a way to introduce you to some of the cooler locals. That reminds me . . . Here." Alex pulled out his cell from the side pocket of his navy pinstriped suit. "I've got a number for you. You were looking for a concierge service to oversee things at Windhaven? I've got someone. She's a friend of ours and Gen ran into her today. Dakota's agreed to meet you at Windhaven tomorrow morning at ten."

"Dakota? Interesting name."

"Her last one's even more interesting." He paused a beat. "It's Hale."

Max raised a brow. "Any relation to Elliott?"

"Niece," Alex supplied.

"Ah." Maybe this explained why Dakota Hale was comfortable calling the shots. Potential employees didn't normally set the time for a meeting.

"But she's refreshingly different from her uncle—and the rest of the Hale family," Alex said.

He would make his own mind up about that. "Elliott Hale was a real prick."

"Yeah. I can only imagine what he was like at the closing."

"He looked like he was sucking a giant lemon. Pocketed the check and left without a word."

Alex grinned as he brought his drink to his lips. "His own damn fault," he said after taking a sip. "He must have started believing the BS he was spouting. His Templar Group gambled way too heavily on China letting its currency float up."

And instead China's leaders had devalued it. Bummer for Hale, new house for Max. One more shiny possession to show he'd made it . . . would it be enough?

"This is just the latest in a string of bad bets Elliott's made," Alex said. "Word is his investors are bailing. Can't say I'm going to shed a tear for his sorry ass. He's not just a prick, he's a snob of the first order. That's why you want to hire Dakota."

"Because, unlike Elliott Hale, she's not a snob?"

"Exactly. She's built Premier Service on her own without a dime from the family. After having had the pleasure of Elliott's company, you can imagine what they think of one of their own running a business that's grounded in property management and catering to people's needs."

Max shrugged. "There's good money to be made in the service industry."

"Absolutely. And she's damn good at what she does. You'll be lucky if you can get her to work for you, so make sure you give a killer pitch to convince her that taking you on is worth the hassle with her family."

Max gave him a long look. "You're giving a pretty good pitch yourself. You by any chance an investor in her company?"

Alex shook his head. "She wouldn't let me. Dakota's a self-made woman."

Another thought occurred to him. "You by any chance playing matchmaker, Miller?"

"God, no." He laughed. "I *like* Dakota."

CHAPTER FIVE

There must have been vodka in Piper's liquor cabinet after all.

Mimi, Piper's older sister, was waving her martini glass as she spoke. "I'll never forgive Mother and Father for leaving Windhaven to Elliott. He's never cared for the house. I *loved* it. I appreciated it. Now the fool has lost it—and who knows what else besides—and sold Windhaven to some nobody from *Michigan.* He's lucky I don't fly to Bermuda and let his neighbors know what he's done. Of course, it's all because of Martha. I warned him she'd spend every last penny he had."

Dakota wondered how many times Mimi had repeated this story of warning her older brother; it was the type she liked a lot. Deep in their family drama, neither woman had heard the front door opening, and Piper had no dog to bark in greeting, one of Piper's favorite adages being, "Never buy anything that shits."

For a moment, Dakota hesitated in the entry by one of Piper's collages, this one composed of fabric and nails. It would be so easy. She could take four silent steps backward and slip away. But if she did, the recriminations would be endless.

Besides, some habits die hard.

She owed nothing to her mother, but never mind. She was the dutiful daughter.

She let her boots land heavily on the hardwood floor.

Mimi looked over from the sofa. "Oh, it's you." She'd adopted the dismissive attitude that Dakota's grandparents had perfected. "Have you heard?" she demanded.

"That Elliott sold the house? Yes." Dakota didn't add that she'd be meeting the new owner in less than twenty-four hours.

Her mother had her feet propped on the coffee table, and was studying her toes. The pedicure was fresh and her legs gleamed. She must have gotten her legs waxed along with her pedicure. Probably a Brazilian, too, in anticipation of her coming date.

"Hi, Piper."

Piper looked up. "Hi, doll. Oh dear, you *do* look tired. You'll never catch a man looking like that."

"Not trying to." During the summer months she'd been too busy to date, and now, with Piper fishing in the same pond—Duncan Harding, her latest boy toy, was only a couple of years older than Dakota—she didn't feel particularly inclined to resume. "I just finished work," she reminded Piper.

Mimi waved her empty martini glass at her. "Your shift hasn't ended. I need another."

Maybe she could dump some arsenic in it. Though with all the venom already pumping through Mimi, the arsenic might be woefully ineffective.

Dakota silently plucked the empty martini from Mimi's beringed fingers. Drink was making them fat.

She reminded herself that she was not her careless, self-absorbed mother and she was certainly *not* her aunt Mimi. She'd fix the damn cocktail and remain for the twenty minutes she'd allotted herself until she'd maxed out her NVUs—natural visiting units. It was a term she'd learned from one of her friends, Hendrick Daube, a professor of psychiatry at Columbia University. NVUs were basically the amount of time one could spend in the company of certain people before losing it. Generally she could tolerate her mother for an hour. When Mimi was added to the mix, the NVUs shrank dramatically, rarely passing twenty minutes before Dakota had to escape.

She'd be out of there soon.

"Do you want a martini, too, Piper?"

Piper had switched her attention to her iPhone. She glanced up. "I'll wait until Duncan comes. He should be here before long."

Another reason to make a quick exit.

"What are you doing with that man-child? I simply can't understand you," Mimi snapped.

Piper smiled lazily. "Can't you, Mimi?"

"Oh, for God's sake, Piper. Is that *all* you think about?"

"You might be in a better mood if you got a little something going on. Have you tried coconut oil? It'll do wonders for you down there, Mimi. I know you must be all dried up—"

Go, Piper, Dakota thought. Her mother had faults aplenty, but as Rae said, she could also be a hoot.

When she returned to the living room with Mimi's cocktail, Piper's infomercial on coconut oil's rejuvenating powers had been cut short and her aunt had returned to her new favorite topic.

"He'll destroy it, of course."

"What's his name again?" Piper asked.

"Really, Piper." Mimi's tone was exasperated. "How many times do I have to repeat it? His name's Max Carr, and he comes from Mason, Michigan, wherever that is. His father was an autoworker—can you imagine?—and now he's living in our house." She grabbed the glass from Dakota and took a slug of the drink.

"Do you think he'll tear it down?"

"He'll try," Mimi predicted darkly. "Can you believe Elliott sold the house for *twenty-eight million*?" She paused as if to absorb the enormity.

Dakota didn't bother to offer a little reality check. The price wasn't that exorbitant, considering Windhaven's location, size, and acreage. Whoever this Max Carr was, he'd known how to negotiate. Moreover, he could probably make a case for a teardown with the town board if he chose. The house had been added to by any number of Hales, which meant that it was no longer the historical monument Mimi believed it to be. But mentioning any of this would be like waving a red flag, and an enraged Mimi was an ugly sight.

"He'll be sorry if he touches even a shingle on our home. James Alden Hale built Windhaven in 1910. It's been lived in by—"

Dakota tuned her out. Her aunt considered herself the family genealogist. Never did she miss an opportunity to mine the glories of her ancestors. Forget the Adamses, Roosevelts, Rockefellers, and Kennedys. According to the Gospel of Mimi, America would be nothing without the Hales.

"—but I'll put a stop to him. And he can forget about joining the Maidstone."

Well, that might hurt. The Maidstone was the exclusive golf club a few miles from Windhaven. It was snooty, but the eighteen-hole course was beautiful, with views of the ocean, and challenging, due to the shifting winds between sea and shore. Dakota wondered if Mimi could really pull off her vindictive blackballing. If Max Carr had friends like Alex Miller behind him, then Mimi might be in for yet another unpleasant shock: discovering that the old Hamptons guard, which she so loudly claimed to represent, had become toothless.

At least when it came to Mimi Hale Walsh, Dakota thought, this was a cause for celebration.

Piper gave a feline stretch, perhaps anticipating her evening with Duncan, and then looked at Dakota. "I wonder who this Carr person will hire to take care of the old place. It's so hard to find good help these days."

And here she'd thought Piper was conserving her energy for the night ahead, or possibly feeling too charitable toward her for having come over to sling any arrows her way.

Those twenty minutes of NVUs were going to have to be cut short, Dakota thought. She couldn't take any more of what passed for quality time with the Hale sisters. "Who knows, maybe he'll hire Premier Service," she said.

Mimi's laugh was loud. "I don't think so. Face it, you're small potatoes."

Dakota smiled.

CHAPTER SIX

At ten o'clock the next morning Dakota buzzed Windhaven's doorbell and willed a calm expression on her face.

She really shouldn't have Googled Max Carr.

After leaving Piper and Mimi last night, she'd been determined to accept any task Max Carr needed done, just to show her relatives that her "small potatoes" company could attract serious bigwigs. Over a bowl of takeout pad Thai and a very nice glass of chardonnay, she'd opened her laptop and typed "Max Carr" into the search engine. She'd learned far more than she wanted to.

The front door opened, and everything inside her warned her this was not a good idea. As in, really not a good idea. Max Carr was even more strikingly handsome in person. His face, chiseled and strong, would have suited a Roman soldier, and his blue-gray eyes shone with a fierce intelligence.

His body spoke of power. His broad chest was outlined in a black crewneck sweater—cashmere, she knew from a glance—

and his faded jeans were just snug enough to emphasize the muscles in his long legs. The bottom three inches of his pants were damp and his bare feet were dusted with sand—something never allowed to enter the house by her grandmother—which told her he'd already enjoyed Windhaven's private access to the beach.

The weekend look, complete with the reddish-brown scruff darkening his lean cheeks, did nothing to diminish the intensity radiating from him. He could probably stroll into a boardroom dressed just like this and cow all the assembled suits with a single lift of his dark auburn brows.

She extended her hand. "Hi, I'm Dakota Hale."

"Max Carr," he replied, shaking it. His gaze swept over her in swift assessment. "Come inside."

The entry hall and the living room to her right were empty and forlorn-looking. The wallpaper was marked with dark rectangles where paintings had once hung, and scratches marred the wood floors. A film of dust covered the windowsills and built-in shelves. The cleaning crew hired by her uncle had missed a few spots. No one at Premier Service would have.

"I gather from Alex Miller that you know the house."

She turned to face him. "Yes. It's belonged to the Hales . . . well, until now."

"Is it odd for you to be here, in your family home?"

"Actually, I can't recall stepping inside Windhaven even once after my uncle inherited it. It was my grandparents' when I was growing up. We weren't close, either."

"So it wouldn't be a problem working for me?"

It would be a lot of things, she thought. After what she'd read online, she wasn't sure she wanted anything to do with Max Carr. From her brief search it was clear he was a MOTU—a master-of-the-universe type. But he didn't just grace the pages of *Forbes, The Wall Street Journal,* and *Bloomberg Businessweek;* he also hit the gossip pages. There'd been dozens of pictures showing him with one model/starlet type after another. Clearly his "I can have anything I want" aura worked well with the opposite sex.

Max Carr was the type of man Piper liked to snag and then shag, and the kind Dakota avoided like the plague.

But this was a business meeting. Max Carr wasn't looking to become friends, as Gen Monaghan and Alex Miller had, and he wasn't looking to date her. She'd be caring for his property. Period.

With luck, she might never have to interact with him again after this meeting. She had a number of clients where for all intents and purposes she was like an invisible genie. She'd prefer to go the invisible route—Dakota the friendly ghost—but she had to get the job first.

"A problem with respect to my family, you mean? They'll be outraged, but that's one of their favorite attitudes."

"I met your uncle."

"Ah, then you've had a taste of the Hale charm," she said lightly. "Wait until you run into my aunt Mimi. She consumes a steady diet of sour grapes." And that was really enough about her wildly dysfunctional family. "Windhaven's a beautiful property. I hope you'll be happy here."

She pulled out her notebook from her leather tote as well as her business card and a glossy folder. Inside was an overview of the company, a list of the jobs her staff routinely performed, and references from numerous clients, Alex and Gen among them. She handed the folder and her card to him.

He tucked the card in the back pocket of his jeans, opened the folder, and scanned its contents. "Very impressive."

This from the man who'd had article after article written about his business coups. "Thank you. Would you like to discuss what you're looking for with respect to Windhaven?" She glanced around and caught herself. *Great.* He had her so rattled, she was actually looking for a chair in a room bare of everything save dust.

From the small smile curving his lips, he must have noticed. "There's not a stick of furniture in the place other than the mattress I had the realtor deliver. I'm assuming you'd rather not sit there."

"No! I mean, yes, that's right." She fumbled for more but came up empty, her mind flooded with images of the two of them on the bed. And where had their clothes gone?

The corners of his eyes crinkled. "How about we sit outside, on the porch steps?"

Had Max Carr just teased her? Yeah, but so what? He didn't have to be professional. She did.

"Perfect," she said coolly.

Windhaven was a sprawling shingled "cottage" that in any other part of the world would be labeled a mansion. The porch steps, in proportion to the house, were wide. They gave onto a manicured lawn, which led to a gate with a planked walkway to the dunes and the sea beyond. She sat down on the top step as far as she could from Max Carr's lean length and drew a deep breath of the salty air.

"As you can see, we offer an extensive list of services." She rummaged for a pen in her bag and passed it to him. "You can check off the ones that interest you."

He took a moment to scan the relevant page again. It was more than enough time to study him in discreet glances. Just because he wasn't her type didn't mean she was blind.

Then he began ticking off boxes next to the menu, and her heart beat faster still.

Silently he handed it back.

There was definitely one thing to like about Max Carr: all the lovely bold checks he'd made. Only two boxes were left blank, the one for babysitting and the other for pet care. "You want all this?"

"No. I want more."

With any other potential client, hearing those words would

have sent her cartwheeling across the lawn, a forbidden joy when her grandparents lived here. But something told her that working for this man was going to complicate her life even more than she'd imagined. "What else can Premier Service provide for you, Mr. Carr?"

"It's Max," he corrected. "I'll need you to oversee the remodeling and furnishing of the house and grounds. Structurally the house is sound but—"

"Excuse me, Mr. Carr—"

"I said, it's Max."

Fine. "Max. There are many interior designers on the East End who'd be happy to work with you—"

"But *I* don't want to work with them. A designer remodeled my New York apartment and believed that was license to pester me every other hour about types of wood and fabrics and delivery snafus. If you can do all this"—his index finger ran down Premier's checklist of services—"I imagine you can oversee any changes to the house and then furnish it."

She swallowed. "Well, yes." The entire house and grounds? This would be her biggest account yet. She should have figured Max Carr wouldn't do things by halves. "Nonetheless, I'd like to consult with someone. You've already invested quite a bit of money in this house. It should come out just the way you want it. I know a designer. Her name's Astrid Shibles. She does beautiful work and has a reputation for getting the job done on time."

"Fine. Retain her. But I want you to be in charge of everything."

"I have a very competent staff."

"I want you. Consider yourself my personal assistant for the foreseeable future. I want the job here done well and I want it done fast. How much will it cost for you to say yes and accomplish that?"

She blinked. "This is a big job. It won't be cheap," she warned, deciding to be as blunt as he.

"I hadn't realized the Hamptons were the place for bargains."

A laugh escaped her. "Good point."

"So how much?"

She stole another look at him. He was staring out at the ocean, a wide strip of rolling gray. The waves had been cranking today at Turtle Cove when she'd surfed at dawn. His profile was as arresting as every other part of him. His nose had a bump as if it had been broken. Had that happened in a football game? she wondered. She'd read that he'd been the starting quarterback at UPenn.

And why was this man so distracting?

It was one thing to be intimidated by his long list of accomplishments and successful business deals, quite another to be hung up on his looks and charisma.

At least he wouldn't be asking for her help in finding dates. The women on the East End were going to go nuts when they got a load of him.

Dragging her gaze away, she fixed her attention on the form he'd filled out. Then she did a rough calculation of how much she'd earn for overseeing nearly every aspect of this man's life in the Hamptons.

"We charge on an hourly basis for our services. Our rates are in the booklet. The personal assistant part of the job is different, so for that my rate would be double. I won't charge a commission on anything we buy for you. Does that seem fair?"

"Suits me. Though you'll probably come to regret not charging me triple."

"I don't take advantage of my clients that way," she said. At double her rate she would do well enough to ensure there'd be no layoffs this winter. She'd even be able to give Rae a promotion and a much-needed raise. And if she did a good job, Premier Service's reputation would soar and her business would grow. She gripped the wooden step to keep from jumping up and down and shouting her triumph all the way to Portugal.

And for the record, she was pretty confident she could handle whatever Max Carr threw at her. After all, dealing with difficult and demanding people was second nature to her. But there was no time like the present to scope out how demanding he'd be. Or how outrageous his demands.

"However, I haven't agreed to take *you* on yet," she said, and was pleased to see him lift a brow in surprised amusement. She suspected he was used to getting his way. "Why don't we go through the house so I can get a better sense of your tastes and what you'd like done? Then I'll know whether I'm right for the job."

They started in the kitchen. Recently remodeled by her uncle's third wife, it had the requisite Viking range and double wall oven, a Sub-Zero refrigerator, carved wood cabinets, subway tiles, and sandstone counters. The kitchen island was large enough to eat at. Mimi had detailed the renovation with her usual criticisms, thinly veiled envy, and boasts that Elliott had hired the top kitchen design company in the Hamptons. Dakota thought the kitchen rather nice and well laid out. The pendant light fixtures could be improved upon, though, and the paint color was all wrong.

Opening her notebook, she placed it on the counter and made a notation. "Does the kitchen suit you or would you like it redone?"

"The kitchen's fine. I don't cook much."

She'd need to find out what he liked to eat, then, but before she could quiz him, he spoke.

"I need an espresso machine. The coffee I found in town was insipid."

"Where'd you go?"

"Can't remember."

"I'll give you a list of places. There's the Golden Pear on Newtown Lane—that's probably the closest. I often go to Sagtown Coffee in Sag Harbor. It's a short drive during the off-season, and they're very serious about their coffee. Any particular brand of machine?"

"I have a Marzocco in New York. It works well."

At a price tag of $4,500, she certainly hoped it did. She wrote the espresso maker down.

"And in terms of food?"

"I'll eat anything." He paused. "Except liver."

"Pâté?"

"No liver."

For some odd reason his answer made her want to ruffle his wavy dark hair. What a ridiculous impulse. He had women aplenty to do that and more.

He was looking impatient. Time to move on. "How about I email you a list of foods, wines, and alcohols for you to check off?"

He nodded. "Sounds good."

She thought of the bells and whistles that Mara Bridges, a realtor who used Premier Service to spruce up the houses she listed, claimed many wealthy buyers now considered absolute essentials. "The basement is large. Would you like a temperature-controlled wine cellar?"

"Sure."

She jotted it down in her notebook and then, with her pen poised, asked, "With or without a tasting room?"

He gave her a long look. "Without."

"And how about a fully automated home system? So the pool

can be set at the desired temperature when you arrive? We can also fit the pool with a retractable cover."

He didn't hesitate. "Yes to all those. And the security system needs to be upgraded. And get an electrician in to check the wiring. Plus I'll need an office. That room off the library should be fine."

Her grandfather's old study. She'd never been invited inside. *Don't think about that,* she told herself. *Concentrate on this man, who's a techie, who's work-driven, and likes snazzy espresso machines.* "I have a hunch the electricity was upgraded to accommodate all these appliances." She indicated the gleaming stainless steel surrounding them. "But I'll have an electrician come out on Tuesday to verify."

"How about today?"

She smiled. "Holiday weekend. I'm good, but I'm not God." She thought of a few more of Mara Bridges's home "essentials." "How about an elevator?" she asked casually.

"This is a two-story house."

"Some people's luggage is too heavy to carry upstairs."

"I think I can manage." A faint smile teased the corners of his mouth.

She was not going to let him catch her glancing at the breadth of his shoulders or the bulge of his biceps for confirmation.

"And then there are elderly parents or in-laws who might have difficulty negotiating steps."

His face became stony. "No elevator."

She wasn't stupid when it came to paddling into dangerous waters. She'd just entered them. Gathering up her pen and notebook, she said easily, "Shall we look at the other rooms?"

They toured the downstairs, Max walking beside her, his expression still remote.

The dining room held no interest for him. She'd figure that room out with Astrid.

Crossing the wide hallway, they entered the library. This was where the Christmas tree had stood, opposite the grand piano that no one ever played yet she'd been forbidden to touch.

The Ghost of Christmas Past was particularly ghoulish in her case. She had a hunch Max's ghosts weren't all that friendly, either.

"This library's beautiful with the pond views. It might be nice to read here on a rainy weekend."

He glanced at the empty shelves lining the walls. "I like history and biographies."

"Any fiction?"

"Mysteries. Thrillers."

Thank God she wasn't going to have to buy books by the foot, she thought as she made another notation. "The room's large enough to accommodate a pool table as well as sofas. Do you play?"

"Yeah, I shoot pool."

They decided that her grandmother's sitting room would become the media room. Dakota pictured her grandmother spinning in her grave.

As she suspected, it was the office that he cared about. To her relief, the tension that had gripped him over her elevator comment dissipated as he told her what size desk he wanted, what style of desk chair, and the need for extra outlets.

"Well, I think I can handle the rest of the downstairs with Astrid." A sudden idea occurred to her. "But how about a personal gym? I read that you played football in college. It could go in the den, which—"

"You Googled me?" The question was sharp.

"Why, yes. It helps if I understand my clients' lifestyles. And I routinely research potential clients' backgrounds and run criminal checks, too. I'm not going to expose my employees to sex offenders or work for anyone with a history of nonpayment or a habit of making deranged allegations. My job is hard enough."

"And what did you discover about me?"

Something in his tone had her abruptly wondering if he was going to show her the door. Her stomach clenched. In these past forty minutes she'd already envisioned Rae's reaction when Dakota promoted her. She'd be over the moon.

But no matter how advantageous working for Max might be, she was not going to be intimidated for running her company diligently and protecting her employees.

"What did I find out? Well, besides the fact that you were a college football star, then traded in your cleats and shoulder pads for a job at an investment bank where you tore through the ranks before moving on to join a private equity firm where you became partner within two years, not much. From all the deals you've negotiated and companies you've guided, I assume you're very, very successful." *And from the photos I've seen, I know you date beautiful women. Lots of them,* she added silently. "You don't, however, have a criminal record. Nor do I," she finished with a tight smile.

"My assistant already informed me." He looked at her in silence. "You'll sign a confidentiality agreement."

It wasn't a question.

"Naturally. My staff and I—as well as the companies I hire for outside work—pride ourselves on discretion."

"Naturally," he repeated. "And yes to the gym. I'll need free weights, medicine balls, a rack system, a bench, a rowing machine, a treadmill, rubber flooring, and a punching bag."

And mirrors.

"What was that?"

Her pen stilled. Had she actually said that aloud? Or had she made some involuntary noise at the thought of all those muscles bunching and flexing? What was wrong with her? She didn't do snark with potential clients or get hung up about their looks. She cleared her throat. "Nothing of importance," she replied. "Shall we continue upstairs?"

*

The last room they visited was the master bedroom. By now Dakota had filled pages with notes for purchases and design ideas. The bedroom was big, with a fireplace, yet with Max prowling it restlessly, the room felt as small as the front closet in her own house. She wondered whether he, too, was trying to ignore the king-sized mattress with its twisted sheets and piled pillows.

When he came to a stop in front of the French windows, which opened onto a deck with a view of the ocean, she took a deep breath. *Focus,* she told herself.

"What do you like in terms of decor?"

He gave a restless shrug. "I know what I *don't* like. Fussy wallpaper."

She froze.

Had Max somehow learned of Piper's great adventure in the bathroom of that apartment in the Dakota? Was he alluding to *that* wallpaper as a way of retaliating for her having Googled him?

She was being paranoid, she knew. She blamed it on the lingering effects of a visit with Mimi and Piper. It always brought out the worst in her.

Then something at the periphery of her vision registered and she looked about her rather than at him or the fantasy-inspiring bed. The walls were covered in a red floral pattern, the wallpaper fussy indeed. More fitting for an old lady with pretensions to royalty. And Max, for all his wealth and power, struck her as refreshingly unpretentious.

"The wallpaper will go."

"As soon as possible. It's driving me nuts. Take all the wallpaper down. Everywhere."

She felt an odd and hopefully fleeting affection for him. But it was very hard not to like someone who was also a member of the I Despise Wallpaper Club.

He'd begun to circle the room again with the same restless energy he'd displayed earlier. He stopped in front of her, and she reflexively hugged her notebook to her chest.

"So did I pass the test?"

"Excuse me?" she asked.

"The tasting room, spa with sauna, elevator, home movie theater, what-have-you test. The one where you tried to assess just how much of a spoiled, self-important dick I was."

She bit the inside of her cheek. She'd thought she was being fairly subtle. "You passed."

A single eyebrow rose in challenge. "So will you take me on as a client and do the job?"

She clicked her pen and transferred it to her other hand, intending to reach out and shake his. Then she thought better of it. He was too potent and that unmade bed too unnerving. She nodded instead. "Yes. You've got yourself a personal concierge service."

CHAPTER SEVEN

Dakota Hale had a voice that was made for hot nights and sin.

Max had been surprised when he opened the door. For all that Alex had hinted at how different Dakota was, he'd nonetheless expected a female version of her uncle Elliott: a blond, blue-eyed country club type. Instead he found himself staring at an Amazon whose olive skin tone would never fade in the dead of winter.

She stood easily five foot ten. In heels she'd be nearly eye to eye with him. It would be easy to lose himself in those gold-brown depths. Her face was as strong as the rest of her. Wide cheekbones were balanced by a square jaw; lush lips were coated with the barest trace of a nude lipstick.

She wore her brown hair in a tousled mop, its front ends grazing the line of her jaw. He thought it was just long enough for him to wrap his fingers around and hold her by as he claimed a first taste.

A weird impulse. He generally went for blondes with long

shimmering tresses, women who wore more than a hint of lipstick, women who did everything they could to accentuate their femininity and sexuality. Dakota Hale was dressed in a beige wool poncho that hung from her shoulders and ended at the top of her thighs, obscuring everything except the tantalizing swell of her breasts.

What kind of woman wore a poncho?

One who didn't want a man checking her out.

Message delivered.

But then, in the two seconds it had taken for him to catalog and acknowledge these details, she held out her hand and said, "Hello, I'm Dakota Hale."

The husky rasp had everything inside him going on alert. Hers was the kind of voice associated with the Lauran Bacalls, Anne Bancrofts, and Kathleen Turners of the world—dames who smoked a pack a day and threw back whiskey like it was mother's milk.

With a voice like that, she could stand on a street corner and read pages from a phonebook and men would empty the contents of their wallets onto her donation plate in the hopes that she might turn her gaze their way and say, "Call me maybe."

He'd been similarly affected. It was why, when he led her into the empty house, that comment about them conducting the interview on his mattress upstairs had slipped out. He wasn't usually a dumbass, but her voice and looks had him thinking of all sorts of things he'd like to discover about her. Not one of them involved the environmentally friendly cleaning products listed on the info sheets or what kind of food he wanted in his refrigerator.

Early on in business school Max had learned an important lesson: a successful entrepreneur was one who identified a pain point—a problem that the prospective business would satisfy.

Dakota Hale had chosen to build a personal concierge service, hard work that was all about anticipating, solving, and fulfilling rich people's needs and desires. It also required effacing oneself, no easy task when one was as striking as she and possessed of a sex goddess's voice.

From the way she'd questioned him about his habits and preferences while they toured the house, he could tell how good she was at satisfying the pain point—as good as Alex had promised.

Perhaps with another client, one of those "Me, me, me!" types, she might actually be invisible. He supposed he should give himself a pat on the back that he hadn't reached that level of self-absorption. As it was, he couldn't help but wonder what was going on inside her head as they inspected her family's former home. The flashes of vulnerability he caught on her face before she redirected her thoughts to ways of transforming the rooms for his pleasure alone told him there was a whole lot more to Dakota than she showed to the world.

Max liked puzzles, and Dakota, with her odd choice of business for someone with that pedigree and her mix of strength and vulnerability, was an intriguing one.

He glanced at her again and caught her stealing a peek at the mattress the realtor had delivered. The temptation to cross the bedroom and see what it would take to tumble her onto it, taste that mouth, and lift up that damned poncho was strong. Would she taste as good as he imagined? How would she feel as they rolled across the feather-topped expanse? If she ended up on top, would she stay or would she go?

He had to stop thinking with his cock.

In the aftermath of Ashley's blackmail attempt, he should be abstaining from sex, not contemplating how to maneuver a complicated woman into getting naked.

After all, she'd openly admitted to Googling him. Okay, everybody Googled these days. It wouldn't be a big thing for him, either, except it reminded him of Ashley and some of the more blatantly grasping women he'd slept with recently. He wasn't sure yet if Dakota's confession made her more trustworthy or simply cannier. Until he figured out her endgame, no nude wrestling on the king-sized bed.

So he remained by the window, staring out at the bank of waves approaching the shore, watching them crash and leave a wash of foam in their wake while he answered questions about what he wanted his bedroom to look like.

Christ, how should he know? Rosie had been the creative one, always carrying around a sketchbook and drawing everything that caught her imagination. *Everything.* He'd been the polar opposite—the jock, the math geek—and yet somehow that had only strengthened their connection. . . .

Fighting the cold grief that threatened to choke him, he made a snarling comment about the hideously ugly wallpaper.

Preoccupied as he was, he nonetheless heard her indrawn breath. The sound of a quick and unexpected hurt. He couldn't believe she liked it, either, not after the things she'd been suggesting to him, which meant something else was going on.

And here was the real reason he needed to stay far, far away from Dakota Hale. The flashes of vulnerability were getting to him.

The last person he'd felt protective of was Rosie. He'd failed her and destroyed his family, and now he was left with a hole inside him that nothing could fill.

He was not going to repeat past mistakes. His caring days were over.

Needing to finish this so-called interview and get her out of his bedroom before he did something stupid, he asked whether they were finished, whether he'd passed her test. He'd been amused by some of the over-the-top extravagances until she'd mentioned how some Hamptons homeowners installed elevators for their aging parents and his humor fled.

Because of course he'd bought this huge old place with his father in mind. But Phil Carr wouldn't talk to Max, let alone step inside his new country house to take an elevator ride, or even sit out on the porch and watch the Atlantic in its ever-changing glory. Max would have installed elevators, escalators, and tasting rooms, even plunked a carousel down in the middle of the lawn, if it would have gotten the old man to come. To change his heart. To forgive Max.

But that was never going to happen.

When she told him he'd passed her test, he decided it was time to close the deal. "So will you take the job?"

As she nodded and told him he had a new personal concierge service, a surge of satisfaction went through him. Despite his instinct to avoid getting involved with someone like Dakota, he didn't want her walking out of his life. Not until he was ready.

Neither of them spoke over the fall of their footsteps on the wide wooden staircase or as they walked out the front door to the U-shaped drive.

Her Land Cruiser looked as if it had some serious miles on it. A surfboard was strapped to the roof rack. Another intriguing detail to file away. He'd never surfed. His youth had been football or fixing up cars with his father. After the accident . . . well, everything changed.

She stood next to him, her face angled down as she returned her notebook to her shoulder bag. He thought of the notes she'd taken. It was weird to realize she now knew more of his dislikes and likes than anybody else had bothered to find out in years.

He balled his hands in his front pockets.

They both spoke at once.

"So I'll have Fred Meyers, my assistant, call—"

"I'll find a Marzocco machine—" she began, then stopped and motioned for him to continue.

"Fred will contact you to discuss the finances. Just tell him what you need," he said.

"The biggest expenses will be through Astrid Shibles, the interior designer I mentioned. I'll try to reach her, but she may have gone away for the holiday."

He glanced at the surfboard. "I guess I took you away from yours."

Her mouth lifted in a half smile. "It may have been worth it."

She was referring to the large chunk of change she'd be making with him as a client. A flash of irritation accompanied the thought, which was ridiculous. Why should it bother him that everything seemed to circle back to his money? And why did it bother him especially with respect to Dakota? Why did he want her to be different?

"Well, I should go ..." She ducked her head again and rummaged in her bag, taking out a set of keys.

She looked at him, and their gazes locked and held. She had beautiful eyes. Maybe he said it, or maybe he simply telegraphed his attraction. Her breath caught in sudden awareness. He heard the metallic clang of her keys hitting the gravel.

One of the things that had made him a good quarterback was his quick reaction time.

He crouched and scooped them up, rising just as she bent down. Their foreheads brushed and her eyes widened in a brilliant flare of gold. She straightened, swayed, and then his hands were on her shoulders and, before he could think better of it, his mouth was covering hers.

He could have stayed there for hours, ignoring everything he'd been telling himself just to stand in the driveway and kiss Dakota, his lips brushing in exploratory sweeps. Cinnamon-spicy, she tasted like fall and the cool wind blowing about them. She tasted as wonderful as he'd imagined.

Damn it.

He released her, letting his arms fall to his sides.

She stepped back. A big, at-the-edge-of-a-precipice step. A flush stained her cheekbones. "This is not the kind of service I offer."

Crap, he'd pissed her off.

Inclining his head, he said, "Understood." He held out the keys.

She snatched them and strode to the SUV.

He stood in the driveway long after she'd left, wondering what had prompted that impulsive kiss. It wasn't like him to lose control. He should have been able to resist the temptation she presented. Yet even as he berated himself for his lack of restraint, he recognized a deeper and more troubling explanation. He'd kissed Dakota because he wanted her to think of him as something other than a way to make a profit.

This only showed Max he didn't need a bedroom. He could do stupid anywhere.

CHAPTER EIGHT

"Good morning, Hendrick," Dakota called out as she entered Hendrick Daube's saltbox house the next morning. "Yes, Arlo, I've missed you, too," she said to the large, black Muppet-like dog that bounded toward her and then spun in a shaggy circle of happiness in front of her.

"Dakota, welcome! You're in time for breakfast. I'm making scrambled eggs for Arlo and me."

"Thanks, but none for me," she said, carrying the newspaper and a few groceries she'd bought into the kitchen. "I stopped for a sandwich and a smoothie on my way back from Turtle Cove."

"So, how were the waves? Good?" He took the newspaper from her and put it on the kitchen farm table where a place was set for one. His partner, Marcus, was away for the weekend.

"The sets were nice and clean. I had some decent rides."

"Crowded?" he asked, stirring the scrambled eggs that were cooking in the frying pan.

"Not too bad. The guys were there. The regulars." Opening the refrigerator, she put away a roast chicken and some salad. On the counter she placed an apple pie she'd baked. Hendrick could bring the leftovers back with him to the city on Tuesday.

The toaster dinged. Removing two thick slices of toast and buttering them, he arranged them on a plate. "And what do you have planned for the rest of your Sunday?"

"I'm invited to brunch at Gen and Alex's."

"Good." He looked over at Dakota and nodded approvingly. "You need to relax with friends more."

She smiled. "You're the best, you know that, right?"

He scooped fluffy eggs onto his buttered toast and spooned a small amount into Arlo's bowl. The dog's tail beat madly. "Don't tell Marcus. He firmly believes that title's his."

If Hendrick hadn't been nearly forty years her senior and gay, she'd have fought tooth and nail to be his partner. In addition to being one of the kindest people in the world, he also had the distinction of having been her first client.

The day they met had been a frustrating one. She'd spent it cycling through the East Hampton neighborhoods near her middle school and Piper's house, knocking on doors and handing out flyers listing the odd jobs she was willing to do—an ancient version of the form she now presented to potential clients. Most of the people who'd bothered to answer the door had smiled stiffly, glanced at the photocopied sheet, and sent her on her way.

Hendrick was different.

He'd actually come out of his house and invited her to sit on a wooden bench at the base of a gnarled tree that grew in his front yard. Taking the sheet, he read it carefully. Then he'd asked why she wanted a job. She explained that she wanted a surfboard. Her friends Lauren and Tom had lent her theirs this past summer, but that had meant depriving them of their rides. She'd done the math. If she got enough jobs this fall, she'd be able to afford her own next summer.

When she told him her name, Hendrick must have known who she was. Or, rather, who Piper was, because he didn't ask Dakota about her father, only whether her mother couldn't help with the purchase.

It had been several months since Piper had decided to share the story of Dakota's conception, and Dakota still had trouble dealing with it.

"I'm getting the board myself. Otherwise it will become all about Piper." She'd already come to recognize that the way to survive her mother was to carve out her own space and find her independence wherever she could.

"Your mom, have you always called her Piper?"

It was funny. When Hendrick asked the question, it didn't make her feel weird, like when everyone else remarked on it. "Yeah." The tree bark scratched, so she leaned forward. "She says parents are boring and that she and I—we're different. More like sisters. Buddies." She stared at the scuffed toe of her sneaker.

"Well, I understand why you'd want to buy the surfboard. It's good to have something that's your very own, that you earned. I don't surf myself, but I love driving to Montauk and watching the surfers."

"Some of them are awesome."

"Indeed they are. As it so happens, I was just thinking that I could use a responsible plant-waterer when I'm in the city teaching and seeing patients."

"So you're a doctor?" He looked like one. He had kind eyes of a soft, faded blue. He sat with his arms folded across his chest as if he could sit there for hours. She liked that he didn't seem in any hurry to end their conversation.

"Yes, I'm a psychiatrist. I have some autumn ferns that require frequent watering and some others that only need a drop or two once a week. I'll show them all to you, of course, but you'll have to remember their needs. Think you're up to the demands of the job?"

She was kind of disappointed that he wasn't a surgeon. A brain surgeon would have been super cool, but since it sounded as if he might give her a job, she decided that his being a psychiatrist was all right, if a little boring. "I can water your plants. And rake your lawn, too. This tree has a lot of leaves." Some were already scattered on the grass.

He looked up, considering the canopy of remaining leaves. "It does. I like your initiative. You strike me as responsible, too. You'll remember to lock up the house when you leave? And you'll put away the rake in the shed?"

She nodded, trying to contain her excitement. "Yes. Absolutely."

"Well, then consider yourself hired."

She hadn't forgotten the thrill of winning that first job. It had also marked the beginning of one of her most important friendships. Hendrick had become a voice of sanity for her.

Piper's reaction had been predictable. "You want to waste your time watering a shrink's plants? Suit yourself. He's queer, you know."

She didn't. When she finally figured out what her mother meant, what *that* meant, she decided that she was fine with working for someone who was queer—it was a lot better than having a mother who overshared.

Not even Mimi, try as she might, could poison the growing friendship.

"So I hear you've become pals with Hendrick Daube. Are you pouring your heart out to him, telling him all about poor little you and your terrible life? You should be grateful you're alive."

Because Hendrick had already begun offering her coping strategies in his gentle and offhand manner, she was able to recognize that the vile things Mimi spewed had little to do with her. She also learned not to engage; Mimi hated nothing more than to be ignored.

On the last weekend before school let out for the summer, Dakota had returned from giving Daisy, Arlo's equally shaggy predecessor, her afternoon walk—the list of jobs she performed had grown steadily over the year—and found Hendrick standing beside his ancient Volvo station wagon. He'd waved them over.

Assuming he needed a hand with the groceries, her mouth had fallen open in an O of astonishment when she saw the shiny long board lying propped against the top of the backseat. The board was a thing of beauty, one half covered in wide navy blue and cream stripes, the other colored a robin's egg blue. A thin yellow line bisected its length.

Speechless, she stared.

"This is for you," he said. "So you'll be able to start surfing as soon as the water is warm enough."

"I—I—" She blinked, her eyes stinging, her throat closed too tight for words.

"No putting me off, Dakota. You've worked hard for me all fall, winter, and spring, never missing a day or coming up with an excuse to leave early. You've earned this."

"I—" She swallowed and tried again. "I've been saving for it."

"I know. But out of curiosity I went to the surf shop in Montauk. Even now that you're walking Daisy, picking up my mail at the post office, and helping in the garden, it would have taken you too long to buy a board as nice as this one. The man at the surf shop said you'll be able to use it for a long time. I want you to have this, Dakota."

She remembered squeezing Daisy's leash so hard the leather dug into her palm. Then slowly she reached out to stroke the rounded edges of the board with her free hand. Too choked with emotion, she hadn't been able to thank him properly, had only nodded, her fingers skimming its cool, glossy surface.

Fifteen years later, and she still had the board. It hung in pride of place over her mantelpiece. While she might have fancier boards and fancier clients now, none meant as much to her as the one given to her by this infinitely kind and wise man.

She took the frying pan from him and began to scrub. "Having brunch with Gen and Alex will be fun," she agreed. "And a huge improvement over the way my weekend started. Just so you know, I'm going to have to recalculate my NVUs with respect to Piper and Mimi, Hendrick."

"Dare I hope this means that you're getting better at tolerating their antics? Coffee?" he asked, lifting the coffeepot in inquiry.

"A half a cup, please." She set the scrubbed pan in the dish drainer and followed Max over to the table. "I'm afraid I didn't come close to my allotted NVUs. My blood pressure was soaring after ten minutes with the Hale sisters. I even fantasized about sprinkling arsenic in Mimi's martini. And for the record, they once again failed the 'share a brew or two' test," she said, referring to another of Hendrick's handy guidelines to life, what he called the "two beers and a puppy" test.

In a nutshell, the test determined whether the family member, acquaintance, or co-worker would be a good candidate to enjoy a beer with, or could be depended upon to help with the important stuff in life, such as caring for a beloved puppy for a weekend. Some people might fall into the "share a couple of beers" category. Others might be trustworthy enough to puppy-sit. A few rare individuals ticked both boxes; they were the truly wonderful people in one's life.

And then there were those who couldn't be counted on for anything, not for good company or a helping hand. Dakota's family were card-carrying members of the "undependables."

She swallowed a sip of coffee. "But in Piper and Mimi's defense, Friday afternoon was rough. Elliott sold Windhaven."

"He sold it?"

"Yup. Mimi's livid. Piper's performing her own interpretation of mourning—which involves lounging on the sofa and inspecting her nail polish. She'll rouse herself quickly enough, though, when she learns I'm going to be working for Windhaven's new owner. Think I should take out a life insurance policy?"

"You'll be working for the new owner? My, my, well done, Dakota."

Her smile was so wide it ached. "Crazy, huh? But he kind of made me an offer I couldn't refuse. He's having me redo the whole house, among other things. It's my biggest account yet, Hendrick. I haven't told Rae the good news—you know how superstitious I am—but she's going to be promoted."

"She'll be overjoyed."

"Yeah." Dakota felt a flush of pleasure and pride.

Finished eating, Hendrick clapped his hands. "Bravo, Dakota."

She stood and sketched a quick curtsy.

Hendrick stood, too, and carried his plate to the sink. "And what's he like?" he asked, adding when she tried to take his plate, "No, Dakota. You were too quick with the pan. I insist on putting my own dishes away."

"You know you're going to spoil me for any other man."

"Quite possibly, and stop avoiding answering my question about your newest client."

Guilty as charged.

She'd spent much of yesterday thinking about Max. It didn't make it any easier to talk about him. He'd swept into her world with enough force to change the landscape. And that was without factoring in his kiss. She couldn't discuss that with Hendrick, either, not when her feelings were so muddled.

It would be simpler if she could just hold on to her anger at

Max. But she was equally annoyed with herself for how much she'd enjoyed it. What Max Carr managed with little more than a graze of lips put all the other kisses she'd received to shame.

This was what came from having an anemic sex life. But during the summer months she was simply too busy to date, and when she did have a free night, she preferred to hang with her friends or catch some much-needed Z's so she could hit the waves bright and early. Few of the guys she dated ranked anywhere near the breathtaking pleasure she derived from surfing at sunrise.

She was going to do her best to forget that Max's kiss had left her just as breathless.

"Dakota," Hendrick said.

"Right. Well, his name is Max Carr and he's rich and successful—he's in private equity. But there's something—I haven't figured out what it is—that might save him from being just another high-maintenance plutocrat."

She told him about the questions she'd asked Max about upgrades to the house. "I don't know whether I've become jaded due to some of my more spoiled clients, but I sounded as snobbish as Mimi. And Max called me on it. For all his wealth, he seems quite down-to-earth. He was basically camping out in the house." It struck her as she said this that Max might not even have noticed the vast emptiness around him. She wondered why.

"It sounds as if you like him."

"I wouldn't go that far." And she was sure the impact of his kiss would soon fade.

"Well, I'm pleased you took the job."

"You may change your tune when I come sobbing to you about Piper and Mimi once they've heard about my new employer. I'm hoping I can fly under their radar for a while. Luckily Elliott's gone back to Bermuda, or he might have to acknowledge me long enough to rip me in two."

He made a scoffing noise. "In all the years I've known you,

you've never once come sobbing to me. And you can stand up to the likes of Elliott. You're one of the strongest women I know."

Maybe, maybe not. But at the moment her family and all their conniving ways concerned her less than how she'd fare when it came to dealing with Max Carr.

CHAPTER NINE

Alex and Gen's house was nestled between Georgica Pond and the ocean, barely a third of a mile away from Windhaven as the gull flew. It, too, was a large house, another Hamptons "cottage." Some cars were in the driveway when Dakota rolled up. She spotted her friend Lauren's among them, which was lovely. With summer so hectic for both of them, they hadn't seen enough of each other.

The front door was open, allowing the crisp air to waft into the house. Dakota pressed the doorbell, called out a hello, and peered through the screen door, grinning when she heard the hurried stomp of feet.

"Hi, Gracie."

"They're out in the back," Gracie said by way of greeting. Pulling open the door, she took Dakota's hand and tugged. "Come."

Dakota glanced down at the small hand holding hers and marveled at how trusting and open this child was, how secure in her world. If Dakota had ever felt that way as a child, it had been only briefly, her sense of security disappearing when her mother abdicated her role as parent, preferring the one of eternal party girl.

Dakota let herself be tugged along. "So did you have another riding lesson yesterday?"

"Yeah. I got to ride Gingersnap. I rode him because Katie wasn't there. She and Ali are at their grandparents'. Lauren said I did really well. She's so nice."

"I like her a lot, too. Do you know we became friends when we were just a little older than you?"

There was a vigorous nod at the level of Dakota's hip. "Mommy told me. She's already here."

"Who, you mean Lauren?" Lauren's schedule was still crazy. Hamptons horse people came out on weekends for lessons and to hack until it was time to trailer their mounts to Wellington, Florida, for the winter show season.

"Yeah. She's having Becky teach the afternoon lessons."

Gracie was a font of information. Dakota smiled and said, "That's great."

They'd just passed the living room, where a portrait of Grace Miller hung over the mantelpiece. Gen had painted it. Dakota paused to admire the canvas. "I really love your mom's paintings."

Another nod. "That was my daddy's great-aunt. I'm named after her but I never met her. I don't think I look like her."

Dakota knew about searching for one's identity in others' faces. In her case it was a fruitless task.

"Well, Gracie, it would have been your great-great-uncle who was your blood relative."

"Oh. That's right."

"I didn't know Mrs. Miller too well, but she was really smart and she loved art."

"I love art, too." Gracie was silent for a second as she studied the portrait of a gray-haired woman with piercing blue eyes. "Mommy's going to have a big show of her paintings in New York. In January. After Christmas."

"I bet she'll sell them all."

"That's what Daddy says." With a final look at the portrait, Gracie hurried on, leading Dakota past the family photographs lining the wide hallway. "Ty and Steve are here with Connor. Lee couldn't come. He's at a sleepover. Lee and Connor ride at Lauren's, too. But they're in a more advanced group."

It was a testament to Lauren's coaching that Ty and Steve Sheppard had chosen her junior riding program for their sons. Steve Sheppard was a former Olympian who trained jumpers at his own private stable, Southwind, in Bridgehampton. His wife, Ty, helped run his show barn and competed on the amateur level. She'd also become one of the organizers for the Hampton Classic, the huge glitzy horse show that was held at the end of the summer. So, a horse-centric family.

It made Dakota happy and ridiculously proud that Lauren was doing so well after her husband Zach's death. Her only worry was that she might be using her stable and its constant demands to avoid any serious relationships with men ... and if Lauren could hear her thoughts, she'd shake her head and say this was a prime example of the pot calling the kettle black.

"Connor and Max are playing football," Gracie said. "I don't like football very much, and ..."

Whatever else Gracie was going to share with Dakota was lost. *Max.* She should have guessed he'd be here. It made sense that Alex and Gen would invite him. But for some reason she'd assumed he'd be back in New York in his swank designer-decorated apartment, setting female hearts a-flutter.

Now she had to calm her own.

*

Gen, Lauren, and Ty were sitting on the patio, their chairs turned in the direction of the lawn that stretched between the back of the house and Gen's painting studio. At the sound of her daughter's voice—Grace was still updating Dakota about everyone and everything—Gen smiled and rose to give her a hug. "Dakota, we're so glad you're here. Gracie, sweetie, could you go tell Tilly that Dakota has arrived?"

"Sure." Gracie took off at a run.

Lauren looked over and smiled. "Hey, friend, long time no see. I'd get up, but Carney's decided I'm a fantastic pillow." A dark gray Irish wolfhound rested its cinder-block-sized head on Lauren's feet.

"Understood. Glad to see you rather than the inside of your fridge."

"Which gleams, thanks to Lupe and Tanya. And those burritos you made last week were amazing. Ali ate an entire one. The lasagna was a hit, too. Katie didn't even pick out the vegetables," Lauren said.

In addition to sending Lupe and Tanya, two of Dakota's employees, to Lauren's farmhouse to clean and do the piles of laundry, which consisted mostly of pairs of breeches and short-sleeved polo shirts, Dakota did a weekly grocery shopping and prepared a few easy meals for Lauren and the girls.

"I'll put the burritos and the lasagna in the menu rotation. Ali and Katie are . . . ?"

"With Zach's parents. A trip to the American Girl store was mentioned." Lauren raised her brows.

Dakota grinned in return. As kids neither she nor Lauren had been very doll-oriented. She turned to Ty Sheppard. "Hello, Ty. It's great to see you again. How was your summer?"

"Crazy but good. And you?"

"Crazy but good," she echoed.

They shared a smile.

Ty Sheppard was the ultimate in cool. Raised by her autocratic real estate mogul father, she'd stood up to him and walked away from her inheritance in order to save Steve Sheppard's horse farm, Southwind, from being sliced into multimillion-dollar lots for multimillion-dollar homes. While Dakota had founded her business on serving these potential homeowners, she didn't want to see the area's natural beauty destroyed or have its farmland lost to the Hamptons version of McMansions.

"Dakota, what can I offer you? Coffee? Tea? A mimosa?" Gen asked, gesturing to a teak table laden with carafes, pitchers, and glasses. A bottle of champagne chilled in an ice bucket.

No mimosas if Max Carr was about. He made her brain fuzzy enough. Would he know she was still obsessing about their kiss? "I'd love a coffee."

"You take it black, right?"

"Please."

"A woman after my own heart." Gen grinned. "I don't like anything coming between me and my caffeine." Handing her a steaming mug, she said, "Come and take a seat next to Lauren and Ty and enjoy the show."

That's when Dakota understood why the chairs had been dragged into a line, all facing the lawn. Some serious male beauty was on display.

The Hamptons were not bereft of good-looking individuals. But the three men playing football with eight-year-old Connor topped the male beauty scale. Alex Miller had the classic, clean-cut features to match his dark blond hair and blue eyes. She knew he played squash, his speed evident as he sprinted down the length of the lawn to catch the ball flying through the air. Steve Sheppard's features were more rugged and his physique honed from the hours he spent in the saddle. But it was Max who made Dakota's breath catch. Taller and more muscular than the other two, he moved with the effortless grace of an athlete in his element.

Connor was his receiver. He'd raced down the lawn as Alex and Steve bore down on Max. Max nimbly evaded them, side-stepping and dodging, while cradling the football in his large hand and waiting for Connor to reach the end of the lawn, the end zone. When Connor turned, Max feinted one more time, slipping past Alex's outstretched hands, and let the football fly.

It was a long pass. Many with less strength would have had to drill it. Max threw it with ease. He knew exactly how much force it would take to make the ball land squarely between Connor's waiting hands without knocking the boy over.

Connor's yell of triumph as he clutched the ball and then slammed it onto the ground before performing an NFL-inspired victory dance had everyone clapping and the mothers cheering loudly.

"All right," she heard Alex call, "now it's getting real. You better wake up, Carr."

"That's right. Alex and I are done being nice to you and Connor," Steve said.

Max made a motion with his hands. "Bring it on."

"Yeah, bring it on!" Connor chimed.

From her chair, Tyler said, "Connor is in testosterone heaven."

"I'm right there with him," Lauren said. "How about you, Dakota? Are you enjoying the show?"

She refused to admit how very much she liked watching Max move. "Aren't we being terribly sexist here? Shouldn't we be out there playing against the men rather than ogling them?"

"Oh no. That would be a terrible waste," Ty said.

"I don't believe in this 'don't objectify men' business," Gen said. "What about Michelangelo's *David*? It's a celebration of the human form at its finest. What we have here before us is the modern-day inspiration."

"Poetry in motion," Ty said with laughter in her voice.

"Hear, hear." Lauren raised her coffee mug. "I hope to see a painting of this scene in the near future, Gen."

"Life size," Ty suggested.

For a minute silence reigned as they watched the men playing and laughingly hurling insults at each other, the comments undoubtedly milder due to Connor's presence, but no less imaginative.

Yeah, a painting depicting the three men in action would be very well received. "Okay, I'll agree that there's a lot to appreciate on the lawn right now, but I still think we should go out there and show them how to play the game."

"You go right ahead, Dakota." Lauren waved her forward with a grin. "I'll cheer you on."

"Sorry, Dakota. I'm having too much fun watching Connor bond with Alex and Max," Ty said.

"And I'm more into baseball than football," Gen said. "Besides, we're going to eat soon. Tilly was just waiting to put the popovers in the oven. They should be ready now."

"Warm popovers. Now I'm in heaven," Ty said.

"Warm popovers with cheddar and bacon," Gen clarified with a smile. "Tilly put Brooke in charge of adding the bacon, so they should be extra delicious. That little girl likes her bacon. I'm counting on the mimosas to balance them out."

"Popovers and mimosas. My stomach is rumbling already," Lauren said.

"Good. We have to celebrate Max's arrival in the neighborhood," Gen said. Turning to Dakota, she said, "So I hear you agreed to help him get Windhaven spic-and-span and looking beautiful."

"Um, yes. That is, I guess so." Maybe it was good that she wasn't out there playing football. She couldn't manage to answer even a basic question about Max without fumbling.

Dakota felt Lauren's curious gaze on her.

"So Max is a new client?" she asked.

Dakota cleared her throat. "That's right."

"Go you." Lauren's smile widened. "I thought you were taking an extra-special interest in him, even with him moving into the family digs."

"Was I?" She kept her voice casual. "Then it was purely for professional reasons."

If they'd been alone, Lauren would have jumped up, letting Carney's shaggy head land with a thunk on the flagstone, and called Dakota on her BS. Instead she demonstrated her restraint, offering a grave "Of course."

"So you heard about Windhaven?" Dakota asked.

"Gen mentioned it when she introduced me to Max. But I should have guessed when I heard the ungodly howling coming from Dunemere Lane."

"Yes, it was quite the scene."

"I wish I'd been a fly on the wall—a happy fly on the wall. Mimi and Piper deserve to be taken down several notches."

"Mimi certainly does."

"And what has Piper done for you lately, and by that I mean in the past twenty-five years?" But, knowing the comment would lead nowhere—she had already told Dakota countless times to cut her ties with her family because none of them, not even Piper, deserved her loyalty—Lauren said, "Oh, look, the game's broken up and your new client is taking an interest in your presence. I'm sure it's merely for professional reasons, of course."

Max had known Dakota would be coming. Gen had mentioned it when she greeted him at the door. "Hi, Max. How's the house?"

"I like it. The view is pretty incredible."

"Yes. I thought I'd landed in paradise when I was invited by Alex's great-aunt to live out here and use the studio. I could paint the ocean every day and it would offer a different scene each time. And the light out here? A painter's dream."

"I can see how that would be. The sunrise was pretty spectacular."

She led him through the house. It was nice. Lived in. "So Alex is on the patio putting out coffee and champagne. A few friends will be joining us, all locals. But you'll know Dakota." She glanced up at him. "Did you hire her?"

"Yes."

Gen smiled. "Alex said you were smart."

He'd been on alert since Gen's announcement. He told himself he was curious whether Dakota would have the same effect on him as yesterday. He had his answer the minute she arrived, walking hand in hand with the older Miller girl. Everything inside him tensed with awareness.

He made sure not to look directly at her. Alex and Steve Sheppard helped. They were decent players, making him focus on the game. And Connor's enthusiasm was contagious. He spent some minutes teaching Sheppard's kid how to snap and giving him pointers on passing. The boy was sharp. Still, Max's gaze kept flicking over to where Dakota was talking to a blond-haired woman named Laura—or was it Laurie? The two seemed close.

Alex must have received a signal from his wife. "Have to suspend the game, guys. Brunch is ready."

Connor grumbled as loudly as any kid taken away from a game, but he quieted when Max promised to work on more moves after they'd eaten. Then he wished he'd let the boy continue his disgruntled squawking. The noise would have been a welcome distraction as he walked toward her.

She wasn't wearing a poncho today.

She was standing with Gen and the other women. A cream-colored sweater revealed mouth-watering curves just south of her collarbone. Her waist was small, her hips sweetly rounded, and her legs, encased in faded jeans, even longer than he'd imagined. Combined with that arresting face and siren's voice, she was a bombshell. He was in trouble. Deep trouble.

"Hello," she said with a slight nod.

"Hi. Thanks for the email." As promised, she'd sent him a list of cafés and food shops close to East Hampton. "I went to the place you mentioned in Sagaponack. Pretty good croissants." The woman had clearly fried his brain. He was reduced to talking about croissants.

"Loaves & Fishes? I'm glad you liked it. The owners are friends."

The words were polite, but Dakota wasn't quite meeting his eyes. So she was still pissed about the kiss.

"I was surprised at how crowded it was."

"Mm-hmm," she said, nodding. "It has quite the following."

"I asked the woman behind the register about setting up an account and putting your name on it."

"Oh." She gave a tiny shake of her head, and it made her dark hair brush her jaw the way he wanted to. "They don't do that."

"That's what she said."

"We keep all the receipts for client purchases. You'll receive a detailed inventory down to the last croissant."

"So you're still working for me."

She looked at him, and from the flare of awareness in her eyes, he knew she was thinking about the kiss, too.

"I said I would, didn't I?"

"Yes. Yes, you did." It seemed Dakota was a woman of her word.

Gen ushered them into the sunroom, where a large round table was set with a blue-checked cloth and yellow flowers in little vases. The pretty, homey arrangement made Max uncomfortable, as if he were wearing a suit two sizes too small. He didn't make a practice of sitting down to a table like this, one that spoke of family and good times.

"Max, why don't you sit here?" Gen gestured to a chair. "Dakota, you take the seat next to him."

Max pulled out the chair that Gen had indicated was for Dakota. She hesitated and then murmured, "Thank you." Her wool sweater felt soft against the back of his fingers as she took her place.

He sat, hyperaware that he was going to be eating a meal inches away from Dakota and listening to her throaty voice. He was half hoping she'd do something like speak with her mouth full of food so he could shake his fixation when a cellphone pealed. The jingly notes were familiar. They were from a popular chick flick Rosie and her friends had liked to watch, getting up to sing and dance at key scenes . . . his signal to run for the hills, round up some guys to play ball, or go and tinker with an engine in the garage.

It was Dakota's phone. That much was evident from the flutter of activity near his left hip as she grabbed at her pocket and silenced the ringing. "Sorry," she muttered.

Across the table, Lauren—that was her name—sent Dakota a look of weary empathy. He didn't get what that was about, but Dakota must have. She lowered her gaze as if needing all her mental faculties to unfold her napkin.

His discomfort with the cozy atmosphere lessened as he ate a stack of waffles and breakfast sausages and something Gen told him was a popover. His awareness of Dakota did not. He felt the space between them acutely. Imagined closing it so his thigh touched hers. The electricity from the contact—anything but simple—would be an instant crackle and snap.

His focus was such that he noticed her reflexive flinch each time her cell vibrated and how afterward it was harder for her to relax and rejoin the conversation flowing around them.

Someone really wanted to talk to her. From the frequency of the calls the odds were that it was a single obnoxious caller rather several at once.

A jealous boyfriend?

Nah. He didn't know Dakota, but he suspected she wouldn't put up with shit like this from a man. So who, then? A client with a burst pipe? Again, that didn't feel right. Something told him she would have taken the call and ridden out to rescue a client who didn't know the working end of a mop.

As he picked up the rustic ceramic mug that Alex had just refilled for him, her cell buzzed yet again.

"Why don't you answer it?" he asked in a low voice.

She started guiltily.

So she thought he wasn't paying attention, hadn't noticed her cell vibrating every few minutes? Good. Let her be clueless. Because it felt as though he were noticing *everything* when it came to Dakota. And he was none too happy about it.

"I can't." Her whisper was fierce. "She'll stop. Eventually."

To have the caller tagged a "she" pleased him. He told himself it was because he liked to be right. "Who is it? An irate client?"

"I wish." Her tone was resigned. "It's my mother."

He took a bite of popover and chewed. "She worried about what you might be getting up to at noon on a Sunday?"

The question surprised a laugh out of her. Its husky sensuality felt like a feather trailed down his abs. He shifted in his chair.

"Piper worried about me? Hardly."

He filed that comment away. "So what's up?"

"Some drama or other. I don't know and, damn it, I do not care," she enunciated quietly. When her cell buzzed again, she picked up her coffee and took a long sip.

"Want me to answer it?"

She nearly spat out her coffee. When the others glanced at her, she made a show of coughing. "Sorry, I swallowed the wrong way."

Once everyone had returned to their conversations, she cleared her throat and said, "Thanks for the offer. But it wouldn't solve the problem. Not by a long shot." After a careful swallow of coffee, she said, "And what about your parents? Do they resemble burrs?"

His internal locks clicked into place. "Burrs?"

"Yeah, burrs. No matter how hard you try, you just can't get unstuck."

"No."

"Lucky you."

He pushed his plate away. "Yeah."

He had to get out of here. A quick glance around the table told him everyone had finished their food and was merely lingering over their drinks. They wouldn't realize he was bolting. "Hey, Connor, want me to show you how to throw the perfect spiral?"

Over Tilly's protests, Dakota and Lauren helped her clear the dishes while the others, including Gracie despite her professed dislike of football, went back outside to watch Max and Connor.

"What's up?" Lauren asked her as they carried stacks of plates into the kitchen.

"Nothing." Except for her complete obsession with Max. Whatever dysfunction her family claimed, it appeared to be nothing compared to Max's. The Carrs must be pretty messed up if he couldn't talk about them at all. He'd left the table far too abruptly for her not to guess at the cause.

"So what were you and Max talking about? It seemed kind of intense."

"Piper was pulling her usual trick with the phone. He was curious." When her phone vibrated again, she sighed. "I wish she'd get a life."

"Like that's going to happen. She loves being the idle rich."

The phone went silent for the time it took to carry a tray of mugs into the kitchen before buzzing again. "This is ridiculous. Why can't I train her, or at least get her to acknowledge the basic rules of calling?"

Lauren made a *pffft* sound. "You know Piper doesn't respond to training or rules. Like jobs, they're for *other* people."

Lauren certainly had Piper's number.

"Excuse me, Tilly. I'm afraid I have to answer this," she said by way of apology. Opening the back door, she stepped outside, and pressed the button on her phone. "Yes?"

"I am beyond embarrassed. How could you do this to me?" Piper's voice was shrill.

"Do what?"

"That I had to find out that you would be cleaning Windhaven's toilets from *Marcy Klein,* of all people."

Dakota was surprised by how fast word had spread. "What would Marcy Klein know about anything?" she asked, hoping to distract Piper.

"Plenty. You've been hired by Max Carr. He tried to sign you up for a charge account at Loaves & Fishes. You really wanted to rub our noses in it, didn't you?"

Dakota sighed. "I didn't take him on as a client because I wanted to embarrass you."

"So why, then?"

Dakota opened her mouth to list the benefits that would come from having Max Carr as a client. Piper cut her off.

"I get it. He must be as hot as Marcy said."

What to say? Impossible to deny that Max Carr was handsome and very hot.

"Just fuck the guy, Dakota. You don't need to be his servant just because you service him."

A garbled noise—a verbal cringe that was a mix of "Gross" and "Ugh"—was all she managed.

Piper was deaf to it. "Mimi is now beyond livid, angrier than I've ever heard her. And I've had a lifetime of her anger."

"Because you told her." It wasn't a question.

"Of course I did. She's my sister."

And I'm your daughter, Dakota retorted silently. But obviously the Hale reputation was more important to Piper than supporting her only child.

"You have to quit," Piper said.

"What?"

"You can't be one of Windhaven's *staff.*"

"I can't earn a living and grow my business?"

"For God's sake, run your precious business if you must. But just let me know when you've called him so I can get Mimi off my back."

"No."

"No?" Piper's voice was blank with incomprehension.

"No," she repeated calmly. "I'm not going to quit working for Max Carr. This account is important to me and it's vital to Premier Service."

There was silence at the end of the line. Then Piper said, "Mimi always did say you were a little bitch." With a click the line went dead.

Dakota stared at her phone in stupid disbelief. Why, she didn't know. After all, she'd predicted how her family would react to the news. They were just being true to form. But, as always, the reality of their actions was like a slap across the face. No amount of prior warning or bracing herself lessened the sting or the shock.

She swallowed the lump that had formed in her throat. Well, it was done. So much for her being an expert at riding waves, she thought. That had been a major wipeout.

On the plus side, she had a hunch Piper wouldn't be calling anytime soon.

CHAPTER TEN

Dakota was used to working with rich people. Max Carr's wealth left them in the dust. Had she been a different type of person, she would have spent his money like a lab rat that's discovered the correct button for stimulating the pleasure center of its brain, pressing until the poor creature expires from euphoria.

Her last name and her pride prevented her from running amok with limitless spending. She didn't want Max to think that she was in any way taking advantage of him or somehow in cahoots with her family and retaliating for his having scooped up the family manse. To do so would be to stoop to the level of Piper and Mimi—who, three weeks after the phone conversation with Piper, had yet to forgive her for working for the "enemy."

Besides, as exciting as it was to stroll into H Groome in Southampton or Wyeth in Sagaponack or to drive into the city with Astrid Shibles, the interior designer she'd hired to help transform

Windhaven, and roam the floors of the New York Design Center and SoHo furniture showrooms and order whatever caught her fancy (and then have it scheduled for express delivery, the ultimate in consumer gratification), she loved hunting for bargains. She and Astrid had found a number of good ones. Between them, they knew all the local artists and craftsmen and were able to buy some beautiful pieces, like the handcrafted dining room table and set of chairs made by a Sagaponack designer.

"I love clients who trust you to do the job you've been trained to do. This house is going to look amazing. I'm so glad he's allowed us to give the old place a makeover rather than razing it to the ground. Too many old homes are being lost." Astrid raised her camera and snapped a shot of Max's newly transformed bedroom. She was taking pictures of the finished rooms—there were five to date—for her portfolio. Dakota had already cleared Astrid's photographing his new home with Max. Considering his penchant for privacy, it had been generous of him to agree.

"The house looks better than it ever did, which doesn't actually surprise me since you and I have better taste than my uncle Elliott and my grandparents. This room came out especially well," she added, glancing about her in satisfaction.

Gone was the ornate red wallpaper. It had been stripped, and after the walls had been repaired and prepped, they'd been painted a pale gray, with white for the woodwork. The light palette made the room appear even more spacious and contrasted beautifully with the dark espresso of the newly finished floors. Astrid had searched her design resources and found a platform bed frame and headboard in a gray velour that was a couple of shades darker than the walls. Dakota did her best not to imagine Max sleeping in it.

Astrid crossed the room to snap a picture from a different angle. "I do like the window treatments, Dakota. They work. And the blue accents you chose are perfect."

Astrid had campaigned to put a patterned fabric by the windows, but Dakota resisted, remembering Max's stated dislike of fussy patterns. They'd settled on a fog-gray textured linen.

Dakota had scoured shops and found pieces in marine blue—throw pillows, white and blue porcelain table lamps—that added a splash of color and broke up the mix of grays without making the room look overdecorated or too feminine. Even with the addition of an oversized armchair and ottoman in a matching off-white twill, which she had decided would be the perfect spot to sip bourbon and contemplate corporate takeovers while staring at a dancing fire, the room was unmistakably masculine.

"I hope Max approves."

"I'm sure he will," Astrid said. "We lucked out, you know. If he were married, his wife would have taken over the decorating and most likely changed her mind half a dozen times over the color scheme. I love my own sex and I'm a card-carrying feminist, but the truth is, his being a bachelor is the only reason we've been able to accomplish so much in so little time."

Imagining Max with a wife made her strangely uncomfortable. "We've also had our crews working around the clock." Starting at seven o'clock in the morning, the driveway was one long line of pickup trucks. The pounding of hammers and the buzzing of power tools competed from different parts of the house.

"So what do you bet he'll make another surprise appearance?" Astrid asked, straightening a faux sable fur throw that lay at the foot of the bed.

The first couple of times Max had shown up out of the blue Dakota had been taken aback. She'd assumed that he'd stay away until the work on the house was complete, down to the last billiard ball. She should have recognized from his willingness to camp out at Windhaven with next to no furnishings and from his decision to hire her rather than one of the Southampton concierge companies that Max did the unexpected.

Luckily, Astrid was as great a neat freak as she, and their crews knew to pick up after themselves. So except for a pile of folded drop cloths in the corner of the mudroom and some power tools lined up in one of the garage bays—leaving plenty of space for the screaming red Maserati should Max show up—the house was far from chaotic. And since Dakota cleaned and dusted after the workers had left for the day, it was actually neater than it had been on the morning she'd toured it with Max.

"No bets. But his office is set up and the wireless system installed. The library's shelves are full and the pool table in place. The living room furniture looks great, and the kitchen now has a full set of dishes, glassware, pans, and gadgets—including his state-of-the-art coffeemaker. Thanks to Fred, his all-knowing assistant, I've gleaned vital information about his food preferences. He likes chicken potpies and rocky road ice cream. Both are front and center in the freezer."

"Chicken potpies and rocky road? I swear the man is perfect."

Dakota laughed at Astrid's theatrical swoon. "Come on, you know he had you at carte blanche."

Astrid smiled. "True."

"The wine cellar now boasts a nice assortment of Italian, French, and California wines, and his liquor cabinet is fully stocked," she continued. "He has towels for his bathroom and Egyptian cotton sheets on his bed. I hung the punching bag in his gym yesterday with one of the carpenters." Indeed, she was so ready for one of Max's surprise visits that this time she was sure her pulse wouldn't soar into the stratosphere should he saunter through the door.

Astrid had crossed the room and was taking pictures of the spacious bathroom. She glanced over her shoulder. "In case he forgets to say it, you and I have done a damn good job so far."

"This is true. We make a good team."

"Remind me again why I haven't approached you about becoming my partner."

A partnership. Joining forces with Astrid would mean that she'd probably never have to worry about getting through the cold desert of the off-season in the Hamptons. But it would also mean relinquishing total control over her business. And if Astrid were her partner, she'd never be able to look back on her success—and she was determined to succeed—and say that she'd done it all on her own.

"Thank you, Astrid. That means a lot to me. But I like being the master of ceremonies of my traveling three-ring circus a little too much. And you'd miss living on that razor-thin edge of having it all under control and losing it completely."

"You're so right," she said with a rueful laugh. "We alpha females and this compunction we have to take on the world . . . Still, if you ever change your mind, you'll let me know?"

"Absolutely."

Max was in a conference room in Watertown, Massachusetts, with the members of his team, which included his firm's corporate lawyers, on his right. The conference room was at the research and development headquarters of Chiron, a company he'd acquired for Chris Steffen, the head of Bentech, another pharmaceutical company. Chris wanted Chiron because of Zeph3, a drug it had developed. Zeph3 had already gone through its clinical trials and was awaiting the results of its new-drug application from the FDA. According to Chris, Zeph3 had the potential to be a breakthrough drug in targeting melanoma tumors and shrinking them. If his prediction was correct, Chiron's stock would soar when the drug hit the market. Buying Chiron meant that a ready-made profit generator would be in place. In addition, the company had a number of other drugs in its portfolio that Chris considered solid workhorses—a neat bonus.

Two months ago, when Max had presented the strategic plan

he and his team had devised to restructure Chiron while Chris handled Zeph3's rollout, all he'd needed to do was recount Chris's previous coups in the industry for Max's Summit Group partners and the firm's limited partners to begin salivating. It had been unnecessary to explain that being early to market would mean cornering it, or how profitable it would be to own the patent to a breakthrough cancer drug.

And now it was happening. The lawyers representing them and Chiron had marched them through the agreement page by page. Beside him, he could feel Chris expanding, pumped with triumph and glee.

Max supposed he was just as pleased. This deal was going to make him a very rich man. Max's CEO, Bob Elders, had called earlier in the morning, as Max was on his way to the airport, to congratulate him once again.

"Kudos on the Chiron deal, Max. You're going to get a big piece of the carry."

Somehow, though, in spite of the hefty performance fee coming his way, in spite of Bob Elders's ringing approval, Max felt a strange sympathy as Mike Kauffman, Chiron's CEO, signed his name and then sat back in his chair with a bittersweet expression. The bucketload of money Kauffman was making today couldn't offset his chagrin at not having been able to steer his company more successfully, or protect it from being snatched away by the likes of Chris Steffen.

It was well known that Kauffman didn't like Chris Steffen. Who did? The guy was a brash ass who liked to get into pissing contests just so he could whip out his dick. But that didn't stop Chris from being eagle-eyed at spotting the drugs that promised to be very lucrative. Thanks to the PR company Chris hired to tout his accomplishments, *Forbes, Financial Times,* and *The Wall Street Journal* treated him as if he were a cross between Gandhi and a Nobel-winning biochemist.

Those who had regular dealings with Chris knew better, Max thought as he watched him sign his name with a flourish on the document making him the new CEO of Chiron and leaving Kauffman to twiddle his thumbs for the next year, due to the non-compete clause Chris had insisted he sign.

The meeting officially over, everyone around the gleaming conference table stood. There was a lot of handshaking and back-slapping on his and Chris's team.

Max went through the motions.

His mind was focused elsewhere, on the eastern tip of Long Island. He wondered what Dakota had done to the house this week, and what she was doing now. It was strange that she knew so much about him, down to what brand of toothpaste he used, while she remained an enigma. An elusive enigma. Every time he arrived at the house, she managed to disappear—after checking that everything was to his satisfaction, of course. He was wondering if he'd have to start manufacturing bizarre needs and oddball requests in order to get her to stick around.

He'd bought Windhaven for a number of reasons besides impressing his unmovable father. The property allowed him to diversify his portfolio and, once all the renovations were finished, both the house and location would be an asset when it came to entertaining associates. In terms of wooing a potential business partner, an invitation to a weekend at an East Hampton estate that was steps away from one of the most beautiful beaches in the world ranked right up there with a case of Dom Pérignon and tickets to an Adele concert. A weekend at Windhaven could seal many a deal.

Numbers worked for Max. So did clear-eyed cost-benefit analysis. But somehow his attitude toward Windhaven had changed since he'd bought it. He no longer thought of it in utilitarian terms or as the place to cement lucrative ventures. Even though she'd yet to finish all the rooms, Dakota had managed to make the sprawling house feel like a welcoming refuge . . . a place he could escape to. A home.

He hadn't even known he wanted one.

"So, Max, you up for some serious celebrating?" Chris Steffen asked, rubbing his hands together. It was one of his signature gestures. A slight man with dark hair and eyes, he tended to overcompensate. Steffen was always ready to get cracking. "I've booked a block of suites at the W for the weekend. We can party upstairs and then head down to the Tunnel or the Rumor. I'm flying Elena and the girls in. On Sunday we can catch the game. A friend's lending me his skybox. The Pats are playing the Jets—can't-miss football," he said, as if Max needed instruction on what teams to follow.

Max had done this kind of partying—weekend blitzes of alcohol, women, and strobe lights—many times before with Chris. Everything done to the nines, or to the "Max Carr," as Chris would drunkenly crow. And the mention of Elena, Chris's girlfriend of two years, and her female posse, was a guarantee of tanned limbs exposed in miniskirts and halter tops. The women would be made up with pouty lips and heavily mascara-coated eyelashes, with notes of Chanel No. 5 clinging to them.

Briefly he considered accepting Chris's offer. The prospect of a night screwing his brains out with an equally ravenous woman and then being able to walk away the next day without a single promise made or string attached nearly outweighed having to listen to Chris bray about his general awesomeness.

Perhaps sensing his hesitation, Chris said, "Want me to call Ashley? I remember she really dug you."

Ashley would be Ashley Nicholls, of the failed million-dollar shakedown. Max only now remembered that he'd met Ashley at one of Chris's parties. He wondered how Chris would react if he told him one of the girls had tried to blackmail him. Probably bust his gut laughing and then say something like from what he remembered, Ashley's blowjobs were totally worth a mil. Maybe more.

The guy might have graduated from Caltech at nineteen; he might be widely hailed as a genius in the pharma world. It didn't make him any less of an asshole. Max didn't believe Ashley would be so stupid as to show up anywhere near him after he'd sicced Roger Cohen on her—the lawyer was as ferocious as any attack dog—but he didn't intend to find out.

"Thanks, Chris, but I have a previous commitment." Utter bull, but Max could lie with the best of them when the situation called for it.

"So reschedule. This weekend's going to be epic."

"I wish I could. Really." He shook his head regretfully. "But I know Andy and Glenn would be totally up for partying with you and taking in the game. Glenn grew up in Beantown." He glanced over to where Andy Reynolds and Glenn Howard were talking to the lawyer who'd handled their end of the negotiations. Ambitious and determined to climb the corporate ladder, they were equally hungry for the glittery perks that went with the job.

Chris's mouth tightened at the prospect of hanging with two junior members of Max's team—second-string players—but since they'd just helped hand Chris a new drug company on a gold platter, there wasn't much he could do about it.

"Your loss," he said with a shrug.

"I'll be sure to clear my schedule next time."

"Do that." His tone was petulant. "So word has it you got yourself a shack in the Hamptons. Great place to party."

Max tensed. Open Windhaven to Chris Steffen? No way in hell. He'd seen the condition of the suites after one of Chris's late-night raves. Heavy metal rockers caused less destruction. "I'm having a lot of work done on the place. It's nowhere near ready yet."

Chris snorted. "Nobody goes out there now, bro. The place is *empty.* We'll come and check out your new digs in the warm weather. Elena loves the vibe at the Sloppy Tuna."

Max had forgotten how much he hated it when Chris started in with the "bro" crap. "Sounds great. Have fun with the guys and say hi to Elena."

"Later, bro." Chris stepped away to round up Andy and Glenn.

As soon as he was out of earshot, Max pulled out his phone and called his assistant, Fred, to arrange a flight from Logan to East Hampton. If he got there early enough, he might catch the elusive Dakota Hale.

CHAPTER ELEVEN

"Damn it, I really do not need this now," Dakota muttered, no longer able to pretend that the funny noise coming from her left front tire was caused by Windhaven's gravel drive. She pulled over onto the narrow strip of grass, careful to avoid the split rail fence that lined this section of West End Road. On the other side of the fence, gnarled pine trees hid the neighboring properties from curious eyes.

The left front tire was so flat, the rubber pooled blob-like on the asphalt.

"Damn," she repeated. It was Friday afternoon. During the off-season, the posh, high-octane Hamptons took on a sleepy, small-town mentality, with many of the local businesses closing early. Who knew if anyone would answer at Joe's Garage, or how long it would take for a mechanic to come out? She was only a quarter of a mile from Max's, but no brawny carpenters remained back there to lend a hand. Dakota had sent her and Astrid's crew off and then stayed an extra hour to put everything to rights.

Whom could she call? Rae and Marcos weren't an option. They were house-hunting in North Sea, an area that lay between Southampton and Water Mill and ended at the shores of Peconic Bay, looking at a cute little ranch that had just had a price decrease. Rae's promotion and raise had come at the perfect time. Housing prices dipped in the fall, when owners realized their chances of a sweet sale had left on Labor Day with the last Range Rover heading west on Route 27.

Lauren was teaching. Besides, her tire-changing skills were as pathetic as Dakota's.

The garage it was. With an aggrieved sigh she pulled out her cell. At least she had reception.

She was searching for the number in her contacts when she heard the rumble of an approaching car. The fire-engine-red blot grew larger and then sharpened into low-slung lines and outrageously sexy curves.

She knew that Maserati.

Embarrassment and excitement warred within her as the car slowed and then pulled up so its hood faced the Land Cruiser's. Its orange hazard lights began flashing. Max climbed out, and her grip on the phone tightened.

His overcoat was open, revealing a dark gray suit, the flash of a red tie, and a stark white shirt. Both he and the Maserati belonged on Park Avenue, Rodeo Drive, or the streets of Milan, where the sleek power of car and driver could be admired.

An empty country lane hardly fit the bill . . . not that she wasn't doing enough admiring for a multitude. She glanced down at the phone's screen.

"Car trouble?"

"Flat." She gave a jerk of her chin in the direction of the sad-looking tire. "I'm just calling the garage now. I have a client's dog waiting for his afternoon walk—"

"You got a spare? A jack?"

"Yes, but—"

"I'll change the tire."

"Oh no!" She looked up, certain the horror she felt was stamped on her face. "Really, that's not necessary."

"It's Friday. Rush hour. Even though it's off-season, the roads are busy. I can have your tire changed before the mechanic arrives." Shrugging out of his coat and jacket, he slung them over the surfboard resting on her roof.

"Wait! You can't—"

"Want to bet?"

"Excuse me?"

"Want to bet?" he repeated. "Go ahead, call your garage. I bet I can change your tire and have you back on the road before the tow truck arrives. Tell you what, to sweeten the pot, I'll pay the garage, win or lose."

"I—I can't bet you."

"Why not?"

She stared, dumbfounded.

"Come on, humor me. I've been locked away in a conference room with a bunch of guys. I need something fun to do."

She shook her head, marveling at his notion of fun. "Fine. I'll take your bet." She moved her thumb over the call button. "You ready?"

At his quick grin, she pressed the button and then brought the phone to her ear and listened to it ring. And ring. Finally, the recorded voicemail message came on. On the off chance that someone might be checking it, she gave her name, number, make of car, and location, explained that she needed her tire replaced ASAP, and then hung up.

While she'd been leaving the message, Max had gone to the

back of the Toyota and popped the rear door. He'd already found the jack and the lug wrench and had laid them by the front tire. Now she heard heavy scraping noises and then a thud as the spare landed on the road. Then he was rolling it around the car and she bit her lip to keep from sighing aloud. He'd removed his tie and unbuttoned his collar. The sleeves of his shirt were rolled to his elbows.

He glanced up as he stopped the tire a couple of feet from the tips of her Uggs and asked, "What?"

"What do you mean, 'what'?"

"Why are you looking at me like that?"

A woman would have to be blind not to look. "Can't help it. The Hamptons are known for amazing sights, but this is a rarity. Private equity types aren't often spotted changing tires, particularly not when dressed in—" She paused and hazarded a guess. "Hugo Boss."

"Armani, actually." He dropped to his knees.

With a squeak of alarm she ran to the back of her truck, grabbed a couple of the towels from the stack stored there, and sprinted back to him. He already had the hubcap removed and the lug wrench fitted over a bolt. The man worked fast.

"Here," she said, dropping them by his crouched form. "We should at least try to save your trousers."

"Thanks." Amusement laced his voice. "It's true, I've never worked on a car in office clothes." He dragged the beach towels so he could use them as a kneeling pad and returned his attention to the wheel.

The white of his shirt was brilliant and the material fine enough to reveal the play of his muscles as he steadily turned the wrench. Her eyes traveled down, taking in the taut line of his butt and quad muscles. Dear Lord.

"So what was your meeting about?" she blurted out.

"Bought a company for five hundred and fifty million."

"No wonder you needed to do something fun and exciting like change a tire."

"Yeah." The smile he flashed over his shoulder was like a blast of warmth in the rapidly cooling afternoon. The first nut loosened, he placed the wrench over the next one and began working those back muscles again.

She cleared her throat. "You, um, seem to know what you're doing."

"Changing a tire's basic. But yeah, I used to spend every weekend working on cars. I'll never forget my first Mustang—a GT Shelby."

The heat was back and he wasn't even looking at her. She cleared her throat. "I think you're supposed to reserve that tone for encounters of a different kind."

"Sex, you mean? Not too different from the rush you get handling and working on a classic Mustang."

"I'll try to remember that when I need a new hobby."

He huffed in laughter.

"But here I'd pegged you for a Tesla kind of guy, 'cause it's all about high-tech innovation and the new new thing."

"Nope. I'm a Detroit boy. I like my cars to roar and my women to moan."

With nothing but a light breeze blowing, the gasp that escaped her sounded loud. If the brief kiss they'd shared was anything to go by, he probably wasn't exaggerating or weaving fantasies to compensate for being a dud in the sack.

She glanced at him. A grin creased his cheek.

Oddly, his remark didn't repel her. With a guiding life principle being to avoid any resemblance to Piper, she was usually turned off by sexual banter, passes, and blatant come-ons. Somehow, though, her set of rules didn't apply where Max was concerned.

But just because he was different, just because he could make her body flush with awareness, or with a casually provocative line have her envisioning them wrapped together in a garden of earthly delights (specifically this one, scented with pines and sea air), just because maybe—okay, yes, definitely—he might well possess the power to wring moans from her, it didn't mean she was going to join the ranks of women who'd succumbed to that penetrating blue-gray gaze and gorgeous body.

No siree, her instinct for self-preservation was stronger than that.

Her heart thudding, she told herself to ignore the comment and to stop picturing all the ways he might make her moan.

"So, this working on cars. You did this back in Michigan?"

There was the slightest pause before he replied, "Yeah."

"How did you get started?"

"My dad. He lived and breathed automobiles. On the weekends he'd hunt the used-car lots for classics, clunkers, anything with four wheels that caught his eye, and then he'd bring them home and rebuild them from the inside out. Even after Dad was promoted to management—he'd started out on the assembly line—and moved us to a house in Mason, where the schools were better for Rosie and me and they had a good youth football program, there was always a car on the blocks in the driveway. I started helping him with them as soon as I could hold a ratchet."

"That sounds like a great childhood," she said, barely suppressing the envy that filled her at the mention of a father, a caring and involved one at that. And Max had a sister named Rosie. How lucky he was.

"Yeah, it was." He must have yanked too hard on the wrench, because the nut he was working on went flying. With a low curse, he shifted to catch it, but it had already bounced out of reach.

She followed it and, picking it up off the pavement, passed it to him, their fingers tangling for a moment. A warm shiver danced through her.

Nothing in his expression revealed that he'd felt anything from that brief contact. With a terse "Thanks," he returned to loosening the nuts. This time a grim efficiency fueled his movements.

How to account for the quicksilver shift in his mood? Was it caused by talk of his father? Dakota thought of the conversation they'd had at Gen and Alex's when she'd asked if his parents were the type to cling like burrs. He'd shut down then, too. Despite the affection in his voice when he'd spoken of learning about cars from his father, she had a sinking feeling something wasn't right with Max and his family.

Her cell rang, interrupting her thoughts. "Hello?"

"This Dakota Hale? It's Danny from Joe's Garage. You called about emergency roadside service?"

"Oh, yes."

She looked at Max. The wheel nuts loosened, he'd positioned the jack and begun cranking it, raising the front end of the car off the road. Hastily she turned away from the sight of his broad shoulders working rhythmically. She didn't want the garage repair guy to get the wrong idea if her voice went breathless. "Yes, I did. But I'm okay. Someone's helping me."

"That's good, because our guy's out on a call. There's an accident on Route 27 outside of Bridgehampton. But come in tomorrow morning, and we'll get that tire repaired or replaced for you."

"I will. Is ten o'clock okay? Thanks." She ended the call and turned around. "Looks like you've won the bet. The tow truck is out on another call."

The car's front end now suspended, she watched him remove the damaged tire, replace it with the spare, and then lower the jack until the wheel touched the ground. After tightening the lugs, he stood. "Glad I could be of service."

Picking up the towels and tools, she followed him as he rolled the damaged tire to the back and lifted it into the cargo space.

"Thanks," she said. "And congratulations on winning the bet so impressively. I hope I can return the favor someday."

He shut the rear door and turned to her. "You can. Teach me how to surf."

The request came out of left field. "You want to learn how to surf?"

"Yeah. I noticed you always have a board on your roof rack, so I figure you must go out fairly often. I asked Alex for confirmation. He said you're hard-core. I'd like to have some lessons."

Teach Max to surf? Not a good idea at all. Surfing was *her* thing, her special, private way of finding her balance in the world. It was where she forgot about the exhausting dysfunction of her family and the demands of her more trying clients. Some of her friends surfed, but as a rule, she didn't invite outsiders to share that special time and magical place with her. She definitely didn't want Max, her too-handsome and too-intriguing employer, out on the ocean with her.

Rattled, she stammered, "I, uh, know some great people who can take you out and show you the basics."

"I'd like to have you."

His easy tone didn't fool her. He wasn't going to back down.

"All right," she said, trying hard not to show how very *not* all right it was. "Once the weather warms up, I'll take you out." By the time June rolled around, he'd have forgotten this sudden whim.

"I was thinking tomorrow."

That startled a laugh out of her. "The water's cold. And the high for tomorrow is—"

"The forecast is for forty-three degrees. I checked."

"I go out early in the morning. It'll be a lot colder than that."

"I've bought a wetsuit. It has an attachable hood if I need the extra warmth. But being from Michigan, I'm used to the cold."

Michigan, the land of roaring cars, moaning women, car-tinkering fathers, and cold.

"How about a board?" she asked. From the knot in her stomach, she already knew the answer.

He checked his watch. "It should be here in half an hour."

Should she be surprised that he'd planned everything so meticulously? Not really. During the past few weeks she'd cobbled together a sense of how he operated. This kind of strategic planning must be one of the reasons he was so good at brokering all those deals she'd read about—and the one he'd signed this afternoon. He'd anticipated every angle and every out that she would seize and had blocked them.

Okay, then. Many people thought surfing was wicked cool and that in a few rides they'd be on their way to becoming the next Laird Hamilton. Then they tried their first pop-up, and their second and third . . . until it was like a GIF: pop up and fly over the board and into the water. And that was as far as the "surfing" ever advanced. It was possible that for all his impressive muscles, Max might be one of those rank kooks.

Clinging to the hope, she decided to be gracious in defeat. "I like to be on the water for the sunrise, but we'll need the light to do a few drills. Be ready to go at six-thirty."

CHAPTER TWELVE

Some people might call Max conceited, but he truly couldn't remember when a woman hadn't wanted to go out with him. Girls liked him in junior high, passing him notes in the hallway and giggling and batting their eyelashes when he walked by them in the cafeteria. He played football, was cute, and wasn't a complete tool. Enough said. High school heated things up several notches. Thongs and the wonders of Victoria's Secret push-up bras replaced notes written in purple sparkly ink. Casual brushes as girls walked by him and "spontaneous" hugs replaced clusters of girls giggling at a distance. Make-out sessions progressed several plays beyond a taste of cherry-glossed lips.

Senior year he was captain of the football team, which effectively conferred celebrity status in a football-crazed state. His cellphone rang constantly. His popularity drove Rosie nuts. She called them his "dopies." Shyer than he was, his sister was happiest reading or writing in her journal in a quiet corner of the library or hanging in the art studio with her artsy friends.

Sisters were born to be ignored. He loved shutting her out when she tried to get in his head with her sweet girl wisdom, knowing it infuriated her like nothing else. He'd been such an adolescent prick.

Then the accident happened. Everything changed overnight. Summer was shrouded in a dense fog of grief and guilt. Their house, once filled with laughter and buzzing with activity—school, football practice and games, Rosie's art and drama classes—was still, suffocating, and silent, save for the weeping behind closed doors.

He could have deferred college, but he needed to escape the sight of his mother and father's ravaged faces as they sat and stared into the middle distance. He couldn't bear knowing he'd caused his mother's heart to shatter, couldn't live with his father's relentless, accusing anger. More, he needed to escape that house so he wouldn't have to walk past the pretty room next to his, with the pink curtains their mom had sewn and the posters of the foreign cities Rosie had dreamed of visiting. He needed to leave so that he could forget what he'd lost.

A hole wasn't supposed to weigh anything. Unless it was a black hole, and his felt as massive as any measured by astronomers. He carried it around with him wherever he went. For the past sixteen years, he'd been trying to fill that vast space inside him.

It was why he always needed more. Another win, another deal, another thing to lift him up.

When he'd been crouched next to Dakota's flat tire, working the tools, his hands relearning the motions, his mind had flashed back to that golden halcyon period when his family had been intact. He'd remembered how it had been with his father, the two of them lying on creepers beneath one of his junkers, streaks of grease on their hands and forearms, the smell of oil filling their nostrils as his dad taught him how to replace an oil pump. For a second he'd remembered how it had been when he wasn't despised.

Luckily, he'd closed the memory down before it could turn acrid and before Dakota could glimpse the impenetrable darkness inside him.

By all that was rational, he should resent Dakota for triggering these memories of his broken family. And maybe he did, but not enough to make him do the smart thing and stay the hell away from her.

He wanted to kiss her again and discover whether she tasted as good as he remembered.

There was a memory he was happy to replay in his head.

He was going to have to work for that next kiss. She was doing her utmost to fight their mutual attraction and keep her distance. If her tire hadn't obligingly gone flat that afternoon, it was possible she would have flitted in and out of Windhaven sylph-like, and he wouldn't have caught her to wrest a surfing lesson from her and give him a morning of her company.

Lacking any real experience with women intent on ignoring him, Max thought it wise to be ready and waiting when Dakota arrived. No point in aggravating his reluctant surfing instructor.

She was her prompt self. She must have spotted his new eight-foot board propped against the garage door and the nylon duffel bag lying next to it, for she pulled up next to the garage and hopped out to unlatch the roof rack. He lifted the board overhead and slid it into place.

"Morning," he said.

Her fleece jacket was zipped to her chin and the dark strands of her hair lifted in the breeze and landed on her cheeks and lips. An impatient hand dragged them back behind her ear.

"Morning." She refastened the rack with grim determination.

"The spare tire okay?" he asked, to remind her of his usefulness yesterday and that his presence wasn't a total imposition.

"Yeah." She shoved her hands in the pockets of her jacket.

"You're going to the garage, right? You shouldn't drive on the spare for too long." The advice came out a little more sharply than he'd intended.

"I'm going later this morning."

"Good. That's good." Telling himself to calm down before she decided he was certifiable, he grabbed his duffel and tossed it in the backseat, next to her own gear bag, and then got in beside her.

She turned on the ignition and shifted into drive. "The coffee in front's yours. Muffins are in the bag."

He glanced down at the cup holders and the paper bag. "Thanks."

"It's important to fuel up," she said, as if worried he might interpret the gesture as anything but practical. "Between paddling, sitting out on the lineup, and trying to catch a wave, you'll be expending a lot of energy."

Figuring he'd appease her and that any muffin bought by Dakota Hale would taste damn good, he took it out of the paper bag and bit into pear, cinnamon, walnut, and brown sugar. "Damn, this is really good. Where'd you get it?"

"I made it."

West End Road was deserted, but she kept her gaze fixed ahead of her. He wondered how long she aimed to pretend he wasn't sitting next to her.

They'd reached East Hampton. Main Street's glittery luxury shops were shuttered. They cruised through the traffic lights, Dakota driving with a competence that put him as much at ease as he could be since the night Rosie—

She cleared her throat, interrupting his thoughts. "Since it's cold this morning and we won't want to hang out on the beach too long, I thought I'd go over basic surf etiquette now. Ditch

Plains, where we're going this morning, has a sign posted with essential surfing etiquette, but it's amazing how many people don't bother to read it."

Ah. Now he had a clue about what was partially responsible for her aloofness. She was worried he'd act like a jerk out on the water.

He picked up the cup and drank. The coffee was strong and hot, so he decided not to be too pissed off at her assumption. "Luckily I have you to enlighten me."

That got her. She slanted a look at him. "Right. So the first and most important rule is, don't drop in on another surfer. At Ditch Plains, the waves there break to the left. If you see someone on your left who's closer to the peak than you, that person has priority. If you try to go for that wave and get in the way of his or her ride, that's known as 'dropping in.' It's a major no-no."

"And then I'd be worse than a kook. I'd be an asshole."

"Pretty much." She glanced at him again. "So, you've been reading up?"

He shrugged. "I do my research like I do my due diligence. I read about snaking, too."

She nodded. "Another jerk move. I've been surfing for a while at Ditch Plains and Turtle Cove. Both spots have some really good surfers who are going to be able to anticipate where the waves are breaking and position themselves accordingly."

They'd reached Amagansett, the next town to the east, and she eased off the accelerator. He'd driven through the town once. From what he could tell, it was more low-key—if anything in the Hamptons could truly be counted as low-key—than Bridgehampton, East Hampton, or Southampton. It had a yoga center and a number of funky little shops. And with the Stephen Talkhouse, which had good live music, the town had a cool vibe. Half a dozen cars were parked outside Jack's Stir Brew. New Yorkers getting their morning caffeine fix.

He picked up Dakota's coffee. "Here," he said, taking shameless advantage of the fact that she was driving to place his fingers over hers until she had a sure grip. The rush he got from touching her was becoming irresistible.

"Thanks, I've got it." Her husky voice had the tiniest and most gratifying tremor to it.

"So it sounds like there's serious potential for scumbag moves in surfing," he said.

"As in life. As on Wall Street."

Max had a hunch the deal he'd closed yesterday, buying out Mark Kauffman and handing Chiron over to Chris Steffens, might be condemned as "dropping in" by Dakota. Being the first to nab a potentially profitable company was the name of the game he played. But he was on her turf—or surf—now, so he'd abide by her rules. Inclining his head, he said, "Point taken."

"Surfing shouldn't be like that, though. But when the lineup gets crowded with everyone wanting to catch a ride, things can get ugly. Who needs that?"

Dakota flicked her indicator light and turned right onto a road that was called, surprise, surprise, Ditch Plain Road. She ignored the entrance to the town parking area and continued east, only then turning onto a narrow, rutted lane that led to the dunes. She parked between a Jeep with stickers plastered all over the cargo door and a beat-up Volvo wagon.

"Looks like we lucked out," she said as she turned off the engine. "It's not too crowded. Let's change into our suits and head down."

Dakota had been dreading this moment. She'd even considered putting on her wetsuit, at least the bottom half, before picking up Max at Windhaven. But the weather wasn't cold enough to justify donning a wetsuit so far ahead of time, and the thought of sitting behind the wheel with neoprene bunched and rolled about her middle while her face grew redder and redder and sweat ran down her temples, with Max there as a witness, was just as embarrassing.

Instead she was presented with the prospect of him watching her wriggle and jiggle her way into her wetsuit. Ordinarily Dakota had no problem stripping down and pulling on neoprene. The guys on the beach were buddies. Dudes.

By no stretch of the imagination would she ever think of Max as a "dude." He was too vital and intense. And unlike the guys she hung out with in the lineup or went with to grab a breakfast burrito and coffee from the Ditch Witch post-surf, Max made Dakota aware of every inch of her body. Worse still, he made her wonder what he'd think about it.

What was almost as disconcerting as being exposed to Max's gaze was how much she wanted to catch a glimpse of him stripped down to his briefs. A sudden thought occurred to her: what if he chose to go commando? She'd heard a lot of guys claim it was the only comfortable way to surf in a wetsuit.

Dear Lord. With a flush warming her from head to toe, she shucked her sweatpants. The morning air nipped her skin as she grabbed her wetsuit, shook it briskly, and shoved her feet into it.

Pulling on a wetsuit was usually no big thing. Now, though, the neoprene felt like a pair of Spanx two sizes too small as she tugged it over her thighs and bikini-covered bottom.

The suit at last over her hips, she put on her booties. Only then did she peel off her fleece and her sweatshirt, sucking in a breath at the cold. She dragged the wetsuit up over her bikini top—achingly aware of all that jiggling—and stuck one arm after the other through the armholes, adjusting and wriggling until the material covered her shoulders. Reaching behind, she pulled the headflap forward and shoved her head through the neck seal.

With a sigh of relief, she zipped the front flap closed. It had taken her less than five minutes to don the suit. It might as well have been an hour.

Casually she glanced across the front seats and through the open passenger door. Max must have practiced putting on the wetsuit last night because he was already pulling the neck seal over his head.

The second his dark auburn head appeared through the neoprene's opening, she directed her attention to their boards, opening the rack.

He'd bought an eight-foot foam board. A smart choice for a beginner. And he'd even done some homework, reading about surfing's cardinal sins. So far, she couldn't help but be impressed with his attitude.

"Here, I'll get that," he said.

She turned and her eyes nearly popped out. Encased in body-molding black, Max looked like a freakin' superhero.

"Oh, sure. Here." She took a big step backward, as if that might lessen his potency. Mutely she watched him lift the board and tuck it under his arm, his biceps bulging against the neoprene.

What had she gotten herself into?

"So do we hit the water now?"

Though she longed for the distraction of the waves, she shook her head. "The beach is the best place to practice pop-ups."

CHAPTER THIRTEEN

The beach had the typical number of hardy walkers and beachcombers, some with dogs running and chasing waves or chomping on seaweed and crab legs. One golden retriever noted their arrival and came over to sniff Dakota's board, then raced back to its owner, barking madly.

Their surfboards lay parallel, the fins buried in the sand, separated by a few feet. Feeling as self-conscious as if she were onstage at Madison Square Garden, she lowered herself onto hers to demonstrate how to move from a prone position to a standing one—otherwise known as a pop-up.

"I've never tried to teach anyone how to surf, so it's best if I just show you. Watch closely," she said foolishly, unnecessarily, since she could feel the weight of Max's gaze traveling the length of her body.

It was silly to be self-conscious. Max had undoubtedly seen plenty of women moving far more provocatively. And when they stuck their butts out, it wasn't to demonstrate proper surfing technique.

She took a calming breath. "A pop-up is kind of like doing a push-up into a squat. The difference is that when you land, you want to make sure your feet are angled sideways on the board. You, um, look pretty strong and coordinated to me"—and wow, wasn't that a massive understatement—"so you're probably going to catch on quickly."

She cleared her throat. "When you see the wave, you'll turn your board to catch it." She pretended to paddle by digging her closed fingers through the sand. "Once the wave reaches you, you'll feel its push. As soon as you do, take a couple of extra strokes so you're moving along with it. Then you'll do like so—" Rocking her body a little for momentum, she pressed up against the board with her arms and jumped forward to land in a sideways squat.

Holding her stance, she said, "See my left foot, how it's up where my hands were when I pushed up?"

"Yeah."

"That's how far you'll need to jump forward. And look at how my right foot's on the other side of the board, a little farther down, and also angled. And when I pop up, I extend one arm out and bend the other like so in front of my chest. It helps my balance. Once I'm steady, I can straighten and start riding my wave." She hopped off the board. "Have you got it, or should I show you again?"

Max would have liked nothing better than for Dakota to repeat the move for the rest of the morning. In her formfitting wetsuit, she resembled a modern-day mermaid, all long, sinuous lines. Performing that pop-up, going from a horizontal position to a balanced crouch in one fluid snap of her body, she displayed grace and strength that were as sexy as anything he'd seen in a long time.

So hell yeah, he could have watched her a couple of hundred times over.

He already knew a few things about Dakota. She was smart and resourceful, and she loved running her business. This morning he was seeing a different side to her, a private side. For all his fierce attraction, he found himself strangely moved by her willingness to share this part of her life.

He didn't want to blow it, and he might if she caught him staring at her like some horny teenager while she demonstrated the surfing technique.

"I think I've got the basic idea," he said, and dropped down onto his board. The push-up part would be easy, but he'd never tried to move quickly and hold a squat in a full wetsuit. He supposed there was no time like the present to find out if he could.

"Hold your head a bit higher when you paddle," she told him. "Too many people lower their head and their gaze."

He did as instructed and pretended to paddle through the sand, feeling more than a little foolish. Then he reminded himself of what his best coach, Stan Walker, had always told their high school team: *Perfect practice, perfect game.*

"Okay, here's your wave," she prompted.

He remembered to give a couple of extra strokes, making the cold, wet sand fly toward his feet, then moved his hands beneath his chest, flattened his palms, and pushed up as he contracted his core muscles and jumped forward. He made sure his left foot landed in the space where his hands had been and that his right foot was behind and also angled. He rose into a crouch, extending his left arm and keeping his right arm in front of his chest.

"Good."

The reluctant admiration in her voice made him feel like he'd just completed a thirty-four-yard pass for a winning touchdown.

"Better do it again, to make sure it wasn't a fluke."

Damn straight it wasn't a fluke. Now that he'd performed one, he realized a pop-up wasn't too different from a burpee, only with a sideways landing, and he'd done hundreds of those. Still, he nodded and dropped back down on the board. After positioning himself, he pretended to paddle, and then repeated the push-up and jump.

Nailing the pop-up, he straightened, and flashed her a cocky smile.

In response she lifted a single brow. But she was fighting a smile of her own. "Okay, then. Let's see how you fare on the water."

They put on their mitts and hoods and headed out. Max was surprised by how warm the wetsuit was, how buoyant he felt as he followed Dakota into the waist-high surf. At her signal, he pulled himself onto his board and paddled in her wake.

The breeze was coming off the shore. As wind met wave, the spray flew up, stinging his cheeks. He must outweigh her by a good sixty pounds, yet he was working to keep up with her. She reached the lineup and sat up. He did the same, careful to control his breathing so she didn't catch him gasping.

Straddling her board, she waved to the two other surfers.

"That's Rick and Kris over there," she said, raising her voice to be heard over the chop of the water and through the thickness of their hoods. "They're cool, and both of them are really good surfers. Rick's going to take off now. He's a good guy to watch. He's got a fast action and decent form."

"The other guy's going, too."

"Yeah." She watched them for a second. "That rule about never dropping in on another surfer? Well, this is the exception."

"Good to know there are exceptions to your rules." He planned to be one of them, remembering how she'd said she didn't get involved with clients.

"They're sharing the wave because they're buddies and they know what they're doing. Plus it's a total blast to work a wave together. Watch how smoothly they transition from lying on their boards to standing for the takeoff. See how they're moving their feet and shifting their weight? They'll slice and cut back and work the wave until it dies." She looked over at him. "Today's sets are nice and regular. Want to try to catch your first ride?"

"Yeah, I do." Anticipation built inside him.

"Okay, then. See the set after this one?" She pointed. "It looks promising. Long boards aren't as easy to maneuver as short boards, so you'll want to start turning now. Scoot back a bit. There, now you're in your sweet spot. Here it comes. Paddle hard. Go, go!"

Her shout of encouragement faded as he pulled his forearms through the water once, twice. Then he felt it: the water propelling his board and lifting it. What a rush. Remembering Dakota's lesson, he brought his hands beneath his chest, pressed up, and jumped his booted feet forward, landing with them splayed and angled.

Fucking hell, the board was *really moving*. He tried to find his balance. For a fleeting second he had it, then he teetered wildly and, in the next breath, flew ass backward off the board.

The water was a cold, humiliating slap to the face. He surfaced, bobbing in the swell like a black cork. Following another of Dakota's rules—never ditch your board—he'd attached the leash to his ankle. He tugged it, pulling the surfboard back to him. Grabbing hold of the sides, he heaved himself up, and then looked around to orient himself.

Dakota was about twenty feet away. Even with the water stinging his eyes and embarrassment blurring his vision, he could see her shoulders shaking.

She was laughing her head off.

Grimly he paddled back to her. Reaching her, he sat up.

She wiped her eyes with the back of her mitt. "Oh, man, that was funny." Her laughter started again.

"Yeah, a real laugh riot."

"You fell off because you were looking down. A surefire way to eat it." Still smiling broadly, she said, "Congratulations, you just executed a classic kook move."

"As a professional concierge, aren't you supposed to fawn over your clients?"

She cocked her head. "I didn't think you enjoyed being fawned over."

He didn't. He wanted Dakota to be different from the women he dated. He wanted her to be honest with him. He even liked that she was laughing at him. He hadn't been teased in a long time.

"Besides, I didn't realize that I was on the clock out here." She paused. "Am I on the job?"

He looked at her, with the tight black hood framing her caramel-brown eyes, her straight nose, and her generous mouth. "I'd rather it was just you and me out here having fun."

"All right." Her smile turned dazzling. He hadn't fully recovered from it when she pointed again. "Another set's coming. Want to go for it?"

It took him three more tries. Then suddenly everything that Dakota had told him when he paddled back to the lineup, dripping and rueful and oh so humbled, finally clicked. He kept his head up, looked in front of him, sprang up and landed in a crouch, arms extended like a surfing ninja . . . and he was actually doing it, riding the wave, exulting in the power of the water propelling him. He even managed to move his feet and shift his weight, discovering what could make the board zig and then zag.

The rush, the sense of accomplishment, was incredible.

Almost as wonderful as Dakota's congratulatory whoop and the smile that lit her face when he ended his ride and paddled back to her.

Two hours later, they carried their boards back up to the parking lot.

"In the summer, the Ditch Witch food truck parks here. It's the hot spot to grab an egg sandwich or a burrito or a lobster roll. Off-season, most people head into Montauk and hit the diners there. They can get crowded, but the food's good," Dakota told him.

"Wish that truck were here now. I'm starved." Max caught her looking at him, a smile lifting her cheeks. "What's got you so amused?" he asked.

"You, I guess. I was just remembering you doing your pop-ups in the cold sand and the countless number of times you got dumped off your board into fifty-degree water."

"I counted all of four times."

"Still. You could have jetted to California and taken lessons in Rincon or Malibu. Florida has some decent spots, too. You could have learned in nice, sunny weather and warm water."

"I like a challenge." He was finding he liked the challenge of Dakota Hale a lot.

"Well, you rose to it, that's for sure. You really nailed that last set. Even Rick was impressed, and he's not a fan of outsiders."

"Rick's a good surfer." Though not as good as Dakota. Max's first impression of her as an Amazon hadn't been far off the mark. She was strong and athletic, and her moves were confident and graceful. Smooth. The waves hadn't been huge or long, but she'd worked each one, eking out every possible second of her ride with cutbacks and board grabs. And yes, he'd watched enough videos to recognize just how well she surfed.

"He is," she agreed. "Rick's on the water every day, either here or at Turtle Cove."

They'd arrived at the car. Dakota propped her board against the rear door and reached up to open the roof rack. She turned, making to lift her board, but Max had already picked it up.

"No, I've got it," he said, feeling a flash of irritation at her surprise. Did no one do anything for this woman? After positioning his board next to Dakota's and closing the rack, he returned to the conversation. "Rick may surf every day, but you're much better."

A rosy flush bloomed on her cheeks. "I wouldn't say that."

So she didn't get a lot of praise, either. "I would. It was great watching you out there. Thanks for taking me and showing me what to do."

"You're welcome. So, are you hooked?"

He looked at her. "Yeah. I think I am." Stepping forward, he framed her face with his hands, gave in to his hunger, and kissed her.

Her lips were cold. She tasted of the sea. Salt and perhaps sweat stiffened the ends of her hair, and the downy skin of her cheeks and throat was coated with a fine layer of grit. Nothing had ever tasted or felt so good.

He angled his head to deepen the kiss, fierce satisfaction filling him when her lips parted and her tongue met his in a slow pass that made him burn. With a groan he slipped a hand to her back, drawing her close until the soft mounds of her breasts pressed against his chest. Arousal drumming through him, he mentally cursed the millimeters of tight neoprene separating their bodies. He wanted Dakota naked, and him caressing and savoring every inch of her long, luscious body.

Lust fueling his brain, he released her lips to whisper roughly, "You're beautiful. I want to take you to bed."

Her response wasn't what he'd hoped for. Stiffening inside that figure-hugging wetsuit, she pulled out of his embrace. Her eyes were enormous, making it easy to read the skittish alarm edging out her arousal. *Damn.*

"I don't think going to bed with you would be a good idea."

"Probably not." Definitely not. "I want to anyway. I think you do, too."

"Then you'd be wrong. I don't sleep with my clients. I'd rather see my business grow. And in my free time? I'd much rather surf than have sex."

"Having sex with me would in no way affect your business. And not to knock surfing, but all your supposed preference tells me is that you haven't had very good sex."

"Again, you'd be wrong. I'm just not interested. Tell you what, though. If anything changes in the next couple of years, I'll give you a call." She flashed a smile colder than the ocean had been each time he'd planted his face in it.

She didn't know him well enough to realize that he excelled at looking for weaknesses and vulnerabilities, whether it was in a rival football team or in a company he wanted to buy. Today it was in a beautiful woman whose kiss was enough to bring him to his knees. When he'd held her, his fingers had found the pulse point beneath her jaw. It was still hammering furiously. "I don't think I'll have to wait that long."

"Why, because you're so irresistible?"

She was even sexier when her back was up. A part of him was grateful that she was fighting their attraction. He should, too. He'd managed to convince himself that he was doing a decent job of ignoring his desire, but he realized he only truly succeeded when he was about eighty miles away from Dakota. The other part of him—the more dominant part—wanted to win and have her admit that she, too, was feeling the charge between them, one powerful enough to light up Manhattan. "Well, you seem to think I am."

Her lips pursed in irritation. "I do, do I?"

He gave an easy nod, which only seemed to infuriate her more. "Yeah. If your kiss is any sign."

"That—that—" she sputtered. "That was shock."

"No, that was desire. You didn't want me to stop."

Her laugh was a fraction too loud. "Now I understand why you're so strong for a Wall Street type. It's from carrying around that massive ego."

CHAPTER FOURTEEN

To think that she'd been on the verge of inviting Max to John's Pancake House for a post-surf breakfast, Dakota fumed as she drove back to East Hampton. Had they gone to the diner, he'd have probably spent the entire time looking across the table with that too-knowing gleam in his eyes and that smug smile playing across his lips. Instead of enjoying the melt-in-your mouth pancakes, she'd have been craving some more of Max's melt-your-whole-body kisses.

It hadn't helped that, after calling him out for his colossal arrogance, he'd merely shrugged and then ever so casually begun peeling off his wetsuit. Roped muscles had flexed under lightly tanned skin, and she'd glimpsed flat brown nipples puckered from the cold. Instantly her own had tightened in response. She'd hastily turned away, but not before catching a flash of his taut abdomen and the narrow line of dark hair below his navel and hearing his amused laughter.

She was pretty sure the image of a half-naked Max Carr was forever seared into her brain.

She glanced at him out of the corner of her eye. Now dressed in sweats and a slate-blue fleece jacket that made his eyes even more intense, he had his cellphone pressed to his ear. The phone had buzzed as they were settling into the Toyota, relieving her of the need to come up with any more useless put-downs.

Eavesdropping wasn't a habit she indulged in often. But alongside her aggravation lived an undeniable fascination. Max was handsome, intelligent, interesting, and successful. She also knew he was far too smart to divulge any confidential information with her sitting next to him. But what had her listening so attentively was the change in his voice, now sharpened to a cutting edge. Inches from her elbow, his fingers drummed impatiently against the seat.

From what she could gather, someone named Chris was recounting his Friday night in lengthy detail. Dakota was forcefully reminded of Piper, who liked nothing better than to entertain herself by calling up to describe a night of clubbing or charity gala mingling, two favorite man-hunting grounds. Ever since Piper had called her a bitch—her unique version of maternal devotion and support—Dakota had been spared any mother-daughter chats. The Hale sisters' pique continued. And the silence was golden. Almost worth the sting of the cut.

This Chris person must be tone-deaf, for he didn't seem to hear the stony disinterest in Max's voice. Then the conversation turned to business, confirming beyond a doubt that Chris was *not* simply an annoying friend, and Max reeled off numbers, mentioned something about restructuring and margins, and said that no, he didn't think Brent Carson would be a better choice for CFO. "Because he's an asshole and a stupid one at that," he answered witheringly. "Yes, Chris, I'll be talking to him on Monday."

A man like Max didn't need to be told whom to contact—no one got to where he was by ignoring important details and calls. That he was not amused must have finally gotten through to Chris. Abruptly the topic shifted. Not that it made Max any more relaxed.

"Yeah, I'm there now. No, not much. As you said, the place is dead. Had to see to some stuff, that's all. Sure you can, once it's ready. I'll call you Tuesday." A jab of his thumb ended the conversation.

For a minute he stared out the window, and even though she knew she was being idiotic, she wished she could come up with the right thing to say to return him to his earlier teasing mood.

She liked seeing him happy.

Because you've been trained since birth to be a pleaser. That was true. But she wondered whether there might not be something special about Max that made her pay even closer attention to his moods and made her wish she understood them.

"Everything okay?" she asked at last.

"Yeah. Just had to listen to someone who thinks I should be doing a lot more for him than making him CEO of a potentially very profitable company."

"Oh. One of the chest thumpers."

He glanced over at her. "Chest thumpers?"

"Yes," she said nodding. "They thump their chests and go, 'Me, me, me' while they're waiting in line at the Seafood Shop or demanding a table at Nick and Toni's. They're as big a problem as the deer population out here. Definitely should be sterilized."

That earned her a chuckle. "I might mention that to Chris next time he decides to bug me." He fell back into silence as she turned left onto Further Lane, the road that would allow her to bypass East Hampton and the morning shoppers. Perhaps realizing they weren't far from Windhaven, he said, "I haven't told you how much I like what you did with the rooms in the house."

"I'm glad it meets your approval," she said stiffly.

"So you're still ticked off at me, huh?"

She gave him a sidelong glance.

"Listen, I'm not going to apologize for saying I'd like to take you to bed. Besides, you seem to have a pretty good BS meter, so what's the point? But as for the renovation, it's terrific, Dakota. The place no longer looks anything like it did when I bought it. I wasn't sure you'd be able to pull it off so well or so quickly."

She softened a bit. "Well, we're not done yet, but I told you Astrid was good."

"*You're* good. After you've finished the house, I'd like you to do the guest cottage, too."

"Okay." She tamped down on the urge to jump up and down in her seat. "I'll have Astrid look at it on Monday. In the meantime, we'll get the spare bedrooms finished."

"I don't want anyone underfoot."

"Oh. So the cottage isn't for friends?" She was careful not to add "family" to her question.

"Friends?" A muscle in his cheek twitched. "No. I need a space for business associates."

It was hard to feel sorry for a man as successful as Max. But she couldn't help but think that true friends might be a rarity for him. Was this the collateral damage of being so wealthy and powerful? Or was there something else that made him such a loner?

They were passing the Maidstone with its manicured golf course. Parts of the course had ocean views. The golfers she knew sang its praises. "You'll want to start working on getting accepted into the Maidstone. Those business associates will appreciate it." Deciding that now was as good a time as any to inform him of what he was up against, she said, "Just so you know, there'll be an attempt to blackball you."

He guessed the source quickly. "Your family?"

"I'd say their grudge grows with every megamillion-dollar

deal you clinch. It won't help when word spreads that Windhaven's looking much better than it did when it was owned by the Hales."

"My hiring you—I've put you in a real bind, haven't I?"

"Thanks to you, I've been able to give my best employee a raise and a promotion. I may even be able to offer my workers healthcare benefits. My business may not be important to my family, but it is to me."

"Alex said you've built it single-handedly."

The respect in his tone meant far more than when he'd called her "beautiful," and a part of her basked in the compliment. "I started doing odd jobs when I was a kid. My list of services grew once I was able to exchange my bike for a car. Being able to stock my clients' liquor cabinets legally was another milestone."

"My hiring you, though . . . that's a tipping point for your family, right?"

"Maybe, but for ninety-nine percent of my family, I've been in the enemy camp since birth."

"Why?"

It was only on account of his genuine puzzlement that she didn't deflect the question and switch topics. "You met my uncle Elliott, right? You may have noticed I don't look like him. I don't look like any Hale."

"So your dad was—"

"Unknown. Another mark against me. My presence in the family is an embarrassment. Luckily, my mom is wonderfully careless. She's always done what she wants. When she found herself pregnant, for some reason she decided that what she wanted was a child. Fortunately, the trust fund she lives on was set up by my great-grandparents and out of my grandparents' reach. Otherwise she might not have chosen to defy them."

"Some family you've got there."

She was not going to have him pity her. "I'm past thinking of them as family, except for Piper—my mother—and she'll get over her snit that I'm working for you soon enough. But when it comes to the Maidstone Club, you have an ace in the hole. Alex Miller will know how to get the votes for you."

He looked out his window. "I don't like imposing on him."

And she really liked him for saying that. "He'll see it as helping a friend, not as an imposition." She flicked on her indicator and turned into his driveway.

"On the subject of impositions, I had a good time today. Can I come out again with you?"

"We're talking surfing, right?"

"The weather's not exactly conducive to sex on the beach."

She couldn't believe she was blushing like a teenager. "Yeah, well, that's definitely not happening."

"A shame." The corner of his mouth lifted engagingly. "But yeah, I did mean surfing."

Growing up with Piper as a mother, she'd been given a master class in the art of getting out of doing anything and everything. But just as she was coming to recognize Max's moods, she knew he was getting good at reading her. If she nixed any future surfing sessions, he'd guess that she was nervous around him, and he'd guess why.

"It wouldn't be right or safe for you to go out without a buddy. You can come with me until you're more proficient and have gotten to know the other surfers and when they're likely to be out on the water." To make sure he didn't read more into her agreeing to surf with him than her simply being friendly, she switched topics. "You might want to pick up another car for your surfboard. I doubt the Maserati would appreciate the potholes leading to the beach."

"I'll add that to the weekend's shopping list."

"The joys of being über-wealthy," she murmured.

"What's that?"

"Nothing," she said, pulling up to the garage.

He opened his door and paused before climbing out. "You're off to get the tire replaced?"

She nodded. "I made an appointment for ten. And I'm thinking it can be patched."

"No. Have it and the other tires replaced. The treads are worn. I checked."

He would have.

"What garage do you use again?" he asked.

"Joe's, on Brick Kiln Road. They do good work. Not sure they're up to tackling Maseratis, though. You're better off with your dealer."

"Right." He paused. "Are you going to Montauk tomorrow?"

It was done. She'd said yes to taking him surfing. But she really wished her heart didn't trip at the prospect of spending more time with him. "I'll pick you up at six."

"I'll be waiting."

Something in his tone told her he was talking about more than hitching a ride to Ditch Plains.

CHAPTER FIFTEEN

Gen and Alex Miller had a tradition of throwing a holiday party on the Saturday after Thanksgiving. With Gen's fame as an artist and Alex's success as a venture capitalist, along with their ties to old Hamptons society, theirs was the coveted invitation on the East End. Much to the fury of Mimi, Dakota was the only Hale on the guest list.

That was only one reason Dakota loved going. For all their dynamism and influence, Gen and Alex knew how to have fun, and their guests, a mix of locals, city friends, and family, filled the house with laughter and interesting conversation.

Dakota and her crew had all worked over Thanksgiving. Splitting into two teams, they'd prepped, served, and cleaned up at the Hogans' and the Ellsworths', both hosting for extended family. It was seven o'clock by the time Dakota exchanged a weary goodnight with Jarrett. They parted, he to hang with his girlfriend, she to drive to Lauren's shingled farmhouse. Holidays were tough for Lauren; memories of her husband, Zach, continued to haunt.

After taking over bedtime duties for Lauren and reading Katie and Ali a story, tucking them in with their favorite stuffed animals, and kissing them goodnight, Dakota changed into jeans and Uggs and accompanied Lauren for a final barn check. Then they settled down before a crackling fire, Lauren's two wirehaired Jack Russells, Monty and Jax, curled on either side of them, and feasted on tacos and tequila while watching *Sleepless in Seattle* so that Lauren could pretend her tears were for Meg Ryan and Tom Hanks.

As nontraditional and melancholy as her and Lauren's Thanksgiving night was, it was far preferable to the times she'd succumbed to Piper's less than subtle hints and prepared a Thanksgiving meal on Dune Road. The marathon of cooking, serving Piper's assorted friends, and then washing up after them would have been fine had her mother ever thought to say thanks. This year, luckily, Piper had Duncan Harding to distract her. For that reason alone, Dakota thought she should like the latest boy toy.

Max hadn't come out. The weekend before Thanksgiving, she'd taken him surfing. He was learning quickly. With each ride, he was more confident, unafraid to experiment with angles and positions as he worked the waves.

Watching him, it was hard not to think about sex.

Even bobbing on the water while they waited in the lulls for the next set to come rolling in, she couldn't help lowering her gaze to take in the broad wall of his chest and the imposing V of his muscular thighs straddling the board.

Framed by black neoprene, his face—with his penetrating eyes, the intriguing bump on his otherwise straight, no-nonsense nose, and lips that were as firm and commanding as she'd initially suspected—was just as distracting. While she would have liked to resent him for disturbing the peace she found on the water, the blame lay with her.

To resist her fascination, she formulated shopping lists and made a mental spreadsheet with the holiday work schedule. Naturally she had to inquire about his plans.

"Will you be needing me on Thursday?" she asked.

"No, the head of my firm holds a Thanksgiving celebration at his place. All four partners and our junior associates are invited."

She had a clear image of what kind of party the head of a successful private equity firm would throw. "Over the top" wouldn't begin to describe it.

"But you'll be going to Alex and Gen's?" She told herself she was asking for professional reasons, but she knew there was more to the question than whether she should add muffins, freshly squeezed orange juice, fruit, milk, and a box of Max's favorite cereal to her shopping list, and another cleaning slot to the work schedule.

"Not sure. Bob Elders's ranch is in Sun Valley, Idaho. Sometimes it snows."

"Oh." She rearranged the mental image she'd formed, replacing crystal chandeliers, marble, and ceiling-to-floor windows with a mega-lodge decorated with elk antlers, stone, and timber. Instead of a panorama of skyscrapers, Max and his colleagues would enjoy a vista of mountain ranges.

But then on Saturday, while she was walking on the beach with Hendrick, Arlo running ahead of them over the hard sand in shaggy, bounding leaps, she received a text.

Arriving @ 3:00.

It was, like all of Max's texts, pared down to the essentials. One word, a symbol, and a number shouldn't make her pulse leap. Or make her stare at the screen for several seconds.

"Good news?"

She raised her head and nonchalantly returned her cell to the front pocket of her down jacket. "Max will be coming out after all."

"Reason enough to smile."

She hadn't realized she had been. "I'm just glad I decided to buy groceries for him after all."

Hendrick nodded gravely.

"It's not what you think."

"Of course not," he said, laughing when she shook her head in exasperation.

For Alex and Gen's party, she chose one of her favorite dresses, one she was careful to hide in the back of her closet away from Piper's grasp. Filching clothes was another boundary her mother ignored when she dropped by Dakota's place on Marion Lane. Invariably she'd wander into Dakota's bedroom, asking over her shoulder whether Dakota had bought anything new because she was so bored with her own wardrobe.

The long-sleeved, scoop-necked dress was a dark metallic gold that ended midthigh and did good things for her legs, especially when paired with high-heeled nude pumps. Dakota knew she'd probably regret the heels before the end of the night, but sometimes Uggs just didn't cut it.

She didn't want to arrive too early, since Rae, Jarrett, and Lupe were working tonight, along with Andrew and George, two part-time employees who made themselves available for the bigger parties. Rae was in charge and it was her show. Dakota didn't want her to feel that she was looking over Rae's shoulder.

The forecast had warned of a heavy fog later, so she left the front lights on in her house and flicked on the one hanging over the door of the barn that served as both garage and storage space for her surfboards and Premier Service's equipment.

Gen and Alex's driveway was already lined with cars when Dakota arrived. She was actually relieved not to see the fire-engine-red Maserati. Once she'd said hi to Gen and Alex and found some people to talk to, her party nerves would settle. Then, when Max showed up, it would be like seeing a familiar face. It would be nice.

The house was filled with voices and laughter and the vibrant hues of women dressed in velvets, silks, and cashmeres. Men were in jackets, some wearing ties, others opting for crewnecks and V-necks under their sports coats. Dakota saw Rae in her crisp white shirt, burgundy bow tie, and tailored black pants. With her long hair pulled back in a chignon, she carried a tray of champagne-filled glasses with the grace of a dancer.

Spotting Dakota, she smiled and mouthed, "Wow." After offering flutes to the other guests, she made her way to Dakota.

"Looking fine, boss. May I offer you some champagne?"

"Thank you." She picked up a flute and sipped. It was delicious. "How's it going?"

"Piece of cake. Why can't everyone be like Alex and Gen? They're so great. And normal."

"I know." She glanced around. "Where is Gen?"

"In the dining room, making sure the kids eat something other than brownies and cake. George and Andrew set out the buffet a few minutes ago. Alex is in the library talking to Astrid Shibles and some Wall Street types. Oh, and don't look now, but your hands-down hottest client just walked in. And yes, the man looks incredible."

"Oh." She took a slow sip of champagne, but it only made the sudden flutters in her stomach that much more … fluttery. To focus on something other than Max, she said, "You'll come get me if you need—"

"Dakota, you're here to have fun. Go have some. Me, I'm here to pay for my new kitchen floor, which is gonna look awesome." Rae's dark gaze slid past Dakota and her smile widened. "Good evening, Mr. Carr. Could I interest you in a glass of champagne?"

"Hello, Rae. Yes, I'd like that."

Dakota willed herself to remain composed. Then she turned and everything inside her went a little haywire. He wore a black suit and a white shirt that was open at the collar, a stunning combination of elegant and casual.

"Nice" was such a vapid word. What in the world had made her believe anything connected to Max could ever be so blandly pleasant?

Then Max spoke again, and his voice sounded even deeper, an intimate rumble. "Hello, Dakota. You look stunning."

"Thank you." The compliment shouldn't mean so much or cause a zing of awareness to dance through her veins.

Caught in the warmth of his gaze and the curve of his lips, a reminder of the drugging pleasure of his kisses, she barely registered Rae clearing her throat.

"If you'll excuse me, I need to refill this tray." As she passed Dakota she whispered, "I will kill you if you go home alone tonight."

Max's hearing was obviously excellent, for his smile widened in amusement.

She pretended not to notice. "How was Idaho?"

"Predictable, unlike here." He took a sip of champagne. "Will blood be shed?"

She raised a brow. "Rae's bark is worse than her bite."

He moved closer, close enough that she could feel the heat of his body, anticipate its hard strength. "Anything I can do to tip the scales?"

"Afraid not." His smile and the light in his eyes, a promise of sensual pleasure she too often denied herself, had already decided her. She was tired of thinking about sex. She wanted it. And she wanted it with Max. She swept her gaze over the room. "There are people here you might enjoy meeting. Shall I introduce you?"

"Sure—unless I can convince you to walk out the front door with me."

"I haven't even said hello to Gen and Alex yet."

"I suppose it would be rude to leave before greeting them. Then again, the way you look right now makes me wonder if I couldn't simply send a case of champagne in apology."

"Let's expand your Hamptons social circle at least a little." She paused a beat. "And by the way, you look pretty good tonight, too."

He cocked his head, as if sensing a change in her. "Do I?"

"Yes." It was time to be honest and frank in admitting her desire. "And Rae won't even have to growl at me. It seems you've won again."

The light that flared in his eyes warmed her. "Thank God." He grinned. "And thank you." Placing his hand on the small of her back, a possessive gesture that sent awareness rippling through her, he said, "For that, I'll follow wherever you lead."

Max was as much a draw as she'd expected. People were curious about Windhaven's new owner. The locals were reassured at having her, a Hale and a bona fide Hamptons full-timer, introduce him. The artists among them, who were active in conserving the beauty of the East End, perked up upon being reminded by her that Max had preferred to keep the old house standing rather than bulldozing it, as many other wealthy newcomers would have done.

Max did the rest. His calm confidence, obvious intelligence, and good looks, combined with the catnip effect of his hundreds of millions had the predictable effect on the moneymen and their bejeweled wives. Gestures and broad smiles said it all: Max had conquered his audience.

She was equally conscious of her own surrender and excitement. Awareness caused her to feel the silky weight of her hair as she tucked it behind her ear, the simple gesture fraught with sensuality. The cling of her dress made her conscious of the swell of her breasts, the nip of her waist, the flare of her hips. Even her skin felt different, hypersensitized.

All the while, conversation continued. Then Max would turn to her with a comment or merely angle his head, focusing on her with that singular intensity, and the rest of the room would melt away.

As they moved from one cluster of guests to the next, his hand would return to the small of her back, making her heart soar like a flock of plovers taking flight.

Gen found them a short while later. Kissing their cheeks in welcome, she said, "Oh, good, Max, you've had Dakota to introduce you."

"Yes. It's quite a party, Gen."

"Thank you. It's a fun mix of people. And how was your Thanksgiving?" she asked him. "Did you spend it with family?"

"No." Max shook his head. "Bob Elders, Summit's director, holds an annual party at his spread in Sun Valley. A command performance for the team."

"It's a shame that you couldn't get home." Although married to a venture capitalist, Gen hadn't bought into the culture. Turning to Dakota, she asked, "And how are you?"

"I'm fine. You look lovely."

"Yes," Max said. "I'd expect you to be a bit ragged around the edges, throwing such a big party on the heels of Thanksgiving."

"I'd be an utter wreck if it weren't for Dakota." Gen grinned.

"Stop, you'll embarrass me," she said.

"It's true," Gen insisted. "When Alex and I first threw this party, I had my sister, Bridget, come and cook up a storm—remember, Dakota? But then her restaurant received a James Beard Award and there went my personal chef. And this party's gotten bigger every year. No way could I do it without Premier Service, especially when I've got an exhibition coming up. I'm still working on a few canvases."

"I've been meaning to ask you for an invitation. I'm hoping to hang a Gen Monaghan on my walls," Max said.

"Funny, that's been my wish for years," Dakota said with a smile. "The show's in January, right?"

"Have no fear, you're both on the guest list. Look for your invitations next week and please, please come to the opening. I'll need as many friendly faces there as possible. The New York art crowd can be savage."

"I can't wait to see the paintings. I'm sure the show will be spectacular," Dakota said.

"Come into the library with me," Gen told them. "Alex is there talking to some people. I'm sure you already know a few of them, Max, but Dakota should meet them. One couple in particular might be great potential clients. I want to introduce you before Alex's sister, Cassie, arrives. She just texted me. The gang should be here any minute."

The round of introductions finished, Dakota was chatting with a couple roughly her age, the wife a corporate lawyer and the husband in advertising. They were house-hunting for a summer place in Sag Harbor, drawn by the architecture of the old houses.

Next to her, Max was talking to Alex and Gen and a man who owned a chain of luxury hotels and lived on Meadow Lane in Southampton, a few doors down from Calvin Klein. He was telling them about a fundraiser the designer had hosted for the Animal Rescue League, and how much fun it had been to see the celebrities and outrageously beautiful models being dragged about by their overexcited pooches. The sight was classic Hamptons: bighearted and well-intentioned, but also crazy and completely over the top. He hoped Calvin would agree to host it again next season.

The sound of several voices reached them. Dakota looked toward the double-door entry and recognized Cassie Miller and her husband, Caleb Wells. In Caleb's arms was a shy-looking little girl with a halo of golden curls who made Dakota's heart melt. Next to Cassie were the older children, Jamie and Sophie—they must be eighteen by now, she calculated, and Dylan, who was seven.

Alex and Gen went over and hugged Cassie and the others, and Alex took Holly from his brother-in-law and settled her against his chest, saying, "Let's give your dad a chance to drink some champagne, okay, pumpkin?"

Dakota was pleased to see that her star server, Jarrett, was right there with champagne as well as nonalcoholic drinks for the kids. Andy followed him with a tray of appetizers.

Alex brought his extended family over to introduce them.

"And you remember Dakota," he said to Jamie and Sophie.

"Hi," she said with a smile. "It's great to see you again."

"Is that the lobster surfing lady?" Holly asked, pointing a chubby finger at her.

"You are a legend in our household," Cassie said with a laugh. "Yes, that's the lobster surfing lady, Holly, but you can also call her Dakota."

"Lobster surfing lady," Max said with a smile that Dakota felt straight down to her toes. "There must be a story there."

"Dakota taught Jamie and me how to eat lobsters at Uncle Alex and Aunt Gen's wedding. We'd never had them before," Sophie answered.

"We were super-deprived as kids," Jamie said.

"Yeah, terribly deprived, because most seven-year-olds eat lobster *all* the time," Cassie mocked.

Dylan piped up. "And one summer, Uncle Alex and Aunt Gen took us to Montauk and we watched you surf. Then we all went to dinner at . . ." He faltered. "Where was it again?"

"The Surf Lodge," Alex provided.

Dylan nodded, his dark curls bobbing. "And we all ate lobsters and Dakota showed me how to break open the claw—"

"Hence 'the lobster surfing lady,'" Alex said to Max.

"—and then afterward there were fireworks on the beach," Dylan finished.

"What a good memory you have. That was a fun night," Dakota said. "Maybe we can do it again this summer."

Dylan's face lit up.

Cassie ruffled her younger son's hair. "Well, the Hampton Classic is on our show schedule. I'm hoping I don't have to ride off against these two," she said with a nod to Jamie and Sophie. "The Miller-Wells twins are making quite a name for themselves on the West Coast."

"You two are twins?" Max asked, his voice oddly sharp.

She supposed he was simply surprised. A stranger might not guess that they were fraternal twins. Though their coloring was identical, curly blond hair and deep blue eyes, Jamie topped his sister by a good five inches. Many would assume more than minutes separated their birth dates.

"Yes," Sophie said. "And I'm pretty sure Jamie was as obnoxious in the womb as he is now."

Jamie was unfazed. "Sour grapes. Sophie can't get over the fact that I'm the older and wiser twin by a whole four minutes. What were you doing in there, anyway?"

"Giving our mother a chance to recover from the sight of your scrunched-up face," Sophie returned. "There's documentary evidence to prove that you were the ugliest baby ever."

Dakota had a hunch these two could lob good-natured insults at each other all day. She glanced over at Max to share her amusement.

But he seemed far from entertained. He looked as if he'd been gutted but had forgotten to fall down.

"Max?" she said quietly, so as not to draw attention to them.

He didn't seem to hear her, and before she could ask again, Steve Sheppard joined them, saying to the twins, "Hey, Jamie and Sophie. Word has it you two are lighting up the West Coast."

Jamie grinned. "Someone had to teach those Californians how to ride."

"You are so embarrassing," Sophie told her brother before turning to Steve. "We lucked out at Stanford. Our coach is terrific and there are a lot of really talented riders on the team. We had a great fall season."

"Stanford's lucky to have you. Did I hear right that you both will be riding in the jumper classes at the Classic?"

"That's right, and ..."

Dakota missed the rest of Jamie's answer, her attention caught by Max when he abruptly stepped away from their circle, his face etched in harsh lines.

She watched him walk over to Alex, who was still holding little Holly in his arms. He leaned in to say something—with all the conversations going on in the room, there was no way she could catch it, but she could read Alex's lips as he formed the words *Thanks* and *See you.*

Then Max strode quickly from the room.

Dakota stared after him in confusion. Had he just left the party without a word to her? Without even a backward glance?

What in the world had just happened?

CHAPTER SIXTEEN

Forty-five minutes later, after saying her good-byes and thanks, Dakota climbed into her car and realized she had to decide whether to be wise or foolish.

There was no good reason to go to Windhaven. Whatever urge or attraction Max had felt earlier clearly hadn't lasted. Otherwise he could have simply looked over at her and crooked his finger, and she'd have trotted after him.

Embarrassing but true.

And now, freed from the seductive web he'd woven, she knew she should simply drive back home, turn off the lights, crawl under her down quilt, and catch up on some much-needed sleep.

Except that she wouldn't sleep a wink.

Not even her tried-and-true remedy for insomnia, cleaning and reorganizing her kitchen cupboards, would prevent her from seeing Max's tortured expression. Something was wrong with him. Terribly wrong. Foolish though it was, she was going to find out the cause.

*

Windhaven was lit brightly, forcing Dakota to discard one explanation for Max's abrupt departure—that his trip to Idaho, which had surely involved late nights and free-flowing alcohol, had caught up to him at the party, exhaustion slamming him like a rogue wave.

She rang the doorbell and waited, shivering slightly in the cold fog, and of half a mind to turn on her heel and leave him to his problems. Who was she to think she could fix what troubled him?

He answered in rolled-up shirtsleeves and bare feet. His hair was mussed as if he'd been dragging his fingers through it.

"Premier Service is making night calls now? How enterprising."

The scent of the peaty single-malt whiskey reached her. Max's words were unslurred, though, so it wasn't drink that was making him hostile. Ignoring the jab, she said, "I came to see how you were."

"As you can see, I'm fine."

Plainly not. Whatever was eating at him hadn't relinquished its hold. The cold night and something even chillier cut through her wool coat, and she shivered again. "Are you going to invite me in?"

With the hall light at his back, his face was shadowed, his expression inscrutable. Seconds ticked uncomfortably while he remained silent. Then he spoke, and his voice was like the roll of stones. "I'm not in the mood to talk, Dakota. I want to fuck you."

The crude admission should have had her walking away. The only reason it didn't was because she could practically feel the tension radiating off him.

She made a final attempt to search his expression. Having gleaned nothing, she was left with an offer far removed from the smooth seduction he'd treated her to earlier, far removed from the promise of a carefree, brilliantly executed sexual romp. Everything—his words, his body language—spoke of a raw need held barely in check, and told her that the sex with him would be as elemental.

Her gaze locked on his shadowed face, she drew a breath and crossed the threshold.

Max didn't allow himself to question why Dakota had accepted his proposition; the only way to deal with what had happened tonight was to shut down his thoughts.

As she stepped into the house, he closed the door behind her. The light and the moisture from the fog made her dark hair sparkle, fairy-like.

Fairy-like. That was the sort of thing Rosie would have said. God, he had to stop remembering.

Clasping Dakota by the shoulders of her damp coat, he spun her around and hauled her up against the wall, plastering his mouth to hers. He kissed her, devouring her lush lips and the sweet, hot recesses of her mouth in hungry bites and lashes of his tongue. There was no finesse, just desperation.

With a moan, her mouth opened beneath his, allowing him deeper access, and her hands joined his frantic quest, grappling with his shirt buttons while he yanked off her coat and then tugged the stretchy fabric of her dress up, dragging it over her hips and waist. "Raise your arms," he growled, and when she did, he pulled the dress over her head and threw it behind him.

He hissed, scorched by the sight of her. Her full breasts strained enticingly against the lacy cups of her bra. Her narrow waist was accentuated by the sweet flare of her hips. He stared hungrily, jealously, at the triangle of lace covering the place he most wanted to be, before lowering his gaze to toned legs that went on for days.

Her body more than made good on the dark, smoky promise of her voice. All-tempting, she made him burn.

He dropped to his knees. In her heels, she was at the perfect height. He wrapped his fingers around the narrow band of lace encircling her hips and dragged it down. As it fell to the floor, he found her with his mouth. Her startled gasp ended on a moan of pleasure.

She tasted as he'd imagined: salty like the sea. He drank her in, licking and sucking and drawing forth soft cries as her fingers dug into his hair, clinging fiercely. Anchoring him.

As if there were any other place he'd rather be.

He brought her to the edge quickly. Pushed her over it when he slid two fingers deep inside her—lust nearly blinding him as her muscles clamped vise-like around him—while he circled her clit with his tongue.

She went wild, her shocked cry of "God, Max!" filling the entryway.

He barely registered his triumph. Nor did he give her time to come down. He couldn't; he would lose his mind if he didn't get inside her and feel that incredible heat, that slick strength around him.

Thank fuck he'd had the foresight to arm himself before going out tonight. He dug a foil from his back pocket and tore it open with his teeth.

His belt was unbuckled. That, and his open shirt, was as far as Dakota had gotten before he'd dropped out of reach. He unzipped his fly and shoved down his briefs, kicking both off.

Unable even to smile at her gasp of appreciation, he rolled the condom on with clumsy hands. Christ, his whole body was trembling, straining to be in hers.

He looked at her. Cheeks flushed a dark rose and her lips deliciously swollen from his kisses, she looked glorious. Beautiful and powerful.

"Take your bra off." He almost didn't recognize his voice, guttural, verging on feral.

She obliged, reaching back and unhooking it, and then lowering the silk straps. Could his heart pound any harder? Her breasts were just the right size, he thought even before he'd cupped them, tested their weight and teased her taut nipples. And then she arched, offering him more.

God, she was perfect. He wasn't even inside her and he was already close to losing it.

He placed his hand beneath one of her legs and wrapped it around his hip. The gold in her dark eyes glowing, she lifted her other leg and hooked her ankles around his back, and he felt her heat against his straining erection.

"You ready?"

When she bit down on her lower lip and nodded, she was the sexiest thing he'd ever beheld.

Locking his gaze on hers, he thrust inside, and his groan of pleasure met her gasp of surprise.

Then everything became a frenzied blur as their trembling bodies rocked and bucked. Their mouths were as reckless in their hunger, teeth scoring and tongues lashing, desperate to taste everything within reach. Their sweat ran and mingled as his hands kneaded and hers clutched, as they drove each other to a fevered pitch.

And when her inner muscles tightened around him, contracting powerfully, an electric pleasure shot through him. With a hoarse cry, he drove his body into hers, sending them flying over the edge in a dizzying rush.

Emptied, he let his head fall against the wall with a soft thud. He lost track of time, aware only of his body pressing against hers, the peppery-floral scent of her damp neck, and the uneven rasp of their breathing.

Slowly Dakota unhooked her ankles and cautiously lowered

one leg and then the other with equal care, as if unsure of their ability to support her.

"Wow," she said in a dazed voice.

He raised his head. "Yeah."

Her hair was tangled, her face was flushed, and her eyes smoldered. With awareness. With desire.

And just like that, the storm of hunger rose inside him again, even stronger than before. Because now he wanted to taste her everywhere, from the arch of her foot to the small of her back to the tips of her fingers, and learn all her flavors. He wanted to touch and stroke her until he knew exactly how to make that supple body arch and flex as pleasure rolled through her. He wanted to hear his name tumble again and again from her lips in throaty wonder.

He wanted her to stay.

He didn't tell her any of that. Instead he asked, "Do you want more?"

She looked at him, and he forced himself to keep his expression impassive. But somehow he sensed that she saw past his posturing to the pain and darkness at his center.

"Yes."

His throat tightened with relief. Dropping his gaze, he busied himself with removing the condom, then bent down to rummage for fresh ones in his trouser pocket. Taking her hand, he said, "Come."

They made it to his bed eventually. But not before he'd led her into the living room and sunk onto one of the armchairs, tugging her hand until she straddled his thighs so he could do justice to her breasts. As he lavished attention on them, she reached between them, stroking him until he was ready to explode.

He grabbed a condom off the side table. "Take me inside you."

She rode him, her every rise and fall wringing a shudder from him. He was so close, but he fought it, never wanting the pleasure of her clamped tightly around him to end. But then her tempo increased and he couldn't stop himself from grasping her hips and urging her on as the tension built and then spiraled out of control as, shattered, she cried his name.

And when she collapsed, quaking, against him, he petted her in slow strokes down her sweat-slicked spine. Turning his face into the hollow behind her ear, he breathed in the scent of her flushed skin, the fragrance of her shampoo, the lingering notes of her perfume, and wondered if this ferocious need for her would subside.

Sometime in the wee hours it did, when their last coupling left them in a heaving tangle of limbs. Exhausted beyond thought, he collapsed onto her. As their breaths evened and slowed, he fell asleep, his body deep inside hers.

CHAPTER SEVENTEEN

Dakota awoke slowly to a room bathed in shadows, a bed much larger than hers, and the combined weight of an arm across her chest and a muscled thigh canted over hers. Dakota doubted she would have moved, even if she hadn't been thus pinned. She knew already that every part of her ached. Deliciously yet unmistakably. Understandable; she'd never had quite the full body workout like the one Max had given her.

She'd been well and truly ravished, she thought with a small smile. And were Piper to see that smile, she would crow in I-told-you-so triumph. But at least this hadn't been one of Piper's exalted anonymous encounters. Dakota knew Max.

And she understood him well enough to recognize that something more than his insane physical prowess and sexual appetite had been at work the previous night. Whatever had caused his sudden tension at Max and Gen's party had also fed the white-hot need driving him.

She'd been happy to offer him the haven of her body, especially when doing so brought her physical pleasure the likes of which she'd never experienced before.

She turned her head to study him. Even at rest, his face, with its dramatic planes and squared chin, was strong and commanding. Up close, his dark auburn lashes were straight and thicker than she'd previously noted. His lips were slightly open, and he was snoring. Lightly, yet unmistakably.

Perversely, that only increased his appeal. In a man who must usually rise early to check the world markets, the heaviness of his slumber meant that she'd worn him out. Perhaps she'd also helped banish whatever was troubling him.

A sudden frown furrowing his brow challenged that hope. With a mumble, he flung the arm that had rested across her chest to the side and shifted his weight. Now he lay on his back.

He took her breath away.

Her gaze roamed over his muscled length, and she colored at the marks on his shoulders where her teeth had scored. She'd been as voracious as he. Her gaze traveled further, past the ridges of his stomach, to follow the narrow line of dark hair that led to his groin. Even semi-erect, he was impressive. At full mast, awesome.

Max and his penis made a very fine team. With their combined talents they must have slain legions of women. Remembering how he had known just how to find the perfect angle, rhythm, and tempo to drive her wild, she knew he could add her to the number.

The last time they'd had sex, his every thrust had inched her up the bed, across very soft linens, until she was bracing herself against the headboard. She'd never given headboards much consideration, but with a man like Max, who could sling her legs around his hips and then hammer into her until she screamed her release even while pleading for him never, ever, to stop, she now fully appreciated their importance.

So kudos to her and Astrid for supplying him with the very best, she thought with a smile.

She seemed to remember the two of them passing out when, after a few more pumps, Max came with a hoarse curse, gripping her hands as if they were a lifeline. With a heavy shudder, he'd fallen on top of her, and she'd been too wrecked to care that he weighed a solid ton.

A sudden thought had her lazy smile slipping. Where was the condom he'd been wearing?

Her gaze moved from his body to hers. The spent condom lay at the juncture of her thighs. How gross, she thought.

"That's a hell of an expression on your face." His voice was a sleepy rumble.

With her thumb and index finger, she picked up the used condom and held it aloft, explanation enough. "Good morning."

"It was certainly a good night." He reached over and plucked the condom from her fingers.

"I can throw that out."

"You're not on the job." He deposited the condom on the floor. "I have fresh ones in the drawer to your right," he said with a nod toward the nightstand.

So that's where he stocked them. Unless specifically requested to clean them, Dakota left medicine cabinets and drawers alone, instructing her crew never to open them. Max seemed to break every rule she had with clients. And though his words had miraculously eased her aching muscles, it would be best if she went home. Safer for her peace of mind and heart. She was growing a little too fond of her employer.

"I should go home."

"That would involve your leaving the bed."

"This is true."

"I'd rather you stayed." He rubbed his hand across the flat of his belly, drawing her gaze. He was fully erect.

That hadn't taken much.

She glanced up. He wore a sleepy look and a lazy smile, but she didn't doubt for a second that he was ready to perform to the high standards he'd set last night. Yet even now, with the early morning light only barely seeping into the room, she sensed that there was more going on here. Which meant he was still using sex to block out whatever was bothering him.

Should she call him on it or play along?

Her gaze strayed to his erection and her inner muscles tightened as if remembering his girth, the deep stroking rhythm he'd been able to maintain, and how he could switch it up, touching her in places that had her toes curling and her back arching off the mattress.

Why not at least start the day on a pleasant note? "I was also contemplating how nice a shower would be." She sat up.

His gaze lowered and lingered on her breasts, then rose to meet hers. "A shower, huh?"

She fought a smile at the husky arousal in his voice. "Yours is quite big," she said.

"Easily large enough for two. Which means I could join you. Perhaps soap those hard-to-reach places."

"That's a very generous offer."

"I'm feeling very generous."

The smile won and spread. "Lucky me."

Max's generosity included dropping to his knees and paying careful attention to a special place that left her trembling and clutching his water-slick shoulders. Then he slid inside her and took her in long, hard thrusts as waves of pleasure rocked her ever higher.

She wanted that pleasure. Already she'd come to crave the skill of his hands and mouth, the strength of his beautifully coordinated body. Yet even as her pleasure mounted ever higher, as he sent her riding the crest of a giant, glorious wave, she sensed troubled waters ahead, there in the deep pain that lingered in his gaze.

Since her clothes—and destroyed undies—lay in a heap downstairs, Max had lent her a pair of sweats that she had to roll at the waist and bottoms, and a cashmere sweater that enveloped her in his scent. While he went downstairs to make coffee, she stripped his bed and remade it. Professional habits die hard. And as dangerous as the impulse was, she wanted to do something for him.

He would thank her for the clean sheets, but not for what truly showed she cared: asking him what was wrong.

It would be so much easier to pretend that all that counted was the truly splendid sex they'd shared, and simply enjoy the excellent and super-strong coffee he'd made, drinking him in with surreptitious glances as she sipped.

Max was eating a bowl of cereal. She'd helped herself to one of the muffins she'd baked for him. Breaking off a chunk, she debated how to ask . . . *whether* to ask.

She was chickening out. Annoyed with herself, she forced the words out. "So what happened last night at the party?"

His spoon stalled in midair, then resumed its trip to his mouth. He chewed a little longer than necessary for a mouthful of soggy cereal. "What do you mean?"

"I'm talking about whatever made you leave the party so abruptly." She recalled his stricken expression. "Did it have something to do with Jamie and Sophie?"

"I hadn't realized they were twins."

It was only because she was watching carefully that she realized he was holding the spoon in a death grip.

"You hadn't seen the photographs of them all around the house?"

"I don't look at family photos."

The very opposite of her. More than expensive tchotchkes, it was the pictures scattered throughout a home that drew her attention. When dusting, she would study the candid shots of mothers and fathers with their kids offering their smiles to the camera as well as the more formal photos—the graduations, the weddings, the award ceremonies—that marked the milestones of a life. She loved the moments captured and the stories told.

"So the twins, why would they—"

The spoon hit the edge of his bowl with a sharp clatter. "Christ, Dakota, I just wasn't expecting it, all right? Now will you leave it the fuck alone?"

There, in stark relief, was the pain she'd only glimpsed before. Then it had been focused inward. Now it radiated out, sharp and jagged as broken glass.

She pushed her stool away from the island.

"What are you doing?" His voice was quieter, yet the strain remained.

"I'm going home. I apologize for invading your privacy." She felt like an idiot. He'd made it clear what the rules were. It was her fault for thinking he needed something more than a one-night stand.

His curse was swift and fluent. "I had a twin sister. Her name was Rosie."

She'd frozen at "had." "She died?" The question hardly made it past her lips.

"Four days after our high school graduation. We had the summer before us. And then college to look forward to in the fall. Seeing Jamie and Sophie, hearing the way they talked to each other . . . it was hard."

He'd averted his gaze while he spoke, but she could see the corded tendons in his neck and the rapid blink of his eyelids, and her heart ached for him. "I am so sorry, Max."

He shrugged, obviously uncomfortable with her sympathy. "It caught me unawares, that's all."

"How—how did Rosie die?"

At her question he turned his head. His expression was bleak, his eyes empty. "Car accident."

There were more questions she wanted to ask. They remained lodged in her throat, along with her aching sadness. "I am so very sorry, Max," she said again.

"It happened years ago."

"Some wounds don't heal."

"Don't play psychiatrist with me, Dakota. I don't want or need one." The scrape of the stool legs on the floor was discordant, like the mood that had settled over them. "I have to read some emails and catch up on work," he said, and strode out of the kitchen.

She gave him time; *she* needed time. Of all the various explanations that had gone through her mind, never once had she entertained the possibility that Max had a twin. Whenever she considered her childhood, how messed up it was to grow up in a family who treated her with a combination of hostility and careless neglect, and how much she'd longed for a father who regarded her as more than a stupid mistake or afterthought, at least she hadn't faced real tragedy or a terrible, wrenching loss, as Max had.

The death of one's twin? Losing the person who came into existence simultaneously? Who shared the same womb? She'd heard stories from Alex and Gen about the closeness Jamie and Sophie shared. Beneath the bickering and teasing existed an extraordinary emotional connection. Sophie, the more forthcoming of the two, described it as a kind of telepathy.

No wonder Max had looked like he'd seen a ghost.

Max had it under control again. Numbers, projections, acquisition potential, bid strategies—those were his comfort zone. He was in the midst of writing an email to Bob Elders and his partners at Summit outlining the exit strategy—in this case a secondary buyout by another private equity firm—for a healthcare company that designed electronic medical devices when Dakota entered his study.

From the corner of his eye he saw the cup in her hand, but she remained silent, waiting while he continued typing. When he finally pressed send and looked over, he made sure to keep a blank expression on his face.

"I thought you might like some more coffee."

He gave a short nod. "Yeah. Thanks."

She placed it on a hammered-tin coaster that she'd told him came from a store in Sag Harbor. He liked it. He liked everything she'd done in the house. And he liked her, which was too bad, because he should be formulating an exit strategy for Dakota as well.

Her shoulders rose as she drew a breath, and he thought of how he'd run his tongue along the line of her collarbone, and then how his hands had cupped her shoulders as she'd lowered herself onto his cock. He'd loved exploring every inch of her last night. And this morning, watching his hands glide over her while the water streamed and the suds ran in rivers, leaving her sleek curves glistening, had been the perfect wet dream.

"Listen," she said. "There's this spot in Montauk, just past the lighthouse, where I sometimes go. Being there, well, it's like the earth has slipped away, leaving nothing but ocean and sky. It helps me."

"That's nice." He injected a bored tone into his voice. "But like I said before, I don't need help. I'm fine."

He'd devised excellent ways of coping. He worked hard and he screwed even harder. Last night was the perfect example and the reason he was weighing the cost versus benefit in having Dakota stick around. The sex between them had been stellar. He wanted her still. Would like nothing better than to take her over to the leather couch and once again lose himself in her deliciously hot body.

But now she knew about Rosie. For that alone he should be hustling her out the front door. He never talked about his sister's death, or any of the rest. Yet he'd looked into Dakota's eyes, lit with expectation and compassion, and confessed that he'd had a twin. And lost her.

His insides twisted as if he'd ruptured something.

He'd even admitted how hard it had been to see the twins. Hard? It had *shredded* him. While Sophie and Jamie didn't particularly resemble Rosie or him physically, hearing them talk to each other had been harrowing. It was as if someone had switched on a recording of him and Rosie goading each other.

He didn't know why Dakota had been the one to extract that confession from him or why he hadn't simply blocked her questions. He could close down a person with a single look. Just as troubling was the fact that he'd fallen asleep inside her. He was the kind of guy who withdrew. Yet he'd spent an entire night with her wrapped about him and his body blanketing hers—as if he needed the connection with her.

His irritation must have showed, for she said, "I can see you're busy. I'm going to head off."

So she was showing herself the door. Good. Perverse bastard that he was, he found himself asking, "What are your plans for the day?"

She hesitated. "I'm going to swing by my place and grab my board. The conditions aren't great, but . . ." She shrugged.

She didn't need to explain. He'd become hooked himself. Dakota would want to be out on the water, hoping to eke out a few good rides. True surfers didn't just hit the waves under ideal conditions.

"And then I've got some homework," she said.

"Homework? What kind of homework?"

"I'm getting an MBA. Online. Through Carnegie Mellon University." She shifted her gaze to a ceramic bowl that was sitting on the mantelpiece, focusing on it as if it contained the mysteries of the world.

He should have guessed. Dakota was smart and serious about her business. Yet he'd assumed that her life as it was, an elegant balance of guiding Premier Service to whatever profit goals she'd targeted and spending her free time carving rides out of shifting arcs of water, was all she was looking for. He wondered what else he didn't know about her and wasn't surprised to find his curiosity reawakened. She did that to him.

"Carnegie Mellon, that's a good program. So what are you interested in doing next?"

"I'd like to get into early-stage investing."

"Start-ups, huh?"

Maybe she'd been expecting him to ridicule her idea of pursuing an MBA. When he only expressed professional interest, her expression lost some of its wariness.

"The courses are helping me learn what to look for in start-up companies and identify the ones that have what it takes to last."

"There's some good profits to be made from early investments."

"There are some excellent businesses out there that need financing and guiding," she countered.

"Ah, a do-gooder," he said mildly.

"Having a conscience and making money don't need to be mutually exclusive objectives, do they? Yes, I want to make a nice profit, but at the end of the day I also want to feel good about my involvement in a company."

"So you didn't start Premier Service because you'd identified a potentially lucrative pain point?"

"Lucrative pain point?" A smile tugged her lips. "Gotta love the lingo you Wall Street wolves use."

"How about this, then: you saw you could make a killing from a lot of fat cats?"

She bit her lip, and he knew it was to keep her smile from spreading. "That's downright nasty. No, I started Premier as an extension of the jobs I had as a kid and because I found I liked being around other families and other people's homes. I figured out that I could do things to improve their lives and make them happier. I still get satisfaction from that. If I didn't, it would show, and there'd be no profit for me and my employees."

For the moment he chose to ignore her comment about wanting to be around families—a land mine of a subject—focusing instead on how sexy he found her ambition to be a venture capitalist. As if she needed to be any sexier.

"Well, I should . . ." She shifted, obviously ready to leave.

"Can I come out with you again? I don't have to head into the city until tomorrow," he said, even though while composing his email, he'd been considering going back in time to hit the bar scene. "I'd like your company."

While he resented Dakota for having witnessed him at a vulnerable moment, he wasn't ready to let her go. And he was in control once more, he reminded himself. There'd be no further contact with Alex Miller's extended family, no reminder of family lost or wished for. No talk of it, either. He was offering simple companionship and unrestrained sex.

Several seconds passed. By this point she could certainly recognize his hunger for her. And in the slight parting of her lips, he saw her sudden awareness. Heard it in the quick catch of her breath as her body responded and the attraction between them flared to life.

"Yes," she said.

CHAPTER EIGHTEEN

They had three weekends together. With Max touching down in East Hampton at eight in the evening on Friday and leaving on a six o'clock flight the following Monday morning, they spent those 174 hours as they pleased: in each other's arms, surfing, walking on the beach, and touring the Hamptons, Dakota showing Max all her favorite spots and sights. With the holiday season in full swing, it was a magical time, the shop fronts gaily decorated, the restaurants serving delicious specials. With each weekend, she fell a little harder and deeper for him. With every smile and laugh they shared, a secret part of her wondered if this might be something more than a strings-free affair.

It was stupid, really, but in hindsight so obvious that a Christmas tree would serve as the death knell to their relationship. She recognized the enormousness of her error the second that Max walked into the living room where earlier she, Rae, and Jarrett had put up a freshly cut Douglas fir in the corner to the right of the fireplace. Dakota had spent the rest of the afternoon decorating the tree with tiny white lights and shiny red and gold balls. She'd found a copper star to top it. A pretty tree. Restrained as well, unlike a number she'd decorated for other clients. Yet from the expression on Max's face—a mix of shock, anger, and betrayal—when he took in the tree and the cheerfully crackling fire she'd lit, the scene obviously screamed domesticity.

She wanted to blame him. Had Max not reverted so seamlessly to the cool and self-possessed Wall Street tycoon, she wouldn't have forgotten how his blue-gray eyes had grown stark with pain when he'd revealed the death of his twin sister, and she would have reconsidered installing a ten-foot symbol of joy in his living room. But the Max with whom she'd spent days laughing and talking about everything from favorite movies to investment strategies and nights writhing and gasping under and over him—that man, wholly in command of all he surveyed, wouldn't be rattled by a Christmas tree.

But Dakota knew she was as much at fault. She'd been selfish. Presented with the chance to create a new memory in Windhaven and banish the horrid ones of Christmases past, she'd grabbed it eagerly. In so doing, she'd willfully ignored the unspoken terms of their time together.

No heavy emotions.

No expectations.

Just sex and good times while they lasted.

So she'd overstepped the boundaries, broken the rules. *Sue me,* she thought to herself, fatalism seeping in. Fatalism colored with resentment. How foolish she'd been to believe that Max might want something more meaningful with her.

He was still standing, immobilized, next to the long, narrow table that backed the sofa. Another Friday would have already seen them half naked, laughing as their hands grappled with their remaining clothes to caress exposed flesh. She might already have sunk to her knees, hungry for his taste and heady with the knowledge that when she took him deep in her mouth, he was completely in her thrall. The fixed distance between them screamed what her heart already grasped: they'd reached the end.

There was no use in pretending she hadn't seen his reaction to the tree or that he looked like he wanted to whip out his phone and arrange for a flight back to the city.

"My mistake. I'll take the tree down," she said.

Her words seemed to take him aback.

What? Did he think she hadn't memorized every emotion that crossed his face when he was suspended over her by mere inches, his body sliding against her, inside her? That she wasn't as hungry for his feelings as his passion? Did he think she didn't watch him over their candlelight dinners at the 1770 House or any of the other Hamptons restaurants she'd taken him to? Did he truly believe she didn't study him when she recounted her week's homework, when they sparred over a professor's or fellow student's pronouncement, or when he gave her advice on how to gauge a company's financial health? Was he truly unaware that she soaked up his carefree happiness while they bobbed on the ocean, and delighted in his fierce anticipation when an incoming set of waves looked promising? Hadn't he realized that seeing him like this and knowing she'd introduced him to this world made her own happiness that much brighter?

She had her answer. He had no idea how much she'd learned about him. Dakota's challenge would now be to *unlearn*. And forget.

"It's just—I'm not big on Christmas trees. Or Christmas. Damn it, Dakota . . ." Max's voice trailed off as he raked a hand through his hair. It had grown almost shaggy, but he'd put off a trip to the barber, saying he liked the way she ran her fingers through it. And, he added with a rakish grin, why waste time sitting in a barber's chair when he could be with her and have her sitting on him?

Was it any surprise she'd begun to think the lines were blurring?

"I understand. I'll have it down and out of the house within an hour." Stiffly she walked over to the tree and reached out to pluck the first ornament off.

From behind she heard him mutter, "Christ." And then louder, "It's all right. Leave it. Just take it down after the weekend, okay?"

She lowered her hand. "Okay."

Except it wasn't.

That night and for the rest of the weekend, he avoided the living room. And for much of that time he avoided her. He didn't simply go for his hour-long run on the beach on Saturday and Sunday. He also hit his personal gym to lift weights for another solid hour to emerge drenched in sweat. Normally he would have reserved his lifting, pumping, and deliciously salty sweat for her.

Another unmistakable sign: his cranking the volume on a seemingly endless playlist that included Nine Inch Nails, Modest Mouse, Incubus, and Linkin Park, erecting a wall of screaming guitars and growling lyrics between them . . . such a guy move.

Meanwhile, she mentally compiled her own gendered response, an ultimate breakup soundtrack heavy on Alanis Morissette, Lily Allen, Kate Nash, Adele, and Taylor Swift, her blistering version of thoroughly pissed off and freakin' miserable.

Rejection was never palatable. For Dakota, the taste was particularly sour. She'd never begged her family for love; she wouldn't do so with her lover, either. She knew Max liked her well enough—if not, then he was the world's greatest actor—but for some reason he couldn't, or wouldn't, give her more of himself.

She told herself she wasn't truly surprised. Early on she had pegged Max as a playboy. But that didn't stop disappointment from weighing heavily. If only she didn't like him so much in spite of his shortcomings.

With the tension reverberating in the air, they should have been able to resist each other. But their physical attraction was too strong. With the end unspoken, the sex between them was also silent. Silent and desperate. Their bodies said goodbye with caresses that lingered, greedily storing memories of the touch of skin, the taste of flesh. Every orgasm he gave her was a poignant gift, eliciting tears that she refused to shed as she clung to him.

On Sunday morning she awoke alone in the bed and to the realization that she had to be the one to make the break. It would be unbearable to hear him utter whatever words he'd been preparing as he raced through the heavy sand or bench-pressed impossible loads. The speech would be polite and depressingly distant, pretty much the way he'd behaved since entering the living room on Friday evening. She almost wished he'd spent the past two days behaving like a total ass. It would make it easier to stop thinking about the way his kisses tasted, his arms felt about her, or his smile warmed her.

She showered the scent of him off and then left the bathroom immaculate. She erased her traces elsewhere, too. There wasn't much to pack up: an extra set of clothing, her laptop, and her toiletry and cosmetics case all fit into an oversized tote. At least she'd never made the mistake of invading his space with too many of her own things. . . .

She pushed the bitterness away. It was an ugly emotion and she wouldn't indulge in it.

Carrying the tote downstairs, she left it by the front door before she began her search for him.

He was working in the office that she and Astrid had taken such care to decorate. She paused, stealing this one last image of him in the comfortably masculine setting with its leather club chairs and sofa, its large mahogany desk and built-in cabinets. He looked so right in it and so very alone.

That was his choice, damn it.

"I've come to say goodbye, Max."

He looked up and, as her words registered, frowned slightly. "You're leaving?"

"Yes, it's time." She swallowed, aware of how much every part of her hurt. "I'd like to end this thing between us now."

Rising, he circled his desk and came to a stop a few feet away from where she stood. "I see. You're sure?"

And there was the relief she'd known would be in his voice if she listened carefully enough. "Yes. I want you to remain my favorite mistake."

He flinched as if she'd landed an unexpected blow.

Had she intended to land one? She didn't really think so. "I'm sorry—that didn't come out the way I intended. I've had fun. Thank you for that."

He recovered quickly, though his smile was a pale ghost of the ones he'd once bestowed. "Me too."

This wasn't the first relationship she'd ended. Breakups often came with a touch of sadness and regret that, for whatever reason, it hadn't clicked. But there were just as many times when she'd walked away with a sense of relief. Max was wrong for her. A commitmentphobe was definitely not on her list of qualities she wanted in a man. And she should be grateful for the fact that he was going to make this the easiest breakup ever.

Why, then, did it feel as if a cinder block was pressing on her chest as she gazed at him?

He'd shoved his hands in his pockets, but she could see that they were balled into fists. He was so good at holding everything tight within him. She couldn't fault him for that. She, too, needed control.

Determined to keep things light, she nodded. "Good. That's what we both wanted, after all."

"Will I see you again?" he asked.

"See me again?" she repeated blankly.

"Here, I mean."

Oh God, he was talking about her *working* for him. She struggled to breathe as the weight pressed harder. "Astrid and I have finished the plans for the guest cottage. She'll be able to oversee the remaining work and the furniture deliveries. I think it would be best if Rae took over readying the house for your visits. She's great, more than able to handle anything you need. I'll make sure she knows to take down the tree. Again, my apologies about that," she said with excruciating politeness.

He gave a restless shrug as his lips flattened in a grim line.

She had to get out of there.

"And what about surfing?" he asked.

He was killing her. She thought of how happy and proud she'd felt watching him paddle toward his wave, knowing that he was going to give it everything he had. And yet he was too freaked out to enter a relationship. "I don't think that would be a good idea."

The angles of his face hardened. "Fine," he ground out. "Right."

"Goodbye, Max."

Would he say something to stop her from leaving, as he had before? Despite everything, a part of her wanted him to try.

Silence answered her.

This time he was letting her go.

CHAPTER NINETEEN

According to the saying, bad things come in threes. Dakota generally ignored superstitions, but in the days following her and Max's brief affair, her life took some definite hits.

First, her mother started talking to her again.

Once more Dakota was subjected to frequent calls and one-sided conversations that, no matter how meandering, nonetheless reached the same end point: Piper, Piper, and more Piper. All too soon she was fully in the know concerning her mother's petty squabbles and outsize dramas.

Why Piper decided to resume contact became quickly clear. She'd ditched Duncan Harding and now needed a larger audience to whom she could enumerate Duncan's failings.

"He really was such a bore, Dakota. In and out of the sack. Utterly vanilla, if you know what I mean."

Dakota wished she didn't, and couldn't help but feel sympathy for the maligned Duncan.

"And he made these funny little noises when he ate. I couldn't bear it anymore."

She tried to tune Piper out, but it wasn't easy. Worse still, each anecdote detailing another of Duncan's shortcomings made her think of her own brief affair.

Max had never bored her, in bed or out.

With his intelligence, energy, and insight, she'd felt smarter in his presence. He stretched her mind, making her think faster and in new ways. Talking with him reminded her of conversations with Hendrick, only with Max there was an added edge and awareness that didn't just stimulate her brain. It quickened the rest of her, too.

She missed him. She missed talking to him. She'd have missed having sex with him, too, if she hadn't been struck down by the nastiest bug ever. It was hard to fantasize about Max when she was battling nausea morning, noon, and night.

She'd caught the virus from Hendrick, who'd been laid low with chills and coughing attacks violent enough to convince Dakota he was a hack away from breaking a rib. She'd nursed her friend with chicken soup, Vicks VapoRub, and hot toddies, and she'd forbidden him to even attempt to walk Arlo.

Because no good deed goes unpunished, she quickly came down with the same symptoms. But her illness was an extra-nasty one, not restricting itself to her upper respiratory system. It traveled south, laying waste to her stomach. Being too sick even to look at food . . . well, it sucked any possible cheer right out of the holiday season.

From Piper she received the expected reaction. Upon hearing her symptoms, she said, "Good God. Well, don't come near me. I've been invited to several Christmas parties in the city that I don't want to miss, and then I'm flying to Palm Beach for a few days of R&R."

"I'm not going anywhere." Huddled on the sofa beneath a mohair blanket, she blew her nose for the umpteenth time.

"But you'll come over on New Year's Day, right? We'll exchange presents then. That reminds me, I'd better find something for you. You're so self-sufficient it's difficult to think of what to buy you." She paused as if considering. "I suppose I could get you a facial with Monique."

"That'd be nice." Maybe Monique could perform a miracle and she'd leave the spa feeling less like yesterday's garbage.

"Then again, Monique's gotten ridiculously expensive. I went in last week for my regular treatments, and I swear, she's upped her prices again. I'm not sure it's worth it—"

Dakota felt too weak and dizzy to roll her eyes. Piper was the only person she knew who took a present back before she'd even given it. "That's okay. Don't worry about getting me anything. I'm not sure I'll be well enough to come over on New Year's Day in any case."

"You'll feel better by then," Piper said with breezy conviction. "And it's Mimi's birthday on the second. You know how she is about people ignoring her birthday."

"It wouldn't be ignoring her if I'm sick."

"So I won't see you for *any* holiday? Carly's coming with Mimi. The girl may bore me to tears, but at least she cares about her mother. Mimi's already on a tear because Matt insists he has to head back to San Francisco directly after Christmas, so I'd show up if you don't want her to be even angrier with you than she already is. It's a shame Matt won't be there. We could have talked about San Fran. I always have such a good time when I'm there. I think I could be really happy on Nob Hill. But Carly? She's terribly full of herself, which is pathetic. I was much more interesting at her age. But you could talk to her about Lauren's stable and, well, horsey things."

It was like a knife was slowly piercing her temple. Squeezing her eyes shut, she said, "Fine," before Piper could voice another observation. "I'll try to come by on New Year's Day."

"Thanks, doll. I won't be getting back in time to do much, so pick up some nibbles on your way. Love you."

While Piper possessed the maternal instincts of a harp seal—and yes, one evening several years ago over mojitos, Dakota and Lauren had Googled "animals with the worst maternal instincts" to see how Piper compared, and the harp seal was the closest match—Rae put Florence Nightingale to shame. She came over with groceries and a constitution of tempered steel, unfazed when a wave of nausea slammed Dakota, causing her to empty her stomach into the bucket beside the sofa. She'd cleaned out the bucket and brought Dakota a moist towel, a toothbrush, and a glass of water.

After Dakota cleaned herself up, she'd let her head fall back on the throw pillow, exhausted from the effort of holding it up. "Oh God. Thank you," she moaned. "You should flee, Rae. I'm contagious."

"And I'm armed with Purell and Lysol. I brought ginger ale, Gatorade, chamomile tea, chicken broth, applesauce, bananas, and some white bread, because I figure that's all you can manage for the near future."

"No future. I'm going to die."

"Tut-tut or whatever it is Mary Poppins would say. We'll get you better. Listen, I've got to run—Astrid called. She managed to get the kitchen appliances for the cottage delivered today."

"The cottage—it's coming along?"

"It's looking great." And because Rae's heart was enormous, she told Dakota what she really wanted to know. "Max hasn't been out. He must be super busy with work."

"Of course." Dakota told herself she was going to stop thinking about him just as soon as she got over her flu.

There were times—like whenever something to do with Max arose—that Dakota suspected her illness might be something more, a kind of physical manifestation of her melancholy post-breakup. She hadn't heard a word from him since that Sunday morning. She wondered where he was, what he would be doing for Christmas, if he ever thought of her . . . and if he'd resumed dating cover models.

As if to prove her theory, Rae's mention of Max's guest cottage had her stomach clenching again, the sensation disturbingly similar to the time she'd eaten one too many hot dogs at an amusement park and then agreed to ride on the cliffhanger. She swallowed hard.

"You'll ask Astrid to take pictures of the cottage?"

"You bet." Rae must have noticed the color of her face, for she nudged the bucket closer to Dakota.

Closing her eyes, Dakota listened to the sounds of Rae moving about her small house, of cupboards being opened and shut, followed by the clang of metal. Then she caught a whiff of toast and swallowed again.

When Rae's footsteps neared, Dakota opened her eyes to find her holding a glass and plate. She set them on the coffee table. "Now, I want to see some of this toast and ginger ale gone when I return, or there will be consequences."

Dakota made a grab for the bucket.

Christmas passed in a fog of exhaustion and nausea. She was vaguely aware that Hendrick and Lauren came over to play nursemaid since Rae and Marcos had driven to Hempstead to celebrate with Marcos's family.

By New Year's Eve Dakota had beaten back the cold to a few

sniffles and the occasional cough. The nausea, however, persisted and erupted whenever Dakota caught an unexpected whiff of food or attempted to eat anything less bland than applesauce, chicken broth, and saltines. Even bananas were too exotic.

That evening she watched her friends—Rae, Lauren, Lupe, and Astrid had come over—munch on the least noxious of foods and sip their champagne, offering toasts to the day when Dakota would no longer resemble Elphaba from *Wicked*. Although she smiled weakly and sipped her chamomile tea, Dakota had long since lost any sense of humor when it came to her illness.

"Thanks for getting all those appetizers for me, Lupe. They're exactly the sort Piper and Mimi like."

"No problem, Dakota. All your mom has to do is pop the mini quiches and the pigs-in-blankets into the oven. And I got little toasts for the pâté. Perhaps you can nibble on them."

"Look at you," Lauren said, shaking her head in a mix of concern and exasperation. "All Lupe had to say was 'pâté,' and you turned several shades greener. How do you think you'll be able to go over to Piper's tomorrow?"

"I'll manage. Going to Piper's is easier than dealing with the repercussions of a no-show. And if I look sick, that's all to the good. They'll hustle me out of there extra quick."

"Take my advice and shower tonight," Rae said. "Otherwise you'll be too exhausted to make the drive."

How humbling to realize that Rae was quite likely right.

"Okay," she said.

"Poor Dakota," Astrid said. "Here, look at the pictures I took of Max's guest cottage. That'll cheer you up."

Ignoring the sympathetic looks Lauren and Rae gave her, she mustered a smile, took the phone, and swiped through the photos. "The rooms look wonderful. He's going to be really pleased."

"Come by and see it when it's finished," Astrid suggested.

Dakota smiled but knew she wouldn't.

It was likely Lauren and Rae saw her increasing quietness for what it was, but they were the best, so instead they began talking about how tired they'd made her by keeping her up until nine o'clock on New Year's Eve. They understood she'd rather be teased for her feebleness than pitied for her aching heart.

After setting the living room and kitchen to rights, they left, blowing kisses and wishing her a New Year free of the plastic bucket she'd spent so much time bent over. She waved and managed a laugh, saying that was one wish she fervently hoped came true.

A model patient, she followed Rae's advice and showered, falling asleep the second her damp head hit the pillow.

The ringing of her phone woke her. Blindly she groped for it, and as her fingers clutched the rectangular frame, her thumb reflexively pressed the green circle.

"Hello?" she groaned.

"'Kota?"

Blinking, she pushed herself up on her elbow. "Max?"

"Yeah." There was a pause. Then, "How are you?"

"I'm—I'm okay." She listened more closely and heard the background noise, a mix of voices, techno music . . . laughter. "Where are you?"

"Some party. SoHo, maybe."

He didn't know where he was? "Max—"

"Wanted to wish you a happy New Year, 'Kota." With that many words, the slide of the vowels and the slur of consonants were unmistakable. Oh God, he was drunk-dialing her.

She squeezed her eyes shut. "Happy New Year." She drew a breath. "Make sure you take a taxi home."

"Nah, I got the town car. Only way to travel. Die otherwise—"

Another voice intruded, this one high-pitched and demanding. "Max, *come on.* Let's dance."

"Yeah, okay. Just a sec. Bye, 'Kota."

She clicked off the phone and stared sightlessly up at the ceiling.

Piper answered the door dressed in tight suede pants the color of buttery caramel, a cream-colored V-neck sweater, and high-heeled ankle boots. Gold hoop earrings and a necklace of beaded glass completed a look that was designed to make Mimi feel very much the older sister.

It even made Dakota feel old.

The foyer light was on. When Dakota stepped inside with her two bags, one filled with presents and the other with the hors d'oeuvres Lupe had bought, the first words out of her mother's mouth were, "God, Dakota, you look terrible."

"Yes. You may remember I've been sick. Would you take this, please? It's heavy." She held out the bag with the appetizers. Neither bag was especially heavy. But sweat nevertheless beaded her brow and snaked down her back.

With a shrug of cashmere, Piper took the bag. Setting the other bag down next to the living room sofa, Dakota followed her into the kitchen. Piper had simply placed the bag on the counter.

"The heating instructions are on the packages," she said.

Piper looked at her. "You don't want to do it?"

"No, I really don't. You don't either unless you want to see me vomit."

Piper's brows rose. "There's no need to be theatrical," she said in a miffed tone. "If you're so sick, you shouldn't have come. You know I hate cooking." She dug out the foil containers and slammed them on the counter to underscore her words.

"You were the one who insisted I should be here."

"I'd have thought better of it if I'd known you were going to be pissy." She pulled off the plastic covers and shoved the appetizers in the oven.

"The oven should be preheated."

"Who cares? Mimi will only want to drink, and I'm fasting. I've gained a couple of pounds. You should count yourself lucky. You didn't pack on your usual holiday weight."

"Thanks, Mom."

Piper shot her a narrow-eyed look. Dakota rarely defied the decades-old prohibition against calling her Mom. But right now she really felt like reminding Piper that for all her facials, scheduled treatments, and exercise classes, she was the mother of a twenty-eight-year-old woman, which made her pretense of being thirty-two biologically impossible.

"You know, Dakota—" The chime of the doorbell cut off whatever Piper intended to say. "Good, they're here, which means I can start counting the minutes until you all leave. I have a massive headache coming on."

Dakota hung back as Piper went to greet her sister and niece and perform the standard ritual of cheek presses. No way was she going to be party to that. Waiting until the three of them entered the living room, she smiled grimly as her aunt and cousin caught sight of her, their eyes widening, Carly's with shock, Mimi's with malicious pleasure.

"You must have really tied one on last night. You look like something the cat dragged in," Mimi said.

"No, I've had the flu. Happy birthday." She took a wrapped package out of the bag and gave it to her aunt. It was a beaded clutch she'd found in Sag Harbor a few months back. It was nicer than Mimi deserved, but Dakota couldn't bring herself to buy ugly and cheap presents. "Carly, I got you something, too."

She handed her a small box containing a purse-sized perfume

atomizer, because Carly's favorite activity outside of riding her horse was clubbing with her crowd at places like AM in Southampton. This was the real reason Piper didn't like Carly—she hated running into her niece when on the prowl for a new boy toy.

Carly took the gift with an awkward smile. "Thank you. I'm sorry I didn't—"

"No worry." Just then a wave of nausea hit her. She sat down abruptly on the sofa.

"What's the matter?" Carly asked.

"I think the appetizers are ready," she said faintly.

Out of deference to her—or more likely because she wasn't interested in eating—Piper kept the assorted hors d'oeuvres in the kitchen. When Carly and Mimi sat down with their plates, Dakota did her best to breathe shallowly.

"I suppose you'll be going into the city for Genevieve Monaghan's exhibit," Mimi said. Not even Mimi could ignore her completely after receiving a birthday present.

The opening was from six to eight on the coming Friday. Dakota had it marked on the wall calendar that hung in her kitchen. She'd been looking forward to attending. But now . . . well, she still felt so awful and so ridiculously weak, and Max, if he was in town, would undoubtedly be there. Pride dictated that when she saw him next, she look her best, not hollowed out and smudge-eyed. "I'll have to settle for seeing the show later on. I don't think my stomach can handle a trip into the city just yet."

"I hope I don't catch whatever you have," Carly said. "I'm competing in Florida next weekend and then heading to Cabo with friends. I can't afford to get sick."

As if Dakota could. But it would take too much effort to point out that Carly didn't have to worry about pesky things like being paid or meeting payroll. Despite having graduated last May, Carly had yet to enter the workforce. There were no signs she intended to, either.

"Don't worry, Carly. I may look like death warmed over, but the nurse I called at the clinic told me I wouldn't be contagious after ten days."

Piper took a sip of her martini. Vodka apparently worked on her fast. "You'd have done better calling your ob/gyn."

"What?" Dakota said.

"Yes, Piper, what do you mean?" Mimi asked.

"Come on, don't you remember how I was when I got knocked up? Exactly like that." Piper gave an insouciant flick of her wrist in Dakota's direction.

"I have the flu," Dakota ground out as Mimi's gaze shifted, studying her closely, like a bird eyeing an especially tasty worm.

"Oh my God, you're right." Her pink-lipsticked smile spread. "You couldn't keep anything down for *weeks,* Piper. Once they figured out what was up, and couldn't convince you to get rid of it, Mother and Father were hoping you'd miscarry."

Dakota was quite glad when her vomit landed on her aunt's leather boots.

CHAPTER TWENTY

Three First Response sticks lay on the white porcelain rim of Dakota's bathroom sink. They were arranged in a neat, regimental row to compensate for the chaos they'd announced three mornings running, making her pregnant, very pregnant, and ultra pregnant.

How had it happened? Okay, she knew *how* it had happened, but Max had used a condom every time. She wondered if one could have torn. Or how about the morning she'd awoken to find the spent condom near her crotch? When it slipped off Max, could those intrepid sperm have escaped and swum their way to her egg?

The thought was enough to make her pivot, bow over the toilet bowl, and retch yet again.

Straightening, she turned on the faucet and rinsed her mouth, then clutched the sides of the sink and tried to breathe. Tried to think. Not easy when her thoughts were as disorganized as her emotions and when nausea still held her in its tight grip.

She wasn't on the pill. She'd tried it but hated how it affected her body—the bloating and the headaches—even if it did make her periods more regular. She'd had another reason to go off it as well: not being on the pill actually made sexual relations *less* complicated for her. While she'd been on the pill there had always seemed to come a point where the guy she was dating would start in about how good it would feel to go "bare." She'd even heard the line about how a rubber made a dick go numb.

Her solution had been simple. If she wasn't taking anything, then there'd be no pressure to go without a condom and no need to explain the obvious. Condoms might be annoying; dealing with an STD was a lot more so.

But Max had never raised that awkward and, for her, lust-killing topic. He'd matter-of-factly wrapped himself up every time he entered her. It would be a question of control for him. And of trust. They were remarkably alike in this, his need for control as great as hers, his ability to trust just as shaky.

She looked down at the three sticks so efficiently blasting her theories and illusions to bits.

A baby. She'd wanted a baby, yes, eventually. But even more, she'd longed for family in the most boring and traditional sense of the word, not because she was morally conservative but because she herself had missed having a father's love, a father's presence, a father's name.

And what of her other dreams and plans? How did a baby fit in with running Premier Service? And what of her long-term goal to go into investing?

How much would she have to sacrifice?

She wasn't going to panic. It was possible the home pregnancy test was faulty. Maybe the flu had done something weird to her body. Okay, that was grasping at straws, but there could be something terribly off, either with her body or with the test's chemistry, to cause a false positive.

Her mother didn't have to be right.

The way to know for certain was to schedule a visit to her gynecologist and have a proper test and exam. If the results were the same, if indeed she was pregnant, then she'd tell Max, though how she'd break the news was anybody's guess. He deserved to know—just as her baby deserved to have a father.

She would not be her mother.

She'd been so careful, had spent so much of her life, starting as a kid, determined *not* to be like Piper, yet here she was, through a manufacturing defect or human error—otherwise known as "improper usage"—possibly in the very same situation her mother had faced twenty-nine years ago.

Had her mother been as scared, as completely freaked out?

Dakota hit the light switch, left the bathroom and the worrisome plastic wands predicting a very different future from the one she'd imagined for herself, and went into her bedroom. Standing in front of a full-length mirror she'd found at an antiques store in Wainscott, she slowly peeled her long-sleeved tee up and over her head, then untied the drawstring on her flannel pajama bottoms.

She stared at her naked reflection, shifting to view her body at a different angle. In a new light. It was hard to reconcile what she saw with what those three sticks pronounced. She didn't look pregnant; she looked hollowed out, half starved from nearly two weeks of an unwilling fast.

She cupped her breasts, testing. They hurt. But so did her entire body. Her hands traveled down to her abdomen. She spread her fingers, her pinkies brushing her hipbones. If anything, the space seemed like an empty cradle rather than one nurturing a life.

But if there was a baby, had her being so sick harmed it? Was it all right?

Grabbing her chenille robe from where it lay at the foot of her bed, she wrapped it tightly about her and then walked over to her bedside table. Picking up her phone, she scrolled through her contact list and pressed the dial button.

"Dr. Davis's office," the receptionist answered.

"Yes, this is Dakota Hale. I'd like to make an appointment for a pregnancy test and an examination.... Yes, I can come on Monday morning."

All day at the office—during the investment committee meeting where Max had presented his proposal to invest in a start-up tech company that specialized in cloud data; during the follow-up calls he'd made to the limited partners; during a business lunch with Chris Steffen, who suddenly and deludedly believed he could renegotiate the terms of his compensation as Chiron's CEO; even while he stared out his office windows at the wintry mix of rain and ice pelting and then running down the length of the glass in long, slushy streaks—an internal debate waged in Max's mind. Should he skip the opening reception for Genevieve Monaghan's exhibition or suck it up and get the inevitable encounter with Dakota over and done?

He couldn't believe he'd called her from a club on New Year's Eve. His excuse? He'd been drunk off his ass and no longer able to curb his yearning to hear her voice. Since the morning she'd ended things, she'd consumed his thoughts. He was unaccustomed to a woman mattering or her absence bothering him so much. Before, he'd always been able to fill the void by finding another woman or sealing a new deal.

But with Dakota it was different. He kept imagining how it might be if he could turn back time. Could he somehow change things and get her back? That question, that foolish fantasy, fueled that night by brain-cell-destroying quantities of cocktails and glasses of champagne, had had him pulling out his cell while he sat at a table with Andy Reynolds, Lewis Brant, Glenn Howard, their dates, and some redhead he'd picked up two bars ago. A woman who had a grating, nasal voice ... nothing like Dakota's.

He remembered how Dakota would cry, "Yes! Yes!" and "Oh God, Max, that feels so good!" in her throaty rasp while she clung to him, how it would make his balls squeeze tight and his hips drive faster with the need to come inside her.

When she'd answered the phone with a husky "Hello?" his mouth had gone dry. Even in his shit-faced state, he'd registered her disoriented tone and knew he'd woken her. But he hadn't cared because he wanted to hear her voice and talk to her again so badly. Only, as drunk as he'd been, he'd had no idea what to say once he actually had her on the line. Could only mumble some incoherent crap while a deep longing rose inside him.

He should be grateful the woman—the redhead—had interrupted him before he blurted out to Dakota how often he thought about her. Even so, the abbreviated conversation in which he'd said God knows what had gone on long enough for Max to feel like an idiot now. A pathetic idiot who kept wondering what would have happened if he'd been able to keep his shit together about the damned Christmas tree.

An idiot who kept thinking how much he'd like to be with her ... which made him as big a fool as Chris Steffen.

Obviously he wasn't going to get back together with Dakota. Once he was back in the groove, he'd find a few women to meet his needs, and life would return to normal. Part and parcel of returning to normal was getting this first post-split encounter with Dakota over and done.

Besides, he had to go to the gallery reception. He valued Alex

Miller's friendship too much to be a no-show at a major event in Gen's career. His internal debate at an end, he pressed the intercom and asked his assistant, Fred, to arrange for a town car to drive him.

So here he was scouring the gallery, the space composed of several large rooms, searching for a glimpse of a tall, dark-haired beauty, straining to catch a note of her throaty voice or the low timbre of her laugh.

Where was she?

Everyone else in New York seemed to be here. While the gallery walls were filled with fields of color and luminous detail, the space in between was dominated by black, the New York art scene's color of choice when it came to clothing. It only took a quick glance at the Japanese and French designs they were wearing, along with the horn-rims and wire-framed glasses and bold, clunky jewelry, and hearing the names Monet and Diebenkorn and Homer being used to describe the land and seascapes surrounding them, to know that he was passing curators for MOMA, the Met, and the Whitney as well as the directors of every modern art gallery worth its salt, and probably every art critic attached to every major news source.

Max paused in front of one of the largest seascapes. It showed a sky of a bright, brilliant blue, clouds white and full, and strong, high waves that raced toward a diagonal stretch of beach. From the bright colors one might think the painting depicted a summer scene. Gen Monaghan's talent lay in revealing the fierceness of the wind that propelled the waves, whipping them until they crashed onto the land. Not even the brilliance of the sun's rays could defeat the bite of the wind or the chill of the angry sea. The painting spoke of the fierce beauty of the Atlantic, a force that could not be tamed. Using only oil and canvas, Gen had captured what it was like to stand on that empty stretch of sand, to feel the stinging spray coming off those rough waves, to hear the heavy roar of ocean pounding the land and be humbled by its awesome power.

He glanced at the price sheet he'd picked up when he entered the gallery. The painting was expensive. No surprise there. Anyone could see that Gen Monaghan was a major talent, and this was a New York City gallery. Because he had a hunch Gen's work would only appreciate in value, the painting would be a good investment. That wasn't why he was buying it, however. He wanted Gen's painting for the stark beauty of the composition, the brilliance of its execution, and the fact that when he looked at it, he couldn't help but think of Dakota and her fearlessness when she rode waves as wild as those depicted.

He looked around the crowded room again, willing her to appear. He wanted to share his impression of the painting and watch her face when she studied it, knowing she'd grasp its visual poetry. And he wanted to see her expression when he told her he planned to buy it, and be the beneficiary of her wide smile of approval. He wanted her to be there when he made the purchase. It was only fair, since she'd chosen every other object and decoration at Windhaven.

She wasn't anywhere in the gallery, damn it.

But he saw Gen. Helpfully, she wasn't wearing black; rather, she had on an emerald-green dress that emphasized her slender frame. She and Alex were talking to a group not far from where a bartender was busy filling glasses. He wove his way to them.

"Hello, Gen. Congratulations on an amazing show," he said, leaning in to kiss her cheek.

"Oh, Max! I'm so glad you made it!" Gen said.

"Yes, Max. Thank you for coming," Alex said extending his hand to clasp Max's shoulder.

Despite all the hotshot art people crowding the rooms, Alex and Gen seemed genuinely grateful for his presence. He'd done right to come. "How could I have stayed away? The paintings are incredible. I'm particularly taken with *Series Number Five.*"

Gen's smile lit her face. "That's one of my favorites—I'm so glad you like it."

"As am I," a woman with a sleek gray cap of hair and round, oversized glasses said. "I'm Alicia Kendall. I've been showing Genevieve's work for—how long?"

"Pretty much forever," Gen said.

"And now we're in a space that can really do justice to your larger works, like *Series Number Five.*"

"I'd like to buy it," Max said.

Gen gave a surprised laugh. "Why, Max, that's wonderful of you."

He shrugged. "I don't know about that. I just know that I want it."

Alicia Kendall's eyes twinkled behind her glasses. "Then you shall have it."

He nodded. "Good. You'll need a check or a wire transfer from me?"

"First let me go put a red sticker next to the painting. The Getty's contemporary art curator was making noises about *Number Five.* I'd like to teach him the cost of dithering. I'll come back and we can complete the transaction and fill out the necessary forms in the office."

"That's fine." Max didn't mind going to the office; it had a glass wall. Anyone who passed by would be visible.

"Thanks again, Max," Gen said when Alicia left. "I'm happy to know you'll have the painting."

"I'm glad, too. I really did know I wanted it the second I saw it."

"Gen's paintings have that effect. They speak to you," Alex said, wrapping his arm about Gen's waist.

"You've certainly made an impression on the people here tonight." Max took the opportunity to scan the room once again. Still no sign of her. "They love the show."

"That's because I pressured all our friends to come. They're drowning out the critics' voices."

"I passed a number of critics. They're far from critical. But speaking of friends, I'm surprised I haven't seen Dakota yet. Is she coming?" There. He'd inserted her name into the conversation, perhaps not as subtly as he'd have liked, but what the hell. And he was going to ignore the matching smiles on Alex and Gen's faces that told him he hadn't been subtle at all.

"I hope so. What with the holidays and then all the last-minute details surrounding the show, I've been shamefully out of touch," Gen said. "I don't even think I thanked her properly for the brilliant job Premier did at our party."

"You may get to do it in person. The reception's not over," Alex said. "She may simply be stuck in traffic. The weather's lousy."

And Dakota was a good driver, Max told himself. Her Toyota was a good car, heavy and equipped with four-wheel drive. She had brand-new tires. She'd be fine.

"Have you called her, Max?" Gen asked. "You might try."

"Sure," he said, knowing he wouldn't. Maybe he could call Rae and find out where the hell she was, and then swear Rae to secrecy . . .

Alicia returned, looking very happy. "*Series Number Five* now has a beautiful red dot next to it. If you'll come with me, Max?"

He smiled at Gen and Alex. "I'll see you."

"Come back here when you're finished. There's some champagne with your name on it. We hold it in reserve for Gen's patrons," Alex said with a grin.

"I will." And maybe Dakota would be by their side, and he could breathe easier knowing that she was all right.

*

It didn't take long to write out the check and fill out his Long Island address on the bill of sale so that Alicia could have the painting crated and delivered to Windhaven when the show came down in late February. But while Max dealt with the paperwork, there'd been a few minutes when he'd been unable to monitor what new guests had entered the gallery. Again he prowled the rooms, frustrated and on edge. But then, as he passed a middle-aged woman, he heard Dakota's name uttered. He froze and turned toward the source.

The woman's face had once been pretty. Now puffy, yet oddly stretched, it was a warning to those considering plastic surgery. The woman's hair was cut short, styled and shellacked into a blond helmet. Her voice was East Coast through and through, its tones clipped and its pitch loud enough to cut through the buzz of other conversations.

For a second he wondered if he'd just experienced an auditory hallucination. Then the woman repeated, "Yes, *that* Dakota. My niece. Have I told you the news? She must have grown tired of cleaning houses and running errands for her so-called clients and discovered an easier way to make money."

Another woman who was with her, a slight, overly tanned brunette who was trying and failing for the Jackie O look, must have obliged with the necessary question.

"Why, on her back, of course," the blond woman answered. "Dakota's pregnant. No doubt she'll be demanding a pretty penny from the father—and there's no doubt about who he is." Like twin lasers, her blue eyes locked on Max, making him realize that she was aware of his presence—and his identity. She smiled triumphantly. Maliciously. "Oh yes, we know very well who the father is."

Dakota pregnant? What the fuck? Max thought as she finally broke eye contact and said something to her friend about needing a drink before she looked at the paintings.

He was conscious of a dramatic shift, as if the ground were tilting crazily beneath him. The last time he'd experienced such a radical disorientation was when he'd arrived home from the graduation party in Annie Bauer's car. From a block away the flashing lights were visible. Closer, he'd seen the patrol car parked in front of his house, the white vinyl siding now a blue and red screen. As soon as Annie braked, he'd jumped out and run past the cruiser parked in front of his mailbox and up the concrete walkway, the sound of his mother's sobbing reaching him through an open window. Before he burst through the front door he'd known from the ice formed deep in his gut that Rosie was hurt.

Only it was worse than that. Way, way worse. The inconceivable had occurred.

Dakota pregnant? He couldn't get his mind around the idea. The ramifications. Shit, the ramifications . . .

The woman's words replayed in his head. She—Christ, this must be Dakota's aunt Mimi—had said Dakota planned to use the pregnancy to enrich herself.

Would Dakota do that? It was unbelievable. But then he recalled Ashley Nicholls's scheme to blackmail him for a million dollars with a sex tape. Dakota was much smarter than Ashley. Could this have been her end game all along?

He had to see her and find out what was going on.

He had to do it now.

CHAPTER TWENTY-ONE

Dakota was watching a rerun of *Friends,* her televisual equivalent to a pint of Ben & Jerry's Chocolate Chip Cookie Dough, and already fighting drowsiness despite its being only ten o'clock, when a knock sounded at her door.

It woke her up in a hurry. Her real-life friends (as opposed to Phoebe, Rachel, and Monica) didn't come a-knocking this late on a Friday night in January, especially when the weather was so crappy. On the other hand, she'd never heard of a burglar knocking, either. And her house was too modest to burglarize, anyway.

A rapist? She wrapped her hand around the baseball bat she kept in the corner of the small entry next to where her Uggs and rain boots stood. Gripping its handle, she peered through the front door's peephole.

Even bowed against the sleet, the dark head with its auburn lights was one she recognized. Astonishment had her straightening, twisting the doorknob, and stepping back. "Max? What are you doing here?"

He swept inside, bringing with him the cold and the wet and a barely leashed agitation. Abruptly aware of her thin cotton T-shirt, flannel bottoms, and bare feet, she shivered and shut the door, returning the baseball bat to its place. Braining Max wouldn't be a very good move.

He's too big for my house was her first totally loopy thought. It wasn't just Max's size; it was the energy he brought with him. It radiated out, buffeting her. Dizziness swept over her, which this time couldn't be blamed on a virus or even the tiny peanut that was perhaps growing inside her.

She wasn't ready for this. She was unprepared to see or talk to Max when she was still unsure of the facts. Those three plastic sticks that she had peed on weren't proof positive; they were more like proof probable. And how totally unfair it was that she was going to have to broach the topic of his possible impending fatherhood when she was looking and feeling like something the cat dragged in, and he was looking so like . . . Max.

He'd cut his hair, she noted, and somehow this fact depressed her as much as all the rest.

Max raked her with a narrow-eyed gaze, as if taking stock of the vast difference in their appearances—not that a worn tee, baggy flannel bottoms, and unvarnished toes ever combined to make a killer fashion choice. "What's the matter with you? You look awful."

"And happy New Year to you, too," she said, wrapping her arms around her middle protectively, defensively, abruptly out of all charity for him. Who the hell did he think he was to storm in here, looking so fantastic in his cashmere overcoat, silk scarf, and stark white shirt? Even his cropped hair looked good, damn him. "At the risk of repeating myself, what are you doing here?" She tried to think of a plausible explanation. "Are you locked out?"

"Locked out?"

She gritted her teeth, wishing he would stop staring at her. "Of your house."

Perhaps it was the word "house" that did it, or he'd finally grown bored of looking at her. His gaze made a sweeping inspection of her living quarters, taking in the sofa with its decorative pillows piled at one end; the eggplant-colored throw she'd been curled under; the box of Kleenex positioned on the coffee table within easy reach, the used tissues forming a balled-up mound next to it. And in the corner opposite the sofa, the TV played a scene with Joey and Chandler. The audience's laughter was jarring.

It was all pretty dreary, which was an adjective she'd never associated with her adorable little house. At least she no longer had the vomit bucket ready and waiting by the couch. By this point she knew the signs well enough to sprint to the bathroom.

He turned his head, taking in the kitchen island and the space beyond. Weeks had passed since anything more complex than reheating chicken broth had occurred, so her kitchen, always tidy, was immaculate, if a little forlorn.

Convinced that his next step would be into her bedroom, where he'd give it the same critical going-over to which she and the living space had been subjected, she said, "Please tell me what you're doing here. I'm tired—"

"Is it true?" he demanded.

She started at his accusatory tone. "Is what true? What are you talking about?"

"I drove out here from New York tonight as soon as I found out, so don't play games with me, Dakota. Just tell me yes or no. Are you pregnant?"

This was so not the way she'd wanted to break the news, with him bristling with antagonism. She'd imagined herself calm and composed, her spine made of steel. Instead she felt like she was about to shatter into a thousand pieces. And Max looked livid.

Carefully she made her way to the sofa, giving Max a wide berth. She sat down, her arms again folding about her middle. How quickly a new habit was formed. "Yes—that is, I'm not sure. It's possible I am."

"Jesus." He dragged a hand through his hair. He began pacing, and there wasn't enough room.

She once again grew dizzy. But no way was she going to be sick in front of him. She fixed her gaze on the box of Kleenex, determined to keep her stomach under control.

"How did you hear about my—" She couldn't bring herself to say "pregnancy."

"At the opening for Gen Monaghan's show. Some woman was talking about you. Loudly. I couldn't help but overhear. She said you were her niece and that you're pregnant."

"Damn you, Mimi," Dakota whispered. Of course her aunt would run to spread the news as fast and as far and wide as possible. There was little if any stigma attached to unplanned pregnancies these days, so it wasn't a question of blackening the Hale name. It would only embarrass Dakota and deprive her of the ability to announce the news on her own terms. Mimi was smart. She'd have guessed there was an excellent chance Max would be at the opening and had known that Dakota wouldn't be. What a perfect way to exact revenge. Dakota abruptly wondered how many people on the East End had already heard that she was pregnant and that Max was the father.

She closed her eyes. "I'm sorry you had to hear the news this way."

"And when were you planning to approach me? After you'd calculated how much money you could get from me?"

Her eyes snapped open. Surely she couldn't have heard him correctly. "Excuse me?"

"You heard me. How much, Dakota?"

"Exactly what are you implying?" she demanded, outrage filling her.

"No need to imply. I'm merely repeating what your aunt was willing to tell anyone within hearing distance. The gist of it was that you'd grown tired of cleaning people's houses and running errands and hit upon an easier way to make money. If getting pregnant and shaking me down is your plan, Dakota, you picked the wrong man. Is the kid even mine?"

She stared at him, trying to recognize the man who'd made her heart turn over with his intelligence and charm. "Is that what you think of me? That I'm the kind of person who would use a child to get money out of you? Or that I'd lie about the identity of the father?" Her voice had risen with every word, reaching a piercing anger.

Something flickered in his expression. "I don't know what the fuck to think."

"If that's an apology, it sucks."

"Christ, Dakota—"

"For your information, the only reason I didn't contact you was because I wanted to make sure of the facts before I spoke to you. I was waiting to see my doctor on Monday and have her confirm the pregnancy. Oh, and here's something else you should know: I regret ever laying eyes on you. Now get out of my house."

Thanks to Max's unexpected visit, she passed a sleepless night. She was almost glad when her stomach announced itself. Retching was better than staring at the ceiling, replaying Max's words, and wishing she'd been sharp enough to come up with a hundred better, more cutting replies.

Finished with the toilet, she brushed her teeth, and then took a good look in the mirror. The confrontation with Max had had a weird effect on her body; she actually felt pregnant today. But so much for the old wives' tale claiming that pregnancy made a woman glow. She looked like she'd been living in a crypt.

She had to get out of here. After Max's invasion, her house no longer seemed cozy and intimate. The space felt suffocating, as if the walls were closing in. It had been too long since she'd gazed out at the ocean, been soothed by its vastness.

So what if the chop of the waves made her heave? She heaved at blank walls, too. And the roar of the surf pummeling the cliffs would be loud enough to drown out Max's words.

Did he really see her as some scheming parasite, waiting for a chance to use him, to *take* from him? She'd figured out that his sister's death had left him damaged. She got that a man of his wealth would be on guard against women trying to bag him, the ultimate in the multimillionaire trophy hunt. But to hear him hurl his accusations and repeat Mimi's vile words without giving them a second thought stunned her. She had believed he understood her.

She showered and dressed in warm layers. Although yesterday's freezing rain had stopped, the wind would be brutal on the Point. Before heading out to Montauk, however, she stopped at Hendrick's.

He answered the door in his navy blue sweats and his worn L.L.Bean moccasins. He didn't question the early hour, merely said, "Dakota, Arlo and I have missed you."

From the furrows between his blond brows and the concern shining from his pale blue eyes, it was clear that the gossip had reached him. "Hi, Hendrick." She blinked furiously. "So that bug that knocked you sideways? It turns out that what I have might be a little different in nature."

He stepped forward and wrapped her in a hug, giving her time to pull herself together or lose it completely. When she sniffed and hugged him back, he understood and released her. "I just made coffee. Would you like a cup?"

"Maybe some tea? That chamomile?"

"Coming right up."

They sat at the kitchen table with Arlo lying by Dakota's feet, his black tail sweeping the floor.

"So you've heard," she said.

"Your aunt actually sought me out."

She shook her head. "She's been busy."

"I do wonder at your aunt's destructive tendencies. I've come to the conclusion that she must have hated competing with Piper, and it all came to a head when Piper got pregnant. It's the only semi-logical explanation for why you're her favorite target when she needs to spew her anger and resentment."

"If that's the case, she's presently in seventh heaven. As I said, she's been busy. She went to Gen Monaghan's opening in New York last night and orchestrated it so that Max overheard her. She must have turned in a stellar performance. Even with the snow and ice, he drove out to my place."

"Ah. And how did that go?"

"Not well. I wasn't ready—I haven't seen my doctor yet, so it's possible I'm not actually pregnant, though the home tests beg to differ." She drew a breath. There, she'd said the *P*-word aloud. "He was pretty angry. He thinks I intend to use the baby to leverage money out of him. I don't know whether that's what he truly believes or whether he was just infected by Mimi."

"Having just experienced a dose of Mimi myself, I'd give him the benefit of the doubt."

"Even so, it hurt, Hendrick. A lot."

He laid his hand over hers and squeezed it gently. "I have no doubt it did. But people often say things in the heat of the moment they don't mean."

"I told him I didn't want to see him again."

"I assume you're reconsidering."

She sighed. "How could I not? While I'd like nothing better than to stick to my guns, you know as well as I that I could never deprive my child of a father. It's like a sick cosmic joke. And honestly, Hendrick, I'm having a hard time dealing with it." She took a sip of the tea, letting the warmth seep through her.

"I can't help thinking about my mother," she continued, her finger tracing the mug's rim as she spoke. "All my life I've tried not to be her and instead be responsible, careful, and conscientious. A grown-up. I felt so superior to her because I had a plan—and not just my five- and ten-year business strategy. I had a life plan. In the next couple of years I'd find a good, solid man, steady and true, to build a life and family with. And what happened? I let myself have a fling with a Wall Street hotshot, a player, a guy I knew from the first is anti-commitment, and I get knocked up because something went wrong with the damned condom.

"I'm basically in the same position as my reckless, irresponsible mom. Actually, mine is worse. At least Piper had a trust fund gigantic enough to put any accusations of wanting to pad her bank account to rest." Wearily she hung her head. "I never saw this coming, Hendrick."

He waited to speak until she'd straightened. "That's life, Dakota. Not everything can be planned. Accidents happen. Unexpected events occur. Men and women have sex. And sometimes, even with precautions, pregnancies result. I've heard of women on the pill and men who are faithful condom wearers conceiving a child. The question is how you deal with the curveballs that life throws at you."

"I'm afraid I'm striking out so far."

"I disagree. You may be questioning your actions now, Dakota, but clearly there was an attraction that brought you to this point. I've heard the way you speak about Max. There are many things you admire about him. So the sex wasn't indiscriminate or reckless. Now you've found yourself pregnant. But there was never a doubt in your mind that you'd tell Max about the child, right?"

Dakota shook her head. "No."

"Moreover, I know that you'll give him the opportunity to be a positive presence in your child's life. What this shows is that you are very far from messing up. Now it's up to Max to get over his shock and make the necessary adjustments."

"It was just sex, Hendrick. At least on Max's part it was," she added, remembering how she'd started down the road to imagining a real relationship with him before blowing it all to smithereens with the Christmas tree. "And Max has issues. He lost his sister, Rosie, when he was eighteen. They were twins. I don't think he's gotten over it."

He was silent as he absorbed the information. "That's a hard thing to overcome. Most studies focus on the bond between identical twins, but losing a fraternal twin can be harrowing, too, the grief a long and troubled road. I don't know Max, so anything I say can only be broad conjecture, but as the surviving twin, he may feel he doesn't deserve the joy that accompanies a new life. But whatever difficulties Max may have adjusting, you can help him with them, Dakota."

"I don't know how."

"Come now, you're strong and you're smart. You'll figure it out. But remember that even if you can't change Max's feelings about you and the baby, this child is going to have a very different upbringing from the one you had. One filled with love and support. This baby will have the best of mothers. And hopefully a wonderful and involved father."

Shifting in her chair, she threw her arms about him. "Thank you, Hendrick. Thank you for being my friend."

"Thank you for being mine, my dear. It's brought me great happiness."

CHAPTER TWENTY-TWO

He'd fucked up. The thought screamed at Max as loudly as the wind howling outside his windows. Walking into Dakota's house last night, seeing her, had been like a one-two punch to the solar plexus; he was still trying to draw an even breath. Still struggling to recognize his world since the moment that woman—Dakota's aunt—dropped her bomb.

As he tore along the Long Island Expressway, the weather having grounded all planes, the aunt's voice, obnoxiously loud and superior, had assaulted his mind, relentless as the wet snow and icy rain pelting his windshield and obscuring his vision. Dakota was pregnant. Pregnant with his child. And she was looking to cash in.

Guided by the GPS, because there was no way he could have found her Marion Lane address otherwise, he'd pulled up to a house that was basically the size of his garage and barged inside the second she opened the door.

A part of his brain had registered the blue-and-cream patterned long board suspended over the mantel, the enlarged photos of the local beaches, the colorful pillows, and the plants decorating the Lilliputian space, while the other part was busy adjusting to a Dakota who didn't look like herself. The first day they'd met at Windhaven, he remembered thinking of her as an Amazon. But gone was her former confidence. In its place was a defensiveness that he'd rashly assumed was guilt; she wouldn't even meet his eye. More disturbing was her frailty. She'd been waiflike, far too thin beneath her shirt and flannel bottoms, and her face had been drawn, exhaustion a gray wash over her features.

The changes scared him.

They scared him as much as the possibility that he could have misjudged her character all along and that she might try to trap him with a baby. Fear became panic, and panic made him stupid. Needing answers, he'd fired questions at her as if she were the stranger she resembled.

He'd been jolted out of his blindness when she recoiled, wounded by his accusations. And then once again she became the Dakota he knew, standing up for herself as she leveled him with a disgust too profound to be feigned. Even before she finished denouncing him by saying that she regretted ever laying eyes on him, he'd recognized how badly he'd screwed up.

And now he had to fix it somehow.

He drove to her house first, frustration giving way to worry when his repeated knocks on her door went unanswered. He kept picturing her drawn features, her shadowed eyes. She was clearly unwell and she might be carrying his baby, and he? He'd seen that and yet been an ass. A total ass. Again.

Climbing back into his car, he drove east. In the parking area for the Montauk Point lighthouse, he spotted her Land Cruiser, and blew out a deep breath. Pulling up next to it, he turned off the ignition and sat for a moment, aware of the racing of his heart, his jitters worse than before any game he'd played or deal he'd negotiated.

She was the only person braving the wind and cold. An ache filled him that he was responsible for sending her here.

"It's freezing out here," he said by way of greeting when he reached her side. He shoved his hands into his jacket pockets, because before he'd have reached out and hauled her close to share his body warmth. He didn't have the right anymore.

At the sound of his voice, she jerked and then stiffened. Her gaze slid sideways, glancing at him briefly, then returned to study the waves slamming into the rocks below. "Feel free to leave."

He ignored her suggestion, letting the punishing wind whistle in his ears and scrape at his skin. At least she'd dressed for the weather in a blue parka, a beige knit cap, and a matching scarf.

"How'd you find me?" she asked after a minute.

He let out a breath he hadn't realized he'd been holding. "You told me you come here sometimes." From the corner of his eye he saw her lips purse—whether in pleasure or in annoyance or simply because it was cold as hell, he had no clue. "How long have you been out here?"

"A while. Why?"

"Your nose is red." And it was dripping, making her look like a lost and lonely kid, and making his insides twist with remorse. "Your cheeks are, too." And why the hell was he talking about her wind-chapped face? The thought had him saying abruptly, "There was a woman I was with a few months back, shortly before I met you. She didn't like it when I broke it off. In retaliation she tried to blackmail me."

He felt the weight of her searching gaze, but pride and embarrassment kept his own fixed on the waves crashing, retreating, and crashing again.

"Even if I held a grudge against you for the way things ended between us, I wouldn't do that. Ever."

He swallowed and turned his head. Her eyes were bright with unshed tears. "Yeah, I know that now. But last night—" He lifted his shoulders and let them fall in a heavy shrug. "Anyway, I'm sorry for what I said. Really sorry."

She looked out at the sea again, and the silence stretched as long as the horizon.

"Okay."

"Okay?" he repeated, not sure if he'd heard her correctly or even what she meant.

"Okay, I forgive you."

He pressed his lips together, rocked by emotion. So this was what forgiveness felt like.

When he spoke, his voice was strangely hoarse. "Listen, can we go somewhere to talk? We need to figure things out."

Dakota drove to John's Pancake House with Max's shiny black Range Rover in her rearview mirror. With the cold weather, the diner was less crowded than usual. She led Max to a booth in the corner, the most private spot.

"Hey, Dakota, long time no see," said Dan, a waiter who'd been working at John's for as long as Dakota had been coming for her after-surfing stack. He set down two glasses of water and menus. "Heard you were laid low with a nasty bug. Feelin' better?"

"A bit, thanks," Dakota said, her cheeks warming. Apparently the news that her nasty bug was actually a determined sperm hadn't reached Montauk. She'd give it until midweek.

"Coffee and the regular?"

"The regular" was a large stack of blueberry pancakes swimming in maple syrup. God, what she would give to be able to devour one with her usual appetite. "Um, no. I'm going to change it up a bit today. I'll just have toast—can you make it dry? And I'll take mint tea, please."

"That's all you want?" Max asked.

"Yup. Still feeling a little off," she replied, handing Dan back the menu and ignoring Max's frown. Was he finally putting two and two together? She couldn't imagine that he, a single guy in his mid-thirties, had ever spared a thought for a pregnant woman's morning sickness.

Welcome to her world.

Her anger had been swept away in the morning wind upon her hearing Max's story of being targeted for blackmail. Yet a sadness lingered. His confession underscored once again how different they were. Now here they were, seated together at a booth, attempting to figure out how to proceed if Monday's visit to the doctor confirmed a baby was growing inside her. Was the effort doomed? Probably, but at least they were trying.

Dan's attention had shifted to Max. "And for you?"

Max glanced at the menu then looked at her. "Just coffee." He handed the menu back.

"Coming right up."

Once Dan was out of earshot, Max said, "So you've been pretty sick, huh?"

She wished she hadn't shrugged out of her parka. It would have offered some camouflage. Then again, he'd seen her last night. "Yeah. At first I had a cold, then it morphed into what I thought was a stomach flu. Only it didn't stop."

His expression turned grim. "So can you eat anything?"

She fiddled with the napkin. "Saltines and dry toast. Chicken broth. Sometimes applesauce."

"And you've been like this for how long?"

Forever—at least it seemed like it. "It started four days or so before Christmas." She frowned. "Maybe longer."

His expression incredulous, he leaned forward. “And you didn’t go to a doctor?”

“I didn’t really think about it being anything other than a flu,” she said defensively. No way was she going to bring up her irregular periods with him. “But then on New Year’s Day I had to go to my mother’s. It turns out she had exactly the same symptoms when she was pregnant with me. Unfortunately, my aunt Mimi and my cousin Carly were at the house when Piper decided to turn amateur sleuth. The next day I bought one of those in-home tests. I got the one with three sticks and I used them on three consecutive days, just to be sure,” she admitted sheepishly. “They were all positive, so then I called my doctor—”

“Here you go. One mint tea, one dry toast, and one coffee.” Dan set two mugs and a plate with two golden slices on the wood table. “Enjoy.”

“Thanks, Dan.” She hoped he hadn’t caught too much of what she’d said. She sat with her arms folded across her middle until Dan had gone behind the counter and into the kitchen before saying to Max, “So don’t even begin to act as if I’ve in any way been negligent or irresponsible.”

He held up his hands. “Okay, okay. I just—I don’t like that you’ve been so sick.”

She gave a short laugh. “Join the club.”

Lifting his mug, he took a slow sip of his coffee, then set it down, his eyes never leaving her. It was as if he were sizing up some complex problem.

She scowled. Breaking off a corner of her toast, she brought it to her mouth, chewing tentatively. She swallowed.

“I want to go to the doctor with you.”

“What?” And then she coughed and coughed some more, the toast caught in her throat, scratching it. Wildly she waved Max away when he made to rise. Despite everything going on, he was still Max; she worried she might still be susceptible to his touch. A thump to her back might be her undoing. She took a gulp of water and closed her eyes in relief when her throat cleared.

"What did you say?" she asked, praying she'd misheard.

"You said the appointment's on Monday. I want to be there."

Damn him for remembering details like that. "No." She shook her head.

"No? Why not?"

"Because—because—" She scrambled for an excuse. "It's personal."

"Yeah, it is personal. And if it turns out the home kit was right and you're pregnant, then it concerns me personally, too, doesn't it?"

It struck her that he was no longer questioning whether he was the father of the baby. In the wake of his revelation concerning the woman who'd tried to blackmail him—and what a scheming bitch she must have been—that he believed her was huge. She wanted him to trust her.

"And if you're not pregnant," Max continued doggedly, "then we have to get you to another doctor and figure out what the hell is wrong with you. What time is the appointment?"

"Nine-thirty. But surely you need to be back in New York—at the office—on Monday. I'll tell you everything that . . ." Her voice trailed off, turning into a heavy sigh as he pulled out his cellphone.

Resigned, she watched as he swiped, scrolled, frowned, scrolled some more, swiped again, and then began tapping out a rapid message. She assumed the lucky recipient was his assistant, Fred, who was going to be very busy rescheduling Max's Monday.

Finished, he returned his cell to his pocket. "There. I can take you."

"You don't have to—"

"Yeah, I think I do."

CHAPTER TWENTY-THREE

At 5:00 A.M. on Monday, with the world outside still dark, Max's study was illuminated by the glow of his PC. He was drafting the exit strategy for a California robotics company the Summit Group had invested in three years ago. He'd already been up for an hour, talking on the phone with Dieter Fischer, the CEO of the German company that was set to acquire AB1 and its nifty prototypes for $800 million.

Over the Thanksgiving weekend in Idaho, Bob Elders, Summit's managing director, had exhorted his partners to start the calendar year with a bang to make potential investors come running. Bob was determined to raise the firm's rankings. If this deal went through, Max had just fired the starting gun.

After he'd sent the draft to Bob, Summit's general counsel, Roger Cohen, and his team, he spent another hour going through emails and memos. Chris Steffen's took the lion's share of his time. It started out fine, addressing the expected topics: the rollout of Zephyr3, ways to evergreen its patent, and Chris's strategies for extending patent protection for other drugs in Chiron's cache by reformulating them or creating combination therapies.

Then Chris decided to veer sharply from the predictable CEO route and head off into batshit-crazy territory, devoting the rest of the email to his continued sense of "betrayal," bemoaning Max's unwillingness to renegotiate his compensation package. He once again trotted out the claim that he'd been led to believe the terms of his equity stake would be 10 percent, not 7 percent.

This was utter bull, as Max had told him over lunch the previous week. Chris had been more than okay with a 7 percent comp because in return he was getting a very hefty salary, with nice perks thrown in. For a man who liked instant gratification, the well-padded salary had been enough.

Wall Street wasn't for the meek and mild. Successful pharma companies weren't steered by wimps. But Chris, with his oversized ego, was taking the "Greed is good" mantra and mainlining it.

Max typed his reply, responding to the business strategies and ignoring Chris's whining. As he signed off, Max wished that there'd been a way to keep Mark Kauffman, Chiron's former CEO, in place. Chris was proving to be a huge time suck.

Especially as Max had more important things to think about, like what the hell he was going to do if Dakota was carrying his baby.

He showered, shaved, and dressed quickly, so as to have time to check the global stocks. Emerging markets were tanking, oil was cheaper than Coca-Cola, and Europe was a mess. Didn't mean there wasn't money to be made; he just needed to dig a little farther off the beaten path to find that nugget. He shut down his computer, stood up from his desk, and went to the window. Today the ocean was a pewter gray, mirroring the clouds above.

He thought of Dakota at Montauk Point, staring at the endless angry sea. She'd been standing with her hands splayed over her stomach. What had she been thinking and deciding as she faced the headwinds and the water crashing below? Had she shared those thoughts with the baby? Would she do so with him?

He left for Dakota's at eight-thirty. The drive across East Hampton was only about five and a half miles, and even with the Monday morning rush of people driving to work and parents getting kids off to school, he made the trip in under fifteen minutes. A nice change from the madness that was Manhattan at this hour.

When he knocked on the door, she answered, her hair damp at the ends and her face drawn.

"You're early. It only takes five minutes to get to the doctor's office."

"Sorry," he said. "Were you sick again?"

She frowned. "You used to have much smoother lines. I tried to eat something this morning. I thought it was a good idea. My stomach didn't. Come in. I'll be ready in a second."

The house in daylight was as tiny as it had been the other night. And just as neat. Dakota had her laptop open on the island that separated the living room from the kitchen. A textbook on investment analysis was next to it. *Catching up on homework?* he wondered.

He circled the living room, taking note of the books, magazines, pictures, and photos, telling himself he needed to learn as much about the private Dakota as he could. In a number of the framed pictures he recognized a younger, grinning Lauren Payne, Rae in some others. She had a faithful and long-standing circle of friends; she read a lot of fiction, everything from mystery to romance, and had a ton of books devoted to the Hamptons. Her decor was colorful but it wasn't girly. He could be okay hanging out here if it came to that.

Dakota emerged from the bedroom. She'd put on makeup, and highlighted her eyes so that they appeared even larger. The blush and lipstick were artful, too. If he'd arrived and seen her this way, he wouldn't have been able to guess that she'd been sick just minutes ago. She'd covered her white shirt with one of those long, drapey sweaters that didn't button. Grabbing her handbag off a side table and scooping her keys from a shallow ceramic dish, she turned to him, all brisk efficiency. "All right, I'm ready."

He hoped he was.

The Healthcare Center was just outside of East Hampton, on a cul-de-sac off Route 27. Dakota led him into the low-slung shingled office building. He followed as she turned right down the carpeted hallway and opened a maroon door with the names of several doctors affixed to it.

Inside, a placard greeted them with the following: *We kindly request that all patients refrain from using their cellphones in the waiting room.*

"Take a seat. I'll go check in," Dakota said, and went over to speak to the receptionist sitting behind a glass partition.

Three women sat in the windowless waiting room. Three very pregnant women. The only other male besides Max was about two years old. He was busy trying to grab his mother's cellphone. She, in turn, was waving it in the air with a distracted, "No, Joey," her eyes never leaving the screen. Whenever she lowered the phone to get a better look at what was playing, the kid made another attempt to snatch it.

Max supposed the woman thought the cell ban only applied to others. He'd have liked to ignore it, too, since there were several messages he should be checking, but he was determined to be on his best behavior.

Max took the seat farthest from the women. But as the chairs were arranged around a large square coffee table, there was only so much distance he could create. Aware that they were studying him, he fixed his attention on the magazines covering the table.

Maybe there'd be something to read or flip through. Among the glossy stacks were *Parents, Fit & Healthy Pregnancy, Child,* and *Women's Health.* He looked away.

Hanging on the wall were pictures of East Hampton sights—a photo of Hook Mill, the windmill located on North Main Street; some swans swimming in the town pond; and a picture of boats moored in a harbor. He assumed it was Three Mile Harbor—he hadn't been out there yet. Unfortunately, there weren't enough pictures to occupy his attention.

The toddler chose that moment to erupt in a full-blown tantrum. Wincing, Max glanced over at the reception desk. Dakota was putting something back inside her wallet. Returning the wallet to her handbag, she picked up a clipboard and walked over to him.

He tried to picture her looking like she'd just ingested a basketball, tried to get his mind around the idea that his kid could be growing inside her. The little boy continued his screaming.

Dakota sat down and began filling in what looked like twenty pages of questions, somehow ignoring the howling that was bouncing off the walls. Max wondered if he had enough cash on hand to bribe the mother into giving her kid the phone.

"Stop," Dakota said quietly.

He cast a sideways glance. Her pen was poised over the form. "Stop what?"

"Your leg. You're jiggling it."

He looked down. She was right. His leg was twitching uncontrollably. He pressed his foot down on the maroon carpet, and Dakota returned to the forms. The kid kept screaming, and he tried to keep it together. If these women could take it, so could he.

Just as he was about to go over to the receptionist and demand that the doctor see Dakota, the door opened. A nurse in pink scrubs called out, "Dakota Hale?"

He jumped to his feet. Dakota glanced at him, gathered her

things and the clipboard, and then rose slowly. "I'll have the nurse call you when—"

"You can't leave me alone here." He hoped she could read lips, since the toddler's shrieks were now as loud as a car alarm. "I promise I won't look at anything you don't want me to see. I won't talk or do anything."

She gave him a look that spoke of disbelief, amusement, and pity. He truly did not care. He'd rather be flattened by a 250-pound linebacker than remain in the waiting room with this screaming child and these women who looked ready to burst.

"Fine." Going over to the waiting nurse, Dakota said, "This is Max Carr, my—" She hesitated. "My friend."

Friend. He'd take that. It was a lot better than many things she could call him.

"I'd like him to be in the exam room so he can meet Dr. Davis," Dakota said.

The nurse smiled approvingly. "Of course. Dr. Davis loves to have the men take an active interest in these visits."

The nurse introduced herself as Trudy and led them to an exam room. Inside, she handed Dakota a plastic cup. "This is for your urine sample. When you're done, you can change into a gown. You'll need to remove everything. I'll weigh you, take your blood pressure and temperature, and draw some blood. Then Dr. Davis will come in and examine you and tell you what's going on."

"Like if I'm pregnant," Dakota said.

"Yes. And if you are, there'll be lots to discuss. The first prenatal visit is often the longest, but you'll have plenty of opportunities to ask questions along the way, so don't worry if you get home and you realize you've forgotten something."

With a nod, Dakota left with the cup.

To Max, Trudy said, "You can take a seat there." She pointed to a chair tucked away in the corner. "I'll be back in a few minutes."

Max did as instructed, and then tried not to wince at the poster facing him. He was all for vaginas, but he preferred to appreciate them in the flesh. Spying some pamphlets in a plastic stand, he stood and snatched a couple up and then sighed. One was about chlamydia, the other a marketing brochure for a progesterone cream.

He replaced them hurriedly when the door opened and Dakota entered. "I'll, uh, step out so you can change."

She nodded.

"You okay?"

She let out a shaky breath. "Yes. It's just . . . weird."

All of a sudden he felt better, marginally less freaked out. "Yeah. Believe me, I know." As he walked by her, he reached out and caught her hand, squeezing it lightly. "Hang in there."

She gave him a surprised look and then a small smile. "I'll do my best."

A smile. That was good, he thought.

Dakota quickly undressed and then shrugged into the gown. At least it was made of cloth and not one of those awful paper ones that scratched and gaped. Still, an examination gown was an examination gown. She tied it securely, striving for maximum modesty. Kind of ridiculous, considering how well Max knew her body.

His presence was unnerving, to put it mildly. She was singularly conscious of how much more he was going to learn about her body, which would have been one thing if they were together—still weird, but perhaps more natural. However, they weren't together.

But since Saturday morning at the Point, she'd been attempting to follow Hendrick's advice and try to find a way to work things out with Max in case the baby became a reality.

So she hadn't insisted that he remain in the waiting room until Dr. Davis finished examining her. It would have been too cruel. Max had kind of melted her heart with his display of nerves, the leg-jiggling, and the barely veiled horror at the prospect of being left with that obnoxious mother who couldn't be bothered to entertain her toddler. She could tell he was trying, despite being freaked out by what was obviously alien territory for him. To give credit where credit was due, Max wasn't merely trying; he was also lending her his support.

She checked the bow she'd tied, giving the loops a final tug. She could do this. It was just an exam, and she liked Dr. Davis.

The knock had her jumping. "Yes? Come in," she added.

Trudy entered, followed by Max. He gave her one of his sweeping, all-encompassing glances, and shook his head, grinning slightly.

"What?" she asked.

"Only you could look beautiful in that thing."

She blushed.

"Aw, that's sweet," Trudy said, not bothering to pretend she hadn't overheard.

It was. Dakota bit her lip to hide her smile. Even if it was untrue, she was pathetically grateful to Max for attempting to bolster her ego when she felt as attractive as, well, vomit.

"All right, Dakota, let's have you step on the scale."

Dutifully she stepped onto the square. Trudy began adjusting the weight, moving it, waiting, and then moving it again, ever leftward. When it was finally balanced, Trudy read out, "One hundred and twelve pounds."

"What? That can't be right. I usually weigh—"

Trudy flipped through the pages in Dakota's chart. "Last visit you were at one twenty-nine."

"I've lost seventeen pounds? How's that possible?"

"Mm-hmm," Trudy replied noncommittally. "Have a seat on the table and I'll get your blood pressure and all the rest so that Dr. Davis can examine you."

Dazed, Dakota hardly noticed Trudy wrapping the cuff around her arm and pumping it to check her blood pressure, sticking the thermometer in her ear for a reading, or drawing the necessary vials of blood. The number seventeen was on repeat in her head.

After updating Dakota's chart, Trudy picked up the tubes of blood and assured them that Dr. Davis would be in directly. The click of the door shutting sounded loud.

Swallowing a lump in her throat, Dakota looked at her bare legs dangling over the edge of the table. She didn't dare glance over at Max, half convinced she might burst into tears and reveal what an emotional wreck she'd become. Seventeen pounds. That was scary weight-loss territory. But it didn't necessarily mean that anything was wrong with her, right? Hadn't Piper said she suffered the exact same symptoms? Had that included losing nearly twenty pounds? Dakota thought not. Piper would have bragged about it—she'd always strived for the whippet look.

A sound that was part laugh, part sob escaped her.

"Hey," Max said. "What is it? Are you worried about the weight?"

Biting her lip, she nodded. "Yeah." She gave up trying to avoid his gaze. "But I was thinking of Piper—my mother—too. She was a lot younger than me when she got pregnant. If I'm this freaked out at the possibility of being pregnant, I can only imagine how it was for her, and then later having to withstand the pressure from her parents to terminate the pregnancy." She drew a steadying breath. Was any part of this going to be easy? No matter; she had to say the rest. "Max, if I'm pregnant, I'm keeping this child—with or without your help."

"I guess I'd already assumed that was how you felt. If there's a baby, you won't be alone, Dakota."

At his words, the tears won. There was still the big unknown, and then so many other things to sort out, but to hear him say he at least intended to be present for the child was a huge relief.

Wiping her cheeks, she sniffed. "Thank you. All this," she said, sweeping her arm to encompass the room and all its paraphernalia, "makes me wonder if I haven't given my mother enough credit."

"After the past thirty minutes, I don't think *any* woman gets enough credit."

His wry comment had her laughing. Her laughter died abruptly as her body went cold and clammy and the skin over her skull tightened. Uneasy, she slid off the table, shivering when her feet touched the linoleum.

"You all right?"

"Yeah, it's just— Oh God," she moaned as the nausea hit her. Rushing to the sink, she leaned over it and retched.

She was still heaving when the door opened. She heard Dr. Davis say, "Trudy, can you get some ginger ale, please?"

CHAPTER TWENTY-FOUR

"Not feeling too great, huh?" Dr. Davis said sympathetically. She had a kind face, with full cheeks and a ready smile. In all the years Dakota had been her patient, her hairstyle, a bright blond pageboy cut, had never varied. Neither had her footwear: polished brown penny loafers. Neither had her calm, steady manner.

"Not really, no." Dakota was back on the exam table, her face washed and her mouth rinsed, and sipping ginger ale from a turquoise Solo cup. Max had returned to the chair, having stood when she introduced him to Dr. Davis. "Am I pregnant, Dr. Davis?"

"You are."

It was real. Her eyes sought Max's. His had grown wide and bright with emotion. She imagined hers were the same.

"Oh. Okay. Well, at least I—at least we—know now." Her mouth dry, she took a sip of soda.

"Yes. So what I'd like to do is examine you and then do an ultrasound to make sure that everything is fine—"

"Because it's not? Fine, I mean."

"Well, as you know, you've lost a significant amount of weight. In addition, your red blood cell count is down quite a bit. Anemia's not uncommon in pregnancy, but your blood pressure is also lower than I'd like to see it. It's at ninety over sixty."

Dakota stared mutely at her. Those numbers had never meant anything because she was always in peak health. Now that she wasn't well, her ignorance terrified her.

"Have you been experiencing any dizziness?" Dr. Davis asked.

She nodded. "Yes."

"Feeling clammy? Weak?"

"Yes. I thought everything was connected to the flu."

"Your symptoms are probably due to a mix of factors. From what you've described and from the amount of weight you've lost, it's clear you've been experiencing rather severe morning sickness."

Feeling battered by numbers and unfamiliar terms, Dakota voiced her biggest fear. "Has any of this hurt the baby?"

"The ultrasound will show us if there's anything to be concerned about—"

She really, really did not want there to be any reason for concern.

"—and it will allow us to estimate the fetus's gestation and your due date. Now, I know your periods have always been irregular, Dakota, but do you by any chance remember the start date of your last one?"

"Around mid-November, I think. The eighteenth, maybe?"

"Okay." Dr. Davis made a note in the chart. Looking up, she said to Max, "I'm glad you're here today, Max, because I'd like to get your medical history as well."

"Of course, whatever you need." From his distracted tone, Dakota wondered if Max was struggling to process the news that a baby was in his imminent future. Or was that fear she heard? Was he as scared as she by the prospect of something being terribly wrong with her body? That the baby might be in danger?

Dr. Davis turned back to her. "Are you comfortable with Max in the room while I examine you, Dakota, or would you prefer he stepped outside? This first ultrasound will be transvaginal, as opposed to abdominal, because it provides a clearer image of the embryo at this stage. As these things go, the ultrasound probe is less uncomfortable than a speculum."

Dakota smiled weakly. "That's good to know. I—I'm all right with Max here." She looked at Max. "Do you want to stay?"

"Yeah," he said gruffly, and nodded. "I do."

Dakota fixed her eyes on the monitor's screen, ignoring the pressure of the ultrasound wand. Max stood by Dakota, as intent on the blackish-gray image as she.

"I'm checking your organs first, Dakota. Your uterus looks fine. And now for the second bit of good news. Here's the gestational sac with the fetus inside, and it's inside your uterus, just where it should be. Trudy, can you please move the cursor so Dakota and Max can see where to look?"

Dakota tracked the white arrow's movement. "That little thing is my baby?" she whispered.

"That's right. And this is the yolk sac and the pole."

Yet more terms Dakota didn't know the meaning of, but that was all right. Just as long as the baby was okay.

She felt the wand move inside her as Dr. Davis continued her examination. Then Dr. Davis spoke, and her voice sounded especially pleased.

"And we have a heartbeat," she said. "From the looks of it, a nice, strong, healthy one."

The cursor was pointing at a pounding dot. "That's its heartbeat?" Her hand reached out, searching for Max's. When it touched his, he caught it and squeezed tightly. At the pressure, she tore her gaze from the screen, and her own heart lurched to see him transfixed by the tiny, beating blip in a gray-black sea.

Dakota had never been in Dr. Davis's office. Come to think of it, she'd never talked to any doctor outside of an exam room. There were the requisite diplomas hanging on the wall, but what really grabbed her attention were the framed photo collages of babies. Smiling, sleeping, crawling, and rattle-waving babies. A frankly thrilling sight. Thanks to Dr. Davis's care, all these children had made a successful journey into the world. She had to believe hers would, too.

Dr. Davis looked up from the notes she'd been making in Dakota's file. "So, from the date you gave me for the start of your last menstrual cycle, I estimate that you conceived somewhere between November twenty-eighth and December sixth. Does that sound about right to you?"

"Um, yes." Her cheeks warmed as she recalled how often she and Max had had sex, not only during that period but right up until their last weekend together. She wondered whether Max, seated in the chair beside her, was remembering as well.

Dr. Davis picked up a printout of the ultrasound. "By looking at the measurements of the fetus—the gestational sac is twenty-seven millimeters, and the CRL, the crown-to-rump length of the fetus itself, is eleven millimeters—I estimate you're almost seven weeks along, Dakota, which should make your due date approximately August thirtieth."

August 30. The date seemed so far away and yet ridiculously soon. How was that thumbprint-sized blot supposed to grow into a baby that quickly?

"And from what you saw in the ultrasound, everything looks all right? Healthy?" Max asked.

"Yes. Actually, I'm more concerned about Dakota's health." Shifting her attention to her, Dr. Davis said, "You've lost a significant amount of weight. We need to get your nausea under control so you can keep your food down, and we also need to get your red blood cell count up and blood pressure back to normal levels to avoid risk of complications. Basically, you're going to have to start taking very, very good care of yourself."

Dakota nodded tightly. "I understand."

"I'd like you to start taking folic acid for your anemia, along with prenatal vitamins. I know how difficult eating is at the moment. There are anti-nausea drugs—"

"I'd rather not take any drugs unless it's absolutely necessary," she said.

"All right, but it's essential that you get enough calories and protein and rest. I don't want you to lose more weight, and fighting nausea is taxing."

"I know. I'll—" she began, but Max started speaking at the same time.

"I'll make sure Dakota gets the rest she needs and the right food. If necessary, I'll bring in a specially trained chef from the city to cook for her."

Dakota looked at Max, taken aback.

Dr. Davis smiled. "I was going to suggest protein shakes. You can sneak lots of calories into them, and Dakota can consume them sip by sip. Small and frequent meals often work best in combatting nausea. But if that fails, a professional chef might be able to create all sorts of extra-nutritious and palatable dishes." She paused to scribble on a small notepad. Then she tore off the sheets and handed them to Dakota along with a folder. "Here are the scripts for the vitamins and the folic acid. Inside the folder is a list of foods to eat and ones to avoid. It also has a list of frequently asked questions. A lot of my patients buy a copy of *What to Expect When You're Expecting.* It's very clear and informative. For right now, let's focus on getting the right amount of nutrition and vitamins in your body, and making sure you get rest and exercise—"

"Will I be able to surf?"

At her question, Max stiffened in his chair. She could practically hear his silent shout of *No!* She ignored it.

"I'd forgotten you're a surfer," Dr. Davis said. "Well, you should use good sense and not put yourself in a risky situation—"

"I'm never reckless," she said, speaking to the tense and silent Max as much as to her doctor.

"—and realize, too, that your center of gravity and sense of balance will change dramatically in the coming months."

"I understand. But I think it would be good for me and the baby to be out on the water—once I can handle sitting out in the lulls without tossing my breakfast."

"Then I see no problem. As you're normally strong and fit, you should continue with all your regular exercises and activities—running, yoga, et cetera. That of course includes sex," she finished with a smile.

"Good to know," Dakota murmured, wishing she could melt into the chair. Nothing in the world could have induced her to look at Max right then.

"Now, you've already given me your family history on your mother's side, Dakota, and we'll simply assume your father's health is unremarkable. I'd like to get some information from you, Max."

Max shifted, crossing his leg so his ankle rested on his knee. "Sure, go ahead."

Dr. Davis began running through a list of conditions. "Any family history of heart trouble?"

"No."

"Any genetic abnormalities?"

"No."

"Diabetes?"

"No."

"Cancer?"

For the beat of several seconds, Max was silent. Then he said, "Yes. My mother had ovarian cancer."

Dr. Davis looked up. "I see. And did she survive?"

"She died a month after being diagnosed. She was forty-five."

"That's far too young." Her voice had softened. "You must have been quite young yourself, Max."

"I was nineteen."

Dakota did her best to hide her shock. Max had told her he was eighteen when he lost his twin sister, Rosie. To then have his mother succumb to cancer so soon afterward?

"Ovarian cancer is a terrible disease," Dr. Davis said.

Max made no reply.

"And do you have any siblings?"

"I had a twin sister. She died in a car crash."

Dr. Davis laid her pen down. "Again, I am sorry."

"Thank you."

Dakota stole a glance at him. His face resembled carved marble. She was coming to recognize that look.

After a moment Dr. Davis continued. "And how about your health, Max? Do you have any medical conditions?"

"I'm fine."

"Good. And how about STDs?"

"None. I have tests regularly. I'm completely healthy and disease-free."

"Any previous hospitalizations?"

"Only for an open fracture of my tibia and fibula."

"And how did that happen?"

"Football. Senior year in college, third game of the season. I was sacked and broke my leg."

"Ouch," Dr. Davis said sympathetically. "That must have been a frustrating end to your senior year."

"Yeah. I didn't like sitting in a cast on the sidelines, unable to make plays. But since I'd already decided I wasn't going to pursue a career in football, at least I didn't have to worry about having ruined my chances as a ballplayer."

"As a member of the medical profession, I can't help but feel that you made the right choice—at least in terms of your physical health." She put down her pen and closed the folder. "Well, I think that covers it. So do either of you have any questions for me?"

As Dakota shook her head, Max said, "Yes, I do. What hospital are you affiliated with?"

"Southampton Hospital."

Max frowned. "My doctor in New York is at—"

Dakota guessed where this was going. "I was born at Southampton Hospital. Jackie Bouvier Kennedy Onassis was born there. Southampton is closer to me than New York, and I *like* Dr. Davis."

The doctor smiled. "Thank you, Dakota. I would of course be happy to deliver you of a healthy baby at Southampton. But I understand Max's concern. Your and the baby's health are of paramount importance. Should any complications arise, I have colleagues who are affiliated with New York Hospital. I will gladly refer Dakota to one of them."

Dakota gave Dr. Davis high points for her answer. It even seemed to appease Max.

"Thank you, Dr. Davis," he said.

"Of course. It was a pleasure meeting you, Max. I hope to see you again. Dakota, I want to see you again in three weeks to check your weight, blood, and hormone levels. You can make an appointment with Susannah at the front desk."

Neither spoke as they left Dr. Davis's office. For Dakota, the sense of a new reality, of a new *her*, had settled over her, and it weighed heavily. She realized she was exhausted.

She murmured her thanks when he opened the Range Rover's door for her.

"Do you mind if I take a moment to check my phone?" he asked once he was in the driver's seat. "I may have some messages that are expecting a reply."

"Of course. Go ahead." He'd missed hours of work today. "I should probably check mine too." Like Max, she'd turned hers off while they'd been in the doctor's office.

She had several. Three were from Piper, because it was barely eleven o'clock and she was probably still drinking coffee and wandering the house in her silk bathrobe. Rae had called twice. There was also one from Catherine Willis. She and her husband, Xander, were clients. They didn't come out very much in the winter, preferring to use their timeshare in Vail. Catherine was ultra-high maintenance, so it was possible she'd called Rae when she couldn't reach Dakota. Best to get the lay of the land first, she decided.

Rae answered on the second ring.

"Hey, Rae, what's up?"

"Dakota. How was the doctor's?"

Dakota's gaze slid to Max. He was busy tapping a message. "I'll tell you about it later. You're still coming by at two o'clock, right?"

"Actually, no, I can't. Catherine Willis has terminated her contract with us. Effective immediately. She's in a snit over our having the keys and alarm code—as if we'd lift a thing in her house," Rae said with an outraged sniff. "I have to swing by their house and drop off the keys. Apparently someone 'trustworthy' will be there to change the code. Then I have—"

"Wait. Hold up. Catherine terminated her contract with Premier? I can't believe it. Did she say why?"

"Um, yeah—" Rae cleared her throat. "She says she can't have employees who are predatory."

"Predatory? She called us *predatory*? After all we've done for her?"

"Um, I think she was sort of singling you out, Dakota. Rich, isn't it? Remember when little Parker decided to turn on every faucet in the house? And when the teenage stepson threw a party when Catherine and Xander were out God knows where? The house was beyond trashed. It looked like a war zone. You rescheduled our other clients for days to deal with those disasters."

"Yeah, I remember. Okay, okay." Dakota's mind scrambled as she tried to figure out what to do. "I'll call her when I get home and get this sorted out."

"There might be a problem with that. I was a little less than polite toward the end of our conversation. She really ticked me off with a comment about you and how she always suspected you had your eye on Xander. I told her it was more likely you were watching him to make sure he didn't get handsy with any of us. Then I kind of said that she was no one to talk about being predatory, since her and Xander's affair started while he was still married to his first wife."

Dakota closed her eyes. "Oh, crap. Well, there goes that account." And how many more would she lose now that Mimi's gossip was making the rounds?

"I'm sorry, Dakota. I know you would have done a better job dealing with her."

"Maybe, maybe not. I'm feeling pretty outraged. We've given a hundred percent to every job she requested. But Rae, we may get more calls like Catherine's, so you're going to have to stay calm and give me a chance to change their minds."

"I'll do better, I promise."

"I know. Listen, I'm going to try to patch things up with Catherine. I'll talk to you afterward." Ending the call, she became aware of the silence. Max was no longer thumb-tapping his cellphone's screen, but watching her.

"What was all that about?" he asked.

She sighed tiredly. "A client just fired us. Lots of firsts today."

"On what grounds?"

Embarrassed on so many levels—suffering a blow to her business, having a family who would knowingly inflict the injury, and Max bearing witness to it all—she turned her head to stare out at a rhododendron bush, its leaves curled from the cold. "No grounds at all. Mimi's rumor-mongering was all it took. Unfortunately, Catherine Willis is married to an investment banker, Xander Willis—"

"Willis. He's with Browning & Reed?"

"Yes." She nodded. "Do you know him?"

"One of my partners has teamed up with Browning & Reed on some deals. I've met him a few times."

"Well, I doubt any of this is Xander's idea. All he cares about is hitting the links when he's here. But Catherine is a classic Park Avenue trophy wife. She and Xander have been together for eight years and she may be looking over her shoulder, spooked by the competition. She'd be the perfect candidate to swallow Mimi's tales." She sighed again. "I'm not looking forward to trying to win her back while she feigns moral outrage. Luckily, not all my clients are like her."

"What about the fallout in terms of future clients?"

"Good question," she admitted. "March is the month we normally add to the roster and when we approach our existing clients about expanding the services we provide for them. It's when houses are bought, rental agreements signed, decisions about summer camps made, and home improvement projects begun, and we can help with each of those. I just have to hope this blows over by then." Unfortunately, in the interim Catherine would be busy running her mouth off to all her Park Avenue friends.

With an effort, she injected an upbeat tone in her voice. "Everything all right on your end?"

He shrugged and pressed the ignition starter. "My team and I have been sourcing a company to assess its potential and are readying another for a sale. Pretty routine compared to what went on at Dr. Davis's."

She laughed softly. "I suppose so."

"So," he said, looking at her. "A baby."

"A baby," she echoed. "I think I'm still in shock."

"You're feeling okay, though?"

"Yeah. How about you? Are you okay?" she asked, conscious of how careful they were being with each other. And now that they had moved on from talking about Premier's troubles, she was aware, too, of how tense Max was.

Was it the baby? Or Mimi's attempt to drag her name through the mud and the very real likelihood the muck would soil him, too?

"I guess I'm—" He paused and frowned. "I guess I'm processing—trying to think things through."

She could understand that. Her head felt as if it was about to explode from thinking about how that tiny galloping heart, that *life,* was inside her. She couldn't get over how small it was. How fragile. She had to get healthier, she simply had to. "I get that. There's an awful lot to think about."

"Yeah." Shifting into reverse, he backed out of the parking space and then headed toward the exit. Braking, he looked at her. "One of the things I've been thinking is that we should get married."

"What?"

CHAPTER TWENTY-FIVE

It was difficult to pinpoint when the idea that he and Dakota should marry had formed in Max's brain. Had it been conceived the night he'd driven to East Hampton to find Dakota wan and forlorn and possibly carrying his child? Had it taken root the next morning at Montauk Point, seeing her standing there all alone with her hands spread over her stomach, as if protecting the life growing within her?

A life, no larger than a penny, with an even tinier heart beating impossibly fast. When he'd looked at the ultrasound's monitor and seen that speck pounding away, his own heart had quickened and then raced with the same mad pace. He couldn't believe that he'd helped make this being.

Later, in the office, listening to Dr. Davis repeat to Dakota the importance of regaining her strength and health, his heartbeat had sped again, only now driven by fear. Not just for that new and vulnerable life, but also for the woman bearing it.

Dakota's astonished "What?" to his suggestion that they wed only underscored what he already knew. It was a crazy scheme. He was the last person who should be contemplating the idea of them getting hitched, let alone voicing it. The very prospect scared him spitless.

But while he'd been sitting in Dr. Davis's office, easily a dozen scenarios had occurred to him that might put Dakota or the baby at risk. He had to take whatever steps were necessary to safeguard them both.

Money, the kind of money he had, brought power. He could use that power for them.

So he buried the panic in his breast and shaped his mouth into a self-assured smile, the one he used when seeking potential investors for a deal. "I said, we should get married."

"No." She shook her head so vigorously the ends of her hair batted her face. "Absolutely not. Why ever would we want to do that?"

He heard the panic in the rush of words that tumbled from her lips, saw it in the flutter of her pulse on the side of her neck. He took that as a good sign. If she'd been completely set against the idea, she'd have laughed her head off. Or, worse, let him down with a gentle, killing politeness. Her agitation signaled she wasn't indifferent. She'd liked him before. Liked him a lot. He could build on that. Turn a no to a maybe, a maybe to a yes.

He pulled out onto the road, driving slowly so he could make his pitch before they reached her house. He didn't waste time with emotions. She wouldn't fall for that anyway.

"Consider the positives, Dakota. Let's take that conversation you just had with Rae. Your aunt's smear campaign is already beginning to have an effect. You can make all the calls you want trying to win back pseudo-outraged clients, but it won't have much of an impact because it won't really change the story. And with March mere weeks away, you can't afford to have the trend continue."

From her tightly pressed lips, he knew she'd love to contradict him but couldn't.

"So what better way to change the story than to take it in a new direction, one where we end up married? Then you're no longer a temptress out to lure men—otherwise faithful husbands included—but the wife of a successful Wall Street financier. Your image changes like this." He snapped his fingers. "So does your status. Being as rich or even richer than your clients will make them come running to *you,* because we all know that's how it works. You'll be part of the tribe."

Aware of how invested she was in her business, he continued to work that angle. "And having access to my money will allow you to expand Premier Service—"

"I wouldn't use your money for my business."

"Why not? And it would have an upside. Hiring additional staff would allow you to get the rest you need. I'd consider that a worthwhile outlay."

"I don't like the idea."

Okay, he thought. He could bring her around to his way of thinking later. He'd enjoy convincing her. It was fun to match wits with Dakota.

When Max went after a deal, he appealed to investors on every level. It was time to make a play for her sympathy. "You know, your aunt's rumor-mongering will affect me, too."

She shifted in the bucket seat. Ah, he'd gotten to her.

"The business with Xander Willis. Will that hurt your reputation?"

"It might." Not that he really cared what others thought, save for perhaps a few friends like Alex Miller. "My director, Bob Elders, is conservative. Very family-values-minded. Until now he's overlooked my, uh, bachelor ways, but fathering a child out of wedlock shines a different light on my lifestyle. Bob will hear about our situation soon enough if Xander Willis is involved. A marriage would smooth the waters. Right now I'm having some trouble with the new CEO of a pharmaceutical company we've just invested in heavily. I need Bob in my corner, and if he has a dim view of my private life, that might weaken his support." This last was truer than he'd like to admit.

He glanced at her. The dark wings of her brows were drawn together. She'd probably been focusing—understandably—on the impact the news would have on her. Now she'd be thinking about him, too. It wasn't necessarily fair, but as the saying went, all's fair in love and war. Not that this was love. This was about looking after her.

"And you know, there are other things to consider. There are straight-up benefits to our marrying."

Her glance was wary. "Such as?"

"Your health insurance, for example. I saw you have an HMO. As my wife, you'll be covered on my plan, which comes with every bell and whistle imaginable. Our child will be on it, too. That's important to me, Dakota. It may not seem like a big deal, but what if something goes wrong while you're pregnant and you need to consult with a specialist outside of your network or have a special procedure—"

She held up her hand to cut him off. "Please don't. I see where you're going with this. I *understand* it's important. It's just—" With a weary sigh, she let her head fall back against the headrest. "I'm really, really wiped out."

His gut clenched. "Let's get you home and I'll fix you something to eat and drink."

"I don't need you to—"

"Yeah, but you've got me."

*

Unlocking her front door, Dakota stumbled across the threshold and made for the sofa. She sank down on it with a moan. The room had begun to spin.

She had a hunch the vertigo was due to Max's ambush of a marriage proposal as much as anything. It was more than sufficient to set her world atilt.

She closed her eyes.

She could hear Max moving about. Then came the muffled bangs of cabinets and drawers being opened and shut and rummaged through as he familiarized himself with her galley kitchen.

Add a man messing around in her kitchen to the list of the day's firsts. She would never have allowed one of the men she dated to root around in her space. But Max didn't follow any of the rules she laid down. Nor did he fit into the life plan she'd envisaged.

And he wanted to marry her?

As proposals went, his was as dry as the toast she smelled wafting in the air. Funny that it had nevertheless caused her heart to squeeze painfully. She told herself it was from disappointment. The proposal was essentially a business proposition, a remedy to silence the whispers circulating throughout the Hamptons and New York City. Yet behind Max's pragmatic pitch she had detected a caring note. And didn't caring entail affection?

She realized how much she wanted that to be true—that while he might not be able to admit it, he did care for her. The wish only underscored how vulnerable she was.

Max had hurt her once before. How would she feel when the time to break up came again, as surely it must?

Another scent reached her. The aroma of chicken soup now mingled with that of toast, and it made her hollow stomach ache.

She caught the sound of Max's low voice. He must be calling someone. He'd lost hours out of the workday. Then she heard some clinking noises followed by the thud of approaching footsteps. She opened her eyes to see him carrying a plate and two mugs.

"Lunch," he said, setting one mug, a spoon, and a plate piled high with toast on the coffee table. He nabbed one of the slices for himself and took a large bite.

She sat up. "You're joining me?"

He chose the off-white accent chair for himself and stretched out his legs under the coffee table. "I'm starving. I chose the chicken soup with noodles." He took a sip. "It's good."

"Rae splurged and went to Citarella." She took a tentative sip.

"I know. I called her and told her you need lots of protein and calories. You don't have a blender. I told her to pick one up."

"Shouldn't you be heading back to New York?"

He smiled, as if fully aware that she wanted him gone from her house, which still felt too small with him in it. "I arranged for a flight back in a couple of hours. I have time."

"Great to hear," she murmured.

He drank from his mug. "How's the soup? Staying down?"

"So far so good." She realized that she'd never had a man warm soup for her before.

"Good."

He let her eat in peace for a few minutes. When she put the mug down and reached for a slice of toast and began to nibble on it, he said, "I'd like to know what you're thinking."

"What I'm thinking?"

"About getting married," he prompted.

"Oh." She ate another corner off the toast.

Finished with his soup, he put the mug down and leaned back in the chair, all relaxed grace. "I realized I left out a number of other bonuses to our marrying."

She eyed him over her half-eaten slice of toast. "And those would be?"

"For instance, I could help you with your homework. I bet you've fallen behind—"

"Are you serious? I am not getting married so you can help me with my homework!"

"I can help you with investment strategies, too, discuss which start-ups show the most promise." The side of his mouth lifted. "I'd be like an in-house consultant."

"In-house?" She put her toast down for fear of mangling it. "Are you saying we'd live together?"

"Why not? I told Dr. Davis that I'd make sure you ate well. My feeling is that promise covers making sure you're getting healthy and strong. I can take care of you better at my place, but if you want me to move in ..."

"Max, I don't—"

"But I can't help but think that your moving into Windhaven would be a powerful counterattack."

"What do you mean?"

"You told me how angry your aunt was when I bought the house. Now she's, shall we say, shown her very limited affection for you. How will she react when she hears that we're married and living in the ancestral pile?"

She met his gaze. "It will absolutely kill her."

He smiled. "Right now, there's nothing I'd like better than for that to happen."

She considered him in silence. Then with a small shake of her head, she said, "You're very good."

He arched a brow. "And?"

"And so I'll think about it. Weigh the *negatives* as well as the positives."

"Fair enough." He rose from the chair. "One last thing to think about, Dakota."

She looked up at him. "What's that?"

"This," he said, leaning over. Sliding a hand behind her neck and tangling his fingers in her hair, he covered her lips with his. Moving his mouth with gentle yet unwavering persuasion, his kiss reminded her how well Max knew how to please her. When at last he raised his head, her fingers were curled into the sofa's cushions, the only way she could prevent them from latching on to him and demanding more.

Still bowed over her, his eyes glittered, bright with desire. "I want you, Dakota. I haven't stopped."

CHAPTER TWENTY-SIX

There were times when one needed a sounding board. Or three. Dakota simply couldn't think logically or clearly. The memory of Max's kiss and of his husky voice saying that he wanted her had cast a thoroughly beguiling spell.

So she called for reinforcements: Lauren, who'd known her for twenty years, their friendship formed one hot July day as they bodysurfed on Main Beach, the two breaking into giggles and matching smiles when Lauren asked if Dakota's tank suit bottom was heavy with sand, too; Rae, who understood her love for Premier Service and shared her determination to make it a Hamptons success story; and Gen, who was not only a friend but also married to a man who had much in common with Max. She would have added a fourth, Hendrick, but he was back in the city seeing patients. And Monday evenings were his and Marcus's culture nights; they had long-standing subscriptions to the ballet and opera.

Under normal circumstances, Dakota would have suggested they meet in Sag Harbor at the Beacon or the American Hotel, but she didn't trust her stomach and loved both places too much to risk forever associating them with an ill-timed bout of nausea. After being sequestered for so many days, she was eager to get out of the house. Gen solved the problem by suggesting they come to her place. She was in the city when Dakota called but assured Dakota that she could make it out by six o'clock.

"I'll leave right after I pick Gracie up at school. Tilly can watch her and Brooke until Alex comes home. The girls love having a night with him to themselves, and it will give me a chance to do some sketching tomorrow morning. It's been madness since the show, and I'm itching to get back to work. Tell everyone to come around six-thirty."

When Dakota rang Gen's doorbell, Gen answered it with a cry of "Dakota!" that was echoed by the others. In the hall she was hugged and exclaimed over, Dakota having already confirmed her pregnancy to the three of them. As they sat down in the living room, where Gen had lit a fire and laid out appetizers, Lauren was the first to broach the gossip making the rounds. "That vindictive bitch Mimi has really gone too far."

"Can you believe she had the gall to crash my opening and spread her lies there?" Gen said.

"I think I should slash her tires," Rae said. "I haven't told you this, Dakota, but I ran into Constance Harvey at Williams-Sonoma—"

"Oh no." Constance Harvey was one of Mimi's besties.

"Oh yeah. She said she felt it was her 'duty' to tell her friends at the Bridgehampton Historical Society about how you trapped Max. How low can she go?" Rae said, outraged.

"When it comes to Mimi and her pals, the answer is subterranean," Lauren said.

"Unfortunately true," Dakota said. "But let's avoid any property destruction, okay, Rae? Your being charged with a felony might be worse for our reputation than my getting pregnant with a client."

"You may be right. I'm just super annoyed with myself that I didn't say something to you earlier. I'd kind of suspected you were pregnant when you first came down with that 'flu,'" Rae admitted.

"You did?" Dakota said.

Rae looked abashed. "I assumed it would occur to you fairly soon. Believe me, I'd have pulled you aside for a little heart-to-heart if I'd thought for a moment it would be Piper spilling the beans."

"That's the thing about Piper," Lauren said. "She lulls everyone into assuming she's too self-absorbed to notice anything. But then she goes and sticks you with a comment that destroys. Mimi's a blunt weapon compared to switchblade Piper."

Dakota choked out a laugh. "I was actually feeling sort of sad for Piper when I was at the doctor's. I wonder whether she regrets not knowing the name of the guy who got her pregnant. Having Max with me really helped."

The news that Max had accompanied her to Dr. Davis's was greeted with "He came to the doctor's with you?" and "Oh, good for him!" and "I remember Zach at our first ob/gyn visit when I was pregnant with Katie. I thought he was going to faint."

"Yes, Max lost a little of his cool," she admitted with a smile. "It was kind of cute. And it made me feel a lot better knowing I wasn't the only one freaked out at the prospect of a baby. But Dr. Davis said the baby's fine so far. And that's the important thing."

"Absolutely. On that note, I have some very fine chilled ginger ale for you." Gen pointed to the plastic bottle chilling in a bucket. Next to it was a bottle of Veuve Clicquot. "We poor slobs will be drinking champagne."

Dakota grinned. "Poor, poor pitiful you."

Once they had their glasses in hand, Gen said, "I propose a toast to Dakota, Max, and their baby."

"Hear, hear!"

"So how are you feeling?" Gen asked.

"My morning sickness is still pretty bad, but I managed to keep down some soup and toast at lunch that Max made for me after we got back from the doctor's. And I ate some vanilla ice cream this afternoon."

"That's major progress," Rae said.

"And how did the doctor's visit go? Did you have an ultrasound?" Lauren asked.

She nodded. "It was pretty intense. We could see the baby's heart beating."

"Ah, man," Rae said. "I can't wait for that moment. It must have been awesome."

"It was."

"Zach cried when he saw the ultrasound for Katie and for Ali," Lauren said softly. When Dakota reached out and squeezed her hand, she sniffed and smiled. "I'm okay. It's a good memory."

"Alex was a basket case, too. Then he went around showing everyone the photo, our doormen included."

"Okay, now I totally get how Max sounded when he called earlier," Rae said. "He gave me a shopping list that filled an entire page, told me to charge everything I bought to him, and then told me to get one of those super-duper blenders—you know, the Vitamix? When you're ready to move on from the water crackers," she said, nodding at the plate of crackers Gen had set out among a half a dozen other nibbles, "I have a protein smoothie waiting for you in the fridge, per Max's strict instructions. He even knew what kind of protein powder I should buy. The man's crazy for you."

Or he was crazy at the prospect of having a child, Dakota thought. She wondered how her friends would react when she told them about his plan. Drawing a deep breath, she said, "He wants us to get married."

She'd expected shock, or at a minimum several seconds of heavy silence while they processed the preposterousness of the idea.

"Yay!" Gen cried as she jumped up from the sofa to hug Dakota. "I've been hoping for this since that brunch we threw. There was just something *there* between you."

Rae's face split in a wide grin. "So happy for you, Dakota. Though I could have called this one, too."

"Not sure there's anyone good enough for my girl Dakota," Lauren said. "But I figure we can have Alex do something like sour all Max's business deals if he doesn't rise to the challenge."

"You may be overestimating Alex's power," Gen said with a laugh. "Though probably not," she admitted when Lauren raised a skeptical brow.

"Wait." Dakota raised her hand. "Hold on a second here. You all are forgetting something. Max and I had a fling. Then we called it off. We were *over*. So for all intents and purposes this is a practical decision."

"Practical in what sense?" Gen asked.

She explained Max's arguments for how their marrying would solve a number of problems: salvage her business reputation, smooth his uptight director's feathers, and give Mimi a conniption fit.

"So you see, it's not romantic by any means." It wasn't love, not like what Lauren had experienced with Zach and what Gen and Rae shared with Alex and Marcos.

"Gotta disagree there," Rae said. "I think Max caring enough to save Premier Service from having any more mud slung at it is pretty darn romantic."

"And taking on Mimi?" said Lauren, "that's beautiful and shows he has the right instincts. Lord knows I've been itching to do it, but I'm vulnerable, too. I can't afford to have her badmouth Hilltop Farm any more than you can have Premier Service trashed. So, three cheers for Max. I hope Mimi develops an ulcer at the thought of you together." Reaching for a prosciutto-wrapped asparagus spear, Lauren took a healthy bite. "Mmm, these are delicious, Gen." And she passed the platter to Rae.

"Thanks." Rae helped herself to a spear. "And don't forget how down in the dumps you were after you and Max broke it off, Dakota. That's not how you usually are when you call it quits—"

"No, it's not," Lauren chimed in.

"—which to me means you really dug him, right? So why not give marriage a go?"

Rae made it sound so easy. They all seemed to think it was the logical step to take. Would they feel that way if they knew about Max's sister, Rosie, and how her death still affected him? But while she'd spoken to Hendrick about Max's loss, it would be wrong to do so with them when Max hadn't shared the story of his twin sister's death with Alex.

But they had plenty of other problems facing them. She focused on one that troubled her most after Max's kiss. "We'd be moving in together. I don't know whether I'm ready to take that step."

"Living together is an adjustment, all right," Lauren said. "But things went well when you guys were together, right?"

Things had been great.

"Pretty good," she said, earning snorts of laughter from her friends.

"So, Windhaven? That's one beautiful house—now that it's had a Premier Service makeover," Rae said. "And you have loads of space."

"And we'll practically be neighbors!" Gen smiled.

"Wow, you, Max, and the baby living in Windhaven. Forget Mimi coming down with an ulcer—we're talking full-blown apoplexy." Lauren lifted her champagne glass. "A second toast to you and Max."

After draining their glasses, Gen said more seriously, "You should move in with him, Dakota. If you don't and you continue to live at your place, that will just cause tongues to wag all over again. And I'm with Rae. I think you care for each other, and with the baby, you have an added incentive to make it work. So why not give the marriage a chance to grow into something real?"

"But what if it doesn't? What if it ends? Won't our marrying have made everything worse?"

"Maybe," Gen replied. "But isn't that the risk every couple faces when they say 'I do'?"

Later, after they'd thanked Gen and waved Rae off, Dakota and Lauren lingered for a moment, staring up at the incredible night sky, a black velvet blanket studded with stars.

"Wow. Reminds me of those nights we spent on the beach," Lauren said.

"Yeah. We only need a fire."

"And a boombox."

"Or your guitar."

"Lord, those were the days." Lauren's words ended in a soft white puff of laughter that dissolved in the inky darkness. "By the way, dibs on throwing the baby shower. Katie and Ali are going to be over the moon when they hear that Auntie Dakota is going to have a baby. A real live baby."

"Thanks. I'd love that. It's all hit me so fast—the baby, Max's idea that we should marry—it's like being rolled by a monster wave." She shrugged inside her coat. "Lauren, the marriage ... do you really think I should do it?"

"Yeah, I do. For both your sakes. And the baby's. Look, the situation's not ideal, I'll give you that. But let me tell you something. Being a single parent is hard and scary. There are so many things I miss about Zach. Losing the one person who cared as much about Katie and Ali tops the list. But you have a chance to see whether you and Max can figure it out, and learn to be partners and parents. I know you'll give it your all. From everything you told us tonight, it seems like Max will, too."

"I just keep wondering about what I'm depriving him of if I say yes. Max wasn't in the market for a relationship, and that's why we ended things. But that could have changed. And if it did, well, he could have had anyone."

Lauren swore softly and swiftly. "See, this is why I hate Piper and Mimi and your whole damned family. I don't care that they're insufferable snobs. That's a common enough defect. What I can't forgive is their using the fact of your birth as an excuse to treat you like a second-class citizen. Even Piper does it with her 'I'm the only parent you've got. It's just you and me kid, so you better love me no matter how selfish I am.' Listen, Dakota, you're beautiful, smart, and a successful businesswoman. And you're kick-ass strong—except when it comes to believing in your own self-worth because your family's done such a good job of hacking away at it. So the same goes for you. You also could have found the most amazing person—"

For that brief period in December, she thought she had.

"—and if what you say about Max being relationship-shy is true, then doesn't he deserve extra credit for proposing that you two tie the knot?"

"Yeah, he does. I was kind of telling myself that earlier."

"Good. So get married to your rich-as-Midas hunk and rock it, Dakota."

God, how she'd needed to hear that. Finding Lauren's hand, she squeezed it tightly. "I will. I love you, Lauren."

"Love you back, Dakota."

*

Dakota was in her kitchen fixing a cup of chamomile tea and munching on a saltine when her cellphone rang. She picked it up, looked at the number, and answered with a casual "Hi," even as a flush of pleasure warmed her body. He'd called.

"I didn't wake you?"

"No. I went to Gen's for a girls' night out with Lauren and Rae. Then I was reading. I downloaded *What to Expect*."

"Oh. And?"

"It's very … well, I guess the right word is 'informative.' And a bit overwhelming. Where are you?" Remembering the night he'd drunk-dialed her from some bar, she strained her ears for some telling background noise. Not that she'd necessarily blame him for tying one on after the kind of day they'd had; she just wasn't sure she could handle a female voice intruding with a saccharine demand of *"Max!"*

"I'm still at work. I wanted to move ahead on some projects." There was a moment's silence. Then he said, "How are you feeling?"

She figured this was as rare a line of questioning for him as it was for her. Needing to steady herself, she leaned her hip against the counter. Raising her mug, she took a tentative sip. *Still too hot,* she thought. "Physically, you mean?"

"Yeah."

"I had a protein smoothie at Gen's that Rae fixed per your instructions. It contained kale, which should have made me puke but didn't. And I'm having a cup of tea and a cracker now."

"Good. That's good." He paused again. "And how are you feeling otherwise?"

She swallowed and wondered whether he, too, was gripping his phone tightly. "About us?"

"Yeah."

"I think—I think you're right. We should get married." And if in her heart she'd imagined a very different scenario when she became engaged, she squelched the secret yearning. She tamped down, too, on the sudden clammy fear that gripped her.

She heard a rush of air, the sound of Max exhaling heavily. So cool Mr. Carr hadn't been sure of her response. Did that make her feel better? Perhaps, but the truth was, she was too nervous to analyze anything properly.

"That's good—that's good to hear," he said. "I, uh, looked into what we need to do. We can get a license at the town hall. All we need is a birth certificate and a driver's license. Once we have the license, we can get married twenty-four hours later. We'll need an officiant—"

"Um, Max, I know all this already. It kind of comes with the concierge service territory."

"Right. Of course." He cleared his throat. "So, any preference? I'll do whatever you choose."

Best to keep the ceremony simple, straightforward, and unemotional. It would make it easier for both of them. "I know one of the county clerks, Martin Geller. We organized a surprise anniversary party for his parents. I can ask him."

"Sounds good. I'll come out tomorrow so we can get the license. Can you ask if he can marry us on Friday?"

Her legs suddenly wobbly, she braced her elbows on the counter. "Friday? This Friday?"

"The sooner we marry, the better the chance we have of changing the conversation quickly and burying your aunt's story."

"Okay, I'll give him a call first thing tomorrow."

"I'll see what can be done about getting the wedding announcement in the papers and posted online. We'll need a good professional-quality photograph to go with the announcement."

She couldn't help but be impressed. He'd thought of everything. "I often use a photographer who's in Bridgehampton. I'll call her." Straightening, she grabbed the notepad she used for grocery and errand lists and jotted down *Martin* and *Greta* and *hair*, underlining the last several times.

"Do you have anyone you'd like to have as a witness?"

If this had been a normal wedding, she'd have packed the place with her friends, but somehow she suspected that she'd be even more terrified about the huge step they were taking—make that a Grand Canyon–sized leap—if she was surrounded by loved ones. "No, that's all right. I saw them tonight, and Lauren's going to throw me a baby shower." She paused. "And what about you? Would you like your father—"

"No. He won't come." His answer was like a door being slammed shut, reminding her of all he kept closed off.

She rubbed her eyes. "Max, we're going to—" she began, just as he said, "So what size—" Both of them broke off. Then Max said, "Go ahead. What were you going to say?"

"Only that we need to talk about how this . . ." She paused to swallow the lump in her throat. "How this marriage will work. You know, what the parameters and our expectations are."

"Such as?"

"Such as I'm not ready to have sex with you."

Okay, that had come out far more baldly than she'd have liked. But at least she'd said it, and at least they hadn't been face-to-face when she did. Because otherwise she wasn't sure she'd have been able to say it, not with her body and perhaps even her heart at odds with her mind.

The silence stretched. Nervous, she picked up her mug and gulped her tea. She grimaced. Lukewarm, it tasted terrible. "Max?" she said tentatively.

"Yeah, sure, I understand."

His tone made her feel compelled to justify herself. "After all, we had broken up—"

"I get it, Dakota."

Abruptly she revised her earlier thought, now wishing she could see his face. Then she might have a chance of figuring out what was going on in his mind. "It's just that I'm not sure where we stand." And didn't that top the list of oddest things to say to the man she was going to wed in little more than seventy-two hours?

She heard him draw a breath and then release it in a loud and weary sigh. "All right. How about we discuss what we want out of this marriage after we've gotten the license tomorrow?"

"Okay." She closed her eyes briefly as she replayed their conversation. Recalling that she'd cut him off, she said, "What were you going to ask me about just now?"

"What? Oh yeah." He gave an odd, muffled laugh. "I wanted to know what size ring you wear."

She bit her lip until the pain matched the one in her heart. How must he have felt, all set to discuss rings, and she went and flatly announced she wouldn't sleep with him?

"So do you know?" he asked.

She lowered her gaze to stare at her bare hands. "I'm a size six. And you?" she said softly, her heart thudding. "Would you like to wear a band?"

"Uh, sure. I guess. Why not?"

He was willing to wear a ring. Her ring.

"Do you know your size?"

"My college ring was a twelve. It still fits."

"Okay, that's good to know." She added *ring* to her list. "Do you prefer gold or platinum?"

"They should match, right? I was thinking you'd look good with a platinum ring. But I'll get you whatever you want . . ." His voice trailed off.

He was breaking her heart, one minute making her doubt that it could ever work between them and the next bowling her over with his thoughtfulness. "I'd love a platinum ring," she said quietly.

"There's a jewelry store in town, right? We can get a sense of styles we like there."

"That's a good idea."

"So this wedding, it's a go?" he asked.

She could still refuse. "Yes, it's a go."

And God help them both.

CHAPTER TWENTY-SEVEN

Dakota waited until eleven o'clock the next morning to call Piper to be sure she was awake.

"Dakota! I've been meaning to get in touch. That stain in the rug? I had to send it out to be professionally cleaned. You'll foot the bill, right? I'd say it's only fair."

That was debatable. But it was a waste of time to argue, and she had dozens of things to take care of before she met Max. "That's fine. Have the rug cleaners call me when the rug is ready."

"And how is the puking?"

"Somewhat better. The mornings are the worst. But certain smells and foods trigger it. I'm getting better at identifying them."

"That's good, I suppose."

"Dr. Davis would like me to regain the weight I lost."

"Be careful you don't get too fat. I didn't, but you've always been a hearty eater. You'll have to watch out that you don't end up looking like Mimi."

Clenching her molars, Dakota abandoned the idea of telling Piper about her anemia and low blood pressure. The sooner she got to the point, the sooner she could hang up. "Listen, Piper. I just called to tell you I'm getting married on Friday."

"Married?" her mother said blankly.

"Yes, married."

"You mean to Max Carr?"

As if I have other candidates waiting in the wings, Dakota thought. "Yes, to Max Carr."

"Really? Well, bully for you, though why you'd want to get hitched is beyond me," she drawled. "I hope you've made sure the prenup is generous."

"I haven't asked for one. Contrary to what Mimi is busy saying, I'm not interested in his money."

"More fool you. If you're going to give up your freedom, you might as well make some money out of it. Because believe you me, when you start to lose your looks and he gets bored with the same old same old, he'll divorce you and leave you high and dry. That's what men like him do. Just think, you and Mimi will be able to swap sob stories. Maybe it will make her like you."

Pain spiked the side of Dakota's face. With an effort she unclenched her jaw. "First, you don't even know Max. He's not at all like George." Among other charming attributes, Mimi's ex was a heavy drinker and a secretary-groper. The bank he'd worked for as VP had finally fired him, deciding that to keep him all but guaranteed having the bank's name sullied with a sexual harassment suit. "Second, unlike Mimi, I know how to work for a living. I don't need a man to support me."

"No need to get in a snit, Dakota. I'm just trying to give you some good advice. But you'll do as you like, as usual."

That was rich. "Right. Look, I was just calling to see if you wanted to come on Friday. We're getting married at the town hall."

"At what time?"

"I called Martin Geller and asked him to officiate. He said—"

"You're having Marty Geller perform the ceremony? How incredibly dull."

"He's a perfectly nice man."

"Yes. He makes Mr. Rogers seem like Andy Warhol."

She refused to rise to the bait. "Whatever. He can do the wedding at two o'clock."

"At two? I'm almost certain I have something then—"

Piper would have any number of standing appointments she could use as an excuse: her trainer, acupuncturist, massage therapist . . .

"But of course I'll come if I possibly can."

That was pretty much a guarantee she'd be a no-show, Dakota thought. Not having her there was a relief, actually. The ceremony would be difficult enough to get through without Piper sucking the oxygen out of the room. "I understand. Listen, can you do me a favor?"

"Sure."

"Don't tell Mimi about the wedding."

"Why? It's not like she won't find out anyway."

"Because she's doing her best to destroy my business and I don't want her to have a chance to spin more tales."

"Destroy your business? Really, Dakota, there's no need to exaggerate. She is family, you know."

In a family that was about as loving as a nest of vipers.

"Please, Piper, if you could just keep it to yourself," she requested, knowing it was too much to expect Piper to stand up to Mimi and defend her.

Piper let out an annoyed huff. "Fine. I won't say a word, never mind that it'll put me in the line of fire."

"I appreciate your bravery," she said dryly. "If you want to come to the town hall at two o'clock, we'd be happy to have you." There, she'd done her duty.

"Do try to squeeze in a facial at least. You're looking decidedly the worse for wear."

Piper was at her most lethal when she was right. "Thanks so much."

"Oh my God, I just realized what this means."

"What are you talking about?"

"You'll be living at Windhaven. Poor Mother and Father." She laughed. "They must be turning in their graves," she said, and gave another laugh. "Congratulations, darling. Not even I've managed that."

Max had scheduled an early meeting with Roger Cohen, the firm's general counsel, so that afterward he'd have time to swing by Tiffany's and then take the helicopter he'd reserved to East Hampton.

Roger's assistant brought them coffee. When the door shut behind her, Roger picked up his cup and asked, "So what are we looking at this morning, Max? Selling AB1? Chris Steffen's contract? Chris is just blowing smoke, you know. The contract's rock solid."

Needing the caffeine to jolt his system after a nearly sleepless night, Max drained his cup in three gulps. He leaned forward and set it on Roger's desk. "Yeah, I know. What I don't get is why he's acting like this. Chris has always been a prick, but he's never been certifiable. Something's definitely off with him. I feel that I made a mistake campaigning to have him run Chiron." He didn't usually doubt himself this way.

"But the board loves him. And he's made a lot of money for Summit before," Roger reminded him.

"Yeah, the board loves him," Max agreed. "And Chris promises he's going to make even more for us." Which was why he wasn't actively figuring out ways to shut him down. "I hope I can keep his ego in check."

"Good luck with that."

"Yeah." He met Roger's gaze, and the two of them shared a cynical smile over the walking cesspool that was Chris Steffen. "But actually, Roger, I didn't come here to discuss deals present or in the pipeline. It's a personal matter."

"Let me guess. Another woman's blackmailing you?"

"No." He gave a short laugh. "I need my will changed. I'm getting married on Friday."

"Oh, fuck!" Roger's face flushed pink with embarrassment. "Christ, I'm sorry about the blackmailing crack. That was in totally bad taste."

"It's okay, really. I'd have said the same thing in your position."

Roger took a slug of his coffee, evidently stalling for time to collect himself. "So, uh," he began, "congratulations, Max. Who's the lucky woman?"

"Her name's Dakota Hale. This is the will I have now." Bending over, he extracted it from his briefcase, then pushed it across the desk to Roger. "The new one should be changed so that the principal beneficiary of my estate will be my fiancée, Dakota." It felt strange saying the word "fiancée" for the first time, even stranger realizing he'd be switching to *wife* in three days . . . a wife who didn't want to sleep with him.

As he'd told Dakota on the phone, he got it. When they broke up, he'd probably made her think he was all too happy to end it. In fact, a part of him had been relieved. She'd been getting too close.

But now he didn't have a choice. He was going to marry her. They'd be sharing a house. A life. So yeah, it irked him that even though he was willing to take this huge step, she was going to deprive them of something that had been good between them. Not just good, great.

What the hell was he to do about Dakota's decree? Damned if he knew.

Roger had finished reading the document. "So you'd like to make, uh . . . it's Dakota, right?"

Max nodded. "Dakota Hale."

"As your principal beneficiary." He cocked his head. "Hale," he said. "Wasn't your house in the Hamptons owned by Elliott Hale?"

"That's correct. She's his niece."

"I see. Well, this is a straightforward change. Your father was the principal beneficiary before. Would you like to leave him anything in the new will?" he asked.

"Yes. Ten million." Though his father would reject that, too. Max had already attempted to win his forgiveness before with gifts. Every check he'd mailed had been returned to his bank. Pretty clear, as messages went. "If my father predeceases me, however, I'd like that sum to be divided among the other bequests." He'd left money to UPenn, to cancer research, and to the Detroit Museum of Art, which Rosie had always loved visiting.

He waited while Roger finished entering his notes on his computer. One of the things he liked about Roger was how thorough he was. Few details escaped him, his connecting Dakota with Windhaven a case in point. "I'd also like to include a trust fund for my child."

Roger frowned. "Why not wait until—"

Time to drop the next bombshell. "Dakota's due at the end of August. If I die before the baby arrives, I want to make sure the trust is in place." Many might deem him paranoid to be imagining his death when he was a healthy male in his mid-thirties, but Max knew too well that death came like a thief in the night.

"A child." Roger cleared his throat. "Well, my sincere congratulations to you both."

Max inclined his head. "Thanks. You have three, right? Kids, I mean."

With a smile, Roger gestured at the picture frames lining the window ledge to Max's left. "Aaron, Leah, and Rachel."

Max made himself look at the pictures he'd always ignored. "So, Aaron—he's what, nine?"

"That's right. A huge Mets fan."

"I'm sorry."

Roger laughed. "I like to think that being a Mets fan is character-building. I'm taking him to Florida to see them practice during spring training. It'll be our first trip alone together."

Max thought of the tiny blob he'd seen on the monitor and how one day it would be old enough to have a favorite baseball or football team and obsess about stats, and he tried not to panic.

"So, Max, with regards to the will, I can get it drawn up by our trusts and estates guy and have it ready to sign by tomorrow."

"Great."

"You and Dakota might want to discuss whom to name as guardian for your child," he said.

"I think we'd both be comfortable asking Alex Miller. I'll get back to you as soon as I've talked with Dakota and him."

"Sounds good."

He began to rise from his chair, already calculating how long it would take to stop off at Tiffany's when Roger spoke.

"Max, one more thing."

He eased back down in the chair and raised an inquiring brow.

"As your general counsel, I feel a responsibility to ask. Have you broached the topic of a prenup with Dakota?"

"A prenup?" He shook his head. "No."

"You're a very wealthy man, Max. It would be in your best interest to draft one. The agreement doesn't have to penalize Dakota, but it would protect you. To marry without one would be to leave you exposed. With the right divorce lawyer, she could take you to the cleaners."

What Roger said might be true. But the memory of Dakota's

stricken expression when he'd accused her of using the pregnancy to get at his money was still vivid in Max's mind. What he'd said shamed him, and his only excuse was that he'd been in a blind panic at the thought of a baby, of his being responsible for another person. He wouldn't have that excuse now, however, were he to present Dakota with a prenup that coldly set out the division of his wealth and holdings should they go their separate ways. It would mean that once again he'd introduced money into the discussion. She would undoubtedly think he still suspected her of being after as much of it as she could get her hands on.

Dakota would sign the agreement; she knew how the world worked. But with the prenup between them, the chance of their fragile relationship succeeding would be that much slimmer.

"That may be true, Rog," he conceded. "But I'm going to have to take the risk." He'd have to trust her.

"Max, please," Roger said. "Please think this through more carefully. How well do you know her?"

"Well enough to know that she's entering this marriage only because I urged her to and because she wants what's best for our child. The only thing I have is money, Roger. If we divorce and she ends up wanting the lion's share, well—" He broke off to shrug philosophically. "It won't be the first bet I've lost."

It would only be the most important.

Dakota was waiting outside the town hall, her shoulders hunched inside her shearling coat, her chin and lips covered by her scarf, when Max arrived. She watched him stride up the walkway, listened to the crunch of the ice melt that had been scattered along the cement, and fought a sense of unreality. She was going to wake up any second and be the Dakota she knew.

"I didn't keep you waiting?" he asked when he reached her. She was acutely aware that he'd stopped a good two feet away and hadn't attempted to kiss her. A handshake would have hardly been more awkward.

She shook her head and tugged her scarf down. "I had some things to do in town." An emergency haircut and manicure, her first stab at looking somewhat less pitiful.

"You ready, then?" His tone was neutral.

She could say no. She could walk down that path, get back in her car, and have a different life. He would still be a father to her child. She wasn't even completely sure she wanted more from him. But as she looked at him, looked past the handsome features, she saw something that made her heart ache. "Yes, I'm ready."

He held her gaze a second longer, as if he, too, was searching for something. She wondered if he'd found it. "Okay, then."

She turned toward the entrance.

"Dakota, wait."

Something lodged in her windpipe at the sudden notion that maybe he'd thought better of it, had recognized how insane they were to be taking this next step. She turned back mutely.

"Here." In his hand was a small box. He opened it, and a diamond reflected the winter light. "Even the shortest engagement in history should be marked by a ring, right?" he said quietly.

She stared at it, the lump in her throat exponentially larger.

"The design of the two small bands—the jeweler said the way they're studded with smaller diamonds is called pavé—encircling the round diamond in the center reminded me of a wave, so I thought you might like it. Tiffany's will be happy to exchange—"

"No. It's beautiful." She looked up, blinking rapidly to stem the betraying tears. "Thank you, Max."

He took the ring out, and she hurriedly pulled off her glove. Deliberately he slid it on her finger, and for a second they both stared at her hand.

Clearing his throat, he said, "Let's go get that license."

*

In the Hamptons, it took less time to get a marriage license than to obtain a beach parking permit. Fifteen minutes later, she and Max walked out of the town hall, the inside pocket of Max's suit jacket holding the completed form that had been duly witnessed by a bored-looking clerk.

"Do you want to go somewhere and talk? Are you hungry?" he asked as they walked toward the parking lot. "Then maybe we can go look at wedding bands."

"Sure." She glanced at her left hand, still stunned at her engagement ring's beauty, at Max's thoughtfulness. "Why don't we go to Babette's? It's on Newtown Lane."

"Yeah, I've seen it. Meet you there."

Life in the off-season meant that parking spots actually existed and tables at popular restaurants didn't require advance reservations. The server led them to a corner table and, since the restaurant was half empty, took their order promptly.

When the server returned with their food and drinks, Max took a huge bite out of his cheeseburger and then a healthy swallow of his beer. Dakota ate her omelet more cautiously and made sure to nibble on her toast between forkfuls.

It didn't take long for Max's burger to disappear. He attacked the mound of sweet potato fries next. "So you mentioned conditions the other night."

Dakota set down her fork and took a sip of water. "Yes."

She should have blurted out everything at once when they'd talked on the telephone, she thought. Then all this would be behind them and not another set of hurdles to negotiate. But then again, maybe this was what marriage was all about.

If so, she had to begin as she meant to go on. "First of all, I'd like to contribute as much as I can financially to our expenses."

His hand hovered over a fry. "You know that's not necessary."

"It is. I meant what I said about not being after your money, Max. I'm working out a budget so that I'll know roughly how much I can afford to chip in and still cover operating costs for Premier Service. Plus, if we're living together, I can rent my house and bring in some revenue there."

"Okay. We can talk more once we have your budget finished and I see your figures."

"Second, I need to be able to surf. I noticed how you reacted at Dr. Davis's," she continued more gently. "I promise I won't take my board out when the waves are dicey."

"And you won't go out alone. I'll come with you."

"But what if you're working or traveling on business? Or what if I just need to get out on the water? It's where I go to find my balance, Max."

He looked like he wanted nothing more than to shut down the conversation. "Then you'll have to make sure one of your surf buddies is with you."

"That's like having a babysitter."

"You've talked about what you need, Dakota. This is what *I* need."

He was right, she thought with an inward sigh. She couldn't be the one making demands and be totally unwilling to compromise. She gave a small nod. "All right, I can do that."

"Next?"

"Oh!" she said, taken aback. Somehow she'd expected him to belabor the point. But then it occurred to her how much he must detest revealing any vulnerability. She scrambled for the list she'd mentally organized and realized she'd covered the most pressing items. "Other than us sleeping apart—"

"Don't worry, I haven't forgotten that one." He picked up his beer and took a slug.

She blushed. "Well, then that's all."

"And the separate beds? Is there a time frame we're looking at?"

She glanced down at her knotted hands and resisted fiddling with her ring. "Yes, I suppose so. But I'm not exactly sure what it is. I know we're getting married. And obviously there's a physical attraction between us. But I just need to feel right about our being together again. Because this is different." She looked up and knew her expression must be imploring him to understand. "Okay?"

"Yeah." He pushed his plate aside. "Okay."

"Thank you. Max—" she began again, but soon fell silent. She hated how awkward this was.

He cocked his head. "What?"

"With how quickly we've been moving to make the marriage official, I realize you might not have had enough time to draw up a prenup. I'd understand if you'd feel more comfortable with one in place to protect your assets."

For the first time since she'd seen him today, the ghost of a smile lifted the corners of his mouth. "My firm's general counsel would like you. He spent a good portion of our meeting this morning trying to convince me of the necessity of having one."

"He failed?" She didn't hide her surprise.

"My gut told me it would be a lousy way to start this marriage. I decided it would be better if I simply trusted you not to take all my worldly goods."

She shook her head and laughed softly.

"What's so funny?" he asked, his own smile growing.

"Piper told me I was a fool not to insist on a prenup and that without one, you'd divorce me and leave me high and dry. That's a direct quote."

"Ah. So would you like a prenup as added security?"

"No, because I trust you."

Something flickered in his eyes. He reached across the table and laid his hand over hers, squeezing it lightly. "How about we prove them wrong? Shall we give it a try?"

"I'd like that. And Max, there's something else. Would you be all right with my taking your name? I've decided I'd much rather be a Carr than a Hale."

CHAPTER TWENTY-EIGHT

Maybe Martin Geller, the county clerk who'd agreed to officiate at their wedding, was as moved by the sight of Dakota in a figure-skimming cream knit dress as Max was. Geller, a pallid, balding guy with a paunch that spoke of too many hours behind the desk of his drab office, turned what Max was fairly certain was normally a routine recitation into a flowery speech about Max and Dakota's love being an inspiration to others and how he hoped it would grow deeper and sweeter with each passing year. He talked about them being helpmates, supporting and encouraging each other on a long and beautiful journey. How they should share both their laughter and their tears along the way.

Max would have much preferred the abridged, cut-and-dried version. He was fairly certain that Dakota, standing next to him with her hands clasped tightly in front of her, would have, too.

Geller's exhortation wasn't the only thing rattling Max. Dakota smelled amazing. Her perfume was the same one she'd worn on the night of Gen and Alex's party. With every breath, the scent teased him and jogged his memory, reminding him of the hours he'd spent exploring the valleys and hollows of her body. He hadn't been with another woman since her—not even when he'd been loaded on New Year's Eve—wanting only to be with Dakota, hear her cries of need and watch her face as she came. That hadn't changed.

And now, to stand so close to her . . . it was torture.

His thoughts were interrupted by the sound of a discreet cough. Max shifted his gaze from the framed map of Suffolk County hanging on the opposite wall to the clerk's bespectacled face.

"Do you have the rings?" Geller asked.

As Dakota murmured a yes, Max fished the band from his suit pocket.

Geller waited as they turned to face each other.

Dakota's eyes were enormous. He felt himself falling into their dark pools.

"Max, if you'll repeat after me: 'Dakota, I give this ring as token and pledge and as a sign of my love and devotion. With this ring, I thee wed.'"

Dakota's hand was cold and trembled in his as he spoke the vow. Reaching the word "wed," he slid the pavé diamond band, a match to her engagement ring, on her finger, and heard her breath catch.

She's mine. The thought filled his head and made his heart pound.

"And now, Dakota, if you'll repeat after me."

Max strained to hear Dakota's voice over the noise inside him as she took his left hand and pushed the platinum band up the length of his ring finger. It gleamed under the fluorescent light. They'd ended up flying into the city to buy it, the offerings in East Hampton not up to Dakota's standards.

When he'd noticed the slight but marked frown on her face as she inspected the men's rings at the East Hampton jewelry store, he'd taken her aside.

"What's the matter?"

"The rings. They're just not what I want for you."

It was funny—he'd expected her to obsess over her band, but it was his own she cared about. "How's your stomach? Is it up to a helicopter ride? Tiffany's—"

She'd brightened. "Yes, Tiffany's should have a much better selection. We should go there."

He made a mental note to get excited about one of the rings at Tiffany's. Otherwise Dakota might decide to scour the city in search of the perfect band. "I'm sure they'll have what you're looking for. But you didn't answer my question about the chopper."

"I'll be fine," she'd replied stoutly.

Even at Tiffany's she'd done a Goldilocks number, studying the width of each ring, comparing flat to rounded surfaces and shiny to matte, while the jeweler patiently brought out tray after velvet-lined tray.

Max had been touched by her fussiness. It was a side of her he'd yet to glimpse.

And now the ring that Dakota had selected with such care was on his finger. It felt weighted by more than the dense metal. She didn't know what he was really like. Would she still want to be with him—

"And now, Max," Martin Geller said, "you may kiss the bride."

Dakota tilted her head to meet his gaze. She looked nervous and achingly beautiful.

His lips settled over hers. His pulse quickened as he tasted her soft lips and then lightly traced the seam between them with his tongue. A fierce exultation swept him when her jaw softened and her lips parted and her tongue advanced to meet him in a caressing slide. God, she was hot and so incredibly sweet. His hand tightened about her shoulder, and if Martin Geller hadn't been standing two feet away, he'd have hauled her close and devoured her, so intense was his need for her.

But she'd said she needed time.

With a silent groan, he released her. Straightening, he stared deep into her eyes, where awareness shone bright. So she'd felt the heat, the fierce pull, even in that too-brief kiss. It gave him hope, because the one thing he understood when it came to what was going on between them was the sex. It worked.

"Congratulations to you both." Geller was beaming, as if he was stupendously proud of what he'd accomplished in this drab office. "I wish you both great happiness."

"Thank you, Martin," Dakota said, and leaned forward to kiss him on the cheek.

"Yes." Max shook his hand, then removed an envelope from his pocket and passed it to the clerk. "Thank you."

"My pleasure. My pleasure." Geller rocked on his heels. "Off on your honeymoon now?"

"Uh . . ." At a loss, Dakota colored.

"We'll be taking our honeymoon later," Max said, covering for her. "Dakota's busy interviewing employees for Premier Service and I have several projects that need my attention."

"Oh! Of course."

"We should be going, Dakota. We've got that photography session."

"Your wedding day portraits?" Geller asked with another broad smile. The man was clearly a closet romantic.

"That's right. Thanks again, Martin, and please give my regards to your parents," Dakota said.

"I will. They were so excited to hear you were getting married. You certainly kept the news under wraps."

"Yes, we did. But it's official now, so feel free to spread the word." Geller seemed like someone who'd enjoy sharing the news of their wedding, and Max wanted people to know not only that Dakota and he had married but also that, far from taking a hit, Dakota's business was thriving.

Her damn aunt was not going to win either the battle or the war.

Max and Dakota had finished the photo session with Greta Krause, who wore her hair in pigtails and dressed in overalls and clogs but behind the camera lens shed her Swedish dairymaid persona. All business, she'd used a variety of filters and lenses and posed Dakota and Max in different areas in her light-filled studio, instructing them to angle their heads closer and for Max to lower his so that their eyebrows would be level—a pictorial style preferred by newspapers such as the *Times*. At the end of the shoot, she promised that the pictures would be in their inboxes later that evening to send off with the wedding announcement. Any prints they wanted would be ready by the end of the following week. Max wondered what he would see when he looked at the photos. Would the awkwardness and tension be visible despite their best smiles and artfully angled poses?

It was when they arrived at Windhaven, with the sun slipping toward the horizon, that it hit him: ever since the visit to Dr. Davis's and looking at the ultrasound monitor and seeing the shape that would become their child, he'd been driving them toward this moment. Now they were here, embarking on their married life, and he knew to the bottom of his soul that they were both feeling utterly lost.

Max was used to taking risks in business, in ball games. In those, the downside was limited. At worst, you lost a boatload of money, and it made stringing together the next deal on the table that much harder. In a ball game, you threw a pass and it got knocked down. You got sacked. Then you'd have to hunker down and figure out how to regain those lost yards. Sure, maybe you'd get your ass handed to you, maybe you'd get carried off the field, but most likely you'd have a chance to rally and pull off another win. He'd studied and trained equally hard for those situations.

Nothing had prepared him—there was no deal book, no playbook to scrutinize—for what would happen if he screwed up with Dakota. And what of the costs if he did blow it?

The click of Dakota unfastening her seatbelt pulled him from his thoughts. Hurriedly he followed suit and opened his door to jog around to Dakota's side. "Here," he said, helping her out.

"Thanks," she murmured, equally polite, equally careful.

The house was ablaze with lights. Among the long list of stuff he'd tended to since getting Dakota to agree to marry him, he'd asked Rae to pack up the things Dakota would immediately want—clothes, toiletries, makeup, surfboards, books, computer, the glass bowl of shells and sea glass that she collected on her beach walks, and anything else Rae thought would make her more comfortable, more at *home*—and bring them to Windhaven. He'd given her their schedule. She must have done the math and realized they'd be returning in the falling light. Dakota had a smart deputy.

Dakota stood stiff and too quiet while he unlocked the front door and pushed it open. When he stepped back she took a step forward. His command of "Wait!" stopped her long enough for him to bend down and scoop her into his arms.

"Max! What are you doing? I weigh—"

"Next to nothing," he finished as he carried her across the threshold. He hadn't the foggiest idea what the tradition symbolized other than to give the groom a chance to flex his muscles and prove his physical strength, but he wasn't going to jinx their marriage by ignoring it. They had enough obstacles to overcome.

Still cradling her, he entered the foyer and set her down slowly, reluctantly.

Her eyes met his for all of a millisecond, then she turned to look about her, as if she'd never stepped foot inside his house. Something caught her attention, and she started in surprise. Rae had placed Dakota's bowl of seashells on the table that stood beneath the stairs.

"I asked Rae to bring some of your things over. Clothes and stuff."

She gave him a soft smile, and he revised his opinion of Rae from smart to brilliant for putting the bowl where Dakota would be sure to see it.

From her gasp of pleasure as she entered the living room, he realized that wasn't all Rae had done. Flowers in lush arrangements were everywhere. Some of the more opulent ones had cards attached with congratulations from Lauren, Gen and Alex, Dakota's friends Hendrick Daube and Marcus Field, and even Roger and Robin Cohen.

The dining room table was set for two with candles and another floral arrangement, this one with huge, deep red roses. Max was starting to think that Rae and her crew must have raided every florist from Montauk to the city.

Yes, definitely, he thought when he and Dakota walked into the kitchen and found yet another bouquet, this one beside a bottle of Dom Pérignon nestling in an ice bucket.

Both the magnificent flowers and the champagne were dwarfed by the wedding cake next to it. The cake was decorated with chocolate seashells and swirls of vanilla frosting made to look like cresting waves. On top, in place of the bride and groom, were two very different figurines: two surfers crouched over their boards, shredding a wave.

"Oh my God. The cake is so great," she whispered, bending over to inspect the details more closely. "I love it."

"Yeah," he said. Dakota had mentioned that Rae had just bought a house. She was going to have her mortgage paid off very quickly. "There's another card," he said, pointing.

Dakota picked up the envelope and then extended it in invitation. "Do you want to read it first?"

"Go ahead. You can read it aloud."

There was a wobbly note to her voice as she began. "'To Dakota and Max—We wish you a lifetime of joy together. To start your first evening off right, in the fridge you'll find caviar and canapés to accompany the champagne—as well as ginger ale for Dakota after her first celebratory coupe. Dinner will be delivered from the Palm at eight o'clock. Enjoy it, Mr. and Mrs. Carr. With all our love, Rae, Lupe, and Jarrett.'"

Dakota put the card down and burst into tears.

Oh hell.

Trying to stem the embarrassing stream of tears, Dakota flapped her hands, surely looking as emotionally wrecked as she felt.

"I'm fine, I'm fine," she insisted, while sniffing and brushing her cheeks. "It's just—"

It was all too much. Max behaving with such unwavering, perfect consideration; the wedding ceremony driving home how serious and real the marriage was, when Dakota had almost convinced herself it was more of a convenience, a well-intentioned arrangement; and, topping it off, a kiss leaving her wanting and needing and so terribly confused about how to proceed.

Here they were in a house they were meant to share, surrounded by gifts from their friends, gestures of hope and support. Their friends believed she and Max were serious about making a go of it, which was what she'd essentially promised Max when she'd agreed to prove the likes of Piper and Max's cautious lawyer wrong. And wasn't that what she'd *vowed* to him in Martin

Geller's office? To share her laughter and her tears as Max's partner? To be his lover and his best friend?

She hadn't simply picked Martin to officiate because she was sure he would be available even on short notice. She'd also asked him because she half agreed with Piper's damning assessment: Martin was kind but as dry as the slices of toast Dakota had been eating and was now heartily sick of. She'd believed his delivery of the wedding vows would be equally bland. Easily digestible, instantly forgotten. Yet he'd surprised her with a ceremony that was emotional and profound. The words had pierced her heart; Max slowly sliding the wedding band onto her finger as he promised to honor and cherish her had shredded it.

How would Martin have reacted had he any inkling as he presided over the service or when he inquired about their honeymoon that, far from celebrating their nuptials, she'd banned Max from her bed?

That was one mark against her already. But even aside from the sex, Dakota had doubts about how much of a friend—forget *best* friend—she was being to Max. At this point he was the one stepping up and exerting all the effort to make this marriage work.

Max was sharing his name and his house, and trying to think of her comfort and the baby's well-being. What was she sharing in turn?

So far it seemed that all she was offering him were her tears, which, despite her repeated sniffing and wiping, kept coming. While she tried to get her emotions under control, Max stood looking on, agonized and at a complete loss.

Was he already regretting signing his name to the marriage certificate?

It occurred to her that she had no template to show her how to go forward. Obviously she couldn't look to Piper, Mimi, or anyone else in her family as a model for a happy union. Nor did stories and movies provide much help. In them, the wedding ceremony, with its sublimely romantic kiss between the couple, was where there was a fade to black. And that was it. The end. The audience closed the book or filed out of the movie theater, convinced of the characters' happily-ever-after.

Dakota wanted a happily-ever-after, too. But could she and Max manage one when they'd done everything backward?

She looked at the wedding cake, so lovely, funny, and perfect, and then at the champagne chilling on ice. This was their wedding day. A bride and groom shouldn't be standing in stiff misery in the kitchen; they should be upstairs, tearing at their clothes and making good on the vows to worship each other's bodies in a physical expression of their love.

And she'd told him she didn't want to have sex.

What if, by some miracle, she and Max defied probability and actually made it as a couple? How would she feel remembering this day, this evening, if it ended by their retiring to separate rooms, perhaps not even managing to exchange a kiss goodnight? How deep and choking would her regret be?

She remembered Max telling her he still wanted her. His words had caused a delicious heat to unfurl low in her belly. In the upheaval of her unplanned pregnancy, she'd welcomed that feeling, had reveled in being desired, in being the Dakota she knew rather than the one she was becoming. When he'd kissed her this afternoon, their first kiss as husband and wife, those feelings were reawakened. His mouth, his nearness, and the warm weight of his hand on her shoulder had effortlessly aroused her.

She wanted him, too.

What would denying him—denying them both—accomplish? She half suspected that as time passed, it would ultimately become about exerting her will and thwarting his, a far cry from the reason she'd given him of needing space to find mental and emotional clarity. Besides, she wasn't sure that spending sleepless nights in a room down the hall from Max was any way to gain peace of mind.

Max had moved to the sink and was running the tap. Quickly she rubbed her eyes and then gave what she hoped was a final sniff. Unfortunately, the noise was amplified in the sudden silence as Max shut off the water. She watched him stand over the sink for a second longer and then draw his shoulders back as if bracing himself before he turned, a glass of water in his hand. He walked over to her and held it out. "This might help."

She accepted it with a quiet "Thank you" and sipped it slowly before setting the glass on the counter. She glanced at the cake and the champagne and drew a breath.

"Max—"

"Listen—"

They broke off. After an awkward pause, Max said, "Go ahead."

"No, you go."

"All I was going to say was that I know how tired you are. Perhaps you want to go upstairs and rest before dinner."

Alone.

"And what about you?"

"Me?" He rubbed the back of his neck as if easing tense muscles. "I'll catch up on some work. Watch the news, maybe." He shrugged.

"That's a terrible idea."

He looked surprised, which kind of annoyed her. Did he really expect her to leave him to source companies and devise investment strategies on their wedding day? Actually, that was probably exactly what he thought. And how depressing was that?

"So what do you want to do instead?" He was still being solicitous, but she heard the fatigue in his voice.

She stepped closer to him. "I'd like to go into the living room and put on some music and dance with you." She laid her hand against the fine cotton of his shirt and felt the heat of his muscular chest and the heavy thud of his heart.

Their eyes met and held. The wary tension in his expression eased. As his face relaxed, he gave her a smile that made her toes curl inside her high-heeled pumps.

"Is that so?"

Her hand slid up and she snagged his tie and tugged, bringing his mouth within reach of hers. She kissed him lightly but deliberately, then stepped back, an answering smile lifting her cheeks. "Yeah, that's so."

"Gotta say, I like your plan a hell of a lot better."

They didn't make it up the stairs, at least not the first time. Dakota happily took the blame. In the half-dimmed lights of the living room, surrounded by the gorgeous flower arrangements with their heady scents, they held each other, their bodies brushing as they swayed to the strains of REM, Brian Ferry, Van Morrison, the Eagles, and the Rolling Stones. Eyes locked, their breath mingled and then joined as they kissed slowly, deeply.

To the wailing of Prince's guitar, Dakota unknotted Max's tie and unbuttoned his dress shirt. Her hands roved, relearning muscled contours. Her mouth trailed, tasting anew. She traced the puckered flesh of his nipples, palmed the heaving ridges of his abdomen, fingered the line of hair that led south from his navel.

He stayed her when her hands met at his belt buckle. "Dakota," he groaned. "Wait."

"I can't. I want you, Max." In admitting her desire, she was now consumed by it. Its flames licked her, drove her.

"I want us to go slow," he insisted. "I don't want to hurt you."

"Max, I need you. We can go slow the next time. You won't

hurt me or the baby." Realizing it was time for more honesty, she said, "I've really missed you."

"Ah, Jesus, Dakota," he whispered. His hands fell away, freeing hers. And while she worked at his buckle, and then the button and zipper of his trousers, his hands moved to her hips. Walking his fingers, he gathered her dress inch by inch, then pulled it up her body and over her shoulders and head.

"You're as beautiful as I remember." Lowering his head to the hollow of her neck, he ran his mouth along her collarbone. With a deft flick, he unsnapped her bra, his hands replacing the satin and lace that had covered her.

She gasped. She didn't know whether it was the acute pleasure of being in Max's arms again, of being lavished with expert caresses and kisses, or if it was the effect of exchanging vows with Max—perhaps it was all combined into one combustible whole—but she was already close to climaxing. Need racked her entire body.

Tugging his briefs down, she wrapped her hand around his erection. He felt bigger. Harder.

A shudder went through them both.

"Max, please, I need to have you inside me. Now."

She sank to her knees and then lay back on the thick Oriental rug. Max followed her down. Bracing himself with one arm, he hovered above her. She wanted his weight over her, wanted him inside her. She opened her legs in invitation, felt the blunt head of his penis, and held her breath in anticipation.

When he froze and whispered, "Damn," she searched his face. "What's wrong?"

"Condom. I didn't— They're upstairs."

"Max." She bit her lip, hard. "I'm pregnant, you know."

"But—"

"You told Dr. Davis you'd been tested."

"Yes, but I've always worn a condom—"

"Me too." She ran her hands down the length of his back and spread them wide when she reached the taut globes of his butt. "So this would be a first ... for both of us."

Something flared in his eyes, beautiful and mesmerizing. "It would."

She lifted her head to brush his lips with hers. "Then would you please be so kind as to rock my world?"

He smiled. "I'll see what I can do."

CHAPTER TWENTY-NINE

It worried Max that he might be falling for his wife. Eight weeks had passed since he'd slipped a wedding ring on her finger, since he'd made love to her, stroking her as she arched and cried his name, clenching his bared flesh so sweetly. The sexual pleasure hadn't merely been heightened; that night it had felt profound. Left him shaken, and yet craving her all the more.

Amazingly, his need for Dakota remained as fresh, as piercing, and as troubling as ever.

Yet no matter how clearly he saw the danger before him and all the risks inherent with caring too much, he couldn't stay away from her. As with their lovemaking, whether straight-up missionary and sweet or wild and raunchy, he found himself wanting it all, from the sublime to the humdrum domestic.

Without either of them consciously creating one, they'd established a routine. During the week, he took an early flight into the city and returned in time for a late dinner. When it was impossible to avoid a business dinner or schmooze a new contact, he would spend the night in the city, but only if the evening ended very late. Otherwise, he far preferred arranging for a town car to drive him back to East Hampton and sleep with his arms around Dakota. On the weekends they surfed and then afterward, following a hot shower and hotter sex, he cajoled her into eating as big a breakfast as she could stomach. In the afternoon, if the weather held, they bundled up for a walk on the beach, sometimes talking, at other times content to listen to the wind and to the roll and scrape of pebbles with each advance and retreat of the waves. She'd bought another glass bowl and started a new collection of shells and sea glass; he refused to analyze how much that pleased him.

When the weather was too cold or blustery, they hung out at home, sitting on the sofa by the fire, he researching potential companies and catching up on his reading, she doing her course work or talking on her cell to potential clients in her low, husky voice. When she hung up, he often had to pull her down onto the cushions and get her naked. Her voice continued to do things to him.

The wedding announcements had done their job, successfully stymieing her aunt Mimi. Dakota's clients had been wowed that she was now married to "one of their own." Dakota had also launched a vigorous counterattack, campaigning hard for new clients by placing ads in luxury mags, as well as on websites and blogs devoted to the Hamptons. In a stroke of serendipity, Tom Hunter, an A-list Hollywood actor who'd been friends with Dakota when they were kids and who was one of her long-standing clients, got in touch with her about overseeing the refurbishment of his East Hampton property. She and Astrid and their crews had been at work on the house for the past month.

Max admitted to being impressed. Hunter had done everything—coming-of-age movies, action flicks, gritty dramas, indie projects—and was always worth watching. Naturally he'd quizzed her about the star . . . to no avail. She'd shaken her head, given an impish smile, and said, "I'm afraid I can't discuss Mr. Hunter with you. I take my nondisclosure agreements *very* seriously."

The day he received the letter from the Maidstone Club offering him membership, Dakota had crowed with delight. The thing that got him was that she didn't even like golf and, as soon as he finished reading the letter, had informed him he'd be on his own—or with his business pals—when it came to hitting the links. No, her satisfaction came from knowing that her aunt hadn't been successful in blackballing him from the club.

In addition to being a vindictive witch, Mimi Hale Walsh was a sore loser. She hadn't stopped trying to make life hell for Dakota, continuing to badmouth her wherever and whenever she could. It was obnoxious and embarrassing, and why Dakota's mother not only sat back and let it happen but also called to whine about how unpleasant this was for *her* and that Dakota should really do something about it, Max couldn't figure out.

It was good that Dakota had such great friends, because she had a seriously lousy family. Since he was hardly in a position to dispense advice when it came to such matters, he kept his mouth shut. But he didn't like how unhappy Dakota was after her mother's calls.

Fortunately, the baby was doing well, and that went a long way toward banishing the noxiousness of Piper's conversations.

Dakota had seen Dr. Davis twice. The first visit had been to recheck Dakota's blood, blood pressure, and weight. As he'd watched the blood being drawn, he'd done his best to remain calm, telling himself that it was okay that Dakota was still puking in the mornings—at least she wasn't losing all her meals—and found himself willing the vials of dark red blood to be healthy.

But he hadn't realized the depths of his anxiety until Dr. Davis entered the exam room with a smile on her face. Dakota had gained three pounds. Better still, her iron level was now within the normal range. The blood was good.

"So we're out of the woods?" Dakota had asked.

Dr. Davis had nodded. "I'm very happy to see these numbers getting to where they should be. Congratulations, Dakota. You're doing a good job taking care of yourself."

Busy dealing with the relief flooding him, he'd concentrated on breathing evenly while he stared at the lines of the tiled floor.

Then Dakota said, "It's Max you should congratulate, Dr. Davis. He's been a tyrant—a benevolent one, but still."

"Well, keep it up, Max, and you'll have a healthy, happy baby and partner."

"Wife," Max had automatically corrected, earning him a surprised smile from Dakota.

The second appointment had been last week, and Dakota had had another ultrasound. He'd been stunned by how different the baby looked at fourteen weeks. Its head was defined, with ears, eyes, a nose, and a mouth—all tiny and all there. It had arms and legs, fingers and toes, and its body curled—furled—tight.

While Max had stared, cataloguing every detail of this new being, Dakota reached out and took his hand. He looked at her, and her eyes were bright with unshed tears. Her wide smile told him they were tears of joy. Somehow he knew he was included in that joy.

It blew his mind.

Because of the baby's position, Dr. Davis hadn't been able to determine its sex. That was okay. He didn't care if it was a boy or a girl; all that mattered was for the baby and Dakota to be healthy.

As for the smiles Dakota gave him, showing her happiness and sharing it with him, well, they were the reason he was presently in Sag Harbor running errands on a Saturday afternoon when he could be doing a dozen better and far more entertaining things.

One of the items on the list she'd given him was to pick up cupcakes—*cupcakes*—for the kids who were coming to the house for Sunday brunch to celebrate Steve Sheppard's making the United States Equestrian Federation's short list for the show jumping team. If he and his horses did well in the designated shows in the United States and Europe this spring, they'd be Olympics bound. Kind of cool. They would also be unveiling Gen Monaghan's new painting, which now hung in a prominent spot in the living room. Last but not least, the brunch marked his and Dakota's first organized party as a couple.

After picking up the ordered cupcakes and buying another cake for the hell of it, he walked back to Main Street, where he'd parked, and, on impulse, went into the jewelry store, where a necklace was displayed in the window. Made of brown and gold-streaked stones, their color reminded him of Dakota's eyes. He thought she might like it. Maybe she'd wear it while he was in California next week, he thought as he thanked the saleswoman, took the gift bag from her, and stepped back outside.

He was flying out for the closing between AB1, the robotics company, and a German corporation that was acquiring it lock, stock, and barrel. Max didn't relish going away, but now that Dr. Davis had reassured them that both Dakota and the baby were doing okay, he couldn't foist the trip off on one of his associates. The sale was his show, and a mega-hit at that.

He should have been excited about it.

Perhaps he would have been if he hadn't been pissed at Bob Elders for taking Chris Steffen's side. Steffen had gone behind Max's back to bitch about him, leading Bob to call Max into his office and lecture him about how brilliant Steffen was—translation: how much money he was going to make them—and how they needed to keep him happy.

On the sidewalk he glanced at Dakota's list. His next destination was Wainscott, where he had to pick up smoked salmon at the Seafood Shop. *Right*, he thought, and shoved the slip of paper back into the rear pocket of his jeans. Looking up, he saw the sign for Sagtown Coffee. The café was tucked away at the end of a brick-lined side alley. In solidarity with Dakota's caffeine-free existence, he'd been cutting back on his intake, but he could really go for a triple espresso right now. Maybe the jolt would remind him of his former self and what he'd been like before he'd gotten hung up on Dakota's smile, before he'd gotten tied in knots over a baby.

The small café was fairly crowded, but he found a table. He had his phone out and was checking his messages and sipping his espresso when a woman's bag, the kind that was nearly as big as the carry-on he'd be packing for his flight to California, banged his shoulder, sloshing coffee over his fingers.

"Shit." He cast an irritated glare at the owner of the bag. She was blond, tall, and thin, dressed in tight jeans and a silver down jacket.

"Sorry," she said in the kind of bored voice that announced she didn't give a rat's ass that she'd nearly sent his coffee flying, and glanced over her shoulder at him. She seemed to do a double take, and then laughed in throaty delight. "Well, well. At long last we meet."

He looked at her blankly, wondering why she would know him. She was older but, like many New York women he'd encountered, impeccably maintained, with glowing skin and few wrinkles, so he couldn't tell by how much. She was quite beautiful, with high cheekbones and a mouth that was now curved in a provocative smile.

His lack of recognition seemed to amuse her, though he detected a hard glint in her bright blue eyes.

"Now that I've seen you in the flesh, I understand why Dakota keeps putting me off. I'd want you all to myself, too." She extended a slender manicured hand. "I'm Piper."

Piper? Dakota's mother? Stunned, he rose automatically and shook her hand. "Hello." He didn't think saying "Good to meet you" quite fit when encountering one's mother-in-law for the first time. And what a mother-in-law, he thought. "Would you like to sit down?"

She smiled. "I would." All lanky grace, she lowered herself into the chair. Then, propping her elbows on the table, she leaned forward as if they were alone in the world. Her leg brushed his.

Max stilled. It wasn't as if he was unused to women flirting with him. But having the mother of his wife do so . . . that was a different kind of beast. He made sure his left hand rested on the table, his wedding band front and center.

"So how is Dakota doing? She looked rather wan the last time I saw her." She didn't sound terribly concerned.

Had Dakota shared Dr. Davis's initial concerns about her low weight, blood pressure, and iron levels? If she hadn't, it probably wasn't his place to do so, which was fine by him. He had no desire to wade into murky familial waters.

"She's doing great. She looks terrific."

She smiled and made an amused sound, as if she thought he was sweet for saying so. Okay, so she was one of those who didn't like to hear another woman complimented. It probably bugged the hell out of her that Dakota was ten times more beautiful.

"Dakota's always been so stubbornly conventional." She lowered a hand from her chin to trace idle patterns on the wood table. "Sometimes I have a hard time believing she's my child. . . ."

Funny, he thought. He was having a hard time, too.

"So imagine my surprise when she went and got herself pregnant. I'd always been sure she'd marry one of her incredibly doltish boyfriends before producing the requisite two children. Has she suggested Haven as a name?"

He was stuck on the doltish boyfriends. He didn't like thinking of Dakota with former boyfriends, whether dolts or Einstein geniuses. Damn, falling for her was bad enough. Was he also becoming jealous of her past? "Haven?" he repeated.

"Well, Windhaven would hardly work, but Haven might. Then she'd be following my example there, too." She cocked her head. "Hasn't she told you why she's named Dakota?"

He'd asked her about it, sure. It had been a Saturday after they'd gotten together. They'd been driving back from Ditch Plains. He'd asked why someone from an old Hamptons family had a given name like Dakota. She'd stared out the passenger window for several seconds before answering. "Just one of my mother's whims."

Clearly there was more to the story. Max didn't like going behind Dakota's back, but he was curious as to what her mother would say.

"No, I don't believe she has," he said.

"Really?" Her jacket made a slithery sound when she shrugged, as if she were at a loss to understand Dakota's motive. "As I said, she's stubbornly conventional. I named her after the Dakota in New York City. It's where she was conceived. I was there for a party, an utterly wild and fabulous bash where anything goes. I'm sure you know the kind."

It bothered him that he did. And that he'd known women just like Piper Hale.

"And there was this fantastic man." She picked up her coffee and took a sip. Setting the cup down, she licked her lip, upping the flirt level to an eleven. "You remind me of him—except for the coloring, of course. Well, we made very good use of one of the palatial bathrooms." She smiled. "When Dakota came along, I thought it only appropriate to name her after the place where she was created. So wouldn't Haven be funny and just so perfect?"

"I think not."

"Oh well." She made a moue of disappointment. "You know, I've been meaning to drop by and see the old family digs."

"Dakota's done a fantastic job with the renovation."

"At least she inherited something from me. But I'll reserve judgment until I see it for myself." Her finger had resumed tracing patterns on the table, inching ever closer to his hand. He thanked God there was a table between them.

"Dakota could use your help." He had no idea why he said it.

She looked at him, her expression quizzical. "What do you mean, 'help'?"

"Help. Support. Your sister's still doing a hatchet job on her. I think Dakota would appreciate it if you stood up for her."

"Sorry to disappoint you, but Dakota will have to fight Mimi on her own. She's made her bed—quite literally, hasn't she? Now she can lie in it." Her smile faded as she looked at him. "You know, you have some nerve butting into our family affairs."

He shrugged. "I call it looking out for my wife. I want what's best for her. What I can't understand is why you don't. Most mothers would."

"My God, you really are full of yourself, aren't you? Where do you get off thinking you can order me about? I was right. You are just like Diego—" Stopping short, she shot him a look that should have left him bleeding on the floor. It was kind of impressive how quickly she shed her charming coquette routine.

With a finger she snagged the sleeve of her parka, exposing a gold watch, and glanced at it. "My, my, I've completely lost track of time. Funnily enough, I'm due at Mimi's. I'll tell her you and Dakota send your love, shall I?"

CHAPTER THIRTY

Max took his time unloading the Range Rover. He wasn't sure what tack to take with respect to his recent run-in with Dakota's mother, and probably would have chosen to keep it to himself had he not been convinced Piper would bring it up in conversation with Dakota.

The house, as always, was clean. Now that he'd met Piper, he understood better why Dakota relished having things neat and orderly. A mother who thrived on discord would have that effect. But as he carried the groceries inside, he noted that today the house gleamed and the scent of flowers, lemon, and beeswax filled the air; Dakota and her crew had gone to town.

Convincing Dakota to follow Dr. Davis's advice and slow down had proved harder than wheedling her into eating a midnight snack. Fortunately, Premier Service had acquired some new clients. The extra accounts plus the revamping of Tom Hunter's house had tipped the scales, requiring Dakota to hire additional staff. It was Rae who had the brilliant idea of training the new employees at Windhaven. It meant Dakota didn't have to drive from house to house to oversee their cleaning methods. Once they'd met Dakota's exacting standards, then the crew was ready to go out and conquer the world.

In the kitchen, Max left the cupcakes and the cake on the counter, stowed the perishables in the fridge and, gift bag in hand, went off in search of her.

The orange glow from the outdoor fireplace served as a beacon. He and Dakota had taken to sitting on the redesigned patio, warmed by the flames that crackled and leapt, to watch the blue-gold sky change and deepen to a rosy silvery purple. The light in the Hamptons was like nothing he'd seen before.

Dakota was on the yoga mat she'd rolled out on the bluestone patio. She must have thought she'd have more time before he returned. He wasn't much for yoga, but he was all in favor of watching her in black leggings and long-sleeved top as she lunged, planked, rose, balanced on one leg, and whatever. The fluid grace of her moves reminded him of when she was on her surfboard, riding the cresting waves with elegance and control.

Looking at her, one wouldn't guess she was pregnant. The only sign he saw so far was that her breasts were larger and even more sensitive. An excellent development. He loved that he could bring her right to the edge with just his hands and mouth massaging and teasing her taut peaks. To his surprise, he found he liked the idea of her body ripening with their child, and was impatient to see more changes.

Before stepping outside, he went into the study and grabbed a wool throw off the sofa. She turned her head at the sound of him opening the French door, and there was that smile again, the one that told Max he was in serious trouble.

"You're back," she said, straightening out of her lunge.

"Yes. Mission accomplished. Don't stop," he said. "I'll just sit here and enjoy the show."

"No, I've done enough." She came over and dropped down on the wicker sofa, tacking on a "Thanks" and scooting closer to him when he draped the throw over her legs. "You know, I really didn't like this house very much before. If you had suggested tearing it down, a part of me might have gone, 'Yeah, let's raze it to the ground.' But it would all be so different if you'd taken a wrecking ball to it." She paused to look about her. "Even this patio."

"Plus the work wouldn't be finished."

She laughed. "There's that to consider. Most likely we'd be sitting next to a cement mixer. But you know what? This house is pretty great. I was thinking that when I was doing the flowers for the living and dining room. Your presence has successfully banished the ghosts of Hales past."

If Dakota wanted to believe it was his achievement, he wasn't going to argue. But he knew it was all her. There were even moments when he thought she'd managed to banish the darkness inside him as well. "Actually, it's our house. I just leave more clothes lying around."

"That's true. You realize the very excellent closets in our house have many hangers, right?"

"Nag, nag, nag."

She elbowed him lightly. In response he draped an arm over her shoulder and pulled her close. They sat in companionable silence for a moment.

"Hendrick called to say Marcus will be joining us."

"Sounds good."

Marcus was Hendrick's partner, but, as an NYU art history professor, he spent most of his time in the city. Max was glad to hear Marcus was coming. It meant Hendrick wouldn't be quite so focused on him. He'd never seen a psychiatrist, not even after the deaths of Rosie and his mother. What was the point of talking for an hour however many sessions a week about his loss? What purpose would it serve? Rosie would still be dead. So would his mother. And his father would still hate him.

There was another reason Hendrick made him uncomfortable. Max couldn't shake the feeling that Hendrick didn't think him worthy of Dakota. That Max agreed with him didn't make for great conversation. It struck Max suddenly that he hadn't felt any sense of unworthiness when he was with Piper. She hadn't made him squirm with a single *Prove to me you're good enough for my daughter* or *Will you promise to treat her right?* How telling.

"I may have to make an extra frittata and salad," Dakota announced, her thoughts clearly traveling down a different path.

"I vote for that pasta salad."

"The one with zucchini and mozzarella?"

"Yeah."

"I think I have the ingredients. Did you get all the stuff, by the way?"

"Everything on the list. And a cake that in my opinion does not need to be shared with guests. And speaking of stuff . . ." He picked up the gift bag and dangled it in front of her. "I bought you this."

"For me?"

She sounded ridiculously pleased. He had a hunch that Piper probably wasn't the type to give presents, unless they had strings attached to them. "Yeah," he replied gruffly.

He watched her lift the box out and open it.

"Oh! It's lovely. Thank you." She turned and kissed the corner of his mouth. Holding the necklace up, she admired it for a moment. "I love tigereye stones. Did you know Roman soldiers wore them for protection?"

He couldn't help but grin. "The things you know."

"All thanks to a seventh-grade science report on quartz and crystals. I made a big chart with illustrations and interesting facts. I got an A." She smiled.

"Of course you did." He squeezed her shoulder.

Unclasping the necklace, she held it against the base of her throat. "Will you fasten it for me?"

He shifted. Taking the necklace from her, he brushed her hair aside and linked the ends. Then, leaning forward, he kissed the knobby bone at the top of her spine and smiled at the catch of her breath.

He'd have much preferred to continue kissing her and then easing her back in his arms so he could slide his hands inside her top and play with her breasts. They didn't need Netflix to chill. But the sooner he got the "By the way, I ran into your mother" story out in the open, the sooner he could feel like he wasn't keeping things from her. Totally hypocritical of him, when there was still so much he was concealing, but there it was.

He settled against the cushion as she turned so he could inspect his gift. "It looks really good," he said and then cleared his throat. "Guess who I met when I was grabbing a coffee at Sagtown."

She looked at him, her fingers running over the stones' smooth facets. "Who?"

"Your mother."

It had to happen, Dakota thought. The Hamptons weren't that big and people tended to keep fixed routines: morning workouts, followed by errands, a trip to the post office, then on to the grocery store. She even knew where to look for people on the beach because they either walked at the same hour—and in the same direction—or lay their towels and loungers in the same area, year after year. Stopping for coffee in the midafternoon at a hip coffee bar was another ritual, and Piper loved her nonfat lattes.

Lowering her hand to her lap, she shifted, the better to study Max's expression. "And?"

"She's certainly something." He gave nothing away.

She made an educated guess. "She hit on you."

"I wouldn't go that far."

She raised her brows.

"Okay, yeah. She was more forward than I'd expect in a mother-in-law."

Dakota wished she could sink between the sofa cushions. "It's like she has this internal switch that flips on. She has to be the center of attention," she explained. "With a man it becomes sexual. She needs to be irresistible."

"I didn't take it personally."

"There you're wrong. She'd like nothing better than to think she has what it takes to seduce you. That we're married and that she'd be showing me up, well, it would be the shiny brass ring."

"Only one problem with that plan. I wouldn't have played along. She's not my type."

She tried to smile normally, she really did. "Max," she said gently, "I did Google you." And she hated every damn photo that showed him with some leggy blond starlet hanging on his arm.

He cocked a brow, silently conceding if not apologizing for his past. "Okay, how about this, then. She's no *longer* my type. Moreover, even if she were, I generally draw the line at accepting overtures from my pregnant wife's mother. Satisfied?"

Hardly, Dakota thought. She wanted a pledge of undying love to tumble spontaneously from his lips. So far all she'd gotten were the carefully uttered words repeated at Martin Geller's instruction.

She knew Max cared. She recognized how well—amazingly

well—things were going between them. But even when they made love, it was as if there was something he was holding back. Not anything physical, but an emotional part of himself.

She was being an idiot for even contemplating pushing him for more when the marriage was still new. She needed to give him time to love her as much as she loved him.

And she'd fallen pretty desperately in love. The problem with love, she discovered, was that it didn't make you selfless. Okay, it did—she'd do almost anything for Max. But love had another side, a greedy one, and she wanted the words, she wanted the knowledge that he'd pick her over every other woman, baby or no.

Fortunately, she had fairly good impulse control, even when her mother was at her most provoking. She wasn't going to be stupid and let Piper's antics, her trial run at being the next Mrs. Robinson, come between her and Max. Not when they had their friends coming over tomorrow, not when he was set to leave for California early Monday morning. She wanted him to miss her, not to be relieved to be flying away from a jealous shrew.

With a sniff, she dredged up a smile and nodded. "Sorry. Piper pushes all my buttons."

"I can see how she would enjoy that."

She felt better when he reached up to toy with the curling ends of her hair. She didn't think he was even aware how often he did that. "So what did you two talk about?" she asked, as if the thought of her mother and Max in a tête-à-tête didn't leave a bad taste in her mouth.

"Let's see. First she regaled me with the story of how you got your name."

"She didn't. Oh God!"

"The story sounded practiced."

"It's one of her favorites. She thinks it shows she belongs to an elite club of sexually daring party girls."

He made a noise of assent. "I got that she was real pleased about it. She thinks we should name the baby Haven. As in Wind."

Dakota closed her eyes. "I am so, so sorry."

"And in the interest of full disclosure, your mother mentioned that your sperm daddy and I have a certain something in common."

"If I tell you I'm going to be sick, you realize it has nothing to do with the baby, right?"

He chuckled and brought his hands to her shoulders, rubbing the tension away. "Will it make you feel better to know that I pissed her off?"

"Infinitely." Though that wasn't exactly true, Dakota conceded silently. Even when she was infuriated with Piper, a part of her always shied away from retaliating, because Piper was fragile and needed her. And Dakota was the ever dutiful, responsible daughter who ignored her mother's bad behavior. And yes, she was quite aware how warped that was. "What did you say?" she asked.

"Nothing terribly shocking. I only suggested that I thought she should support you and stand up to your aunt Mimi."

Dakota gave an appalled laugh. "That must have gone over well."

"Yes, she took definite exception," Max said.

"Doing things for others, that's not how Piper rolls. She resents the very idea. And she's not into standing up to Mimi at all, at least not directly. I know I have a messed-up relationship with Piper, but hers and Mimi's is equally dysfunctional. It goes leagues beyond mere sibling rivalry."

"Well, she told me where I could stuff my suggestion. Said I was just like Diego."

"Who?" Frowning, she turned her head.

"She told me I was like some dude named Diego. Not a compliment. I assumed he was some overbearing bully she dated who refused to dance to her tune—or made the mistake of telling her what to do."

"That's weird. I've never heard her mention anyone named Diego—and believe me, I would have. Piper overshares. She'll call to tell me how long a guy ogled her at a bank. Are you sure that was the name?"

"Yes," he said. "Diego."

She shivered suddenly.

"Hey, you're getting chilled," Max said with a frown. "Let's go inside. I'll warm you up and make you forget about your damned mother for a while."

CHAPTER THIRTY-ONE

Max was as good as his word. Back inside, he'd made love to her, sweeping her up in the power of his body moving in her, against her, and with her. Her morning sickness had at last begun to abate, and she found herself not only regaining her former energy but also in sudden possession of a heightened sensuality. Her body had always responded to Max. Now his touch made her quicken as desire flowed through her like honey. Golden, rich, and so sweet.

He'd distracted her some more while she prepared a dinner of chicken with roasted grapes and shallots and a salad by suggesting various companies and start-ups she might want to strap her angel wings on and fund. One was a green start-up that was researching ways to clean the oceans of the plastic befouling them. Another business he mentioned, though somewhat less poetic and grand in scale, piqued her interest, too. The owner had devised a way to recycle asphalt shingles with a 100 percent raw recovery. Over the cake Max had bought—the man had a seriously sweet tooth—they'd discussed how much waste would be reduced if a company like that could grow and reach new markets.

When they went to bed that night, he lit a fire in their room. By its dancing light, they undressed each other slowly, taking the time to taste and stroke revealed flesh. Naked, he eased them down on the mattress and then lifted her so she straddled him.

Holding his gaze she rode him, rising and then falling with a low moan as he filled her. As pleasure welled, she increased her tempo, resting her hands on either side of his sweat-slicked chest. When he fondled her breasts and tweaked their aching tips, she arched and tightened around him, her climax rolling ever closer. Sensing her need, he reached down and rubbed her straining nub. His touch a trigger, it set off streaks of electric pleasure shooting through her. Overcome, she collapsed with a soft cry, her fall broken as he caught her and held her close.

Dazed and replete, she lay in his arms and watched the fire's embers dull to gray. Then there was only the warmth of his muscular body against hers, the slow, even rhythm of his breathing, and the velvety blackness surrounding them. Her heavy lids slid shut.

The next day's brunch and its preparations should have provided Dakota with an equal distraction from thoughts of Piper, but putting together Max's requested choice of pasta salad and the other dishes she'd planned, laying the table, and setting up a room for the kids to play in were Dakota's areas of expertise. Besides which, she had help from one of her new employees. Dakota was training Lucy to work at parties. Later she'd be keeping an eye on the children once they grew bored of sitting at the table.

As Dakota grilled zucchini slices, Max's account of meeting

Piper replayed in her head. Not the stuff about the origin of her name. Cringeworthy though that was, Dakota was practically inured to it. No, what she was stuck on was the identity of this mysterious Diego. Conceivably he was a new man in Piper's life—though from the sound of it, already come and gone. It was possible she'd missed hearing about him during the worst of her morning sickness. It was possible, but she didn't believe it.

Dakota was aware of the irony in her interest with this mystery man when normally her only aim was to block her mother's every utterance and act from her mind.

The brunch was as boisterous as one might imagine with nine adults and six children and congratulations being exchanged on so many fronts. But she found an opportunity to ask Hendrick, who'd arrived first with Marcus, whether he could recall Piper ever dating a man named Diego. They were in the kitchen fixing Bellinis—and a seltzer spritzer for her—while Max showed Marcus Gen's painting. Marcus was hoping to write a monograph on her work.

Hendrick paused in the midst of pulsing the frozen peaches with lemon and orange zest in the Vitamix—he was an instant convert to the super-blender. "No, I can't say I do. Should I?"

And when Dakota explained the context, he said, "Bravo to Max for saying that to her. I agree with you, whoever this Diego is, he must have left quite a mark on her. But I can't recall any gossip involving Piper and any man by that name. And you've never mentioned him." Accustomed to listening to his patients and keeping hundreds of people and story lines straight, Hendrick had a prodigious recall.

Passing the simple syrup she'd made to Hendrick so that he could blend it into the fruit and then pour the mixture into the waiting glasses, Dakota said, "Oh well. Let's not spoil the day with talk of Piper. Come and admire Gen's painting. It looks especially amazing in the morning light."

Later, after all the guests except Lauren had taken their leave and Dakota had sent Max off to his study so he could get a leg up on some work in preparation for his trip to California, she and Lauren went into the living room. Lauren had gratefully accepted Gen and Alex's invitation to take Katie and Ali for the rest of the day.

"An afternoon free. What luxury." Lauren let her head fall back against the sofa's cushion.

"What are you going to do with it?" Dakota asked, mimicking Lauren's relaxed pose.

"You know, I may saddle Rowan and go for a ride. Just a simple hack for pleasure. I rarely get to do that these days, and he'll enjoy it. Then it will be catching up on paperwork and sending out confirmations for the summer pony camp applications. We've been swamped."

"That's good, though, right?"

"It helps pay the bills. And some of the kids are adorable. The trick is weeding out the horrors." She turned her head. "And what about you? Do you and Max have any plans?"

"Nothing concrete. After he's done working, maybe we'll take a walk on the beach, maybe a nap."

"Uh-huh." Lauren's tone was knowing. "I loved those kinds of days with Zach. I'm so happy to see you like this, Dakota. It's good between you two, right?"

"It is. I've fallen for him pretty hard, Lauren," she said quietly. "I just hope he feels the same and it works out for us. I realize things were different for you and Zach. You two were so in love."

Lauren gave a little smile. "What we had was special. *Zach* was special—a wonderful, kind, and truly good man."

"He was," Dakota agreed. "I know how much you miss him."

"Every day. But he's still with me. I only have to look at the girls. Ali was just a baby when he died, yet amazingly she has some of his mannerisms. And Katie looks so much like him. I honestly can't imagine ever being with someone else because I don't think I could ever find another love like the one I had with Zach. And that's okay, because he's there in my two beautiful girls."

Dakota took her hand. For several minutes they enjoyed the quiet.

"You know I'm working on renovating Tom Hunter's house," she said.

Lauren didn't answer immediately. Then she said, "It's going well?"

"I think Astrid and I will be able to get it done by the end of May, which is the date he gave me."

"Is he selling it?"

"I don't know. Maybe he's coming back."

"After all these years? Why would he?"

"I can think of a number of reasons, like maybe because he misses the Atlantic, or seeing his old friends. Remember the fun the three of us had? Those were good times."

"They were. But we're not kids anymore, Dakota."

"Still, it would be great to see him."

Lauren made a noncommittal noise. "I have a feeling we may be too tame for the likes of Tom Hunter," Lauren replied. "Piper, on the other hand—"

Dakota gave a horrified laugh. "Stop! That image is too awful. And you're right, she would fall over herself to land Tom, Hollywood's most bankable star. But, hey, Lauren, speaking of Piper, do you remember if she ever dated a guy named Diego?"

Lauren thought for a moment. "She tends to go for the Chip, Blake, and Derek crowd, doesn't she?"

"Pretty much."

"I think I would have remembered if you'd ever told me a Diego and Piper story."

"Hendrick couldn't recall him among Piper's horde of lovers, either. It's weird. Max ran into Piper. And to answer the question that's on your lips, his being my husband didn't deter her from indulging in a little flirtation. But it was short-lived. Max ticked her off by suggesting she put a muzzle on Mimi."

"Oh, man, I'd have loved to have been there for that."

Dakota smiled. "Me too. But here's the strange part. Piper accused Max of being just like this Diego. I can't figure out who he could be. If this guy left such an impression on her, I should know a ton about him, including his favorite position."

"Huh." Lauren was silent while she digested this last bit. "You're right. That is odd. Very un-Piper-like. So are you going to ask her?"

Dakota sighed. "I don't know. I've been avoiding her. There are only so many comments about swollen ankles and the wonders of support hose for women like me that I can take."

Lauren snorted. "Support hose? She's scraping the bottom of the barrel with that one. Just in case you haven't passed a mirror lately, let me tell you, you look amazing. You've got the glow, although I'm not sure whether it's from your pregnancy hormones or the effect of falling in love with your brand-new spiffy husband. Just remember when she starts playing her mind games that beneath her tan and the layers of Crème de la Mer she applies to maintain that youthful glow, she's green with envy."

It was a wifely thing, Dakota decided, to wake up hours before dawn and make Max a bracing cup of coffee and a plate of scrambled eggs and toast before the car service arrived to take him to JFK airport. It was on par with watching him pack his bag and sneaking peeks while he shaved, dressed, and knotted his tie, and she secretly relished each, storing away the memories.

She was touched that he'd chosen to stay with her at Windhaven rather than head back into the city, where the drive to the airport would have been shorter and he could have traveled with his team from the Summit Group.

He picked up his coffee and drained it. "You'll be careful on the water?"

"If I go out at all this week. The surf report's so-so at best. And I have a ton of stuff to do over at my house before Jarrett moves in." She'd decided to rent the house to Jarrett and his girlfriend, Kyra, preferring having locals who worked in the Hamptons living in it to some Goldman Sachs–Sloppy Tuna type who'd only want it for the season. While she wouldn't be making as much money on rent, she'd be able to continue to store Premier Service's equipment in the barn behind the house. A big plus. "And at some point I'm supposed to drop by Dunemere Lane."

Her mother had called, asking her to come over with the Land Cruiser. She had boxes of books for the East Hampton Library.

"So are you going to ask her about this guy Diego?"

"Maybe, probably." A part of her felt like it had to know. While she'd strived to gain emotional independence from Piper, for twenty-eight years her mother had been the single greatest force in her life. How could she not be curious about a mysterious man who was apparently exactly like Max? Yet another part of her was reluctant to go anywhere near the topic. Asking would only feed Piper's egomania. And Dakota knew only too well what a colossal energy suck listening to her mother's description of a present or past lover could be. Was it really worth it?

"Well, be sure to give her my regards," Max said dryly as he stood up from the breakfast counter. "Gotta grab my bags. I'll be back in a sec."

She put the dirty dishes in the dishwasher, wiped down the counter, and was making herself another cup of mint tea when Max returned.

"The car's here," he said.

She nodded, biting her lower lip lest a plaintive request that he call her slip out. He hadn't even left and already she was missing him.

They walked to the front door. Drawing a breath, she said, "Hope the closing goes well. And have a good time celebrating with your team and AB1." There, that sounded upbeat, even though she was fully aware of the sorts of places newly flush Silicon Valley techie types frequented.

He put his bags down and stepped forward, framing her face with his hands, and kissed her. He tasted of toothpaste. Clean and minty and hot. She moaned in pleasure, kissing him back urgently.

"I'll call you," he whispered roughly when he broke off the kiss.

Thank God. "Okay, that'd be nice. And you'll be taking a helicopter from JFK to East Hampton on your return?"

He nodded.

"Let me know when you take off from JFK so I can meet you." She paused, then decided, *To hell with it.* "I'll miss you."

His teeth flashed as he grinned. "Good."

CHAPTER THIRTY-TWO

Between work, getting her house in order for Jarrett and his girlfriend, Kyra, and Piper's erratic schedule, Dakota didn't get to Dunemere Lane until Friday, which she decided was all to the good; nothing Piper said or did could make her more miserable. A week without Max had left her in a thoroughly cranky mood. Texting, FaceTiming, and engaging in some admittedly steamy phone sex, while all well and good and exciting, came nowhere near the pleasure of being with him. She wanted to touch him, kiss him, at the very least reach out and smooth the furrow between his brows when he'd told her yesterday that he had to cut their conversation short. In a weird coincidence, Chris Steffen, the CEO of Chiron, was in San Francisco for a conference and wanted to meet up with Max. If she hadn't already been predisposed to dislike Chris for his endless demands—Max had mentioned that the man, while smart, was also a bit of a diva—his stealing her precious FaceTime with her husband guaranteed it.

The fact that she'd be picking Max up at the airport later in the evening was the bright spot on her horizon. But too many hours remained.

Dakota let herself into her mother's house, calling out, "Piper, I'm here."

"Dakota?" her mother's voice came from upstairs. "I'm getting dressed. Down in two shakes. The boxes are in the garage."

Dakota turned around and headed back outside to the garage. Maybe she could simply put them in the Land Cruiser and drive off. Why waste her time trying to ferret information out of Piper? She punched in the code for the garage, and when the door had finished its rumbling ascent, she saw the boxes. All empty.

She rolled her eyes. Why hadn't she realized that when Piper said she had boxes of books to donate to the library, it meant that there were boxes and that Dakota was supposed to fill them, schlep them to the SUV, and then drive them to the library while Piper luxuriated in being Piper? With a sigh, she picked up six empty wine cases and went back inside.

Piper was in the smaller living room. "Oh, there you are."

"Yes, here I am." Dakota set the boxes down and looked at the books lining the built-ins. Piper had yet to remove from the shelves the ones she intended to give away. Why should she when Dakota could? "You haven't sorted the books."

"I'm getting rid of them all."

"All of them?"

"I'm in the mood to redecorate. I want a fresh and airy look for this room. Uncluttered. And no one actually reads books anymore, do they?"

"That's a lot of boxes." Not to mention work hours.

"I'm sure I have some more in the basement," Piper replied.

"I don't know whether I can get to all of them today." Unable to help herself, Dakota indulged in a little passive aggression. She waited, not making a move toward the bookshelves, wanting to see whether Piper planned to pick a single title off the shelf.

"I'll be here all day Sunday." Piper sat down. "Lord, I am utterly exhausted. I've been running around all day and I'm going into the city tonight to meet Miles. Have I told you about him?"

Dakota gave her a long look and then with a shake of her head went and plucked book number one off the shelf and stuck it grimly inside a box.

By box number three Dakota had learned a lot about Piper's newest boyfriend. Miles was an entrepreneur of some sort—Piper was vague on the details—and had recently sold his business for an astronomical sum. He liked to spend money on her. They were going to St. Thomas for a few weeks, so Piper would need Dakota to check on the house.

Dakota had reached the shelves behind the TV. She had to move gingerly so as not to get entangled in the cable wires. "I do have a life, you know," she said through gritted teeth. "I have a business. I have a husband—"

"Yes, I met that husband of yours. Quite delicious. I was surprised. You don't normally go for that type. Did he tell you how well we got along? I think we'll be good friends."

Dakota was about to turn and tell her to keep the hell away from Max—yes, Piper had gotten under her skin in near record time—when her gaze landed on the gold spine of Erica Jong's *Fear of Flying*. The book occupied the same spot it had for all these years, all the way back to the night Piper had pointed to it and then recounted her own fabulous zipless fuck with Dakota's father.

And suddenly, in a horrible epiphany, she knew. She *knew*. Her mother's story was precisely that, a fiction to rival Erica Jong's.

She shifted, turning around just far enough to see Piper's face. "Who's Diego?"

The truth was there in her mother's reaction, in the way her gaze shot to Dakota, then ricocheted away; in the quick blankness that came over her face; in the studied vagueness of her voice—when anyone acquainted with her understood there was nothing vague when it came to Piper Hale's interest in men—as she asked, "Diego? Who in the world is that?"

Dakota grabbed the copy of *Fear of Flying* and stepped out from behind the TV. She was icily calm. It wouldn't last, not with the blistering fury roiling inside her, rising, ready to erupt. "Diego, the man you said Max was like. Who is he?"

"Oh, him." Piper tried a shrug. "Nobody important."

Dakota let the book fall on the glass coffee table. It landed like an angry slap. "Remember the story of the zipless fuck you told me and anyone else with two ears, the one that resulted in my coming into the world nine months later? That wasn't really an anonymous encounter, was it, Mom?"

She could tell how much Piper wanted to deny it, wanted to continue with her perfect story where she had the starring role, where no one else had a line, let alone a name.

The rage engulfed her. She felt it shooting from her eyes and was surprised Piper didn't burst into flames on the linen-covered sofa.

"Don't give me that high-and-mighty look, Dakota."

"I have the right to look at you however I want. Who was he?" she demanded. "Did you even meet him at the Dakota?"

"Of course I did," she snapped, her tone affronted.

Dakota gave a mocking snort. Derision was far preferable to devastation. "Do tell."

Piper's pretty blue eyes narrowed. "Fine. You want to know about your biological father? Here you go. We met at a party at the Dakota, just as I described. Diego was there with a group of friends, like me, only his pals were all foreigners. Polo players. He was on the team, too. They were having some matches here in the U.S. He and his friends were enjoying a weekend in the city before heading home."

Her heart was pounding so hard it hurt. "Did you get his last name? Where he lived?"

Piper rolled her eyes like a teenager under interrogation. "His last name was Salinas and he was from Argentina, and no, I don't remember what town he came from. It wasn't Buenos Aires, that's for sure. Besides, he told me he traveled constantly. He came and played in Bridgehampton once."

The casualness with which this last was delivered left Dakota reeling. Her father had been nearby, mere miles away? "When was this?"

"*Years* ago. You were barely three."

"But he was here and you didn't tell him about me?" Dakota's throat felt raw.

"As if an international polo player would want to be saddled with a toddler. And what if I had brought you to that match so that during halftime while everyone was stomping on divots I could present him with his by-blow? Then I'd have had to *share* you."

"But maybe you'd have marri—"

Piper cut her off with an incredulous laugh. "Married him? Are you for real? We're not talking Prince Charles here. A Hale would never marry a Salinas. What would my friends have said? It would have been like marrying one of the Latinos who shovel shit at your bestie's barn. Diego might have been a very talented fuck, but after all was said and done, he was little more than a gaucho with a big stick. I was bored stiff after a weekend of listening to him—"

"You spent a *weekend* with him?"

Wrapped up in her tale, Piper seemed not to hear her. "Everything was about *him.* Such colossal arrogance. I should have known better than to see him again after our bathroom romp, but, well, that big stick of his . . ."

"You never cease to amaze me," she said, her voice dripping with disgust.

"Why? Because I'm honest?"

Dakota's jaw dropped. But she didn't even manage a strangled laugh before Piper was speaking again.

"Even if Diego weren't a complete nobody, I'd never have married him. Why would I shackle myself to a man who'd only tell me what to do, and expect me to cook and sit at home like a good little wife, a patient Penelope, while he traveled the world having all the fun, riding his precious ponies and partying with his polo buddies? I'm not that woman—I'm Piper—and I live my life precisely as I choose."

Dakota tried to breathe. It was funny; she was gasping, yet she couldn't seem to draw any air into her lungs. "What about me?"

"What do you mean, what about you?" Piper asked.

"Did it ever occur to you that maybe I would have liked to have a father?"

"Don't be silly. You had me. You came out just fine—"

"And that I wouldn't have cared if he were a Latino groom, a Jamaican line cook, or a Moroccan rug merchant? He'd have been my father and a far better parent than you. I always considered you at best a mediocre mother, but I forgave you because I thought you were weak and spoiled and that deep down inside you regretted never knowing my father's name. Now I find out you've been lying to me my entire life, depriving me of a chance to have a relationship with him. All these years I thought Mimi was the vicious sister. I was wrong. You're far more cruel and vindictive. I hope you enjoy the rest of your miserable life."

She walked out, leaving her mother with her lies and her books and taking the shattering truth with her.

*

Max was still in a foul mood when the helicopter landed in East Hampton. Chris Steffen and his endless BS were to blame. He'd wasted a night dealing with him, making him "happy" when he could have spent it coaxing Dakota into giving him a FaceTime strip show, his new favorite long-distance activity, and then later have met up with the guys on his team to celebrate a good week's work.

Instead, he'd been forced to cut short his conversation with Dakota and send Andy and Glenn off to a dinner on him at Quince, all so he could go stroke Steffen's ego. Hoping it would improve his mood, he'd walked from the Fairmont, where he was staying, to meet Chris at the Ritz. It didn't.

The lighting in the hotel bar had been muted, but Chris was on the lookout and waved him over imperiously. Sitting down at the table, Max realized it wasn't Chris's first whiskey of the night. He knew the signs. With enough alcohol sloshing about in his system, Chris, unlike some people, didn't get loose-lipped or sloppy. He got aggressive, even more competitive than normal.

Chris was in town for a conference, a big pharma event, all well and good and part of his job description as CEO of Chiron. Something major must have gone down—a meeting with another pharma honcho or perhaps a stirring keynote speech—and it had triggered Chris's very smart brain and rapacious soul.

"We're going to make a killing, Max. An absolute fucking killing." Chris raised his glass and clinked it against Max's as yet untouched Grey Goose.

Generally those words were music to a private equity partner's ears. When uttered by Chris with a nasty gleam in his eye, Max wasn't inclined to start dancing. "You mean with Zeph3, the melanoma drug?"

"Yeah, that too," was Chris's cryptic answer. He raised his glass, toasting himself. "And when Chiron's raking in the bucks and we get gobbled up by a lovely pharma giant because our profits are through the roof, maybe you'll remember to thank your old friend. Maybe you'll remember how to be a friend. 'Cause you've been a real disappointment lately."

Max gritted his teeth and smiled. "Who's sitting here with you right now? Cheers, buddy," he said, and took a slow sip of the icy vodka, hoping it would temper his urge to squash Chris like a bug. "So you've come up with some new angles to make Chiron even more profitable? Let's hear 'em."

Chris smiled again, and Max wondered whether he'd been enjoying some white lines along with his whiskey. "You know what? I think I'll save sharing my ideas for our meeting in New York with Bob Elders."

Max cocked his head. It wasn't like Chris to be coy. "That's scheduled the day before the board meeting. Doesn't give us a lot of wiggle room if we need to tweak anything. Don't you want to run some numbers, make sure your projections are airtight? We've always gone over the playbook together in the past."

And they'd had some good runs, with impressive scores, he and Chris. Max wasn't sure what had happened. Had Chris simply grown more insufferable with each company he helmed, or was it Max himself who had changed?

Chris seemed to be mulling over the same question, only he had an answer. "Yeah, but that was then. You're not passing the ball to me anymore. It's like you don't trust me to carry it into the end zone. That hurts, Max."

"Hey, didn't I help you get the keys to Chiron?" Which he now regretted.

Chris ignored the comment. "I'm not the only one who feels burned, you know. I was talking to Ashley—"

"Jesus, Chris."

"She thought you and she had something real. And then you went and handed Ashley her walking papers. Harsh, Max. Really harsh."

"What can I say? I realized she wasn't my type."

Chris tossed back his whiskey and signaled to the waiter for another. "Oh yeah? That's funny. I thought you looked real good together."

His glass halfway to his lips, Max froze. Chris's smirk was telling. He wasn't talking about how Max and Ashley had looked standing side by side or even how they'd moved on the dance floor. He was referring to different positions altogether. No clothing required.

Shit.

So either Ashley hadn't deleted the sex tape, as Roger had demanded, or she'd let Chris watch it at some point before taking it into her greedy little head to blackmail him.

"She's here, you know," Chris said, nodding at the waiter, who placed another lowball glass in front of him.

Max took a slow sip of his vodka. No way was he going to let Chris faze him. "Who, Ashley?"

"The one and only. She's got a part in a new reality show about rock and roll. Some director approached her about it because she's been seeing Ryder Stevens—you know, *the* Ryder Stevens. He and his band have a gig this week at the Fillmore. I could call her. Even though she's doing the nasty with Ryder, I'm sure she'd be happy to reconnect with you. For old times' sake." That smirk made another appearance.

Why, so Chris could jerk off watching another sex tape? "I'm married, Chris."

"Yeah, and you didn't even invite your best bud to the wedding."

"It was private."

His shrug was indifferent. "Word around town is you knocked her up. Always thought you were super careful—in that respect at least."

Max stood and dropped some bills on the table. He noticed his hands were trembling. Hell, his entire body was shaking with rage. He wanted badly to rearrange Chris Steffen's face and permanently wipe the smirk off it. "You might want to be careful yourself, Chris. You're pushing your luck."

"Am I, bro? Or maybe it's that yours has run out. We'll see, won't we?"

Max spotted Dakota's SUV in front of the airport's small terminal. His carry-on and briefcase in hand, he strode quickly across the tarmac toward it. Shaking off his fatigue and blocking out his anger and frustration over Chris's veiled threats, he focused instead on his need for Dakota, his outrageous and undeniable need.

She had the window down and he could feel her gaze on his as he closed the distance. He quickened his pace. Reaching the car, he jogged around to the rear and lifted the tailgate, tossing his bags into the cargo area. Then he was opening the passenger door and reaching for her as he slid in.

The kiss was fierce, a fevered mashing of lips, as if they couldn't get close enough, her hunger as frantic as his. He was immediately, painfully hard.

He tore his mouth from hers. "Let's go," he said roughly.

She fumbled with the gearshift and then shoved it into drive. In the dark confines of the SUV, the harsh sawing of their breaths spoke for them.

He had thought he could hold on for the few miles to the house. He'd thought wrong. Dark woods bordered the road. No lights shone from houses, signaling the presence of potentially curious homeowners. Few cars passed them.

"Pull over and cut the engine, Dakota." He didn't explain; she didn't question. The sexual tension gripping him was obvious.

The engine silenced, he said, "Get in the back."

The opening and slamming of metal echoed.

He met her in the back, his hands already pulling her down and beneath him. She was wearing a skirt. She shivered as his hands traveled over her smooth legs, pushing the material up. Reaching her panties, he dragged them down, replacing them with his mouth.

He reveled in the creamy-salty taste of her, in the scrape of her fingers as they dug into his scalp, in the clamp of her thighs about his head.

His tongue lashed and probed, demanding she come apart for him, needing to hear her throaty cry of wonder. He needed that as much as he craved his own release. Another long, hard stroke and she bore down on him, screaming his name and bucking helplessly.

Before she'd even quieted, he'd shoved his trousers down. Grasping her legs again, he lifted them and shifted his weight forward. Feeling her welcoming heat, he gritted his teeth in anticipation and thrust inside.

He tried to hang on and prolong the exquisite pleasure, but it was too intense. Everything drew tight inside him, and then he was pumping and grinding his hips and coming in a violent rush that made him see stars inside the car.

Trembling, he placed a hand on the leather seat and levered himself up. His sluggish mind cast about for an explanation of why he'd gone at Dakota like a madman. His only excuse was the utter shittiness of the past eighteen hours and the recognition that once he was inside Dakota, all of it would go away. Because that's what being with her did for him. She made the stinking rot disappear.

He looked down at her, hoping that whatever came out of his mouth might exonerate him. Her head was turned. But her profile revealed the wet spikes of her lashes, the tight compression of her lips. "Dakota?"

She turned, and her ravaged expression was like a gut punch. Had he done that?

"Christ, are you okay? Did I hurt you? Is it the baby?"

"No." When she struggled to sit up, he helped her and then quickly righted his clothes as she pulled her panties back on and tugged her skirt down. Done, she wiped her eyes with the back of her hand and sniffed.

"Dakota, I'm sorry. I didn't mean to—"

"You didn't. I wanted it to be just like that, to be swept away. It's just that—" Her sentence left unfinished, she looked out the window at the black trees.

He waited for her tension to ease, for her hands in her lap to unknot. Neither happened. "What is it, then?" he asked.

Her shoulders rose as she drew in a ragged breath. "I have a father." And she burst into tears.

There were two people Max could cheerfully murder: Chris Steffen and Piper Hale.

It occurred to Max that they were like two sides of a very bad penny. Both were narcissists who didn't care whom they hurt. They simply differed in their approaches to inflicting mayhem.

But at the moment, Chris and whatever nasty little schemes he was concocting were irrelevant. It was Piper who topped Max's shitlist.

Upon hearing her tortured statement, he'd pulled Dakota onto his lap, and while she cried herself out, he rubbed her back and stroked her hair, helpless to do much else. Minutes passed and slowly she calmed, sporadic hiccups and sniffles replacing broken sobs. Then, opening the front passenger door, he got her settled and her seatbelt fastened. As he drove them back to Windhaven, she told him in a voice quiet with pain how she'd figured out Piper's decades-long deception. Listening, he imagined how satisfying it would be to wring Piper's neck. But maybe that would be too quick. He wanted her to suffer just as Dakota had suffered all these years.

He recalled the day he and Dakota had filled out their application for a marriage license. In the section where she was required to provide information about her father, she'd written *Unknown* in neat block letters. How many similar applications and forms had she filled out? And each time she did, had there been that slight but telling stiffness in her posture?

And then to discover that her mother had lied to her all these years, keeping her father's identity a secret from her? Unbelievable. What a hell of a thing to do to a loved one . . . except Max didn't really believe that the likes of Piper and Chris were capable of love.

But what about him? Was he any better? He'd fallen in love with Dakota, yet he, too, was keeping a secret from her. True, his secret was of a different kind, and he wasn't actually lying to Dakota by withholding it. Nor did it involve her personally.

Yet in light of Piper's deceit, his concealing important information from her made him feel dishonest. It was a condition he'd have to live with, however, because he couldn't bear to reopen those wounds.

CHAPTER THIRTY-THREE

If not for Max and the baby growing inside her, Dakota would have been a complete wreck. Piper's reluctant revelation was like a bomb blast, tearing apart everything inside her and destroying the relationship with her mother, dysfunctional though it was. Piper was all the family Dakota really had, her dealings with the other members of the Hale clan too toxic to endure. With Piper's lie exposed, Dakota lost the mother she'd clung to. And the father she'd longed for? The one she'd dreamed about? Well, now she had a name to attach to those fantasies, to whisper at odd moments when she was walking on the beach, the wind carrying it off to the sea.

Thanks to Max, she was able to replace fantasies about her father with facts about Diego Salinas. He'd suggested she approach Sam Brody, a friend of Alex Miller's, who ran a highly respected security firm. He could hunt down the correct Diego

Salinas and relay any information to her much more quickly than if she attempted to investigate on her own.

Two weeks later, Sam Brody mailed Dakota his findings in a twenty-page report complete with photographs and links to where she could discover more about her father.

The photographs showed Diego was indeed a handsome man. That was to be expected. Piper was far too shallow to ever be attracted to someone of merely average looks. But the physical similarities between her father and her nonetheless came as a shock. Dakota had inherited his eyes, his dark hair, and his olive skin tone. Like her, he was tall and athletic.

Her father came from Villa Dolores, a town located in the province of Cordoba, and he still played polo, though only on the weekends. The three restaurants he owned, popular with locals and tourists alike, demanded much of his attention, as did his wife and four children, the eldest of whom was twenty-four.

When Dakota reached that section of Sam Brody's report, it was too much. To read about her younger half brother and sisters and think of all she'd missed not growing up with them in her life, even if they were five thousand miles apart, was devastating.

Setting aside the document, she'd gone to Max's study and announced that she needed to catch some waves at Ditch Plains. One look at her face, and he'd closed his computer and gotten his gear and long board ready. They'd stayed out on the water until the sun was a gold ball sinking into a dark lavender sea, until she could breathe again. Then he'd brought her home and made love to her and held her in the comforting circle of his arms.

Max's patience was incredible during this awful period where it felt like her head was going to explode and her heart shatter. He listened while she recited all she'd learned about Diego and his family. He let her vent her rage over Piper. And once she'd finished, he let her rewind and start all over again.

Her obsession was such that she took to checking flight schedules from JFK to Buenos Aires. She'd sit at the computer, her finger moving the cursor until it hovered over the purchase button. But instead of clicking it, she would abruptly close the laptop and dash upstairs to the shower, where she could cry about the father that she'd learned of far too late without Max hearing her anguished sobs.

Of course he knew what was going on. On the third night when she came back downstairs, hollow-eyed and damp-haired, to fix dinner with him, he casually offered to carve out time from work so he could accompany her to Villa Dolores. "It might make seeing your dad a little easier for you."

"Thank you. I'll think about it," she said, shutting the oven door on the lasagna with more force than necessary.

He paused in the midst of adding sliced cucumbers to the salad. "But?"

"But I *can't.* It's too late. I can't go to Argentina and show up on his doorstep and say, 'Hi, remember that party at the Dakota in New York City you went to almost thirty years ago? The one where you hooked up with a beautiful blonde and then spent a weekend with her? Guess what—I'm the result.' "

"Maybe there's another way you could introduce yourself to him."

"It would be hard to leave out those crucial details. And the outcome would be the same." Grabbing the loaf of Italian bread, she sliced it down the center, pulled it apart, and spread a paste of olive oil, butter, parsley, and freshly minced garlic on the insides, her movements quick and angry. So very angry. "My showing up, my *existence,* would cause turmoil for six unsuspecting people. I can't inflict that kind of chaos on them. Chaos and pain are the Hales' stock in trade. I refuse to follow their example. You've seen Piper in action. It's exactly the sort of thing she would do—hop on a plane and barge in on the Salinas family and to hell with the consequences."

He came over to stand behind her so he could loop his arms around her waist, which was now curved in a little bump that seemed to fascinate him. She felt her shoulders relax slightly when he kissed the side of her neck.

"Okay, I get your point, not that you could ever be confused with Piper or any member of your putrid family. So how about you write him instead? Just to let him know. You could say that you'd understand if he didn't feel comfortable introducing you to his family. Which would hurt, of course, but at least he'd have the choice. And he'd be aware of your existence."

"I—I'll see." She sighed tiredly. "I think it's best if I give myself more time before I make any decisions. I'm still processing it all. I don't know where I stand or what the right thing to do is. Damn Piper."

And while Max's idea of writing a letter was tempting, she could already anticipate the difficulty of finding the proper words and tone when she reached out to her father for the first time. The challenge would be to introduce herself in a way that didn't shock him into hostility. If she failed, the silence of his rejection would be awful, worse than the pain she was going through now. For the umpteenth time, she told herself that she'd be better off simply letting it go.

Suddenly she caught her breath and the debate raging in her head went silent. Inches beneath the loop of Max's forearms, something moved: a delicate flutter brushing the inside of her stomach.

"Max," she whispered as tears made the kitchen swim before her. "I think I felt the baby."

He went still and was silent for a second, doubtless as shocked and surprised as she. Then she felt his arms close about her protectively. He cleared his throat, but his voice was nevertheless rough and thick with emotion when he asked, "It moved?"

She nodded. "Yes."

"What was it like?"

"Light. Delicate. Fluttery. Like a bird in flight. Like nothing I've ever felt before." She grinned, the anxiety surrounding what to do about her father and how to handle the betrayal by her mother eclipsed by the wonder of her baby stirring. "I can't wait for you to feel it," she said. "You're going to be such a good father, Max."

He gave an odd laugh and his arms dropped away from her stomach as he stepped aside. "I appreciate the vote of confidence." He made it sound as if she were foolish to have faith in him.

"So how long until dinner?" he asked.

"We can eat whenever you want."

"Can you give me another half hour? I have some emails to write."

"Of course."

Her smile slipped as he left the kitchen. For all Max's affection, support, and interest in her and the baby, there remained barriers between them. He almost invariably withdrew, distancing himself emotionally when the topic of his own impending paternal role arose.

She couldn't help but be frustrated. Fathers were on her mind a lot these days. After poring over Sam Brody's report, reading page after page about Diego Salinas, her sense of loss was more acute than ever. One way she dealt with it was to look at Max and see all the potential in him. He was a good man. The evidence was everywhere, no matter how many times he shied away from her.

Her gaze fell on the Vitamix, a gleaming symbol of the care he'd taken when she'd been suffering the worst of the morning sickness. He no longer needed to concoct easily digestible protein-rich smoothies for her to sip, but she continued to use it nearly every day for the simple reason that it reminded her of his efforts. She had half an hour, more than enough time to make an apple crumble for dessert with the help of the super-blender.

She went to the cupboard, pulled out the ingredients, and carried them to the counter, placing them next to a ceramic bowl piled with fruit. Plucking several apples and then grabbing a paring knife, she got to work.

Given her current preoccupation, it was natural that she should wonder about Max's father, as well. She remembered how Max had spoken of him—the one time he'd mentioned him at length—on the afternoon he'd replaced her flat tire. There'd been affection and respect in his voice as he'd described the two of them working on the old cars his father brought home to restore. How could Max have cut all ties with the man who'd been so important to him? What had caused the rift?

The optimist, the fixer, in Dakota wanted to help him bridge the divide. How to approach Max about his nonexistent relationship with his father wasn't clear, however. She understood too well the lacerating pain associated with family conflicts. Things were going so well between her and Max; would it be wise to press him about his father, especially when he'd demonstrated such patience and forbearance in dealing with her family drama?

Plus Max had a lot of work and it was clearly preoccupying him. Even in her meltdown over Piper's lie, she'd noticed that when he wasn't consoling her, he was on his phone with Roger Cohen and other associates she couldn't identify. Now that she was living with him, she had an even better sense of the pressure cooker that was the life of a Wall Street financier. But recently there had been an added sense of urgency about him. When she'd asked him about it, he'd responded with a verbal shrug. He was just making sure Chris Steffen was doing an able job at Chiron's helm.

If that hadn't been enough, Max's firm had suffered a disappointing IPO with one of the companies they'd acquired—not one of Max's, thank goodness. The graveyard silence broken by the chirp of a lonely cricket that had greeted the company's public offering had put the onus on the rest of the Summit Group's partners to perform beyond expectations.

Max had told her the Summit Group's chief, Bob Elders, was a type A personality to rival all others. He wanted the Summit Group to squash the competition.

Max obviously thrived on the intensely competitive environment; he wouldn't be the success he was otherwise. But it was clear he was juggling a lot of balls, both professional and private. Would it be right to toss another one at him by bringing up the topic of his father?

She had her answer when she went to Max's study to let him know dinner was ready. He was on the phone, standing by the window and staring into the black night.

"Roger, he's setting the stage for some kind of major showdown, I know it—" Perhaps catching her reflection in the glass, he broke off. "Listen, I've got to go . . . Right. Thanks . . . Yeah, you, too." He ended the call and turned. "Hey."

"Hey. The lasagna's done. Are you ready to eat or do you need more time?"

"I'm ready."

They went into the kitchen. She'd set places at the island, where they often ended up eating. She'd opened a bottle of Sangiovese for him and a San Pellegrino for herself. She gave him a healthy portion of lasagna and filled the remainder of the plate with salad. Since she still felt better when she ate lighter meals, she cut a far smaller square of lasagna and heaped a mountain of salad next to it.

He lit the candles, sliced the garlic bread, and then held out her barstool as she climbed onto it.

"Thanks." She waited until he, too, had settled behind the island. "New headaches at the office?"

His fork stalled over his food. "Same ones. Roger and I are trying to make sure Chris doesn't suggest anything foolish to the board next week. Chris can sometimes be a little too clever. Unfortunately, Bob Elders might be too willing to listen." He dug into the lasagna.

He seemed to really like the lasagna, so she let him eat in peace. When he'd finished and picked up his wine, she spoke again. "From everything you've told me, Bob Elders seems really smart. Why would he be taken in by a too-clever pitch on Chris Steffen's part?"

He lifted a shoulder in a restless shrug. "Bob's looking for a Twinkie."

"Excuse me?"

Max set his glass down and speared an avocado slice. "A Twinkie, you know, as in the Hostess Company. They made those prepackaged pastries—Twinkies, Devil Dogs, Ho-Hos."

"Oh. Okay, but I'm still clueless as to why your CEO would want one."

"When Hostess went bankrupt, an L.A. private equity group acquired it. They cleaned up the company, cut inefficiency, improved production and distribution, and marketed new products. They even figured out how to expand the Twinkie's shelf life. The PE firm's initial investment was around four hundred and ten mil. By the time they announced the IPO, the company was valued at two point three billion."

She put down her fork. "Wow. That's some Twinkie."

"Yeah." He smiled. "And the equity group kept a forty-two percent stake in the company. All told, a very nice return on investment."

"Well, I guess I can't blame Bob for wanting a Twinkie, too."

Max nodded. "I'm pretty sure Chris's going to try to give him his sugar fix."

"By being too clever by half." She picked up her fork again. "But surely you can stop Chris if he gets reckless."

"Yeah, maybe. Bob and I have a meeting with Chris next week in advance of the Chiron board meeting."

She passed him the bread. "When is that?"

"The meeting?" He tore his piece of bread in half, and a waft of garlicky steam teased her nostrils. "Thursday."

"If you have to prepare for it, don't feel that you have to come to Dr. Davis's with me."

"And that's—"

"On Wednesday, at one o'clock."

"This one's for another ultrasound, right?"

"Yes."

"I can make it. Bob's out of town until Wednesday night in any case. After the doctor, I'll head into the city and probably spend the night."

She hated the nights when he was in the city. She'd grown used to being lulled to sleep by the heat of his body curled around her and by the deep and steady rhythm of his breathing. "That's fine. Maybe I'll invite Rae over for a working dinner—" Abruptly she froze and then said in a hushed voice, "Max, it happened again. The baby. Come here."

He jumped off the stool and came around to her side of the island. When he was next to her, she took his hand. Slipping it under her blouse, she willed the baby to stretch or wriggle or somersault, so Max might feel it. "Oh!" she said when the strange fluttery movement came a second time. "Did you—"

The awe on his face was a perfect match for the marvel occurring inside her body. "Yeah, I think I did." He pressed his splayed palm over her belly a little more firmly. "There, it moved again, right?"

"Yes." She placed her hand over his, praying she never forgot this moment.

"It's amazing."

"It is." And her love for Max and the baby inside her grew that much bigger.

CHAPTER THIRTY-FOUR

Max's arms quivered, his muscles screaming in protest, but he didn't let go of the bar, instead hauling his body up until his chin met metal. He made himself do five more reps while the sweat poured off him and AC/DC blasted his eardrums before dropping to the floor, his sneakers hitting the rubberized floor in a heavy slap.

He grabbed a towel lying on the adjustable bench and wiped his face and arms before going over to the rowing machine. He'd had Dakota order one for the gym for the days when he didn't feel like running on the beach or the roads. Or for times like this, when it was still black as pitch outside.

He sat down on the wooden seat. Strapping in his feet, he grabbed the handle and began rowing to Old 97's "Let's Get Drunk and Get It On." It sounded like an ode to the good old days. It sounded great. He paused for a moment to crank the volume and then resumed his stroke.

It was a good thing that pregnancy caused Dakota to sleep like the dead. First, because she didn't like AC/DC or Led Zeppelin or Guns N' Roses, and this playlist featured a lot of all three, and in his present mood, he intended to keep the volume cranked. Second, because while she was sleeping the sleep of the just, Max was hardly getting any shut-eye at all. He didn't want her worrying about him or guessing that he was being torn apart like some poor bastard strapped to one of those medieval torture devices.

Once again Max recalled how it had felt when he'd placed his hand on the curve of Dakota's belly and beneath his palm, beneath her taut skin, he'd caught the faint movement, the grazing caress from the baby they'd made. Extraordinary, and extraordinarily unnerving, it was doing weird things to him, messing with his mind and with his sense of self. With each new stage in Dakota's pregnancy, he got sucked in deeper, losing sight of the man he used to be.

For instance, last night, when he'd felt the baby, he could have happily stood there with his hand on Dakota's stomach for the next twenty weeks, monitoring the baby's every waking movement.

Had he become a sap? Steffen obviously thought so. Distasteful as it was to agree with anything that little shit insinuated, Max had a hunch he was right.

It was one thing to worry about how much the presence of Dakota and the baby was changing him. It was a whole other truckload of worry to realize it was affecting his business sense.

Only a short time ago, listening to Chris crow about raking in megabucks wouldn't have bothered him in the least. That was the name of their game. Max would have cheered him on, urged him to search high and low to eke every penny they could from Chiron. Now, trying to figure out what the hell Chris was up to was making him lose sleep.

There was a part of him that wondered whether he shouldn't

just play the game as he always had and forget his misgivings. After all, they were mere pangs compared to the pain of his straining muscles in his chest and legs now that he'd been rowing all out for God only knew how long. He could focus on the dollars that would rain down on the Summit Group and their partners, and do a fist pump in victory when Chiron's profits brought him that much closer to his goal of stepping into Bob Elders's shoes and making his first billion by forty.

He could do that and block out the rest, just as he'd always done.

At last he slowed to a stop and sat bowed over the rowing machine, his chest heaving. Setting the handle in its cradle, he turned his hands over and stared at the matching lines of shredded blisters across his palms. His conscience was in far worse shape.

Dr. Davis's waiting room was blessedly empty. Dakota had cleverly booked the first appointment following the office's lunch hour. With luck they'd be in and out.

He nodded at the nurse—it was the same one, Trudy—when she called them back to the exam room and then listened to her and Dakota engage in small talk. The routine was familiar to him now. Dakota had to pee, get weighed, have her blood pressure checked, and have vials of blood drawn . . . the amount they took from her was downright ghoulish.

Scooping up the vials and Dakota's chart, Trudy excused herself, saying Dr. Davis would be in shortly. Dakota began unbuttoning her white shirt. He watched as she shrugged out of it and hung it on the hanger they provided. From the back it was still impossible to tell she was carrying a child. She looked as lean and strong as ever. Bending over, she peeled off her black leggings, and her full breasts spilled deliciously over the cups of her bra.

He had a sudden fantasy of playing doctor with her, doing his own thorough exam of her luscious breasts, her adorable little bump that wasn't even as big as a football (which he'd proved to her when she mentioned how big she was getting), and below.

He indulged in his X-rated fantasies while his wife stripped off her undies and bra and then slipped on the gown.

Turning, she caught his eye, and then shook her head. "Tell me you weren't ogling me."

He grinned unrepentantly. "Guilty as charged."

Being horny was infinitely preferable to being on edge and frustrated, which not even his punishing workout had tempered. Thinking about how the exam table was the perfect height for one of the scenarios that had flashed through his mind was much better than obsessing about the futility of whipping on his Superman cape and trying to stop the inevitable train wreck that was Chris Steffen driving Chiron.

Dakota hopped onto the exam table, her bare legs dangling over the edge. He liked her feet. They were long and strong like the rest of her. She'd painted her toenails a deep cherry red.

He rose from his chair and went over to stand between her legs. Yup, the table really was the perfect height. Reaching up, he fingered one of the gown's ties. Because she was Dakota, she'd knotted it with a perfect bow. "Want to know what I'm thinking?"

Her hand closed over his. "I'm not sure I do." Laughter made her husky voice even sexier than normal.

"I'm thinking you should pinch one of these exam gowns. Then we could play doctor at home." He tugged, and his piss-poor mood improved a hundred percent when the bow came undone and the flaps of the gown parted.

"Max . . ."

"What?" With his finger he traced the deep valley between her breasts, smiling when her breath caught.

A quick knock on the door had him cursing and stepping back

as Dr. Davis entered, tailed by Trudy. Damned inconvenient of them to be on time.

"Hello, Dakota and Max."

He shoved his hands in his pockets and nodded at the obstetrician while Dakota greeted her with a sunny hello.

"How are you feeling, Dakota?"

"Really good. A little sleepy in the evenings."

Max stifled a snort. A major understatement. Dakota's eyes started to roll into the back of her head by ten o'clock. It was funny as hell. The upside was that it was a terrific excuse to lead her upstairs and then have slow lullaby sex.

"And I—Max, too—we felt the baby move."

Dr. Davis was generous with her smiles. "That's wonderful. You'll be feeling the baby move more and more from here on out. At times this will be less than comfortable. But when it does, remember that you're more than halfway through your gestation."

"Yay." Dakota grinned.

The next ten minutes were devoted to Dr. Davis examining Dakota. Max listened to them chat as she measured Dakota's belly and answered her questions. Then another knock sounded and the sonogram technician entered—Max thought her name was Marcy—and took a seat in front of the machine.

"Are you ready to see what the baby's up to this afternoon?" Dr. Davis asked. "Today's the day we check on the baby's anatomy, make sure it's growing properly."

Max's gut clenched. *Please let everything be normal. Please let the baby be all right.*

Dakota didn't seem fazed by the fact that the stakes had risen ever since they'd begun feeling the baby move. Turning her head, she smiled at Max and stretched her hand out in invitation. He hesitated to take it for the simple reason that he desperately wanted the contact. But if he refused, Dakota would notice and then perhaps realize just how nervous he was.

He closed his fingers around hers. This time, unlike during that first visit, Dakota's hand was warm and steady in his.

"Brace yourself, Dakota. Here comes the revolting jelly," Dr. Davis warned as she smeared a glob of clear goop on Dakota's exposed bump.

"As slimy as anything in *Ghostbusters*," Dakota joked.

He felt a spurt of annoyance that they were being so freaking casual.

He fixed his eyes on the monitor and the black field. The sound, the *whoosh, whoosh* that reminded him of a washing machine churning away, was reassuringly familiar. Out of the black, he distinguished the shape of the baby.

"Oh!" Dakota said, seeing it, too. "It's so much bigger." And she laughed in delight.

"Yes," Dr. Davis agreed. "A lot of development has occurred in the past few weeks. Today Marcy's going to check and measure the baby's skull and bones, count the vertebrae in the spine, and look at the chambers in the heart to rule out any abnormalities."

Christ, I shouldn't have come, he thought as panic washed over him. His lungs constricted while he waited for the technician to finish, unable to draw a proper breath.

At last Marcy broke the excruciating silence. "Everything looks to be developing normally. And we've caught the baby between naps. It's moving its legs and arms. See?" The cursor hovered, and Max saw a tiny leg shift.

"That's amazing," Dakota said.

His heart took off.

"Oh yes, that's very good," Dr. Davis said.

Max and Dakota spoke simultaneously: "What?" and "What's good, Doctor?"

"At the last ultrasound I couldn't properly determine your baby's sex. But I got a good peek this time. If you'd like, I can tell you now."

Dakota turned away from the screen to look at him. Her eyes shone with excitement.

He wasn't sure about this. But how could he deny Dakota? He gave a small nod.

Beaming, she returned her attention to the monitor. "Yes, we'd like to know."

"Well then, I'm very pleased to tell you you're going to be the parents of a baby girl."

"A girl." Dakota's voice quivered with emotion.

He couldn't speak. Couldn't swallow. A girl. He shifted his feet, hoping to find his balance.

A little girl. She'd be vulnerable. There'd be so many ways she could be hurt. She'd need his protection and his care. He'd failed on both counts with Rosie. Who was to say he wouldn't again?

CHAPTER THIRTY-FIVE

Dakota was deliriously happy. It bubbled up inside her as she changed back into her clothes, folded up the cotton exam gown, and slipped it into her hobo bag, making sure to keep it hidden from Max as she checked out at the front desk and scheduled her next appointment with Dr. Davis.

A girl, she thought. She'd have been pleased with the news of a boy, too, but a girl felt special. Felt right on so many levels. While Max drove them home, she kept glancing at the printout of the baby: her tiny little nose, the curve of her ear, her perfect little feet. Dakota's mind quickly filled to overflowing with the things she would teach her, the things they would share.

Her happiness made her expansive. Possibilities became boundless.

Max seemed distracted. That was all right. Expecting him to match her euphoria was unrealistic—he wasn't carrying the baby inside him, nurturing her body with his. But he was going to make such a wonderful father, of that Dakota was certain. Their little girl would learn to throw a perfect spiral and change the oil in her car and understand how to analyze a price/earnings ratio. Again, so many possibilities for joy.

They pulled into Windhaven's driveway. Even with the detailed ultrasound, the doctor's visit had only taken an hour and a half out of their afternoon. She recalled the light in Max's eyes when he'd toyed with the ties of her gown. How, at the glide of his finger, desire, delicious and tingly, had coursed through her.

She hadn't thought of her baby as a gift before. She did now. Gratitude had her wanting to reciprocate.

There was the obvious gesture, but then, in a flash, a more lasting gift occurred to her, and she smiled, for the idea felt as deeply right as everything else that had happened this afternoon.

But first things first.

She followed him into the house. Entering the living room, she went to the mantelpiece and propped the picture of the baby on it. She'd buy a frame for it tomorrow. Their first family photo.

She turned to find Max leaning against the doorjamb, his hands fisted in his pockets. Despite the casual pose, there was a distant, preoccupied air about him. *Time for present number one,* she thought, confident it would help put a smile on that beautiful mouth.

She went up to him. "Do you have to leave for New York right away?"

"I've reserved a five o'clock flight."

More than enough time for everything. "You know, I kind of thought Dr. Davis rushed my exam today."

"What?" He straightened. "What do you mean? Is something wrong?"

She bit her lip at the sharp concern in his voice. It was sweet. "Maybe."

"*Maybe?* Jesus, Dakota—"

Before he could hustle her back into the car and head straight for the doctor's, she injected a husky note into her voice. "I was hoping you could take a look at me." Slowly she reached into her bag and pulled out the filched gown.

His reaction—alarm followed by confusion and shock, then all three replaced by dawning appreciation—made laughter bubble up inside her. She tamped it down. "Please, Dr. Carr? I think I need to be seen by an expert. I've heard you're the best in your field."

Playing the game, he stepped into the role, assuming an authoritative air. "To properly evaluate you, I'll need to do a complete examination."

"I'd be ever so grateful. I know you must be a very busy man."

"I am." He glanced at his watch. "Luckily for you, I've had a cancellation. My exam room is on the second floor, at the end of the hall. You can change there."

"Shall I take everything off, Doctor?" She batted her lashes, trying for a mix of coy ingenue and blatant tease.

He cleared his throat. "In order to make an accurate prognosis, it's absolutely necessary."

"I understand," she said solemnly. "It's such a relief to be in good hands." She stepped closer. "I just know you'll make me all better."

"I won't rest until I do."

Max fell back against the mattress. With her inspired role-play, Dakota had blown his mind and then another equally appreciative part of him. When she landed in a sprawl on top of him, he exhaled a tired but grateful huff. Even in his depleted state, he loved the feel of her breasts cushioned against his torso.

Opening his eyes, he caught her satisfied smile and knew it originated as much in the pleasure she'd given him as in the way he'd made her arch and writhe, then cry his name, begging him not to stop.

He let his eyelids drift shut, the better to enjoy the idle patterns she was tracing across his pecs. From the twitchy response of his cock to the slow drag of her fingernail, he knew that were her fingers to travel toward his navel and then meander down and take hold again, she'd have him hard, aching, and desperate in a matter of minutes. Such was her power.

She dropped a kiss on his collarbone. "That was fun. I'm sure Dr. Davis won't mind that we borrowed the exam gown for such an excellent purpose."

He grunted to preserve his words for when he got to the office. With luck he'd have recovered a few brain cells by then. But to prove he wasn't a complete Neanderthal, he allocated precious energy to lifting his arm and letting his hand settle on her ass, squeezing it lightly.

She squirmed a little and her breasts rubbed against him, and that was good. But then she shifted back, presumably to look at his face, and the absence of that lush weight had his brows drawing together.

"So I've been thinking."

"Yeah?" he managed, his voice sounding like a car rolling over stones.

"About names," she continued.

"Names?"

"For the baby."

He gave another grunt, this one of avoidance. Not yet fully recovered from his earlier bout of panic at the doctor's, the last thing he wanted to talk about was the baby.

She must have misinterpreted his response, for she continued, all blithe confidence. "I've been compiling a mental list. Now that we know we're having a girl, it's so much easier. I've got a couple that I think are great, but the one I like best of all and think would be really lovely, is Rosie. For your sister."

It was as if she'd punched through his chest, grabbed hold of his heart, and was squeezing it mercilessly. He sat up, forcing her to roll off him, and swung his legs over the edge of the mattress.

"Max?" she asked as he stood.

Ignoring her, he stalked to where his clothes lay in a discarded heap. He dressed, shoving his limbs into his clothes with quick jerks.

From behind was a rustle. Then he heard the pad of her feet as she came up to him, either stupid or fearless in her approach. He didn't turn. He couldn't.

Her voice was close. "Max? I thought you'd like the idea of naming the baby after your sister. I know how important she was to you."

His clothes felt weird against his skin. Then he realized why: he was shaking inside them.

"It would please your father, too, wouldn't it? The news that you're going to have a baby girl and that you intend to name her Rosie as a way of honoring her memory—that would help things between you and him, wouldn't it?"

God, she was relentless in her do-gooder optimism. He had to stop her. Of all the scenarios he'd imagined in which he told her about Rosie and his father, this one was the worst. "No, it wouldn't. My father doesn't want anything to do with me." He spoke through gritted teeth as he rounded on her.

She stood before him naked, yet it was he who felt vulnerable, exposed, and, worse still, out of control.

"But a baby—*your* baby, Max—that changes things. Your father will—"

His baby. God, it had been so much easier when he'd thought of the child growing inside Dakota as hers. "No, he won't. Listen,

I get that you're hung up on your newly discovered father. I understand how torn you are about approaching him. But don't start thinking that because you can't find a way to bond with Diego Salinas, you can dream up some nifty plan where I'll be reunited with my father. There's a really good reason we don't speak."

She'd gone over to the chair by the fireplace, picked up her clothes, and begun dressing. Fastening her shirt, she looked at him. "And you don't believe that anything can change that?"

"I don't simply believe, I *know* we can't mend fences or whatever it is you're envisioning."

"Why not? He should be proud to see the man you've become."

He dragged a hand through his hair. Would she ever quit? "That's a laugh." His mouth twisted. "My father's the furthest thing from proud."

"But why—"

Enough already with the damned whys. "You want to know why, Dakota? I'll tell you. He fucking hates me, that's *why*."

"But—"

"But why? The answer's simple. Because he blames me for Rosie's death."

She lowered her hands from the last button on her shirt. "You said Rosie died in a car accident. How's that your fault, Max?"

He'd expected her to crumble under the blast of his rage and pain. But she continued to stand tall and calm and strong. It infuriated him.

"I left out a few details. Let me tell you about Rosie. She was everything I wasn't. Creative and dramatic and sensitive. She could draw for hours, memorize lines from Shakespeare, and belt out Broadway show tunes at the drop of a hat. What she couldn't do is drive for shit. Driving made her nervous. With her active imagination, she envisioned accidents and the horror of hitting someone or running over a chipmunk. So I drove us. To school and back. To the mall. Wherever. In the evenings, if Mom and Dad were busy, I'd pick her up at her art or drama classes. And I was fine with it. I loved getting out of the house and cruising the streets of Mason. Even if Rosie had been cool with driving, I probably would have fought to stay behind the wheel, 'cause driving was awesome and studly. Yeah, that was me in my Camaro—captain of the football team, ace driver. One hundred percent chick magnet."

He realized he was pacing their bedroom like a prosecutor before the jury, meticulously laying out the closing argument. Ironic, since he was not only the prosecutor but also the accused. But who better to plumb the depths of his guilt?

"But Rosie never asked to drive. Dad tried to get her to take the car out and practice, but she always had excuses. Valid ones. She was an A student, served on the student body, and was involved in a ton of extracurriculars. Her day started at six A.M. and ended at midnight. Senior year she was even busier getting her portfolio ready in order to apply to college. In April, when she got into Michigan's BFA program, she renewed her promise to practice; she wanted a car at college to drive home on weekends—Ann Arbor's only a little more than an hour away—because she was going to miss our parents like crazy."

They'd reached the worst part, the part that made it impossible for the hole inside Max ever to heal.

"So Dad laid down the law. Rosie would drive us to school. And sometimes she did, but mostly she whined that she wasn't awake yet or complained about the Camaro's hood and how she couldn't see past it and how she didn't want to arrive at school all stressed. Like I said, Rosie was real dramatic.

"I let her get away with it. Along with everything else, Rosie drove at a crawl, at least five miles below the speed limit. And I wanted to roll into the school parking lot as cool as Tom Cruise and impress the hell out of Annie Bauer, because Annie was hot and I wanted in her pants.

"I was getting there, too," he said, careful not to look at Dakota as he passed her before doing a 180 on the wool rug on his trip across the room again. "Annie and I had gone on a few dates. We'd necked, fooled around, each time going a little further.

"A few days after graduation, there was a party at a fellow senior's lake house. Although Rosie and I ran in different circles, we were equally popular, so we both got invites. I made sure Annie had accepted before I committed.

"Our parents were cool with our going. Rosie was a straight arrow. They counted on Rosie to stop me from any wild partying and on me to look out for her. Because brothers looked after their sisters. And while Rosie knew about Annie and me, Mom and Dad didn't.

"I'd wanted to take Annie to the lake house, like on a real date. But Rosie's friends didn't have room in their car, so she insisted on going with me. No way was I going to do something as lame as drive my date to a party with my twin sister in the backseat cramping my style. Both of us were pissed, and it set the tone for the ride to Nate Hicks's lake house. I needled her about all her broken promises to be more independent and drive herself places. She gave as good as she got, telling me Annie was way too smart to go all the way with a horny toad like me.

"Nate's house was rockin'. I scoured the place until I found Annie. I got us some pop—she wasn't a drinker and I wanted to show I was more than a beer-slugging jock—and we wandered down to the lake and sat down on the dock. We were talking, really talking. You know, that adolescent soul sharing that goes down on a spring night under the stars? And I was halfway in love with her. From the way she kissed me, I was hoping she felt the same.

"I was kissing her again when the dock behind us bounced and then steps came toward us. It was Rosie, saying she needed to talk to me. From her voice I could tell she was miserable, but I didn't care. I was too pissed off at her interrupting us. I hadn't forgotten her taunts about me and Annie on the way to the party, either. I told her to spit it out.

"Long and short of it, Rosie's gang had all bailed on the party before we arrived and were over at someone else's house. She needed a ride back to Mason.

"No way was I leaving Annie and giving up the chance of making it with her to chauffeur my sister to her friend's place. I dug the car keys out of my front pocket and jangled them in front of her. 'Here,' I said. 'Your very own set of wheels.' I didn't need to see her face to know how tight it was. Her cheeks and mouth got all scrunched up when she was upset. I didn't care. It wasn't a long drive and she wasn't going to be on any highways. She could deal.

"She snatched the keys out of my hand in silent fury. See, I wasn't the only one who liked Annie. Rosie thought Annie was super-cool because she'd traveled to Europe the previous summer with her parents and visited the foreign capitals, seen the monuments, and explored the museums, everything Rosie longed to do herself one day. It would have embarrassed her to reveal to Annie she was a dork who couldn't drive. This was Michigan.

"While Rosie was too angry and freaked out to say anything, it didn't stop me. As she turned around, I offered a parting shot, determined to win the evening's feud. 'Hey, Rosie,' I called out. 'Make sure you don't get caught speeding.' Those were the last words I spoke to my sister."

He stopped in his tracks and swallowed hard, forcing back the bile, a composite of self-loathing, regret, and never-ending sorrow.

"It was a ten-mile drive back to Mason. Four miles from Andy's family's weekend house, a drunk driver plowed into her, ramming the car into a tree. She'd bled out before the emergency crews could cut her out from the wreckage. My mother died of ovarian cancer less than a year after Rosie's death. At her funeral, my father finally said what was in his heart. I was responsible for both their deaths. Rosie had died because I didn't look after her the way I should have. And if my mother hadn't been grieving over Rosie, she wouldn't have ignored her symptoms until it was too late.

"And those were the last words my father has ever spoken to me. So I don't plan on ringing him up to let him know I'm having a baby girl and want to name her after his dead daughter. Not that it would change anything if I did."

He looked up at Dakota. Tears magnified her eyes.

"How do you know if you don't try—if you don't give him a chance?" Her voice vibrated with emotion.

Hating the sound, unable to bear her sympathy when she couldn't ever understand, he reached for numb detachment. "He's had fifteen years of chances."

"I don't think you believe that any more than I do."

"What?"

"I'm guessing it's been more like fifteen years of regret over every rash word he uttered. Your father was obviously inconsolable with grief when he said those things."

"He was obviously *right,* damn it. I wasn't the brother I should have been. I was the stronger twin, and I gave Rosie the keys knowing and not caring that she was inexperienced—"

She held up her hand. "Stop it, Max. It was the drunk driver who shouldn't have been behind the wheel. Who's to say that if you'd been driving you'd have been able to react any quicker? Then both of you might have died. You know that. I also think you know your father carries just as much guilt inside him for not insisting your sister practice her driving skills. Then he lost his wife. Don't you think that added to his despair and rage? So he did something terrible. He lashed out at you."

"He told me I killed my sister." His voice hurt his ears.

"A horrible, horrible thing to say to your own child. But after his grief waned and he recognized what he'd wrought and whom he'd hurt, his remorse must have been paralyzing. Maybe he feels what he's done is so terrible he can't make the first move. He's waiting until you can forgive him. You're a good man. A brave man, Max. Don't you think it's time you tried?"

"I did try. I sent him money to repay—"

"Oh, Max."

The heavy sympathy in her voice made his head pound viciously, as if a nail was being hammered through his skull. He had to get out of here. "This is utter bull. I can't do this. I didn't *ask* for any of this. Not you, not the baby, not marriage, not all this reconciliation crap." He flung out an arm to encompass the totality of what he was dealing with.

Anger was a gold flame in her eyes. "I didn't ask for any of this, either," she said, standing her ground. "Yet I'm trying my best. I'm trying to make it work."

You're fucking tearing me apart, is what you're doing, he wanted to scream in retaliation. Instead he made his voice as cold as a tomb. "That's great. But see, I've never claimed to be a good person like you. I don't help people. I source companies. I negotiate deals, and I reap the profits. I make lots and lots of money. I'm not like you, Dakota. I don't need a father. I don't need a family." He glanced at his watch, glad it was nearly time to leave for the airport, where he could go back to the world he knew and the life that worked for him.

He bent down and pulled on his shoes. Straightening, he spared her a glance, and told himself he didn't care that the tears had escaped her eyes. "I'm outta here. I'll call later."

CHAPTER THIRTY-SIX

The next morning Max sat next to Chris, the two of them facing Bob Elders. His desk, a big, black rectangle, separated them. Max had his ankle crossed over his thigh. The sheen of his polished shoe caught the reflection of the recessed light shining from above. While he sipped the coffee that Bob's personal assistant had brought them, his white French cuff and silver and onyx cuff link peeked out from the sleeve of his gray suit. His dark blue silk tie had a bold geometric pattern. He was the portrait of a Wall Street warrior, the picture of chill.

Only he knew of the caffeine he'd poured into his system to combat the sleepless hours he'd passed, he alone aware of the war raging inside him.

"So Chris's told me he wants to use this meeting to bring us up to speed on how things are going at Chiron before the board meets tomorrow. What have you got for us, Chris?" Max said.

Chris was looking relaxed. Very relaxed. Max wondered whether it was a sham on his part, too.

"Things are going according to our restructuring plan. We've closed one manufacturing site, which will allow us to make further cuts in the workforce in addition to the initial management layoffs we made. At another site we've retrofitted a tablet press, increasing production volume for several of the drugs."

So far Chris was sticking to the turnaround strategy the Summit Group had devised for Chiron: cutting labor, consolidating physical plants, and upgrading technology.

Max tried not to think about the cuts that had been made on the manufacturing side. A key part of business was to pinpoint inefficiencies and redundancies and eliminate them. But Max's father had started out on the assembly line. Even after being promoted to management, he'd liked to hang with the guys who worked on the floor. He said they were the heart and arteries of the auto factory.

He blamed Dakota for making him think of his father. He reminded himself that there was no room for sentimentality in big business; he reminded himself that, given Chiron's shaky financial health, those jobs would have been in peril no matter who bought the company. He reminded himself that he didn't do sentimentality. At least he hadn't, not for years. Not until he met Dakota.

Not trusting himself to rein in his anger, he hadn't called her last night, instead texting when he arrived at his office to say he wasn't sure when he'd be returning, letting her draw her own conclusions.

He'd felt like the jerk he was when he received her instantaneous response: *I understand and am sorry.* Yet he didn't reply with either a text or a call. He couldn't. Not until he could talk about Rosie and his father without being shredded to the bone.

Bob's ascetic face was looking positively jolly. "Higher volumes, cheaper production costs ... I'm liking this, Chris. You're hitting it out of the park."

"I haven't even shown you my good stuff, Bob." Chris was sucking up. He knew how much Elders loved baseball analogies.

Bob glanced at him, and Max lifted the corners of his mouth to demonstrate his amusement.

"Well, then, Chris, bring it on."

From the eagerness of Bob's tone, Max knew he was picturing the big, golden, cream-stuffed Twinkie he so craved right in front of him. There for the grabbing, there for the gorging.

Chris assumed a cocksure position, leaning back in the leather and chrome armchair, his hands clasped behind his head, ankles crossed. "Zeph3 is on schedule for its rollout in January. We have reps around the country talking it up, so doctors and hospitals are aware of when it will become available. We've hired Taylor & Gibbs to run the ad campaign. They charge top dollar, but they're totally worth it."

"What's your pricing strategy for Zeph3?" Max asked.

"For total treatment duration, eighty thou."

"On the high side."

Chris blew him off with a shrug. "We've got the corner on the market. Have to take advantage of that."

Max glanced at Bob. He didn't seem fazed.

"And while I was at the San Fran medical conference," Chris continued, "I talked to a bunch of consultants, doctors, and insurance reps. They got me thinking about some of the other drugs in Chiron's portfolio. I went and took a good, hard look."

This was it, Max thought, straightening in his chair. What had left Chris gloating with barely contained glee the night they'd had drinks in San Francisco.

"And what did you find, Chris?" Bob asked.

"That while Kauffmann was Chiron's CEO, the drugs were

way undervalued. Their pricing history? Flat as my grandmother's ass." He paused to chuckle. "I've spotted one that's just crying out for a little padding," he said with a smirk.

"Which one is that?" Max asked.

"Mitrilocin."

Max had spent the night reviewing his files on Chiron. It was better than thinking about what Dakota had said to him or replaying the night of Rosie's death and the terrible twelve months that followed it, or allowing his father's words to echo in his head.

"Mitrilocin, that's the cystic fibrosis drug." At Chris's nod, he continued, "Mitrilocin is a macrolide antibiotic, Bob, that's proven very effective in fighting lung infections in patients suffering from cystic fibrosis. It's still got five more years under patent, right?"

"Yeah." Lowering his arms, Chris shifted in his chair.

What, had he thought Max wouldn't come prepared?

"I'm already taking steps to extend its patent. But in the meantime, the drug is overdue for a price increase. We should act while we control the market," Chris said.

"What are you thinking of in terms of an increase?" Bob asked.

"It's at one hundred and forty dollars. I'm going to up it to one thousand five hundred and forty."

"Jesus, Chris, that's a thousand percent increase."

He shrugged. "Mitrilocin's track record justifies a higher price point. After all, we ain't in the charity business. We can't just give it away."

"One hundred and forty dollars a dose isn't exactly a giveaway," Max shot back.

Chris ignored him. "What do you think, Bob?"

"It sounds to me like not taking advantage of a more aggressive market price might be a big reason Mark Kauffmann got his company taken away from him," Bob replied.

Max looked at him. Bob, an avid cyclist, had never been sick a day in his life. Even on the grueling century rides he entered, a type A personality's favorite race, when his heart was pumping and his lungs working overtime on the long, mountainous climbs, he doubtless exalted in the moment. Understandably so. Having to suck in air while his chest worked like a bellows showed his fitness, his toughness, his unsurpassed drive. Moreover, those moments were temporary, sought after by a fitness junkie. Taking his strength for granted, Bob wouldn't wonder what it would be like to be afflicted with a disease where that condition was permanent, the act of breathing a constant effort. To live a life plagued and weakened by chronic lung infections.

There was another thing about Bob: he specialized in media and communication companies. Nobody died in those transactions. He didn't research deals where he had to look at stats that showed what the company's drugs did to help people with diseases and illnesses.

But Max did.

And he knew that if a patient with cystic fibrosis had an insurance plan that refused to cover the drug after its price was raised a thousand percent, that person—a child, perhaps—might die.

If he didn't protest this price hike, that death would be partly Max's fault.

Fuck. Fuck. Fuck.

It was as if he'd cursed aloud.

Chris looked at him, his eyes as flat and menacing as a shark's, and smiled. "Exactly." Then, shifting his attention across the black desk, he said, "Mark Kauffmann didn't have the balls to make Chiron a major-league player, Bob. I do."

"Bob, Chris, I gotta tell you, I don't think this is the right move to make. Such a dramatic price hike is a mistake."

"I disagree, Max. I don't see any problem with Chris's plan. I don't believe the board will, either," Bob said, the twin lines between his brows adding severity to his face. "Chiron's producing a much-needed and beneficial drug that eases suffering. Yes, the insurers and some patients will have to pay more for it. But a portion of the revenue generated will be going toward R&D. Chiron's chemists have already developed a drug to fight cystic fibrosis's symptoms. Perhaps they'll find a drug that actually cures the disease."

Bob might not do pharma deals, but it hadn't prevented him from picking up the industry's standard line. It was the stock response companies parroted over and over again to justify jacking up prices: Discovering new and successful drugs and then putting them through the rigorous trials required for FDA approval was lengthy and costly. Immensely so. Raising drug prices was necessary, *vital,* for the companies to survive.

Anyone who'd looked at the year-end profits for the majority of pharma companies knew that was a crock.

God, why couldn't Chris have made Max's life easier by picking a drug that treated acne? Toenail fungus? Male pattern baldness? Max wouldn't have cared if that drug's price had been raised through the roof.

But this plan was going to hurt people. People who were already suffering.

Max knew better than to press the issue in front of Chris, however. Bob hated any show of dissent.

Bob glanced at his watch. "I think we've gone over everything we need before we convene tomorrow," he said, a clear signal that any further discussion was unwelcome. For the sake of propriety, he added, "Unless there's anything else?"

Rising to his feet, Chris shook his head. "Nope. All good on my end."

Max stood but remained silent.

"Again, Chris, really pleased with what you've accomplished so far. Keep it up," Bob said after they shook hands.

"Glad you approve. Only wish Max here weren't so down in the mouth. Looking a little hangdog, bro."

The little prick, thought Max. "Not at all, Chris."

Chris's eyes widened. "My mistake. Hey, want to grab a bite to eat?"

"Sorry, I have a meeting out of the office. Don't know how long it will take."

"Maybe after the board meeting, then."

Not if he could avoid it. "Sure thing."

"Then see you guys *mañana.*"

Max waited until Chris was out the door and out of earshot. "If I could speak to you for a moment?"

"Sure, Max. Shoot."

"Bob, I've got to level with you. It's a really bad idea to increase Mitrilocin's cost so dramatically. The drug *works,* Bob. That means for the patients whose insurance companies refuse coverage for it, they'll have to look for alternative treatments that might not fight the infection as effectively. Or they'll go bankrupt paying out of pocket because it's the only treatment that helps. That's kind of adding insult to injury, don't you think?"

"Actually, I don't." He leaned forward in his chair and, propping his elbows on his desk, steepled his fingers together. "Who'd have thought it—Max Carr sounding like a bleeding-heart liberal? Next you're going to be arguing for socialized medicine. Max, you know as well as anyone you don't make billions by being nice."

"Chiron will be making a profit on Zeph3 alone, Bob. A thousand percent price hike for a Mitrilocin is outrageous."

"I disagree. The Summit Group's principal duty is to our investors. We have a fiduciary responsibility to maximize our profits. You *know* this, Max. What's gotten into you lately? First you piss off Steffen—when he was the one you put forward to run Chiron—and now you're actively going against him on a business decision that, as CEO, is *his* to make. I'm having trouble recognizing the team player I depend on."

Dakota had gotten to him. Her words yesterday, arguing that he wasn't to blame for Rosie's death or his mother's, that he was a good man, had found their way inside him. He might not be the direct cause of Rosie's death, but he'd nevertheless failed his twin in a crucial moment. Max could blame immaturity for his unthinking selfishness. But how would he ever justify being part of a plan to hike the price of a drug used by people already fighting a terrible disease? Impossible. Impossible, too, to pretend that he was even remotely a good man if he went along with this.

Since he couldn't persuade Bob with a moral argument, he decided to try a regulatory one. "There's another thing to consider. A thousand percent price increase is going to raise a hue and cry among patients and industry watchdogs. The last thing we want is to attract the attention of the feds. That will cost Chiron not only in legal fees but also in reputation. It could lead to a PR disaster. That in turn could affect Zeph3's rollout."

"Again, I disagree. Steffen's not stupid. He knows the market and what he can get away with. If he'd gone and jacked up the amount by four thousand percent, well, then we might have a problem on our hands. But a thousand percent? That's the sign of an aggressive CEO who's fully prepared to wield the pricing power he holds. Time to get on board, Max."

CHAPTER THIRTY-SEVEN

Max returned to his office, sat down at his desk, and opened his Chiron files. He reread everything he had on Mitrilocin and cystic fibrosis to make sure his gut reaction at the meeting with Bob and Chris hadn't been a sloppy side effect of all the emotions—the guilt, the regret—resulting from his and Dakota's fight.

He checked stats, compared competing drugs, looked at follow-up studies on the drug, and cursed as frustration and anger grew inside him. Mitrilocin was as effective as he'd thought. The majority of patients given the drug were free of chest infections for up to six months and reported weight gain, as well—because with CF, it was damned hard to keep weight on when the lungs and gut were being attacked. Adverse effects were minimal.

It was small consolation that Max didn't believe Chris had intentionally duped him. He didn't think that Chris had set his sights on Mitrilocin from the get-go rather than on Zeph3, the melanoma drug that Chris had originally touted as their goldmine.

And what if Chris had recognized the potential for Mitrilocin to be an amazing windfall and shared it with him when they first sat down to talk about acquiring Chiron? Max might very well have decided that it only made the deal sweeter.

Because nine months ago, Max had been a different person.

He had a wife now. A pregnant wife. Yesterday the ultrasound tech had said that everything seemed fine with the baby, but so much could still go wrong.

Restless, he stood and went over to the bank of windows overlooking Park Avenue. It was midmorning in midtown, so the traffic had crawled to a stop, idling cars and delivery trucks spewing exhaust into the air.

He thought of how he'd come to love stepping outside Windhaven and drawing the salty air deep into his lungs. For people afflicted with cystic fibrosis, their lungs were filled with thick mucus; it was a battle to draw any kind of air at all. He thought of his daughter, his tiny perfect daughter. Her lungs were still developing.

How would he feel if, by some horrible twist of fate, it turned out that she had the genetic mutation and developed the disease? His wealth would allow him to afford every treatment available. But how would he live with himself knowing so many other parents, sisters, and brothers couldn't do the same for their loved ones? How could anyone live with that?

Max shouldn't have let Rosie, an inexperienced driver, take the car home that night. The knowledge would probably haunt him forever. He couldn't repeat the mistake and sit back, doing nothing while Chris raised Mitrilocin's price sky-high.

Unless he convinced Bob to back him, Chris's performance as

Chiron's new CEO would likely receive a standing ovation at tomorrow's board meeting. After their conversation, Max knew what a long shot it was.

For so long, Max's world had been shaped by deals and dollar signs. His route had been linear, straight to the top. He was on track to achieve the goals he'd set for himself, raking in millions with each successive and successful deal and burnishing his image in Bob Elders's eyes, essential to taking over as the Summit Group's next managing director when Elders stepped down.

Refusing to go along with Chris's plans could very well derail his own. And he had no map for what that world would look like.

A knock sounded on his open door. He glanced over his shoulder to see Roger Cohen enter.

"Hey, Max. How'd the meeting with Bob and Steffen go?"

He turned away from the windows and shrugged. "Fucked six ways to Sunday." Removing his hands from his pockets, he gestured for Roger to sit and then dropped into the chair angled opposite him. "Remember how I told you about the drink I had with Chris in San Francisco, and how it was clear he was up to something? Well, he just shared it. He wants to take a drug Chiron manufactures that's frequently prescribed to cystic fibrosis patients to fight lung infections and up its price tag by a thousand percent."

Roger whistled softly. "Bob's on board with that?"

"Yeah. And he told me I'd better be, too." Max rubbed his face wearily. Damn, he wished he were home on Long Island with Dakota, far away from this shit storm. "I laid out the drug's role, argued the negatives against the price hike, warned about the potential for a federal investigation, and told him that already sick people might very well die if Chiron takes this step. Bob talked about fiduciary responsibility."

"What are you going to do?"

Max's laugh was bitter. "You're the lawyer, Rog. You tell me.

I'm not about to leak Chris's plan to the media." That kind of move was for rats. Besides, what Chris was doing wasn't illegal; it was simply loathsome. In short, not especially newsworthy. "What the hell *can* I do except go into Bob's office and try again? If he's not willing to second me, then I have no chance of swaying the board."

Roger's silence told Max what he already knew. They had both observed Bob's responses to criticism. There was no way to come out of this battle unbloodied.

"Hell of a time to develop a conscience, right?" Max said.

"Better late than never."

Max managed the semblance of a grin. "It's been good working with you, Roger."

Roger cleared his throat. "Listen," he said. He reached into the inside pocket of his suit and pulled out a business card and a slim silver pen and scrawled on the back of the card. "Here's the name and number of a good lawyer. Your shares in Summit are fully vested, Max, but you'll still need top-notch representation. Mike Gaddis is your guy. Before you head into Bob's, call Mike. Drop my name and make sure you've got him on retainer before you hang up the phone."

Max took the card. "Thanks, Roger."

They stood and shook hands. "Fuckin' Steffen," Roger said with weary disbelief.

"Yeah."

Roger smiled sadly and moved toward the door. Then he stopped and turned. "Look, you're smart. You've been wildly successful. You have enough money to live out the rest of your life in champagne and caviar. You can do anything. What is it you really want, Max?"

What sprang to Max's mind wasn't what he had expected. But he knew it was the truth. He smiled.

Roger returned it. "Good luck, man."

"You too. And hey, you and the family should come out to East Hampton and stay with us this summer. Dakota's not due until the end of August. There's plenty of room at the house."

"We'd like that."

Max nodded. "I'll be in touch."

Max murmured "Thanks" when Susan Hughes, Bob's assistant, ushered him back into the spacious corner office. On the phone, his long legs propped on his desk, Bob held up an index finger to indicate that the conversation would be wrapping up shortly.

Max lowered himself into the chair he'd occupied only an hour before.

While Bob talked about media market growth drivers to whoever was on the line, Max let his glance travel around the office, its gleaming surfaces reflecting power.

His phone vibrated. He reached into his jacket pocket, pulled it out and glanced at the screen. It was a text from Dakota. *Hope the meeting went okay. Thinking of you.*

Damn, he needed her. He'd only begun to realize just how much.

This wasn't the time to reply. There was too much to explain. He swiped the screen and saw that he had a voicemail, from Chris of all people. As if he wanted to hear anything that punk had to say.

Finished with his call, Bob lowered his feet and swiveled his chair to face Max. "So, what have you got for me?" he asked with a nod at the file resting on Max's thighs. "New deal you're sourcing?"

"No." Slipping the phone back into his pocket, he half rose and set the file in front of his boss. "I want you to look at this. I hope it will change your mind."

Bob's eyes flashed in irritation. Opening the folder, his lips thinned in a line of displeasure.

A heavy silence descended, broken only by the deliberate slap of papers being turned.

Reaching the last page, Bob looked up. A muscle twitched along his jaw. "What the hell are you trying to prove, Max?"

"When I was interviewing at PE firms, Summit was my top choice. I wanted to be here because of the way you ran the group and encouraged your partners to go after deals with everything they had. Bob, I've loved working for you and with you. I'm proud of this firm. I'm proud of the deals—big and small—we've made. But this thing with Mitrilocin, it's different. Look at the stats on the drug. Look at the photos of an occluded lung. Do you really want Summit Group to be linked to a decision that will make a drug too expensive for people who already struggle to breathe on a daily basis?

"We have to stop Chris from taking this step. Chiron will already see a substantial increase in earnings from the price he's set for Zeph3."

"And that margin will be even greater if we let Chris do his goddamn job."

"In a few months I'm going to have a little girl, Bob. When she comes into the world, I want—I *need*—to be able to look her in the face and know that I've tried to be a good man."

Elders's face flushed red. "What are you saying?"

"It's your choice, Bob. Him or me."

"Are you giving me an ultimatum?" Elders asked in astonishment.

"The only reason I am is because I care about our firm and its reputation. I want to make deals and money for you, but not like this."

Fury replaced astonishment. "Son of a bitch," he cursed. "I

taught you. I looked out for you. I groomed you for this office. You could have had all this." The wave of his arm encompassed the office. Max knew he believed it stretched further still, to the great beyond. Bob was wrong. Dakota was his all. He realized that now. She and the baby were his everything.

"And this is how you show your gratitude to me?" he concluded.

Max stood. "I hope you change your mind about Chiron and Chris, Bob. He's slime. Don't let him dirty you and what you've built here. I'll let the guys know so we can set up a transition team—"

"Like hell you will. *I* call the shots here. You walk out that door, then just keep walking, Carr. There's no coming back."

Roger had nailed it, anticipating exactly how this would play out. Thank God he'd done as Roger suggested and called Mike Gaddis. It looked like he was going to need a really good lawyer.

"Goodbye, Bob."

CHAPTER THIRTY-EIGHT

Dakota was in the paper products aisle of the Bridgehampton King Kullen, stocking up on supplies for her clients' homes. With Easter around the corner and the weather warming, her regulars were coming out in larger numbers on the weekends. By June, the madness of the summer in the Hamptons would be in high gear.

She plucked down a triple pack of white Bounty—no matter the brand, her customers all favored white paper towels—dropped it in her cart, grabbed the same in Viva in a six-pack because the Morrisseys had a huge storage area, and resisted looking at her phone.

She'd only sent the text minutes ago, after she'd entered the store, grabbed her shopping cart, and then watched Rae push hers toward the canned-goods aisle. It was ridiculous to expect that Max, as busy as he was when at work, would reply so soon.

For all she knew he was still in the meeting with Chris Steffen and Bob Elders.

He'd reply when he could. When he was ready.

She'd made a mistake. The adage went that love made you blind. Here was a new one to add to the list: happiness made you stupid. She was twice doomed.

Love hadn't necessarily made her blind to Max's character flaws, but it had made her lose sight of the wounds he carried, wounds that had never fully healed. Her happiness at discovering they were going to have a baby girl had been as heady as the perfume of a bouquet of peonies in full bloom. Lush and exquisite, happiness had turned her head. Made her ignore lessons previously learned.

She'd seen how he reacted when reminded of his family. He couldn't handle a little old Christmas tree in his living room, yet she'd expected him to be delighted with the idea of naming their daughter after his deceased twin.

Aglow with her own contentment, she'd missed the signs that Max was far from okay, far from nonchalant following the doctor's visit. In her happiness, she'd callously disregarded all she knew about the festering pain of family-inflicted wounds.

Had she not had such experience herself, had she grown up cocooned and cherished and unmarked, her ignorance might have served as a plausible excuse.

Piper had done a terrible thing. Dakota wasn't sure she could ever forgive her for lying all these years. But her mother's transgression paled to a morning mist compared to the accusation Max's father had leveled at his devastated son.

It was a testament to Max's strength that his heart hadn't withered from the corrosive effects of those words.

She grabbed three separate Brawny rolls because John Warner preferred spending extra money and having everything neatly wrapped and organized, the way everything in his house looked.

She dropped them in the cart and made her way down the wide aisle.

She wanted to despise Max's father for what he'd done to his son. But when she considered how he must have been suffering, how some people in their grief and pain lashed out rather than embraced, she couldn't bring herself to wish him any further ill. Under the supermarket's bright fluorescent lights, it was easy to picture the elder Carr: frozen in loneliness, unable to connect with the person he needed most.

That Max so closely resembled this state as well was heart-rending.

She remembered her sadness when he revealed that he'd sent his father money. Max must have been too hurt and too afraid of yet another cutting rejection to approach him in person. The money, while such a sorry solution, would have been a way to show his father his success and prove his sense of responsibility. Just thinking of what the Carrs had suffered made her heart ache.

She stopped her cart by the facial tissues section, grateful for the distraction of matching Kleenex boxes' patterns and colors to all the bathrooms and spaces in her clients' homes.

She would not break down and call Max to apologize for her tactlessness. They could name the baby Augusta for all she cared. And if he could never bring himself to forgive his father, she'd be sorry, but she would understand.

The essential thing was that Max make peace with himself.

Rae's voice broke into her thoughts. "What, are they missing that blue color you like to put in Theo and Freddy's bathroom?" she asked, pulling her own cart alongside Dakota's. Hers was filled with olive oils and vinegars, jars of peanut butters, jams, and mayo, cans of tuna, and packages of sugar and flour.

Dakota shook off her preoccupation. "No, just spacing out."

"I can do the rest if you're tired."

Dakota laughed. "I'm fine. The baby's fine. And if it wouldn't bring down the wrath of King Kullen's manager, I'd challenge you to a race down the aisle."

"That sounds like fun. Let's—" Rae's reply was interrupted by the chime of Dakota's cell.

She held up a finger. "Sorry, just a sec." She grabbed her phone from her vest pocket.

Sharp disappointment filled her when the message she'd hoped for was instead from her aunt Mimi—what was she doing, texting her?—but then she read the text: *Your husband got bored of you awfully quick.* A link followed.

Her thumb was clicking on the link before her intent even registered. A video filled the screen. A man and a woman were naked on a bed. The woman straddled his naked thighs, rising and falling onto his lap as the man stroked her breasts and played with her nipples. Moans and grunts punctuated their thrusts and grinds and then, with a full body shudder, the woman let her head fall back on an ecstatic cry.

"WTF is that?" Rae asked leaning over.

Instinctively Dakota turned off her phone, but the noises coming from Max—it was him in that video; she knew that body, that profile, recognized even the sounds he made—with the woman echoed, pummeling her.

She swayed. *Oh God, oh God.* She blinked against the bright, mocking orderliness of the aisle. It seemed especially cruel that all the products remained neatly stacked on the shelves when her life was so thoroughly wrecked.

"Dakota? Are you all right?"

No, she really wasn't. "Actually, Rae, I'm feeling a little off," she said vaguely. A terrible loneliness filled her as she realized she couldn't share what had happened with her friend. Not yet, maybe not ever. "Let's get out of here, okay?" She let go of the cart and walked away from it.

"Dakota—" Rae's eyes were wide with shock.

"What?"

"You mean to just leave all this stuff here?"

"Yeah." Because if she didn't get out of there right away, she was going to start screaming, unleashing her rage and pain, and hurling every damned box of tissues as far as she could throw them.

Knowing that Bob would immediately be on the phone with Ed Jackson, Jim Bayles, and Lewis Brant, the three other partners at Summit, informing them of Max's desertion, he ignored Bob's fury-injected edict and returned to his office, summoning his two associates, Andy Reynolds and Glenn Howard, to break the news that he was leaving the firm. He kept it short and sweet, stressing that his was an "amicable departure." The guys were sharp. They knew Chris had been causing trouble. They would draw their own conclusions once the news of Mitrilocin's price spike became public.

Because sure as shit, there would be an uproar. Bob and Chris were sadly mistaken in thinking that industry watchdogs wouldn't be sniffing around this very crappy move.

He was unexpectedly moved by his assistant's shock and dismay at the news. Fred blinked rapidly behind his tortoiseshell glasses. "And—and—your appointments?"

"You'll have to discuss that with Bob and whoever takes over for me. They'll either keep them or reschedule."

"Yes, yes, of course." Fred nodded tightly. "And Mr. Miller?"

Damn, he'd completely forgotten today's meeting with Alex Miller. Alex wanted his take on a clean-energy start-up. "That's soon, right?"

"Your appointment is in half an hour. At his office."

"I'll keep it." He'd explain to Alex what had gone down and cut the meeting short. They could talk about the start-up over the weekend. "But Fred, one last thing. Can you call Blade and book a flight for me to East Hampton at two o'clock? And then can you pack up my stuff here and have it sent to my apartment?"

"Of course, Mr. Carr."

Max smiled. From the very beginning when Fred was assigned to him, he'd tried to break him of the habit of calling him "Mr. Carr," but the older man had always been adamant. "Thanks. Thanks for everything, Fred. You know, Andy and Glenn are good guys. One of them will most likely be moving in here." If he had to bet, he thought it would be Andy, who was just a little more aggressive, that much hungrier to close the deal … a true believer. Bob would be looking for that.

He pulled out his wallet and removed the ID card that got him past lobby security and handed it to Fred. Then he took the office keys off his key chain and passed them to him as well.

"It'll take a couple of weeks for the dust to settle, but you've got my number, and you know you can contact me for anything."

He extended his hand.

Fred shook it. "Thank you, Mr. Carr. It's been a pleasure working for you."

Max walked down the carpeted hallway, aware of the hushed atmosphere in the office, a blanketing, damning silence in answer to his defection. In a firm this small, his move would be taken personally, and despite how well he and his partners had always gotten along, there'd be a dose of schadenfreude that the heir apparent to Summit Group was toppled; the race to take his place was on.

Sherri, the receptionist, had abandoned her desk, but Max had no doubt that everyone in the office knew the exact moment he opened the door with the engraved plaque on its front and then let it close behind him with a soft click.

Standing in front of the elevators, he fought against the disorientation. He was no longer Max Carr, partner at Summit Group. He'd made the right decision in resigning, but that didn't prevent him from wishing things were otherwise.

His phone rang. He looked at the number and frowned in surprise. Pressing the green button, he said, "Hey, Roger."

"Max." The way Roger said his name put Max on instant alert.

The elevator doors opened, and Max stepped inside. It was blessedly free of occupants. "What's up?" he asked, pressing the button for the lobby.

"That tape of you and Ashley Nicholls? It's out." Roger named one of the Internet sites that vied with TMZ and Gawker for scandal and dirt. "And it's gone viral."

His stomach dropped faster than the elevator. "Fuck."

"Ashley Nicholls has put out a statement claiming she got hacked. But she hasn't said anything else."

Max's laugh was hollow. "Of course not."

"Unfortunately, I can't handle this for you, but I've called Mike Gaddis. He's on it. He'll get the video taken down."

The damage was done. *Jesus, what if Dakota saw it?* Max thought.

"Did you know this Ashley Nicholls is in a reality show? That's apparently what's spurring the interest . . . aside from the obvious."

Chris had told him about Ashley's new career back in San Francisco. Suddenly he recalled the crack Chris had made about them looking good together. Preoccupied with discovering Steffen's plans for Chiron and caught up in Dakota's distress over her mother's deception, Max had forgotten the taunt.

"Chris is behind this somehow, Roger. I'm sure of it. I don't know if he put her up to making the tape in the first place or just decided to take advantage of its existence, but let the guys know to watch their backs around him."

The elevator reached the ground floor, finally catching up

with his stomach. He stepped into the lobby with its polished marble floors and high ceilings.

"I will. You know nobody's going to care about the tape except for Bob. Smart of you to resign when you did. You took away any ammunition Bob would have used against you. You outmaneuvered them both."

"Rog," he said, striding toward the lobby doors and waving to the security guards, "I don't give a fuck what anybody but my wife thinks about this." He passed through the revolving door, and then he was out on Park Avenue competing with the lunch-hour crowds and traffic. "Listen, I've got to go. Thanks for the heads-up. I owe you."

"No problem. Call me when you can."

Hanging up, he immediately called Dakota, cursing when her voicemail picked up. She'd turned off her phone. He didn't bother leaving a message because he needed to *talk* to her. A recording of him babbling how damn sorry he was wouldn't help.

At the curb, he punched in Alex Miller's number and hailed a taxi with his free hand. A cab pulled up. Max yanked open the door and gave the address for the Blade helipad on East Thirty-Fourth Street as he listened to the rings.

He breathed a sigh of relief when Alex answered. But relief was replaced with shame when Alex immediately said, "Christ, Max. What the hell?"

So Roger hadn't been exaggerating when he said the tape had gone viral. At least his friend—*Dakota's* friend—was still talking to him. "I know. Long story and an old one. The tape was made before I even purchased Windhaven. I'll tell you about it later, but I've got to catch a flight back to East Hampton ASAP. I'm hoping Dakota won't have seen it."

"Are you kidding? Mimi Hale has been very busy. Gen got the link in her inbox an hour ago. Rest assured Dakota's beloved aunt was as generous with her."

"Crap." So the video had been uploaded an hour and change ago. Chris must have arranged with the "news" site to have it released shortly after their meeting, which meant he'd anticipated that Max would object to the price hike for Mitrilocin and planned to use the video to rouse Bob's puritanical damnation—and generally screw Max over. "Alex, I messed up. With Dakota, I mean. We had a fight. It was over some personal stuff and I got angry. I split and I didn't call her, not even after I cooled down. And now this happens." He dragged a hand through his hair, staring out the window and wishing there weren't so many stoplights between him and the East River. "I keep blowing things with her."

"You love her, right?" Alex asked.

"More than I ever thought possible." And he hadn't even told her yet. He'd pay quadruple the fare to get the chopper to leave as soon as he arrived.

"Glad I don't have to kick your ass. Okay, then. Go make it right with Dakota and see to it that she knows how you feel and how sorry you are. She's strong and I know she cares for you."

Max hoped she still did. He certainly hadn't made it easy for her.

CHAPTER THIRTY-NINE

Dakota had let Rae drive.

"So, you going to clue me in on what's got you so upset? 'Cause if it has to do with the baby, I'm heading west and not east."

Dakota continued to stare out the window with her lip squeezed between her teeth. The pain was keeping the tears at bay.

"Come on, Dakota," Rae said quietly. "You've always been there for me."

She released her abused lip. "It's a sex tape. Of Max and some woman. Mimi sent it to me—"

Rae's reaction blistered her ears.

"I—I—" Dakota's voice faltered as a fresh wave of pain rolled through her. "I just didn't think he'd do that to me. Not now." *Not ever,* she added silently.

Abruptly Rae pulled off on the side of Snake Hollow Road. Killing the engine, she turned in her seat and extended her hand. "Let me see it."

"What? No. Why?" The words tumbled out, a verbal recoil.

"Because it's bogus. We just have to figure out why. Max would not do this to you, Dakota. I've watched him with you. Never once has he acted like the kind of sleazebag who cheats on his pregnant wife. And you know before Marcos and I got together I had plenty of experience with two-timers. That's not Max. Not by a long shot. And no, I'm not just saying that because he's the best thing that's happened to my bank account and Premier Service in forever."

Dakota laughed sadly. "As if you would."

"So give me the phone. Otherwise I'll just Google it on my own, and I bet it would be even worse for you to see how quickly it comes up."

Dakota drew a shaky breath. She'd never felt so alone as in these last minutes since she'd clicked on the link sent by her aunt. If she couldn't turn to her friends, whom did she have left? And Rae was right. If Mimi had found the tape—she'd doubtless set up a Google alert for Max's name—it must be making the rounds.

She dug her phone out of her pocket, turned it on, entered her passcode, and handed it to Rae. "It's in the messages," she said dully.

Rae was much more methodical than she had been. She pulled up the link, then tilted the phone so the screen would be horizontal, and read. "'Reality Star Ashley Nicholls and Max Carr, Wealthy Financier, Get Frisky.' Who's this Ashley Nicholls?"

Dakota rubbed her forehead. "No idea," she said wearily, thinking back to when she'd done a routine search on Max. All those pictures showing beautiful women hanging on his arm. Had Ashley Nicholls been one of them? How long had he been seeing her? Had he ever stopped?

"Well, we can find out who she is later," Rae said. She leaned closer to Dakota, holding the phone so that it was between them, and tapped Play.

Dakota kept her gaze averted. But then the sounds reached her, and it was like with a train wreck: no matter how much she wished to resist, she couldn't help but look. Even though she knew that in this case the wreckage was going to be her heart.

It was just as graphic and distressing as the first time, and she hated watching Max's body moving with another woman's, watching his thighs and buttocks clench as he thrust upward . . .

"Stop the video," she said, her heart racing.

"I'm sorry, Dakota." Rae's voice was small. "I had no idea. I didn't realize it would be so—"

"No—no, that's not why. Just let me have the phone."

Rae passed it to her. Dakota held the screen, angling it so she could see the colors more clearly. Relief made her feel faint. She let out a long breath and then said, "He's got a tan, Rae. Look at his butt and thighs, how much paler they are than his torso and lower legs. But Max has been wearing long sleeves and sweats whenever he's run outside this spring. He's *lost* his tan."

"Oh, thank fuck." Rae sank back against the seat. "I was worried I was going to have to chop off his balls for you. So the video isn't recent."

"No, it must have been made last summer." Or even before that.

"You okay, then?"

"Yeah." It still hurt to see the tape; it was upsetting to know it existed. But it wasn't *personal.* She couldn't let it be.

Dakota groaned in resignation when she saw Piper's car parked in front of her house.

"I don't suppose this is a coincidence, Mimi sending you a raunchy video and Piper camping out on your doorstep?"

Dakota shook her head. "Consider me singularly blessed."

"Want me to play wingman?" Any affection Rae felt for Piper

had disappeared when she heard about Piper keeping the identity of her father a secret from Dakota. That Diego Salinas was a fellow Latino was further outrage. "Or would you rather I make a U-turn and finish the shopping?"

On their way out of the King Kullen, Rae had told the store manager that her pregnant friend had an emergency but that she would be back for the items in the two carts they'd left in aisle three.

"That would be great. Sorry for the freak-out back there."

"Completely understandable. You sure you'll be okay with her?" She thrust her chin in the direction of Piper's car.

With her and Rae camped out in the Land Cruiser and Piper yet to emerge from her own car, the scene reminded her of two enemies preparing to do battle. "Yeah, I can handle it. Piece of cake after Mimi's surprise. I just want Piper gone already."

She wondered where Max was, tried not to worry that he hadn't even messaged her. She sighed. "I should get this over with."

"Good luck. I'll bring the car back tomorrow morning, okay?"

"Perfect. And Rae?"

"Yeah?"

"Thanks." She reached out and squeezed Rae's jean-clad leg.

"*De nada,* kiddo."

Piper opened the door and climbed out, a cellphone attached to her ear, as Dakota approached. "She's just arrived. I'll call back later."

Dakota wondered whether it was Mimi on the other end or one of Piper's many gossip buddies, who'd doubtless spent the morning replaying the video, the better to ogle her husband. Rage simmered. "What are you doing here?" she asked, pulling her house keys from her bag.

"So you've seen it," Piper said.

"Seen what?" Dakota used her shoulder to push open the door. Unnecessary but satisfying. She wanted to flatten any number of people on the East End right now, starting with her family. She considered the door practice.

"The sex tape. I must say, that husband of yours is very impressive."

If she said another word about Max, Dakota would make her sorry.

Piper must have guessed she was walking on razor-thin ice. Either that or she was distracted by her first glimpse of her old childhood home.

Dakota hung up her vest, pointedly not inviting Piper to remove her coat. The lack of invitation didn't stop her mother from making herself at home. She wandered into the living room and began circling it, trailing her fingers over the backs of chairs and sofas, the tops of side tables. Pausing, she'd pick up one of the decorative pieces Dakota had found to add warmth to the room, study it, and then set it down, each time in a slightly different and *wrong* place.

"I told Mimi not to forward the link, you know. I did try." She glanced over her shoulder at Dakota as if expecting her thanks for acting like a human being.

Maybe this was as good as it was ever going to get with Piper. If so, could she—should she—try to accept Piper's severe limitations, the shattering disappointment she was as a parent? This was her mother, after all.

"Too bad Mimi didn't listen," Dakota said.

"She never does." Piper shrugged. "I'd have put a different painting there," she said, gesturing to Gen Monaghan's seascape. "But I suppose you want to make her happy."

"I love it there. I think it totally makes the room."

"If you say so. Mary Dillon had a very good lawyer. I could get his name for you."

"Why would I need a lawyer?"

"You'll divorce him, of course. You'll need someone who's a shark if you want to keep Windhaven."

"A video of my husband having sex with some woman is making the rounds on the Internet, and this is what you offer as sympathy?"

"You should never have married him in the first place. I'm only trying to save you further humiliation. Dump him and take him to the cleaners. Now, do you want me to call Mary? I'm sure she's back from Florida—"

With sudden clarity she understood the purpose of Piper's visit.

And she knew, too, that there'd be no apology from Piper, not for hiding the identity of Dakota's father, not for hoping that Dakota's marriage would fail, and not for undermining it whenever she could. Piper would never acknowledge that deep down she wanted Dakota to end up alone. That a divorce might hurt Dakota and the baby wouldn't signify, not when weighed against Piper's desire to reclaim her dominant role in Dakota's life.

A calm that came from finally letting go settled over her. "I'm not going to divorce Max."

"Don't be a fool, Dakota. He'll leave you as soon as the baby's born, and everyone will laugh, and you'll have lost everything—Windhaven, the money—everything."

"I think you should leave now."

"What?" Piper's eyes widened in disbelief, and then she laughed. "Are you seriously throwing me out of my family's house?"

Dakota smiled. "You've got that wrong, too. You see, Windhaven belongs to my family now. And you're not welcome. I'll show you out."

CHAPTER FORTY

Max didn't listen to Chris's voicemail until the helicopter touched down in East Hampton and he'd climbed into the taxi and given the driver his address.

It was easy to picture his face from his mocking, pseudo-sympathetic tone. "Hey, Max, buddy. Wow, just saw the tape. What a shame about Ashley's phone being hacked. Those cyber geeks must have had quite the surprise when they stumbled upon you and her. Can't imagine Bob's going to be too happy about his top partner in a skin flick." He clucked in faux concern. "Life really sucks sometimes, don't it?"

Max turned off the message and stared out the window, absently noting that the trees were beginning to show color, bright greens and rosy pinks. The message confirmed his suspicions. Chris had known about the tape's existence—most likely from the beginning. It would have amused him, made him laugh his ass off, to know that Ashley was trying to shake Max down. Max wouldn't be surprised if he'd conceived the idea of selling the video to the celebrity news site. He'd have told Ashley that by doing so she'd make some bucks and heighten her visibility, always a plus for a reality TV star. Best of all, it would hurt Max. A win-win for both Chris and Ashley.

Their supposed victory over him, a trumping of sorts, left him oddly indifferent. At some point he'd retaliate and would surely find the revenge quite sweet, but after speaking with Roger and Alex, Max realized he was at a crossroads, with new concerns pointing him in a different direction. As he'd told Alex, he loved Dakota more than he'd ever thought possible. He loved her truly, deeply, completely. It was time to show her.

He leaned forward in the seat and said to the driver, "Can you step on it, please?"

A strange car was parked in the driveway; Dakota's was missing. He frowned as he paid the driver and climbed out just in time to see Piper Hale emerge from the house, Dakota a step behind her.

Both women froze. Max looked at Dakota, hoping like a fool that, despite everything, he would see her smile.

It was Piper who beamed a flash of bright white amusement at him. "The porn star returns. But those moans, they sounded quite real, didn't they, Dakota? I'll get the number for that divorce lawyer for you, doll."

She breezed past Max, close enough for her perfume to envelop him, but that wasn't the reason he suddenly couldn't breathe.

Dakota wants a divorce?

When he looked back at the house, she was gone.

The downstairs rooms were empty. In his panic, he had a sudden vision of her simply vanishing from his life and taking everything she'd brought to it. He'd be left empty and adrift, and this time he would recognize the feeling and know the cause … and know who was to blame.

He had to make it right.

Glancing through the windows, he caught sight of her. She was at the far edge of the lawn, where the seagrass grew up from the dunes.

She must have sensed his approach. He saw her shoulders rise and then fall as if she was steadying herself. Bracing herself for the ugliness he'd introduced into their marriage.

He came to stand beside her. "Dakota?"

She didn't answer. She didn't need to. The look she gave him spoke volumes, covering anger, hurt, and sadness.

"I'm sorry, Dakota. I'm sorry about so much that's happened in these last few days. We need to talk—I need to explain everything that's been going on. But please, can I just hold you and the baby for a second?"

He'd expected her to refuse. It was what he deserved after two days of radio silence in which he'd behaved like a petulant boy. It was to be expected after the embarrassment and pain she'd suffered from the video going public. Her turning toward him underscored her resilience and maturity, her basic generosity; they never failed.

She was so beautiful. He stepped forward, first cradling her face and simply looking into the dark gold of her eyes, then wrapping his arms around her and drawing her close until her rounded belly was nestled against him. Lowering his head, he pressed his lips against the side of her neck and inhaled the scent of her. How would he survive if he lost this?

He held her as her shoulders began to quake and the tears ran down her cheeks. When eventually she quieted, he wiped the last of their traces with his thumbs and said, "A lot has happened. A good deal of it is really shitty. I'll start with the worst, okay?"

She nodded. "Okay," she said, her voice husky with emotion.

"You saw the tape?"

"Mimi. May she rot in hell."

"Amen to that. I can't tell you how sorry I am that you had to see it." He couldn't say sorry enough. "I know how much it must have hurt you. Dakota, do you remember the woman I told you about, the one who tried to blackmail me? It was Ashley Nicholls. We were together for a while, four months or so, and then I ended the relationship. Nothing unusual there. But then last fall, she contacted me and told me she had a tape of us together. She wanted a million for it. I had Roger Cohen deal with her and make her understand what would happen if the tape ever surfaced. I didn't hear from her again."

He paused. Would she believe this next part? "Dakota, the tape, it was made a couple of months before I met you."

"I know."

At his start of surprise, her lips curved in a small, fleeting smile. "Rae made me watch it a second time. It was then that I noticed you had a tan, and I realized it couldn't have been made recently."

He was damn lucky she had such a keen eye for detail. "I haven't been with anyone since you. Not even after we broke things off. I've only wanted you, Dakota. That hasn't changed."

She was silent for too long. "Are there other sex tapes?"

He hadn't expected that question. "Honestly? I'm not sure. It's possible. But Ashley, she was part of Chris's crowd. I should have known better than to sleep with her." And wasn't that a hell of an awkward thing to say to one's wife? Feeling the desperation rise in him, he blurted out, "Dakota, give me a chance to prove myself to you. I don't want a divorce." He clasped her shoulders. "Please, I—"

"It's okay, Max. You don't have to prove anything. I believe you. And I don't want a divorce, either."

He felt weak with relief as her words sank in. "You don't?"

She gave a tiny shake of her head. "No. Back there in the driveway? That was Piper playing one of her games. I'd already told her I didn't intend to divorce you over the tape. She was retaliating for my refusing to go along with her plan to hire a divorce lawyer to make sure I ended up with Windhaven. Then she'd have probably tried to guilt me out of it or make my life even worse by moving in. She was probably trying to get back at me, too, for kicking her out of the house."

"You kicked her out? God, Dakota, well done." Unable to resist, he hauled her close and kissed her, pouring his feelings into the embrace. When they broke apart, he put them into words. "You're incredible," he whispered fiercely. "You know that, right?"

The small smile she'd given him reappeared and stayed a little longer. "I have my moments."

The breeze lifted the ends of her hair and played with them. Abruptly aware of the cold, he whipped off his jacket and draped it over her shoulders. "Here, put this on."

"Oh! That's not—don't you need it?" she asked.

She still had trouble accepting things from others. And there was so much he wanted to do for her. Not because she was weak—far from it—but because he cared so damn much.

"No, I don't need it," he said.

He looked at her in his custom-made Brioni jacket. The jacket was absurdly big on her. He wasn't sure it fit him any better right now. He wished he didn't have to talk anymore, that instead they could head inside and he could simply show her how much he loved her.

How would she react when she learned that he'd walked away from a multimillion-dollar career?

He swallowed. "Dakota, there's more I need to tell you. Like I said, a lot's happened."

*

"Okay." Dakota looked at Max. He stood beside her, his gaze directed at the beach below and the gentle rise and fall of the waves as they approached the shore. From the tense set of his shoulders, she knew that whatever he was going to say would be as difficult for him as telling her about the video had been.

Feeling her own apprehension mount, she reminded herself that he didn't want a divorce. That was what mattered. "What is it, Max?"

"I quit the Summit Group."

The pain she heard belied the quietly spoken words. "How? Why?" she asked in confusion. "You loved it there."

"Yeah, I did. But I suppose I've changed. At least my priorities or values have. You know the meeting I had scheduled with Bob and Chris?"

She nodded but remained silent, not wishing to interrupt.

"Well, I'd guessed Chris was up to something—he'd dropped some hints when we met in San Francisco. I didn't know whether it had to do with restructuring the company or something to do with the new melanoma drug Chiron was preparing to roll out. Instead he announced he was raising the price of an antibiotic by a thousand percent. Dakota, this drug's used to fight lung infections and is especially effective in patients with cystic fibrosis."

Suddenly restless, he dragged his hand over his face before shoving it into the front pocket of his trousers. "This whole thing with the baby, Dakota, it's brought up a lot of stuff for me. On the day of your ultrasound, you and Dr. Davis were so relaxed, and I was a fucking basket case, terrified the ultrasound tech was going to pause the cursor over some part of the baby and say, 'Uh-oh.' But then, finding out that it was perfectly healthy and that we were going to have a little girl, well, that was even scarier because I knew it would be up to me to *keep* her healthy and perfect. After what happened to Rosie, I don't think I'm good at that."

She laid her hand on his arm. "Max, I'm so sorry for bringing her up—"

"It's okay."

"No, it wasn't right."

"Then it was necessary. I'd been trying to find the guts to tell you about how she died. You're the first person I've talked to about what happened to Rosie and my mom, and the fallout with my dad.

"Dakota, my dad had it rough. His father walked out on his mother and him when he was a kid. To help his mother out, he got a job at a garage when he was sixteen. Then Vietnam happened. He got called up, one of the last rounds of draftees. Dad didn't talk about what happened during the war. But I think it made him hard, quick to anger. But Rosie? She melted him, even more than my mom did.

"Sure, Dad was proud of me, teaching me about cars, coming to my games, and all, but Rosie could make him smile. He didn't seem the type who'd appreciate art, but I swear, when Rosie showed him one of her drawings, it was like he was holding a Leonardo in his hands." He turned to her. "You were right, Dakota. I was angry at him for accusing me of helping cause her death, because I loved her just as much as he did."

"I may have been right, but I was wrong to cause you such pain, and I'm so very sorry, Max."

"Forgiven." He reached for her hand and brought it to his lips. "Facing all that again was bound to hurt. But I'm glad you made me. Otherwise I might not have been thinking of our baby, of Rosie, of my father, or of *you* when I went into that meeting. But because I was, I knew that I couldn't go along with Chris and Bob's plan to rake in millions while others suffered. I wouldn't be able to look my daughter in the face if I did."

Max had quit his high-powered job because he was worried about being a good enough man for their baby girl? Dakota's heart pounded, ready to burst with love. She leaned forward and kissed the corner of his mouth. "I think our daughter is going to know how incredibly lucky she is to have you as her father. You did the right thing, Max."

He gave a short laugh. "You may be the only one who feels that way. Private equity guys don't just quit because the CEO of one of their companies makes a morally questionable move to increase profits. Strangely, though, I don't give a rat's ass what the PE world thinks. And I have a strong suspicion that walking away from the Summit Group feels a hell of a lot better than getting fired, which is what Chris was trying to pull off by releasing the sex tape."

"Wait. *He* released it? I thought it was this Ashley—"

"I figured it out on my way here. Ashley probably told Chris about the tape some time ago, and likely showed it to him. He basically implied as much in San Francisco, but I was too focused on Chiron to see the threat behind his sleazy comments. Then I got a voicemail from Chris, sent just after today's meeting. I think he orchestrated the tape's release to damage me in Bob's eyes. He knows Bob's character and was counting on him to be so livid over the tape that he'd fire me—or at the very least take me out of the running to succeed him as Summit's CEO. The one thing Chris hadn't counted on was my quitting."

"But," Dakota said, trying to process it all, "you made Chris CEO of Chiron. Why would he turn around and do that to you?"

"Petty vindictiveness." He lifted a shoulder and let it fall. "He obviously got his nose out of joint when I didn't give in to his demands to name a CFO of his choosing and to renegotiate his compensation package. And honestly? I think he was pissed that I wasn't hanging with his crowd anymore. I hurt his feelings."

"I'm sorry Bob Elders didn't support you," she said.

"Yeah. But you know what? When I looked across that big black desk of Bob's, I realized I didn't want to end up there."

She found his hand and linked her fingers with his. The ocean was calm today, the waves negligible compared to the ones she and Max had negotiated these past forty-eight hours. "So what do you want to do instead, Max?"

He let out a deep breath. "I've got a few ideas. I'm thinking of striking out on my own and investing in companies I believe in, ones that I feel are really worth supporting." Still holding her hand, he turned toward her and looked at her solemnly. "But first I want to take some time off and do some other things."

"Such as?"

"To begin with, I want to take my wife to Michigan and show her the town I grew up in, the football field I played on, the streets I cruised. I want to show her the house I lived in, and I want to introduce her to my father. Dakota, I can't promise that my dad will want to have anything to do with me, or that he and I will ever be able to forget and forgive, but I'm willing to take the first step."

She blinked the tears away. "Oh, Max," she said, planting kisses on the corners of his mouth, his cheeks, and then his mouth again.

Smiling, he kissed her back.

"I'm so, so proud of you," she said.

"I haven't finished my list yet."

"Oh, right." She bit her lip to keep from smiling foolishly. "Do go on."

"And then, when our baby girl enters the world, I'd like to name her Rosemary Frances. Frances was my mom's middle name."

"Rosemary Frances Carr," Dakota said, sounding it out. "It's perfect." She nodded enthusiastically. "I love it."

"Good." He smiled. "Also on my list, after Rosie's born and you're up for it, I want to get married again. This time I want to renew my vows to you in front of Rosie and our friends. I'll push

Rosie in a baby stroller or wear one of those carrier things if necessary. The important thing is for everyone I care about to know how much I love you. And that my love will last forever and forever again." Framing her face with his hands, he gazed into her eyes and repeated, "I love you, Dakota," and then he kissed her.

When at last they separated, their breaths mingled in quick pants and soft laughs. "So what do you think of my plan?" he asked huskily. "Are you up for all that?"

"I am. Very much so."

Taking her hand in his, they began walking toward the house. "And what do you want, Dakota? I'll do anything to make you happy."

"I already am. You've given me so much, Max. I can't wait to meet our baby. I knew I wanted a child someday, but this baby girl growing inside me feels so special and so right. And while I hope that things will work out between you and your father, we're making our own family, Max. It's going to be a good one."

He squeezed her hand. "I think it already is."

She stepped in front of him and gazed into his eyes. "I love you, Max. With all my heart. You know that, right?"

"I do now." His smile a thing of beauty, he drew her close and kissed her slowly because they had all the time in the world.

They'd resumed walking and were almost at the house when she stopped again. "Max?" she said.

"Yeah?"

"Actually, I do want something."

"Name it."

"That tape of you and Ashley? It's going to be bothering me for a while. I don't like to think of how long it will take for me to unsee it."

His brows drew together in dismay. "Ah, sweetheart—"

"So I think we should make our own tape. Maybe several."

Surprised laughter burst out of him. "Dakota, love, I'll make as many sex tapes with you as you wish. Whenever you want. I'm yours."

Yes, she thought with a smile. He really was.

EPILOGUE

It seemed that Rosie Frances Carr was as impatient to come into the world as Dakota was to see her, and then to watch Max's expression when he held his daughter for the first time.

She and Max were in his study when the first contraction came, a cramping low in her belly that reminded her of the achy days when she would pop ibuprofen to combat her period. Dakota was propped on the sofa, her legs stretched out, with a plump throw pillow on her lap and her computer perched upon it. With her belly now as big as a basketball and very much heavier, it was the easiest way for her to type. At the moment the setup performed an additional service, effectively hiding her from Max's gaze as she arched and shifted against the cushions until the discomfort had passed.

There was no reason to alert him yet. She'd let him know when things started getting serious, and right now she thought that listening to him on the phone with Mike Gaddis while they discussed how to structure Carr Capital, the venture capital fund that Max was forming, was the best thing for her. She loved how excited he was at the prospect of starting his own fund and calling the shots.

Roger Cohen had done Max a solid when he'd recommended Mike Gaddis. The lawyer had fiercely negotiated Max's exit from the Summit Group, making sure Bob Elders felt the pain of refusing to stand with Max and pressure Chris Steffen into backing down on increasing Mitrilocin's price by such an astronomical sum.

And now Elders and Chris were feeling even more pain. As Max had predicted, the price hike had caused industry watchdogs to sound the alarm. The news reports detailing the price gouging had made the Summit Group's limited partners very unhappy, as many of the funds came from university endowments. Among those universities, a number of them had medical schools; others had their names attached to the country's leading hospitals. It didn't look good to have their institutions investing in a company that so blatantly and callously chose profits over the needs of seriously ill patients.

The stories surrounding Mitrilocin spread quickly and generated enough public outrage that lawmakers took notice. Word had it that come September Chris Steffen was going to have to explain himself to a congressional committee. Dakota hoped the members raked him over the coals.

So Max was in a good place. *They* were in a good place.

It had started with the trip to Mason. She hadn't thought she could love Max more, but after he'd driven to the modest split-level house with its detached garage in the back and walked up the cement path, birdcalls marking their measured approach, he'd stood on the front stoop, staring at the door, obviously steeling himself for another rejection. When he pressed the doorbell, she knew it was the hardest thing he'd ever done.

Seconds stretched as they waited. Then they heard the slide of locks being turned, and Dakota's hand grew numb from Max's grip.

The door opened and Max's father was there, a stooped, lined, and grizzled version of his son. The men stared in silence. It was the elder man who broke it.

"You're here." His voice was thick with disbelief.

She'd given a subtle pull of her hand so Max would release it. "It's a nice afternoon. I'll go sit on that bench under the tree." She pointed. Rising up on her toes, she kissed the corner of Max's mouth, offered his father a polite smile, and left.

If there was a future meeting with Max's father, then she'd join them. To do so now would be an intrusion.

A half an hour later Max came for her. She suspected neither man could withstand the emotional toll of a longer visit. He sank down beside her and his hand found hers. "Rosie used to sit here and draw."

They sat on Rosie's bench while Max cried out his grief. When his tears stopped, he dried his face with a rough swipe of his arm.

She gave him a few minutes more to recover. "It went okay?"

He gave a tired shrug. "As well as it could. I said I was sorry I'd stayed away for so long and that I hoped he'd want to be part of our lives. God, Dakota, the house? It looked exactly the same. I didn't have the heart to go into Rosie's and my rooms, but I know they're untouched, not a CD moved or a trophy disturbed. I've been such an ass to leave him alone all these years." He leaned over his folded legs as if his heart were weighing him down.

She stroked his back in slow soothing circles. "He hurt you, too, Max," she reminded him gently.

"He looked so much older. No matter what, I'll take care of him somehow."

*

Max's father must have been watching through the window, for he came outside as they made their way to the car. Like Max's, his eyes were red-rimmed. "You're Dakota."

"Yes."

"Max said it was your idea to name the baby Rosie. Thank you."

His accent was different from Max's, she noted. Max had probably lost the Michigan in his speech after living in New York for so many years. "Rosemary Frances—that was Max's idea. She's going to be very much loved," she said gently. "Like your own daughter."

At her answer, his lips trembled. Pressing them together, he nodded.

"We very much hope you'll come and visit us, Mr. Carr. You will always be welcome." She left it at that. Max had extended an olive branch, she an invitation.

Reconciliation was a process. Max and his father now spoke once a week on the phone, and the conversations were gradually losing their awkwardness. The biggest milestone had come only a week ago, when Max's father had said that he'd like to visit them after Rosie arrived. He thought he still remembered how to change a diaper and hold a bottle. He might be able to help with some of those changings and feedings.

Later that day she overheard Max on the phone with the mechanic at her garage, asking where he could get an old clunker to rebuild. It was so adorable that she had to leave the room so she wouldn't embarrass him by throwing her arms around him and smothering him with kisses. Now it occurred to her that she'd better tell Max to buy one of those wrecks quickly, because it looked as if his father would be coming east sooner than they had all expected.

Max's courage in going to see his father had inspired her to write to hers. She'd drafted the letter four times and then had shown it to Max. "It's good, babe," he'd said with a smile. "Just right. It may take him a while to get over his shock."

"Only natural."

"Only natural," he agreed. "But then I think he'll contact you. Including the photo is a good idea. You do take after him."

Thank God for that. She wanted nothing more to do with the Hales. "And you're okay with my mentioning you?"

He'd cupped her chin and covered her lips with his. "Absolutely," he said when the kiss had ended. "Actually, the only thing I'd add to your letter is an invitation to him and his family to come to our celebration."

They'd decided to renew their wedding vows at Windhaven, taking one more step in obliterating the Hale presence. Hendrick was delighted at the prospect of officiating. She and Max had initially discussed holding the after-ceremony party at the Maidstone Club, knowing this would be another humiliating blow to Mimi. But in the end Dakota had decided she preferred having the party at Windhaven. The house was more than big enough to accommodate all their guests, and having the entire affair there would stick in Mimi's craw just as much as throwing the party at the Maidstone. After all, living well was the best revenge, and Dakota and Max were living very well indeed. Besides, Dakota had another and far more important thing to consider than how to strike back at her aunt: she wanted to be able to put Rosie in her crib once the baby tired of celebrating with her parents and their friends.

As if on cue, Rosie chose to make her presence very much felt. Another contraction gripped Dakota, this one stronger than the last, powerful enough that she absolutely needed to get up or else the jig would be up and Max would be hustling her to the hospital, where they might very well be told to return home until the labor had progressed.

She couldn't see Max taking that well.

Closing her computer, she set it on the coffee table and stood, rubbing the small of her back as she did.

"Hold on a sec, Mike." Cupping his hand over the phone, he motioned her to come over to his chair. "Everything all right?" he asked, looping an arm around her belly.

"Absolutely." She pressed a kiss against the top of his head. Would Rosie have his auburn-tinted hair? "I just need to stretch. I'm going to take a short walk on the beach."

"This shouldn't take much longer—"

"No rush." At least not yet. And she wanted a few minutes alone with her daughter by the sea. She smiled. "Finish your work. I'll be back in a bit."

She walked a little ways on the beach, wincing when the next contraction hit her. They were coming regularly now but were still bearable, and she'd much rather be watching the lazy rolls of the incoming waves and letting the wash cool her feet than be stuck in the maternity center's delivery room. She did, however, call Dr. Davis's office to inform her that she'd started having contractions and how fast and intensely they were coming.

She crossed paths with an older couple walking with their black-and-white French bulldog. They were marveling at how fast their dog ran along the wet, hard sand and laughing when it dodged the waves lapping the shore, beating a retreat to higher ground.

Perhaps because of all Max and she had already been through together, she could easily picture the two of them in forty years' time doing much the same thing, enjoying a late afternoon walk with their beloved dog . . . though Max would probably want a bigger dog. Once they and Rosie had settled into a predictable routine, she'd start researching breeds, she decided with a smile.

Her smile faltered as another contraction took hold. The pain was replaced by surprise and excitement when she felt a wet warmth slide down the inside of her legs. She glanced over her stomach to where her flowing skirt ended, and her suspicion was confirmed: her water had broken.

She walked a few steps into the surf and, cupping her belly, took a deep breath. "Rosie, I just want you to know that you're going to be loved and cherished. I can't wait to meet you and show you all the things I love to do. I hope you'll enjoy coming out here as much as I do, that you'll learn to ride the waves and also be brave enough to make some yourself." Then, giving her belly a final rub, she said, "This is a good day to be born, Rosie. Let's go tell your daddy we're ready to do this."

She turned back to see a runner approaching. Unlike the others on the beach, he was in jeans and a faded UPenn T-shirt. She waved and, grinning, watched as Max picked up his pace. She, too, hurried to close the distance.

She could see Windhaven's roofline and chimneys when they met. A good thing, because the next contraction stole her breath and left her groaning softly. Still, she couldn't resist reaching up to sink her fingers into Max's hot and sweat-dampened hair and drag his mouth down to hers. She kissed him fiercely, passionately. With a growl, he gathered her close.

"I'm done with work," he said huskily. "Feel like going upstairs and making a very sexy video to add to the collection?"

She laughed. "I would, but there's someone we have to meet." She took his hand and began leading him back to the house.

His brows drew together. "I thought we were free today. Who is it?"

"Our daughter."

"Our what?" He stopped in his tracks.

"That's right, my water broke and the contractions are getting slightly intense."

"Your water broke and you're having contractions? Jesus, Dakota—"

"Not to worry, Max. I've got this and I've got you. It's all good."

"No, it's excellent," he corrected, pressing a tender kiss to her lips. "Because you're the best thing that ever happened to me. I know I may have mentioned this a couple of times, but I love you, Dakota."

"Feel free to say that as often as you want. And by the way, I love you madly and deeply." Her smile turned to a grimace as a band tightened about her belly.

"Another contraction?"

She nodded.

"Right. Let's get you to the hospital." Before she knew what he was about, he'd bent and scooped her into his arms, carrying her through the deep sand.

"I could definitely walk, you know."

"I know, but give me a chance to be manly here, since you're about to perform a miracle, an incredibly grueling miracle, while I basically hold your hand and offer you ice chips."

"Well, when you put it like that, carry on."

"It feels like a long time since I've said this: I love you, Dakota. Thank you for giving me everything that matters."

With her arms circling Max's neck, Dakota smiled into the deep blue sky.

ACKNOWLEDGMENTS

Writing is a surefire way to teach me how little I know. This book could not have been written without the help of many friends who fortunately know far more than I. My thanks to David Olney and Carol Nulman for their business tutorials; to Tim Duggan, John Buttrick, Mark Goodman, Mike Gillespie, and Peggy Davenport for giving me such good ideas; to Sophia Shibles and Dan Horton for allowing me to incorporate their businesses into these pages. I only hope I did justice to the wealth of knowledge each of you shared with me.

Several people took the time to read the manuscript in its earlier stages. Their comments and insights made this story infinitely better. I am so grateful to Sally Zierler, Anne Woodall, Marilyn Brant, Anne Cotton, Paul Mooney, and Jamie Beck.

I also want to thank my agent, Emily Sylvan Kim, who cheered me on when I doubted. I'm very happy to have you in my corner, Emily. To the wonderful Gina Wachtel, my publisher, and Junessa Viloria, my editor, I consider myself a very lucky writer to be able to work with you. My deepest thanks go as well to Ballantine art director Lynn Andreozzi, for yet another dazzling cover. I am also grateful to Alex Coumbis and Ashleigh Heaton for their energy and savvy in handling the publicity and marketing for *Making Waves.*

As for my family—my parents, my husband, and my children—well, I wouldn't be the writer I am without them in my life.

PHOTO: STACEY DOYLE

LAURA MOORE lives in Rhode Island with her husband, their two children, and their Labrador retriever. She loves to hear from readers.

lauramoorebooks.com